GRAB BAG

11

A Gay Erotica Anthology

FOR LITERARY HEAT

This book is copyright © habu 2016
habu asserts his right to be known as the author of this work.
Published by BarbarianSpy in 2016
Cover design © S Bush 2016
Cover image: Manipulated, © Wrangel | Dreamstime.com
ISBN E-book: 978-1-925190-92-2
ISBN Paperback: 978-1-925190-93-9
All rights reserved

BarbarainSpy
Toronto, Australia

Grab Bag 11

by

habu

Table of Contents

Introduction 7

Man Across the River 10

A New Path 28

The Philanthropist 49

Never Mentioned Again 67

Home Alone 75

A Question of Restraint 85

Five-Year Reunion 112

Slap of Realization 123

Taken Hiking 137

A Funeral and a Wedding 154

Martin's Hundred 175

Edge Teetering 186

Business Cruise 211

Iran in USA 229

The Horse Master 257

About the Author 275

BarbarianSpy Books 276

Introduction

Eleventh in the series of eclectic gay male short story collections by habu, the fifteen stories of *Grab Bag 11* offer a variety of gay male stories in terms of theme, sexual interest and fetish, setting, and time period. Laid out in the order in which they were written rather than grouped by theme, these are stories composed during the spring and early summer of 2016. Although mostly contemporary pieces this time, these stories take us from the early history of the United States ("Martin's Hundred") through vampire hunting grounds in the early twentieth century ("A Question of Restraint") to a mafia fishing expedition ("Business Cruise") right up to the most recent summer Olympics ("Iran in USA"). In geographical coverage, although most are set in the United States, others take us to Spain ("Man Across the River"), Germany ("A Question of Restraint" and "The Horse Master"), and Brazil ("Iran in USA"). Some are romantic; more include habu's penchant for writing hot, steamy, rough sex. Most explore the nature of the complex relationships between men who desire other men. All are written to entertain, inform, and arouse the reader of gay male stories.

The first story, "Man Across the River," is set in Galicia, Spain, where a young New York singer/song writer has gone into hiding to escape a controlling relationship only to find the attraction of being dominated by a hot Spanish footballer he observes living in a villa across a river. In an abrupt change back to the states, at his Romance novelist wife's funeral, a male model begins the journey back to his sexual reality from a life of convenience and lies in "A New Path." Continuing with the Richmond, Virginia, setting of this story, in "The Philanthropist," a major donor of a downtown gay men's recreation center uses his gifts to gain access to the center's staff and clientele.

The fourth story, "Never Mentioned Again," finds two sailor buddies, Chuck and Ryan, bar cruising in the snow on the Philadelphia ship repair docks following a long deployment in the Persian Gulf, where the guys not only find something different from what they thought they were getting but also a revelation about themselves and each other.

"Home Alone" is a straightforward invitation from Aaron for a hulking blond he meets at the gym to come to his home when his family is away for the inevitable, unsubtle sexual romp. In a completely different vein in a Halloween offering, vampires fight to control their appetites in early-twentieth-century Bavaria in "A Question of Restraint."

In "Five-Year Reunion," a recently uncloseted movie heartthrob returns to his five-year high school reunion to hand out punishments and rewards for getting him to where he is. "Slap of Realization" is another relationship and "facing the reality" story. In this story, a young Baltimore man is at the brink of acknowledging who he is and who he loves on a visit to his downstate Delaware family—and on the cusp of screwing up his life over his lack of perception, indecision, and inaction.

"Taken Hiking" takes us to the Blue Ridge Mountains of Virginia, where an angelic Shenandoah University college student falls into a way of making mountain hikes profitable.

"A Funeral and a Wedding" is one of habu's Cyprus-based stories, in which the death of a former Turkish lover lures an American into further entanglements on the Turkish side of the island. The next story, "Martin's Hundred," flips back four centuries in time and across the ocean to the Virginia Peninsula, where a young settler and Native American warrior fall into a relationship as the world about them goes up in flames.

In "Edge Teetering," an aging male model flees to the Mediterranean in fear of being seen by his set as losing his sexual edge. A rent-boy gets the business on a mafia business cruise out of Baltimore in "Business Cruise." "Iran in USA" was written during the 2016 Rio Olympics and features an American platform diver going for the gold in sexual encounters.

The collection ends with "The Horse Master," about a university student taking a summer job of "companion" to two cultural icons in Bavaria and being attracted to and possessed by a rougher horse handler.

As usual, the eleventh *Grab Bag* collection provides a varied and rich romp through time, across geography, and into the fertile mind of habu. We hope you enjoy reading it as much as he has said he enjoyed writing it.

Man Across the River

"... and I'll need to be at the Santiago de Compostela airport by eleven in the ... are you getting this, Sean? Your thoughts seem so far away."

"Umm, yes, Phil. You'll need to be at the airport by eleven tomorrow morning for the flight back to New York, so you'll have to leave here at ..."

"No later than eight. I know you aren't a morning person, so you needn't ... but what are you staring at so intensely? Do you even know I'm sitting here with an arm around you and feeling you up?"

"Yes, of course I know that, Phil. You're making me hard. Do you want to go in now?"

"No, not yet. I want to get you off out here first. It's nice out here. My last night with you for a while in Veiga. I want it to be special. But you seem so distant. I don't want you to worry about Chet. He isn't going to find out that you're tucked away here in Galicia. He doesn't know I have this house in Spain."

"Thank you, Phil. You've been a lifesaver," I murmured, as I cupped his neck with one hand to bring his face to mine in a kiss and unzipped my shorts with the other to signal my surrender to his attentions. My singer/song writer agent, Phil Hendricks, had been wanting to get into my pants for a couple of years now. My psychotic boyfriend in New York, Chet Clayton, had been dulling my creative juices for several months with his antics. When Chet beat me up, Phil whisked me away to this hideaway in Spain. I had given myself to him for the last week in gratitude. He was going back to New York tomorrow and I was staying here, attempting to reestablish my song-writing groove without the drama that Chet had brought into my life.

While we were kissing and with one arm around my shoulders holding me close to him out on the stone terrace overlooking the Rio Neira, a tributary of the Minho River, Phil fished my cock out of my shorts, pressed a thumb into my piss slit, and started to stroke me off.

He was an expert in this, I'd discovered. Although I'd known he wanted me, I hadn't been giving him much thought. He was more than twenty years older than I was. He was a handsome devil and tall and muscular enough, but he was thickish around the middle and old in my eyes, with salt and pepper hair that extended into his mustache and goatee. I just hadn't considered a man his age. I hadn't considered that age would have given him an expertise in technique that a man nearer my age, like Chet, didn't have. I guess what had really turned me off about Phil previously was his New York accent and cockiness. He'd always said he'd have me one day, and that always had irritated me.

But I guess he was right.

Chet would stroke me off, but he wouldn't have that sensual technique of making love to my piss slit with his fingers while he did it. Phil could make me come before he did every time, and he wasn't a long-distance endurance runner in that department. He was a quick reloader, though.

"I wasn't thinking about Chet," I said, speaking in a low, hoarse voice as Phil's stroking of my cock had me purring. I was just noticing the light on in the villa across the river from here. That's the first time I've seen any sign of habitation, although the stone villa looked like it was in good condition and the grape vines covering the property down to the water's edge looked tended well.

Phil looked over toward the river. "Ah, he must have a few days off. I haven't looked at the football schedule. All I've had eyes for this week have been for you."

He was acting like he was smitten with me. I was, of course, very grateful that he'd pulled me out of that mess with Chet and hidden me away with the hope I'd return to churning out songs we both could profit from. So, I'd let him fuck me for a week—with the result that each taking had boosted my creative juices and I already had the makings of three songs. But I had no intention of being with Phil forever. It was just a "thanks" interlude.

"Football schedule? What does that have to do with the house over there?"

"Xavier Vicario owns the house and that vineyard. The vineyard pays for itself. He comes up here from Madrid when he can. He's the center-forward for Atético Madrid, of the Spanish Primera Division football league. They were runners up in the Europe Cup the year before last—1974—largely through his effort. He's still a hero in Spain."

"Ah, I'll have to look him up . . . oh, god, Phil. Shit!"

Phil was kneeling between my thighs, fisting the root of my cock. His mouth was covering the bulb of my cock and he was flicking the piss slit with his tongue and making little stabs with the tip of his tongue into the entrance to my urethra canal.

"Oh, fuck, Phil. Take me inside. Take me to bed. Fuck me!"

He did.

* * * *

He was lying on his back on the bed, on top of the sheets, when I came out of the bathroom. His body wasn't bad, I thought, especially in this lighting. Moonlight from across the river was filtering into the bedroom through the open French doors out onto the terrace.

His body was mature, certainly—thick in the waist, but not exactly fat. His pecs didn't sag, and his legs were muscular. The salt and pepper hair swirled around his pecs and descended his sternum down across his belly and into an unruly bush. He wasn't hung, but his erection stood straight up from his bush and did protrude beyond the fist that was encasing it. He had a leather cock ring tight around the root. His age gave him a bit of trouble keeping an erection very long otherwise.

I padded over and sat on the side of the bed beside him. He turned to me and encased me with his arms around my waist. He sat up and moved behind me, his lips going to the back of my neck. I groaned as one of his hands encased my cock and I discovered that he had turned one of the rings he was wearing around. The ring had a gold bead in it.

"Oh shit. Oh fuck," I whimpered, as he pressed the bead into my piss slit, his hand gripping my shaft, holding it prisoner, while he moved the bead in and out of the piss slit, fucking my cock with it.

"It's my last night with you for now," he whispered into my ear. "I'm going to make you come five times. Something for you to remember when you think of me."

Moaning, I lay back in his arms and surrendered to him.

"One," he murmured when, at length, I brought up an orgasm from his bead-fucking of my cock slit.

He nudged me to one side, toward his feet, and reclined in the other direction. I went down on the surface of the bed on my shoulder with his now half-hard shaft at eye level. Understanding what he wanted, I took the root of his cock in my hand, opened my mouth over the shaft, and started sucking him off. His mouth took my cock in, cleaning it and alternating between sucking it and tonguing and swallowing and rolling my balls.

We worked each other until each had come. I moved my mouth to his balls as he nudged me to move over him and to rise on my knees. He half sat up, pulling my butt cheeks apart and sticking his tongue in my ass. I moaned and lay my cheek on his thigh, losing contact with all else other than him eating my ass out, lubricating and opening me, while he milked my cock again with his hand.

Separate notes and then chords, and finally harmonies and runs began forming in my brain and connecting with other chords and harmonies as Phil ate my ass out and milked my cock. I was exhilarated. My brain was creating music again. The blockage that had been caused by the drama of Chet was being put aside by the insistent sexual loving of Phil. He was being gentle, if relentless—controlling and using me expertly. Most important, I was being freed to compose again. The music going through my brain was that of a ballad. I specialized in pop tunes, but the slow, sure way in which he was working me, preparing me, evoked a ballad.

When I came again for him, I pulled away and rose from the bed.

"Piss break?" he asked. "That was just three."

"No, I have something I have to get down in the computer," I said, walking over to where my laptop was sitting on a desk and taking it out onto the terrace.

"I understand. Good," he said. "But come back before I sleep."

I sat, naked and in erection, on the terrace, overlooking the river as I entered the notes of the tune that had exploded into my mind as Phil had worked my ass and shaft. I was erect as I often was when I was composing but also because I wasn't any more finished with Phil that night than he was done with me. When I'd gotten the basic tune into the computer, I turned it off. Refinement could come later—and would be light. I tried not to mess much with my initial creations. I wanted to get back to the bed and ride Phil's cock.

Before I rose from the chair on the terrace, I looked across the river. Lights were still on on the second floor of the villa, and I thought I discerned a figure walking around inside and crossing behind the curtainless windows. The house was too far away to be sure. I made a mental note of digging out the binoculars Phil said were somewhere in the house.

Phil was still on his back, dozing, when I returned. I climbed on top of him, astride his pelvis. He smiled up at me in a half daze and held our cocks together, frotting them to full erections.

"You've written something?" he asked.

"Yes, I think so. A ballad."

"Good."

14

I sucked my breath in as he docked our cocks, bringing the tips of them together in a kiss and pulling the uncut foreskin of his down to cover the bulb of my shaft. I moaned as he stroked the two cocks together. He worked them slowly but without letup until I arched my back and shot my load inside his capturing foreskin.

"Four," he whispered.

His cockhead lathered in my cum, he moved his hands to my waist, lifted me, brought my channel down on his shaft, and, arching back and grabbing his knees with my hands, I rode his cock in deep-penetrating undulating movements until, with a series of gentle flows, he creamed me at the core.

There was a flurry of jerks and pressure from his hands at my waist at the point of the rolling ejaculation, but he had otherwise been holding steady as I had, both of us concentrating on the shaft moving inside me. With a sigh, he relaxed back onto the bed and into the first tendrils of sleep, as, with no objection from him, I rose again and went out onto the terrace.

The music that had run through my brain as I was riding his cock wasn't as obvious to me as it had been the first time, but there were hints of note combinations and rhythms of another ballad. I sat on the terrace for a couple of hours, capturing those in the computer as best I could and doing some polishing and enhancing of the first ballad tune.

I kept looking over at the villa on the other side of the river as the sky began to lighten up, but there were no lights shining then.

I plugged the term "Xavier Vicario photos" into the search engine and photos of a luscious stud, dark and sensuous and well-muscled as so many Spanish men I'd see were came back at me, gripping my libido and making me hard again. He obviously had a propensity of tearing his shirt off and running across the field when he'd made a particularly good play—and the cameras obviously enjoyed capturing those moments. He was one sexy man. The music in my brain became more of a rock tune and with the bite of castanets to it, but the tune was fleeting. What was there had a beat to it—an obvious accelerating beat like Ravel's "Bolero," the international anthem of fucking.

Feeling the danger of what I was seeing—I had wanted him to be just a man a river away from me, not a character in a wet dream—I snapped shut the lid of the laptop, visited the bathroom, and then returned to the bed, pulling the sheets over both Phil and me. Phil was lightly snoring, a beatific smile in his face.

Good, I thought. He indeed had pulled me out of a bad situation. I knew my well-being and productivity were important to his own bottom line, but he had gone beyond any expectation I could have. I had never intended to let him fuck me—it had started as a New Yorker thing and then festered—but I owed him that, and was pleased that he seemed to be happy with it. I just didn't want to make it more than casual and occasional sex.

I closed my eyes and the next thing I knew it was later in the morning, surely after 6:30 a.m., when the housekeeper, Isabella, came to work. I could hear her singing in the kitchen. It was a catchy tune—obviously a Spanish ballad. And it seemed to go so well with the first tune I started composing the night before. My mind started to meld chords from what she was singing into my tune.

Phil snorted and came half awake. He turned to me, throwing an arm across my chest and a heavy thigh across my pelvis. He didn't seem to be awake, but his thigh was moving, rubbing my cock, and certainly bringing my shaft alive.

The cock shriveled a bit out of embarrassment, though, when a humming Isabella came into the bedroom, all smiles and carrying a tray with two mugs of coffee on it with a pitcher of cream and packets of artificial sugar. She put the tray down on the nightstand, looked down at the two of us in bed together, obviously naked, as the sheets had been pulled down to our waists, and Phil's arm across my chest. She looked on benignly for a couple of seconds like there was nothing unusual in encountering two men in the bed—and indeed she'd found us here every morning for more than a week—and then turned and waddled out of the room, closing the door behind her, as if it wasn't too late to hide what was going on in the room.

More awake now, Phil moved his body over mine, pinning me to the bed with his greater weight. His lips went to mine, and I opened to him. He nudged my thighs apart with a hand, the palm of his other hand pressing my forehead back into the surface of the bed as we kissed.

"Raise your ass to me. Give me a good angle, I want to take you deep," he whispered, and bending my knees and raising my pelvis with the leverage of my feet flat on the bed, I responded.

I groaned and he grunted as he slid deep inside me and started a slow pump. He wasn't gigantic but he was big enough to strain at taking without preparation. I willed my passage walls to open to him, and they did so as if a series of gates, opening in progression down into my soft, spongy core. I moaned when his bulb reached me there, and I clutched at his shoulder blades, rhythmically pressing my nails into his flesh to the tune of his slow pumping of me at my most vulnerable core. Several minutes later, we both gave a low exclamation and jerked, as we came together, me by stroking myself off as he slow pumped my ass.

"Five," he murmured and immediately went back to sleep on top of and still inside me.

When I woke, he was gone. I hoped he'd made his plane to the States, but I had refinements of the tunes I had written exploding in my brain, so I didn't give him much thought. I did laugh when I saw he'd left me a note on the bureau: the name "Carlos Guerrero," a phone number, and the note that he had a farm on the right near the junction with the main road, that he would take good care of me on demand, and that he was on a retainer at Phil's expense.

* * * *

The man had the physique of a young god, I told myself, with a sigh, as I lowered the binoculars. I'd spent as much time as I could over the past several days out here on the terrace. Little work was being done on music composition. I'd polished what I'd drafted out the night before Phil left to death, but little new had risen. There was the folk song—well, two, after lying under Carlos, but not the production I'd hoped for.

I'd gone three days without sex after Phil left, which was no big deal, except that I'd been hard and wanted sex at least twice a day. Those were times when I'd caught glimpses of the Spanish footballer Xavier Vicario working in his vineyard across the river. He was out there almost constantly, and he liked to work stripped down to the waist. And at the end of his work day—a time I always tried to be out on the terrace and looking across the river—he'd use an open, outdoor shower by a door into his villa to sluice off his body.

After the first few days I saw this, I saw that he was stripping down entirely to do it. That's when I dug out the binoculars. The man was hung—a thick, uncut sausage of a cock hanging down between his legs, seemingly meatier at the middle than at either end—and his body was absolutely magnificent. I found myself unzipping and working myself while he was showering.

It was frustrating in sexual terms. On the fourth day, I picked up the note that Phil had left on the bureau with the name of Carlos Guerrero. I wondered what he looked like. I really wanted to know that before I called him. But I really, really needed to be taken care of.

I took a walk on the road toward the junction with the main highway. The note had said he farmed to the right almost to the road. There was a man out there on a tractor when I approached the junction. He was smallish and had a wiry body. He also was somewhere past his mid forties and had a grizzled appearance. He certainly was no beauty. I wondered if Carlos was his son. I had brought my mobile phone with me and rang the number. There was ringing sound coming from the tractor and the man stopped the machine, pulled a mobile phone from somewhere in the tractor, answered it, and looked in my direction.

Carlos fucked me on the mossy ground under a tree in a stand of trees at the side of the field he was plowing. And he plowed me good too. He was a bantam rooster of a guy, but he was strong as an ox, he had the dick of an ox, and he had the manners of an ox. He mounted me like a dog and banged away on me for a good twenty minutes. He was humming some sort of Celtic-type song—the Celtic influence was strong in Galicia—and muttering in some dialect that wasn't Spanish as he pounded away on my ass. It was all I could do to hold in place.

I had moaned when he'd pulled my leather belt out of my trousers when I'd stripped them off. He doubled the belt over and snapped it on the palm of his hand. I flinched and groaned, looking at the belt in fear but also experiencing some other sensation running through my body—something arousing. He hadn't missed the spark in my eyes.

When Chet had beaten me, it had been pain, but mixed in that had been some pleasure too. Chet had seen something in my reaction too. He knew he could abuse me and I'd still come for him—sometimes more explosively then. When Chet slapped me around, I'd go straight to the floor, open my legs to him, and take him deep, meeting his thrust with counterthrusts of my own. He had exploited that, thinking that even more pain would trigger sexier reactions. What I grew to fear was that he may have been right. I had the same urge to present my ass with just the snap of the belt.

I think Phil saw it too. He didn't take advantage of it himself, but it gave him impetus to pull me out of Chet's clutches.

When Carlos had mounted my ass and was riding my channel, he flicked my biceps and flanks with the belt. He laughed at the feel of my reaction to that. My passage opened more to him, pulling him deeper inside me; my moan was lower, more guttural in the throat. He reached under my belly and grasped my cock. Snap, snap against my flanks and my cock stiffened further in his hand. Wham, wham, wham, the strike on my buttocks were harder. I spouted for him, moaning hard. I came for him three times with the kiss of the belt as he seeded me twice in quick succession and left me panting and groaning on the ground under the tree.

I lay there and watched him finish plowing his field, after which he drove the tractor back over to the tree line, climbed down, approached me, gripped my ankles, split my legs, and plowed me as well in a vigorous missionary fuck, almost splitting my ass channel.

He rose, smiling, declared me a "good lay," said he'd be in this field every day that week and that we should go for a drink in a couple of bars he knew in Veiga. Then he mounted his tractor again and drove off.

As I watched him go, my mind was filled with a cacophony of sound—primitive Celtic runs, with a Spanish folk song edge to them. He had been rough, but I was completely satiated sexually. I went back to the house and wrote out what I could remember of the tunes he had fucked into my mind.

To refine them, I went to the field again three days later, and, knowing I'd come back and presumably could manage him, Carlos pounded my ass even harder that time. I decided I couldn't go to him very often, but I knew that if I needed it, he would provide it and I'd stagger away moaning in satisfaction but not needing it again for a while.

Shortly after I had used the binoculars to watch Vicario working and showering, the footballer caught on to me. I nearly swallowed my tongue one afternoon—and my tongue had almost literally been hanging out watching him soap up his shaft and balls—when I realized that he had a pair of binoculars and was watching me as well.

When he was sure I was still watching him, he did a full frontal for me, and, holding the binoculars to his face, he jerked his cock off. I, of course, stood, dropped my shorts, and joined him in stroking my cock off. The two of us were having sex with each other, even though we were separated by a river.

On succeeding days, he toyed with me—pulling me into the mutual ejaculation thing again the next day. The day after that, he had a young man working in the field with him—and showering, under the pipe outside the villa door, with him. There was a wine barrel on its side by the door, and the hunky footballer put the young man on his back on the barrel, split his legs wide, and missionary fucked him. After getting off, he lifted the binoculars to make sure I was watching. Of course I was.

The next afternoon, bondage and toys were introduced. The young man was put on the barrel on his belly, with his wrists and ankles tied together, and after he'd writhed under the torture of being reamed with a dildo, Vicario doggie fucked him. The next day, the naked young man was bound to a tree and Vicario whipped him lightly as the young man tried, unsuccessfully to writhe away from him. The lashes rained a little harder, with the body of the young man sagging from the tree. The footballer dropped the whip, stepped up to the young man, jutted the man's buttocks back, and fucked from behind. I fancied I had been able to hear the snap of the whip from across the river, and I reacted to each one, giving a little moan and feeling my cock lurch. When he'd finished, he checked to assure himself that I'd kept with him. Of course I had. I couldn't blame him for assuming I was interested in that level of sex myself.

That was overwhelming for me—both fearful and arousing—especially since, although there was a river separating us, I still felt that it was I who had been lashed and fucked. I didn't go out on the terrace for the next two days. To be truthful, it was raining for much of the time, but I felt justified in denying myself what had become both a pleasure and a frustration.

The evening after that Carlos took me into town in an old Peugeot, to an outside café and bar, where he said it was easy to hook up with men. For most men, seeing that I was with Carlos, other men kept their distance. I saw after a few minutes, though, that Xavier Vicario was there, at another table. There were a couple of young men at his table too, including the one Vicario had been spiking for—I thought— my benefit. The young man was wearing a low-cut muscle T-shirt, and I could see the evidence of faintly red welts here and there on his arms and neck. I barely was able to resist the urge to go over there, run my fingers along the welts, and ask him if the pain and overridden the pleasure, even though, from experience, I knew this could be so. Whatever the level of pain, he was mooning over Vicario, so he couldn't have felt too violated.

I wasn't sure, though, that the feeling of being violated wasn't part of the arousal with me. That may have been why I hadn't left Chet sooner.

Vicario saw Carlos and me, and his attention obviously shifted from the young men he was with to me. My attention was drawn to him too. If an understanding could be arrived at and a deal struck just by the exchange of looks across a bricked square, that's what we accomplished. He even started to rise to come over to me, but just then football fans realized that he was there, and he was swamped with young men who wanted to talk with him, get advice from him, touch him—and, I could see in most, lie under him. He left with four young men—two in addition to the ones he'd been with, and I ran fantasies in my mind of how he was going to plow them all in his villa that night. Interestingly enough, I never questioned to myself that he would be able to do it.

For my part, Carlos came home with me and plowed me all night. He was still on top of me, banging me in a missionary, when Isabella came in with two mugs of coffee on a tray. As always, she just gave us a benign look, muttered a "Good morning, Carlos," and turned and waddled out of the room. Carlos didn't waver in the rhythm of his thrusts. This obviously wasn't the first time Carlos had been in this bed, and it dawned on me how Phil would have known to contract Carlos to fuck me. I managed to recall that Phil had told me he swung both ways, although he hadn't done so with me.

During the night, while Carlos was mounted on my ass and keeping me from sleep, I had looked out of the open French doors onto the terrace and out across the river. Xavier's villa was lit up like a torch. Figures were flitting across the windows and I fancied that I saw some coupling, one bent over and another bent over his back. Quite definitely someone was being fucked over the barrel outside the villa door, as the door was open and light was cascading out, putting the two undulating figures in a spotlight. Flashes of the reflection coming off the raised and downward flicked strands of a hand whip made me moan. My response was to start thrusting my hips back at Carlos and straining to open totally to him and to take him deeper than he'd ever mined before.

The next morning I finished off the three Celtic-style folks songs I had been writing.

* * * *

I stood there on the terrace, naked, my hand working my cock, and lifted the binoculars to my eyes. He was there, across the river, also standing, facing me—also naked and also with his binoculars trained on me. He was holding something with leather thongs hanging down from it in one of his hands. The whip from the other day, I wondered. I shuddered at the thought, almost dropping the binoculars. When I put them back up to my face, Xavier was gone from where he'd been standing outside the door into the villa. In panic, I moved the binoculars around, the view becoming wild, as even the slightest repositioning of them covered a great deal of ground in the focal point and blurred the whole effect.

I found him at the river's edge, going into the water. Swimming toward my bank of the river. I put the binoculars down and started walking down the slope toward the river.

We met near the river bank, as he stumbled up out of the water. A stand of trees was nearby. Included in what he brought across the river in his swim were wrist restraints connected with a leather lead and a multistrand hand whip. He bound me, naked, to a tree, my arms stretched up to the notch in two branches where I was bound. I nearly had to go up on my toes to remain standing, but before long my body was sagging down toward the ground, held fast by my up-stretched, bound arms, as I cried out in slight pain but great passion at the sting of the lash on my back, arms, buttocks, and thighs. The lashing was more symbolic—at least for most of the time—than torture, but I did feel the sting, increasing in intensity and quite biting before he was done, and the whip did raise slight welts. I hardened even while he was binding me to the tree and came the first time during the more stinging bite of the whip.

He tongued the welts, coming ever closer to the crease in my buttocks, until, at last—long after I wanted him there—his face was buried between my butt cheeks and he was eating my ass out. The tongue was followed by his huge cock being rubbed in my crack and over my increasingly open entrance. This was followed by him gripping my thighs and lifting me, pulling me away from the tree, my body parallel to the ground, slowly entering me with his throbbing cock, and fucking me to, first mine, and then his, ejaculation.

He let my body fall and lashed me again until he was hard again. Then he released my wrists—but only momentarily—rebound them, draped me on the front of his body, his arms trapping me in a full Nelson hold, my wrists bound behind his neck, and my thighs held over his, my ankles hooked on his calves. With his cock buried deep in my ass, he strutted around the grassy area between the terrace of my house and the river's edge, jostling me up and down on the cock—until he had seeded me again.

Beyond grunts and occasional murmurings of "Good," "Take it; Carlos says you can take it—that you want it rough," "Fuck, yes," "You want it," and "Nice," Xavier was running more or less silent.

I was screaming the top of my head off—mostly being contradictory: "Please, no, not the whip," "Fuckkkk!" "Oh, god, don't stop!" "Shit, it's too big; you'll split me," "Oh, Fuck yes," "I can't take it," "Nail me, spike me, split me!" "I'm going to commmme!" "YES!!!"

Already totally exhausted, cowed, and conquered, I let him sling me over his shoulder and walk me up to the terrace and then through the French doors of the bedroom, and to slam me down on my back on the bed. He had taken up a belt from my slung trousers as he entered the room, and I cried out as he doubled it over and snapped me twice on the chest. Immediately, he was on top of me, slapping my thighs apart with the sting of the belt, grabbing and palming my buttocks, and pulling my pelvis up to his where he was kneeling between my thighs. He thrust inside me and began pounding hard and deep. The gates to my passage sprang open for his shaft as he relentless marched the cock deep, into my soft core and even further, deeper into my vulnerability than any man had sunk before. I continued hearing and feeling the snap of the belt but all of my attention had gone to the monster cock filling and churning in my passage.

Loud music was thundering through my brain. Trumpets and kettle drums. The twangy runs down the strings of an electric guitar. The whip-snapping sound of the slapstick clapper. The deafening, high-pitched screaming of a lead singer.

We were rock and rolling. And we both were definitely getting our rocks off.

In the morning, when Isabella came in with two coffee mugs on a tray, she still wasn't batting an eyelash at what she found. We were both on top of a tangle of sheeting that looked like a battle zone. Xavier was on his back, his muscular, vein-popping arms bent, his hands gripping the sides of my chest. I was pressing into the mattress at all four points—the palms of my hands, the soles of my feet—as I was suspended, as if levitated, above Xavier's magnificent body, in the crab position. His cock was thrusting up into my passage, and I was bearing down with my pelvis to meet him thrust for thrust.

Not even Xavier and I in high heat had given Isabella pause. Well, of course not. Xavier had known right where the bedroom was. He knew where he'd find the dildo. Phil knew that I wouldn't have just Carlos to keep me satisfied and churning out songs.

Afterward we slept until shadows were stealing into the room through the French door. I woke, on my back, beside the nightstand, holding the ten-inch dildo Xavier had pulled out of a drawer and used on me the previous night, me huffing and puffing, pushing up on my feet to raise my pelvis to him and palming and separating my butt cheeks as much as I could. Me crying out, "Yes, yes, all of it!" before collapsing under the strain of him giving me what I asked for.

Xavier was lying beside me, turned on his side, his head propped up on an elbow, watching me as I sleep.

"You're on my side of the bed," he said.

"What?" I asked, not being sure I was fully awake.

"If you want me in your bed from now on, you'll have to let me sleep on that side—when I'm not sleeping on top of you, of course."

"Oh, yeah. Well, sure, no problem." Of course he'd been in this bed before and knew which side he preferred. I moved to roll over his body to the other side, but, of course, never made it that far. He put me under him, belly down, and started doing one-handed pushups on my sore ass. He had pulled a short hand whip out from somewhere and flicked it with the other hand against my flanks, back, and arms as he fucked me, the snap of the leather strands making me flinch and groan. All I could think of was the "Hallelujah Chorus." I had a real man in my bed.

* * * *

"He's not here. He's not going to be here."

Chet Clayton gave Phil Hendricks a hard look, but then he pulled the chair out and sat down at the big, round table anyway. He looked around the table. No, Sean wasn't here. "He's going to be here; I know it. He sent me an invitation. He's coming back to me."

"Sean didn't send you an invitation; I did. And he's not coming to the Grammies. He's pinned down elsewhere." At least Phil thought his song writer client was still writhing under the Spanish footballer—and baller in other ways too—Xavier Vicario. Phil hadn't heard anything but good news from Isabella about how those two were getting along in the bed he'd provided for them in the Galician villa. And the great songs kept on coming out. Sean was taking this new song niche by storm.

"You sent it? Why would you send it?"

"To gloat, of course. To gloat when Sean's Grammy is announced."

"What is it with this bombastic Rock and Roll stuff from Sean now. And the other songs he's put out this year—ballads and folk songs. Pop is his niche."

"Sean is following new avenues now," Phil answered. In spades, he thought. Who would have known that Sean would take so well to bondage and a bit of sadism. It had been a bit too much for Phil, but he liked a taste of the hunky Spanish footballer occasionally.

"I denote a Spanish element through everything he's writing now," Chet said. "That's where you have him stashed, isn't it? South America. Argentina? Rio? You know I'll find him one of these days."

"You had him and lost him. You shouldn't have flogged and beaten him." But what am I saying now? Phil wondered. Xavier wasn't beating Sean, as far as Phil knew—well, not more than heightened his arousal. But he was fucking him rough. Isabella had said the noise had gotten too much for her from time to time—and that they spent most of their time fucking. "But it doesn't matter, Chet. Sean isn't here; he's not going to be here. I'll accept the award for him. And you won't find him."

"What makes you think he's going to get an award?" Chet asked, with a snort. "The title doesn't even go with the lyrics. Unless you have the fix in on the award." Chet gave Phil a hard look. "You do, don't you? You already know he's won."

Phil just gave him a sweet smile. "Shhh, they're announcing it now."

And with that, a voice wafted down from the stage. "And for best rock song of the year, 'Man Across the River,' by Sean Sinclair."

A New Path

It was peculiar to feel being the stranger and interloper at the funeral of the woman you'd been married to for fifteen years, but that's exactly how I felt as I stood graveside at Denver's Fairmount Cemetery and listened to the priest drone on talking about who must have been some other woman than Emily. This was particularly so, as every time I looked up, across the grave, beyond Emily's first family—her "real" family I'm sure they thought—my eyes met those of Diego's, who stood on the fringe of the crowd.

There was a bit of a crowd. Emily was—or had been—a fairly well-known Romance novelist. And, although she'd enjoyed my escorting her to big events, I'm sure that most here at graveside thought Kenton Boyd was her husband. Emily's children were gathered around him and his shoulders were shaking as the casket was lowered into the ground.

Why weren't my shoulders shaking? Why couldn't I assert myself as Emily's husband? Their divorce hadn't been amicable. He had been a womanizer. Why did Emily's children gather around him today rather than me? I'd been lovely to them—the self-centered, grasping brats.

Which reminded me—I'd have to look again at the date I'd said I'd be out of the house—our house in Breckenridge, Emily's and mine. Already there'd been a wrangle over her half of it. So, I'd just said, "Screw it; I'll move out. Sell it and send me half." It's not like I was a kept man, even though Emily was ten years old than I was. I worked and made good money. In fact, I had another house to go to that didn't have a mortgage and was all mine—Emily and I had pretty much kept our finances separate other than the Breckenridge house.

Who would have known, standing here, wondering whether the priest would shut up before it started snowing, that I'd come to the decision that I was flying back to Richmond next week—to the family house I owned in the Fan District there? I could live pretty much anywhere. I'd only come to Denver—to Golden, really, up into the Rockies west of Denver—because it gave me access to both coasts for my male modeling career. And my book editor job was all handled electronically anyway—I could live anywhere. That had been my stumbling block over the last week. I could live anywhere, so it had been hard deciding where that was. Skiing had been what Emily and I had shared as passions; publishing was what we shared as career context. My passion for skiing had died rather quickly, though, on crutches, with a broken leg—as, I had to admit, had my passion for Emily, if I'd had that to begin with. It too had hobbled along on crutches for too long. And even in publishing, we were in two different worlds.

But I had changed my life for her. It hadn't been anything like my former life—before meeting her. I'd been faithful our entire marriage, unlike Kenton Boyd, standing there and receiving the condolences due the spouse.

I involuntarily looked up again, my eyes searching out Diego Cruz. But he had gone. He wasn't there. It had been in guilt that I had looked up—guilt that was probably largely responsible for my disconnect from this event—the burial of my wife. But I could still say I had been faithful to her to the end—to her end.

I just couldn't say I'd been faithful to her much past the end—shockingly so.

Diego was crying at Emily's funeral, which made me feel all the worse that I was stoic. He had been devoted to Emily for those two years that it took cancer to take her. We were wealthy enough to have round-the-clock nurse companions. Emily didn't have to go into the hospital at the end. We had nurses to do for her what Hospice would, in our own home. Diego had been one of those nurses. He was the nurse who was with her—and me—at the end.

Diego had been as solicitous of my needs and of the effect of cancer on us as he was of Emily's needs. We had grown very close, Diego and I. I hadn't been married to—and faithful to—Emily for so long that I didn't recognize the source of my good relationship with—close attraction to Diego—or that it was reciprocated. Diego hadn't made any secret of his preferences. I, of course, had. I'm not even sure Emily ever suspected. I was seeing other women when we met. I am bi, really, I can get it up and carry through with it with a woman as well as a man. Emily and I had a sex life— just not a robust one and certainly not one that produced children. She was already too old to risk that, or to fit children into her schedule, when we married.

There was no reason—no need—for me to tell her about the affairs equally with men before we met. Bisexuality wasn't something people talked about in relationship to themselves in the early 1960s. They were told it didn't exist, so they tended to try not to even think about having such urges themselves. Emily certainly didn't join in with the innuendo hanging in the air when I told acquaintances that I modeled male underwear and swim wear for International Male—which I still did a year shy of fifty, thank you very much. She had no interest in the world of male modeling, so she probably had no inkling of the suppositions many people made about male models—somewhat akin to male dancers and male figure skaters.

What was important was that there had been no affairs, no falling off the wagon at all, in the fifteen years we had been married. That I fell—and fell big—within hours of her death, though, was what was making me feel so guilty as I stood out here in the cold cemetery, aching for the ordeal to be over—anxious to get onto another path in life, even though I had little idea what that would be.

Two hours after Diego came to me in tears and informed me that he had found Emily dead when he'd taken her dinner tray to her, Diego and I were in the guest room, on the bed, and I was fucking him.

Neither of us, I'm sure—I'm sure more about Diego than myself—had imagined us doing this—ever, probably, but certainly not when Emily's body was still warm. But I was in shock. She had been doing so well. Nobody told her blood clots that she was doing so well, though. And Diego was in grief, both for Emily, genuinely, and in panic that it had happened on his shift.

We came together, really, with me comforting and assuring him. He was the one with the tears. I was the "everything will be all right" one. Why was it that I couldn't cry for Emily, even then, I wonder. I was concerned for the living, though—for Diego in those moments. I held him in my arms. I stroked and then kissed away his tears. He clung to me, his body fitting perfectly into mine. He returned the kisses more fervently than I had intended, but with all of the shared neediness of the months we'd been together, concentrating on Emily, but working closely together and sharing our fears and interests—and our secret knowledge.

I don't know if I pulled him over into my lap, facing, me or if he straddled me. It doesn't matter, we both were equally guilty and equally compelled. I don't know who unzipped who, either. I do know that I was holding our hard cocks bundled and stroking them together as we hungrily kissed.

We wound up on one of the guest beds, me on top of him, both of us pulling at the clothes of the other, becoming intimate with our hands. Diego telling me how much he'd wanted me for months, gagging at the thickness of me in his mouth, begging me to fuck him. And so I did, nudging his thighs open, kneeling between them, pulling him up into my lap; entering, entering, entering him as he moaned at the thickness and length of me; and fucking him deep, hard, and long before I creamed him at the core and he blasted up my belly.

We lay there, panting, afterward, bringing ourselves back down to earth slowly. Neither one of us apologized or expressed regret. My guilt didn't set in until later; I don't know if Diego ever felt guilty. Mine wasn't because I had released my control after fifteen years of holding myself in check. And it wasn't from fucking him that once. It was more that I fucked him again, after I was completely in control of myself, taking him from behind and above, him writhing on the bed on his belly, crying out how thickly and deeply and gloriously I was possessing him, before I did anything about Emily lying dead in our bed on the other side of the wall.

And now, what about Diego? I had just made the decision to move back to Richmond. I just then realized that Diego had figured in my indecision on where to go from here. Something in the back of my mind had been telling me that I needed to do something about Diego. But wasn't that part of the guilt? I hadn't been with Diego since that evening, although we had talked on the phone—or at least sat through long silences on the phone, neither one of us being the one who wanted to disconnect. Could I be with Diego, though? Did I need to continue with the comfortable, convenient lie I'd lived the last fifteen years? If I met with him again, fucked him again, would the guilt rise up of the evening I fucked him twice with my dead wife in my bed just on the other side of the wall from us?

I looked up again, hoping that Diego would have returned to where I could see him and that something in his eyes would tell me what to do. But he still was gone. So were most of the other mourners, including Kenton Boyd and Emily's children. Most were walking back to their cars. So was the priest, his cassock flapping in the breeze that had come in to deliver the first of the snowflakes. I knelt by the still-open hole and put my hand on the railing of the elevator mechanism. I bowed my head.

Anyone looking back at me would assume I was showing my grief. They wouldn't know how hard it was for me to give up the comfortable, convenient lie of the last fifteen years.

* * * *

I was driving south on Brook toward the heart of Richmond, trying to beat the effects of Hurricane Frederic back to my Monument Avenue townhouse in the Fan District, when I saw him huddled in a bus shelter. I was acquainted with Neal from a new place for gay guys, the Rainbow Connection, being established downtown in a warehouse district where Interstates east-west 64 and north-south 95 converged. I'd served him dinner and played basketball with him a couple of times. I didn't know him well, though, and didn't want to, as I was attracted to him, but I didn't want to have that complication with any of the guys at the shelter. It wasn't a snobbish thing; it was a complicated relationships at a place I'm volunteering thing. So I drove on by.

I thought we'd made eye contact, though. I thought he had recognized me. So, I didn't make it more than two blocks farther on when guilt got to me and I turned around and went back.

I don't know for sure how I'd gotten roped in to helping out at the Rainbow Connection, which was everything I had been trying to avoid when I'd moved back to Richmond from Denver seven months earlier. I did not specifically seek out volunteering there, of course. I'd gone back into the church and one of the young priests there, Father Thomas, had latched onto me, declared I needed to get involved in the community, and had pulled me into the Rainbow Connection. It was sort of a perverse thing for him to do, I thought, as he was the first one to take confession from me since Denver, and I had confessed to my proclivities and about Diego. The penance he had given me was to march into the jaws of the lion.

The priest was young, athletic, modern-thinking, and hyperactive in the community. He also was handsome, with dark, sultry Mediterranean looks, and, like me, had done modeling before he went into the priesthood. That gave us mutual pasts to connect us, but it also made me uncomfortable and antsy. I had regretted that he had been the one to take my confession. Any of the other priests in the church, older and more plodding, would, I assume have accepted that I wanted to escape my sins and was being a recluse for that reason. They wouldn't have pulled me out of the renovation projects I'd steeped myself in in the old Monument Avenue townhouse and forced me to face my demons.

Father Thomas said he'd faced demons too. That didn't make me one bit more comfortable with either what he told me I needed to do or how I reacted to him personally—and as my priest.

The Fan District of Richmond in the late 1970s was deep into urban renewal. The district was named thusly because the streets fanned out west from the state capitol center. Monument Avenue, where I lived, was a promenade with a tree-lined grassy median with a parade of statues of southern Civil War generals and figures running between the two sides of the street. All of the houses were set abutting each other or set close together and most were large piles of brick, many with multistory porches on the front of them. The Fan District had once been the prominent residential center of the city and once more was becoming that as the wealthy moved back in from the suburbs. I had returned in time to know that the value of my property—a three-story, fifteen-room mansion set on an English basement with a separate entrance—would go up exponentially if I did some restoration work.

Since I wanted to work myself to a frazzle to avoid thinking about what I really wanted from life, I'd put every working moment that I wasn't editing a book or zipping off for a photo shoot in bringing the house back to life and health. Father Thomas had cut into that after five months of being the recluse by pulling me into the Rainbow Connection, which included a clinic, a soup kitchen, a shelter, and a recreation center for the city's gay homeless and down and outers.

That's where I'd come into contact with Neal, a young blond guy in his twenties, who availed himself of all of the Rainbow Connection's services and who could always be counted on for a pickup basketball game. In that aspect, the Rainbow Connection was a godsend for me too, as I started counting on getting my exercise there while I was helping out in soup kitchen. I'd played pickup in the church's gym with Father Thomas, and the prospect of better gym facilities as he described them at the Rainbow Connection had been the lure he used to get me involved in his pet community project.

I pulled up beside the bus shelter, crossing to the other side of the street, pointed the wrong way, and rolled down my window. It was only then that I saw the small dog huddled by Neal's leg. Neal was huddled over too, several backpacks around him. It was raining already and the wind was pulling rainwater into the shelter.

"Is that you, Neal?" I called from the window I'd rolled down. I damn well knew it was Neal, and he knew I knew it was. The look he gave me hinted that he'd known I'd passed him by the first time too. "Hurricane's almost here," I said, although, thank god, most of the pizzaz of Hurricane Frederic had been knocked out of it before it got to central Virginia. "You need to get inside. Hop in. I'll drop you off at the shelter."

"Can't go there," Neal answered. "They won't take Petey." he gestured to the small mutt pressed into his leg and trembling.

"What have you done with Petey before when you've stayed at the shelter?" I asked.

"Just got him last week. Or he got me, I guess."

"And you've been sleeping outside since then?"

"Yep."

"Well, get inside the car—both of you—the hurricane's almost on us. There's a motel nearby that will take a dog, I'm sure. I'll treat you to the night. No one should be out in weather like this."

By the time we pulled into the motel lot, a motel that was seedy enough that Neal wouldn't think I was putting myself out too much to stand him a room here, the streets were awash with water the drains couldn't handle and the wind was bracing. There wasn't any trouble in having a dog in the room, as I had hoped there wouldn't be. It wasn't the

Ritz, they had the room, and there wasn't any prospect of anyone else dragging in to rent it in this weather. In fact, they probably were pleased to be renting the room for the entire night. It was the kind of motel where rooms usually went by the hour and the biggest charge was for changing the sheets.

I helped Neal and Petey into the room with Neal's backpacks. The wind had come up enough that it was a struggle to get out of the elements. As we entered the room, a tree came down across the motel entrance in back of us. It was obvious I was spending the night too. Fortuitously, I had been driving home from a photo shoot in Washington, D.C., so, after ascertaining from Neal that we'd be OK doubling up—tripling up, if Petey was taken into consideration—I fought my way back to the car and brought my suitcase in. By then I was soaked to the skin, my clothes clinging to me.

Neal gave me an appraising look when I struggled back into the room, making me realize that being soaked to the skin was quite revealing. He'd seen me in the altogether in the locker room before, but here, like this, was much more embarrassing. I excused myself and took my suitcase into the bathroom with me, drying myself off with a threadbare towel that was hopeless at wicking off moisture, and redressing in shorts and a T.

When I came out of the bathroom, Neal had stripped down to his briefs and was sitting on the end of the bed. It hadn't occurred to me, but he, of course, had been soaked as well.

"Finished in the bathroom, if you need to get on something dry," I said, my voice tighter than I wanted it to be. He was a beautiful young man. A bit thinner than he should be, but well-muscled and in perfect proportion. He was blond, with blue eyes, and looked both vulnerable and worldly wise at the same time.

There was only one bed in the room, a double. Neal was sitting on the end of it, his arms outstretched and his fists pushed into the mattress on either side. Petey was nestled up by his bare leg. "So, I owe you thanks from getting me out of that storm," he said, giving me a saucy look.

"As I said, no one should be out in a storm like that. Just sorry that I have to stay here too," I said. I looked around the room, trying to think how we were going to do the sleeping arrangements. Maybe the storm would let up enough that I could check on whether there was another room I could get. Chances on that were slim, though, at the guy in the front office was obviously in the midst of closing up when we checked in.

"I'm not."

"You're not what?" I asked, looking back at him, not entirely on his wavelength, but close enough to be a bit concerned and off center.

"I'm not sorry you have to stay here too. And I don't think you're really sorry either."

Blushing, I cleared my throat and grasped at a change in topic. The only chair in the room was covered with backpacks, so I stood there, probably looking as lost and uncomfortable as I felt. "Do you have any idea what you can do after tonight, if the shelter won't take Petey? Can I make some phone calls to see if there's someplace else that—?"

"Rainbow Connection is convenient to my work," he said.

"You have a job?"

"Yes. I work in construction. We report to a warehouse not far from the rec center and get sent out from there. It's just not enough to pay for room in addition to food—food now for both of us."

"Maybe Petey isn't—"

"Not an option," he said, his face taking on a look of panic. He was very arousing with the vulnerable look. I felt myself hardening up. "I don't have anyone. Now I have Petey. And Petey's got me."

"OK, I can understand and appreciate that. Construction, you say?" Again I was anxious not only to keep a conversation going rather than what I really wanted to do with Neal and snatching at solutions to his problem. The solution dropped into my mind, and, unfortunately, leaped out of my mouth before I could analyze it for danger. "There's an apartment in the basement of my house that's not finished, but it's functional. Better than a shelter certainly. And my house is on Monument, within a walk of where you report to work. Maybe . . . if you're interested . . . you could live there for now . . . until you found someplace else. You could work off any rent by working on the apartment . . . you say you're in construction."

I hoped that didn't sound as suggestive and strained as I felt it was when I said it.

"I think I'd like that," he answered. "So . . ."

I watched in horror—not the least horror because of the effect it had on me—when he rose from the bed and slipped off his briefs. "So, are you going to fuck me now?"

"What?" I said, my voice strangled. "I don't . . . I hope you don't think—"

"That you picked me up and brought me to a motel and have said I can come live in your house . . . that you are nice to me at the Rainbow Connection and play ball with me there . . . and that you shower with me and show off how low you're hanging. That you get hard when you look at me? That you are hard now? With all that, do I think that you want to fuck me? Yeah, I do. And you *can* fuck me if you want."

"Neal. I didn't . . . I don't . . ."

"It's OK. I want you to fuck me. You got a great body for your age and you got the biggest dong I've seen at the rec center. All of the guys there want you to fuck them. We got a lottery going on who gets you inside them first. Looks like I win—unless you been ballin' some of the other guys and they haven't been boasting about it."

"That's . . . not . . . why . . . I brought you here, Neal. Maybe I should just leave."

We both tuned ourselves into the whistling of the wind outside and the raindrops slamming into the window like missiles.

"You're not going to go out into that tonight," Neal said. "It's OK. I want you to fuck me. I'm hard for you. And you're hard for me too."

Of course I was.

"Is there a sleeping bag in what you brought in, Neal?"

38

"Yeah, of course."

"Well, you can roll that out on the floor over there, and that's where you'll sleep tonight. I didn't bring you here to fuck you. I'm not offering you a temporary place to sleep in exchange for some construction work to fuck you. This isn't the way I'd do that."

"But you want to fuck me, don't you? I want you to fuck me. What's the problem? You volunteer at the Rainbow Connection to hook up, don't you? That's what the volunteers do. That's what Father Thomas does. Jarid, that big black dude? He fucks Father Thomas. I've heard even Father Thomas talk about the size of your cock and how he'd like to—"

"I . . . don't . . . want to hear this, Neal. I'm going to take a shower now. Then you can. I'll be in bed when you get out of the shower, and you and Petey can sack out over there. Tomorrow, when they've gotten the tree cleared out the parking lot, I'll show you the apartment. If you want to stay there until you make other arrangements, that's fine. No strings attached. I'm making no demands of . . . or moves on . . . you. I want to be very clear about that. We can forget any of this was said."

"But you're a top, aren't you?" he asked. "Maybe you'll do me sometime? It doesn't have to be any tit for tat. I'd like for you to top me."

I was having trouble breathing. I didn't want to answer. But for some reason, I did. He looked a little downcast, like I was rejecting him. Like he wasn't good enough for me. And that wasn't it at all. "Maybe sometime, Neal. Yes, you take my breath away. Yes, I want . . . but I'm going into the bathroom now."

I was in the shower, soaped up, when the power went out. There was a small square of a window, high up on the wall, at the back of the building, so the flashing of light in the fury of the storm kept the room from being totally dark, but the interior lights were out and the air conditioning, such as it was, had kicked off. The water was still running in the shower, though, so I started to rinse off.

But then I wasn't alone. Neal was in the shower cubicle with me, on his knees, taking my half-hard, but quickly filling out, cock in his mouth. Moaning, I leaned back into the tiled wall, widened my stance to give him plenty of room to kneel close in between my legs, and held the unruly blond curls of his head between my hands as he expertly sucked my cock.

He took his mouth off my cock long enough to murmur, "I knew you wanted it."

Yes, I wanted it. Grasping his head between my hands, I pulled his mouth back onto my cock.

When I had pulled him up, turned his back to the wall, and settled his channel on my cock to the sounds of his grunts and groans and his "You're so big; you're splitting me. Yes! Fuck ME!" he hooked his knees on my hips and I pushed his back up and down the soaping tile wall as I fucked him hard and deep.

On the bed, I covered him, doggie style, the palm of one of my hands on his belly, pulling him up to his knees, mounting him, and fucking him hard, while I milked his cock with the other hand. He stayed right with me, thrusting back as I thrust forward, egging me on to "give it to me good." I gave it to him good—the first total, all-out fucking I'd done since Diego in Denver nearly eight months earlier.

I woke in the morning, on my back on the bed, under a sheet, no sounds of a storm coming from outside the room. The sheet was rustling and rising and falling before me. Neal was under the sheet, between my thighs, giving me a blow job. Petey was sitting on his haunches beside the bed, cocking his head back and forward, looking quizzically at the rise and fall of the sheet. Feeling suddenly free and amused by the sight of Petey and wondering what he was thinking, I relaxed and luxuriated in the masterful job Neal's mouth was doing on my cock and on how he was squeezing, rolling, and distending my balls with one of his hands.

It was only after I creamed his tonsils and he started to move up on my body . . . after Petey began to whine when he saw that his master was in the room, coming out from under the sheet . . . and after Neal voiced an "Oh, shit. I

40

know he's got to get out to take a dump" . . . and after I was alone in room, Neal's parting, "When I get back, I want you to fuck the shit out of me again" resonating in my brain, that I was coming back to earth. I knew this wasn't the path I intended to take. I had to return to reality.

When Neal and Petey came back, I'd already packed out of the room and was sitting in the car.

"The IHop OK for breakfast?" I asked, trying to keep my voice cheery. "There's one nearby, and we can get something for Petey too. Then I'll show you the apartment. Deal's still on offer, but last night didn't happen. OK?"

"This morning didn't happen either? I thought you liked the blow job."

"I loved the blow job. Nope, this morning didn't happen either."

"If you want to pretend it didn't," Neal said. Something in his voice, though, told me that he didn't believe that for a moment.

I wasn't sure I believed it, either. But I'd be damned if I would give in so easily. It wasn't the path I needed to be on.

* * * *

I held off for two weeks. Neal wasn't persistent, but it was like he knew. He was fine with the apartment the way it was, had better ideas than I did on how to upgrade it, and he was a good carpenter. He must have really had a construction job, because he left in the morning on a regular schedule and returned in the evening at about the same time. At my insistence, he left Petey behind and I walked him regularly. The apartment had an outside entrance but it also had an internal staircase running down from the cross hall between my kitchen and dining room, with a door at the head of the stairs with a lock on my side. So, I'd just go downstairs, leash up Petey, and take him out the apartment's outside entrance. When we got back, I'd leave him downstairs, go back up the stairs, and lock the door behind me.

Petey became attached to me—and I to him. I admit I let him up into my part of the house more often than not until it was close to time for Neal to return. Neal and I were OK, too, though, with Neal calling me downstairs from time to time in the evening and on Saturdays and Sundays to check what he was doing on the construction of the apartment and to give me lists for supplies. He was good about not calling me down too late or running power tools too early on Saturday and Sunday mornings. While he dressed skimpily and gave me "those" looks while I was down there, he didn't press the issue. He did, though, say more than once, "Anytime you want it. All you have to do is signal."

And that, ultimately, is what happened. I, of course, told myself it was unintentional. But I knew it wasn't.

One evening two weeks after Neal and Petey moved in, I walked Petey late, my bringing him back coinciding with Neal coming out of the shower, where he'd immediately gone upon returning from work. He'd had a towel around his middle when he'd come out of the shower, but when he saw me come in from the street with Petey on the leash, he dropped it and didn't pick it up. He asked me if I wanted a drink. I was just wearing tight jeans myself that evening. The day had been hot. I stripped off my T and stuck it into the back waistband of the jeans before coming inside. I'm sure I knew what I was doing.

I accepted the drink, but I pretended that all I wanted to talk about was what color the walls in the bedroom there should be painted. We were in the bedroom, looking at each other across his bed. He was naked and in erection. We each had a glass of scotch in our hands. I was hard too, which I'm sure he could tell.

"Well, I think it's time I went upstairs. An early night tonight. Not going out. You?"

"No, I'm not going out either," Neal answered in measured tones.

He probably expected me to fuck him there on his bed, then. But I didn't. Saying it was good to see him—which was a little ironic as I could see all of him, and a significant piece of him was erect—I bid him goodnight.

He stood at the bottom of the stairs, watching me walk up them. He didn't hear the door at the top of the stairs close or lock—because I left it wide open.

Twenty minutes later, we were on my bed on the second floor of the townhouse, Neal under me, his legs spread and bent, my knees pushed under his buttocks, raising his pelvis to my best penetration angle. His arms were splayed out from his body, his fists gripping the fabric of the bedspread, his back arched, his head arched back too, with his eyes open wide, his mouth forming a big O, and him crying out, "God, it's huge. You're killing me! Yes, fuck me. Fuck the shit out me!"

I was thrusting hard and deep, relieving two week's worth of tension and frustration, both of us having known all along it would come to this. It may have been the grinding noise of the brass headboard against the wall or the scream of bedsprings, as, crouched over him, I held him pinned to the bed with my fists pressed into the curves where his arms attached to his torso and pounded him deep and hard, that drew Petey up to my bedroom out of curiosity. When he arrived, though, he just crouched down beside the bed, crossed his front legs, and looked up to where I was moving on his master's body. Petey gave a calm, "it's about time" expression.

I had to acknowledge that Petey was right.

Over the next month, Neal slowly worked his way up into the house and into more control of our relationship. The door to the basement remained open. Neal started showing up for dinner upstairs, so I more than doubled the portions I cooked. He roamed the upstairs at will, advising me on how the nearly untouched third floor could best be restored. He was in my bed, under me, most nights—at least for the first couple of weeks—with Petey taking up station beside the bed.

As Neal became more comfortable with our relationship, the relationship loosened up. He started to bring other men home. These were usually older men—not as old as I was, but older than Neal was. It became obvious to me that he was renting himself out to them. Some of them were there for fun, though.

Then came the evening that he brought one upstairs—a young black man. Very good looking, slightly effeminate, but very well put together.

I was already in bed, in sleeping trousers, reading a book, when they appeared at my bedroom door.

"Trax here wants to see it," Neal says. "He doesn't believe it's bigger and thicker than his." Both obviously had been drinking. Both were just in their briefs.

"Neal," I said, but he already was at the side of the bed, pulling my dick out of the fly.

"Holy, shit, that is big, man. I want a piece of that," the black guy exclaimed. He was between my legs, taking my cock in his mouth, while Neal took my head between his hands and took me into a kiss.

I wound up giving them both what they wanted. I fucked them both, first Trax and then Neal and then, embarrassingly, watched Trax, who did, indeed, have a really big one, fuck Neal on the bed beside me. I couldn't help myself, and I had one hell of a time while it was going on.

After they left, though, and I'd had time to think about it, I crept down to the kitchen. The door to the basement was open. At the bottom of the stairs, Neal was on his back on the floor. Trax was holding Neal's legs out and up with grips on his ankles, and was fucking Neal again.

I closed and locked the door to the basement when Neal and the black stud had gone downstairs. It wouldn't be open again while Neal was in the apartment. I didn't throw him out but I told him that the police would surely be calling if he kept bring men home and taking their money. After that, it was only the younger men he brought back to the apartment—presumably the ones who didn't pay.

I didn't throw him out later either. I had grown too fond of Petey. I didn't want to lose the dog. And although I told myself that I couldn't give Neal and his friends the run of the house anymore or be just another of Neal's johns, I couldn't rule that out either. I just didn't know.

* * * *

Giving up with a sigh, I surrendered to him, letting my body fall back on the bed and letting my senses concentrate on the shaft he was fully sheathing as he rode my cock in long rises and falls, his claws digging into my pecs, his breath coming in fast pants, his eyes slitted in lust.

"I have to. I must," Thomas hissed as he rode me. I couldn't think of him as Father Thomas under these circumstances, just Thomas. As his vigor lagged a bit, having ridden me for over fifteen minutes, turning to a reverse cowboy and gripping my knees for a few minutes before turning back to face me, lowering his face periodically for a kiss, I accepted responsibility. I gripped his waist and slammed him up and down on the cock, loosing seed deep inside him as he arced his own ejaculation up to my chin and neck. Lowering his chest, matted with black, curly hair, down to mine, with its salt-and-pepper mix, he licked his cum off my throat and chin and we shared it in a kiss.

I hadn't any conscious idea when I invited Father Thomas to the house for a late dinner after a Rainbow Connection board meeting that we'd wind up on my bed. But I guess I should have seen it coming. I didn't know whether to believe the taunt Neal had given months ago in that fleabag motel about Father Thomas taking cock and wanting mine, but the idea bugged me and festered inside me.

It turned out that Neal was right. I don't know which of us pushed this over the edge, but neither of us had resisted it.

"We can't come together like this again," he whispered into my chest hair.

"No, we can't," I agreed.

"This has to be the only time."

"Yes."

"But since we're here now, anyway."

"Yes," I agreed.

I was still inside him. I already was hardening again. He obviously knew that. As if by unspoken agreement, he raised his torso off of mine and arched his body back as I scooted us both down to where my butt was on the end of the bed, my spread legs reaching down to the floor, where I could leverage thrusts off the balls of my feet. Thomas' head reached the carpet below the bed. He extended his arms out from his side in a cruciform, completely open and surrender stance. His ankles went to my shoulders, and I pulled him on and off my shaft by gripping his waist until, with a sigh, we both came again.

Later we sat on stools at the kitchen island, drinking coffee and looking sheepishly at each other. We both were in terrycloth robes—and nothing else. Both robes were gaping open, revealing that we both were hirsute and muscular—Thomas dark and sultry; me more of a Scandinavian build—both with cut cocks, both of which were half hard.

"Look at us," Thomas said with a slightly nervous voice, looking straight at me over the rim of his coffee cup, his gaze quizzical. "I think we performed marvelously. I know you did. Biggest cock I've ever had."

I sat there, looking straight at him, feeling a little sad, knowing I showed that, not responding to him.

"What? What's wrong?" he asked. "You knew we were building to this. It's just biological urge. We both can intellectually get past this."

"Oh, really?" I asked. "I am sitting here wondering who I confess this to. You have been my confessor."

"I do suggest that you hold it until you take a trip out of town," Thomas said. And then, when I didn't laugh, "This has to be the only time, Wade, but this did no harm to anyone, and you need this wake-up call. You need to accept that this is what you want, what you need—being with a man. You need to accept that there's no harm done, no one to answer to if you take a man. And you need to realize that you need a man permanently in your life. Not me, unfortunately—I'd like that cock of yours inside me every day—but of course I'm not free for an open relationship. But you are. And that's the point. You're capable of an open relationship and you need one. Not with Neal, of course, you need a greater commitment than he will provide. But, dammit, Wade, find yourself a man to live with you here and share the rest of your life with—openly. I wish I had that freedom. It's a freedom you can have. You need to fully get on to a new path, one that you know you want to be on."

"Are you finished with the homily?" I asked, giving him a reassuring smile. The message had sunk in. I knew exactly what to do.

"Yes, why?"

"You said we couldn't do this again after tonight. So, I was thinking of fucking you again right here on the floor."

I lay on top of him, between his spread and bent legs, as he clutched my shoulder blades in his hands, and cried out with each hard thrust. The third time was just as sweet as the first two—and accompanied by far less guilt.

* * * *

I went straight from Stapleton Airport to the hospital, having called his service and found out that he was there with a terminal patient.

I arrived after the patient had died and while Diego was sitting on a bench outside of the door into the hospital room. He looked a little dazed when I sat down beside him.

"Wade," he said, as if maybe I was someone else and he was just conjuring me up because he wanted me to be there. It had been a year. We had exchanged letters—letters that hadn't talked around our feelings but didn't, really, hide them from each other.

"Yes, it's me. Are you—?"

"She's gone," he murmured. "I've lost another patient. Almost a year caring for her."

"A year that both you and she knew would end here, wasn't it?" I asked. "It's OK, Diego, you were there. You provided what she needed. Did she go peacefully, with a smile on her face?"

"Yes," he said, sniffing back a tear. "She was clutching my hand."

"There you go then."

"It's hard," he said. "I'll have to start again . . . knowing . . ."

47

"You don't have to do this alone, though," I said. "I want you to come with me."

"Yes, of course. I want that. Do you have a hotel room. We can't go to my place . . . I have roommates."

"Yes, I have a room we can go to, and I'm glad you're willing to go there with me—I want to take you there—but that's not what I meant. I want you to come back to Richmond with me. I have a big house and it's within walking distance to a major hospital. We can do this together. Any hospital in the country would be glad to have a nurse who does what you do. We can be together. Will you come home with me?"

"Yes," he said without much hesitation at all.

"There's one thing, though. I have to confess. There's a young man living in the basement apartment—and I've had him in bed. But that's over. But I thought you should know."

"And you are going to let him stay?"

"I'm afraid I have to. You see, he has a dog I've grown very fond of."

"Oh, well, then. I can see why he has to stay."

"I knew that you would be able to," I said. "That's a big reason why I love you."

The Philanthropist

"There's someone I want you to meet. Just as soon as he separates from the battle-ax."

"The battle-ax?" Kyle Kendricks asked, a bit confused. He was standing with Trent Taylor at the opening of the Rodin exhibit at the Virginia Museum of Fine Arts in Richmond. Trent was the curator of the exhibit. He knew Kyle because both served on the board of the Rainbow Connection, a gay men's recreation center/clinic/shelter located in the downtown warehouse district close to where the east-west 64 and north-south 95 interstates met. Trent was the board treasurer. Kyle, a young assistant professor of art, taught classes in art at the Rainbow Connection as well as dance, and he directed the Richmond Gay Men's Chorus, which practiced there.

"Mrs. Battle-ax. It's his wife, Margaret. That's him there, the tall, distinguished-looking dude, Derek Colson. He's among the highest-drawer philanthropists in this town. She's the dowdy one standing beside him. A DuPont, of course. That's where much of their money comes from."

"And you want me to meet him because . . . ?"

"To help them disperse some of that money they're building up, of course. He's willing to give a chunk to the Connection. We just need to be friendly to him."

"So you want me to be friendly to him?"

"You're about the friendliest-looking board member we have. He's a director of the Virginia National Bank. He gave a fourth of the money for this exhibit. Need I say more? Ah, I see she's wandered off. Put on a smile and let's get over there before that dreadful woman from the Richmond Symphony cuts in on us. Here. Take this flute of bubbly over to him. His glass is nearly empty."

"What sort of friendly do you want me to be?"

"You know what kind of friendly."

"He's a married guy. He wouldn't—"

"Don't believe that for a minute. Why do you think he shows interest in the Rainbow Connection? Why do you think he gives money to us? He's a cutthroat businessman. Don't be so naïve as to believe he gives anything to anybody without the expectation of return on his investment."

Trent brought Kyle together with the banker, managed smooth introductions, and wafted off. Kyle and Derek engaged in a bit of chit chat before others arrived, including the executive director of the Richmond Symphony, who was determined to monopolize the banker. Derek Colson gave Kyle a sheepish look and a wink before he turned his full attention to the woman and Kyle, wanting to avoid another man who had been dogging him throughout the opening and who was walking their way, joined the fluid group.

Kyle hadn't been standing beside the banker long, but it had been long enough to get the impression of a big, fuzzy polar bear. He was, as Trent had said, distinguished. He also was imposing, being a full head taller than Kyle, who was on the short side and lithe, albeit well-muscled, like the gymnast he'd been in college and the ballet dancer he was with the Richmond Ballet, just one of the set of artistic talents he had. Colson definitely was a man to be noticed—large boned, tall, broad in the shoulders, and not exactly thin in the waist either, although not really fat. He had wavy gray hair of a silvery texture, bushy gray eyelashes over striking, hazel eyes, and a mustache leading down into a goatee, both of which were professionally tended. He obviously was a man who was obeyed.

When he went home to his second-floor apartment in one of the old mansions of the Fan District lining Grove Avenue, not far from the Fine Arts Museum or many of the other artistic venues in Richmond, Kyle thought back on his few moments with the banker. The man had a magnetism about him and Kyle regretted not having had longer to talk with him.

He needn't have held regret about that, though, as the following Saturday, when the Richmond Gay Man's Chorus gave a Christmas concert in one of the Jefferson Hotel ballrooms, Trent Taylor appeared by Kyle's side, with Derek Colson in tow, to congratulate Kyle, the chorus' director, on a successful concert.

"Raised a big chunk for the Connection," he said. "Derek has written a very nice check too. He wanted to congratulate you personally."

"Yes, it was a fine concert," Colson said, giving Kyle what could only be described in this season as a jolly, sparkling smile.

"I'm glad you enjoyed it," Kyle said.

"Perhaps we could celebrate a bit after you have been properly hailed by all of your admirers," Colson said, as Trent wafted off and other admirers were honing in on Kyle. "Would you do me the honor of meeting me in the hotel bar after you have been exhausted here? I would like to have a chance to exhaust you myself."

Kyle felt a little chill run up his spine even though he was sure that the meaning that jumped into his mind was just his imagination. He couldn't help being attracted to the man, who exuded a dominating, overpowering personality. "Yes, I would like that," he answered.

Colson was charming and dominated the conversation in the bar. They sat across from each other with a tiny, round table between them that let Colson make the most of his height and bulk. He leaned over the table, giving Kyle the impression of the big bear of a man covering him from three sides and drawing him into his embrace. Kyle found that warming and arousing. He didn't bat an eye when Colson touched the hand he had on the table with his fingers or let the fingers move on the back of his hand. Kyle felt a shudder of pleasure when he looked down and saw that the man's knuckles were hairy. Kyle was aroused by hirsute men.

Somehow during the conversation, Colson managed to get his middle finger under Kyle's and two of Kyle's fingers loosely wrapped around Colson's. Kyle wasn't aware of it until Colson started moving his finger slowly in and out of the loose grip. Kyle blushed and started to move his hand away, but Colson's other hand covered his and held it there.

"Am I embarrassing you?" Colson asked.

"No, not at all," Kyle answered. And it occurred to him that Colson's overtures didn't, in fact, turn him off. He looked directly into Colson's eyes and repeated, "No, you aren't embarrassing me at all. You're flattering me."

It had become quite evident that Trent had been right about the man's interest despite him being married. It also was evident that it wasn't so much that Trent had been throwing Kyle at Colson as that Colson had pressed Trent to get him hooked up with Kyle.

"And I hope I am enticing you. I have a room booked upstairs. Will you come upstairs with me?" Colson asked in a low, gravelly voice.

"Yes," Kyle answered simply.

"I am going to fuck you; you are going to be submissive to me," Colson said, pinning his intent down, watching Kyle's reaction closely with his eyes.

"Yes," Kyle acquiesced, lowering his own eyes in submission.

* * * *

"Strip for me, please, and stand there and let me take you in," Colson said. He was sitting on the end of the bed in the hotel room and Kyle was standing in the middle of the room, facing him. The command was given in a calm, low voice, but it none the less was a command. Colson had called Kyle correctly. He was a submissive. As long as he was in the arousal zone and the commands were given calmly, he would accede to them.

Their disrobing was almost a mirror play, with both of them going after the bow ties of their tuxedos simultaneously. Colson stopped, though, with his shirt and undershirt off, mesmerized at the beauty of Kyle's dancer's body, as Kyle continued slowly stripping down. For his part, Kyle couldn't take his eyes off Colson's hairy, barrel chest.

"You are a gorgeous young man," Colson said when Kyle was naked. The older man sat down on the end of the bed. "How old are you?"

"Twenty-five."

"Half my age."

"Not from the look of you," Kyle said.

Colson was obviously pleased by this. "You look like a dancer. I thought you taught art—and, of course, direct a choir. You could be a model."

"I do that too," Kyle said, pleased now himself at the compliments. "I dance with the Richmond Ballet, but I'm getting a little old for that."

"Will you turn around for me? Does it embarrass you that I ask that?"

"Not at all," Kyle answered, and he turned to show Colson his backside.

"Nice. Plump. You're perfection. Would it be too much to ask you to bend over . . ." Kyle did so, ". . . and to spread your cheeks." Kyle did that too.

Colson rose, walked to Kyle, and ran his hand down Kyle's flank and over his rounded buttocks. Kyle flinched when Colson penetrated his ass with an index finger and held it there, both of them focused on Kyle relaxing his sphincter muscle and opening to the finger, both sighing when he did, but neither said anything. Withdrawing the finger, both of them knowing that Colson could have mounted Kyle right then and fucked him and would have been received submissively without demur, Colson went back to the bed and sat down.

"Beautiful. I hope you don't mind my expressing my admiration for what you've done with your body this way."

"No, of course not."

"I wish to worship your body. Are you going to let me fuck you repeatedly? I'll pay you $500 to let me cover you as often as I like tonight."

"Yes, if you want. You don't have to pay me anything." The approach had been smooth, even if bald, and just right—Kyle was narcissistic. He worshipped his own body. He was lost to another man who would do so as well.

"Thank you. Will you kneel to me to start with?"

Kyle turned to see that Colson had unzipped himself and had a beefy cock out, more than half hard, and in his hand. His thighs were spread as he sat at the end of the bed. Kyle knelt between them, took the cock in his mouth, and made love to it as he opened up the tuxedo trousers at the waist, flared the trousers open, and let his fingers dig through Colson bush, finding and grasping, squeezing, and rolling the man's balls as he sucked the cock, running his tongue over the piss slit.

Sighing, Colson leaned back on the mattress on his elbow and enjoyed the blow job, which was over all too soon, as he ejaculated into the back of Kyle's throat.

"I will come quickly, I'm afraid, as I've just done. But I can come often," he murmured, a statement rather than an apology.

He pulled Kyle up effortlessly—Kyle sighing at the powerful, big bear aspect of the man—and turned him onto his back on the bed. Crouching over Kyle, enveloping the young man close with his body, instinctively knowing that this aroused and kept the young man submissive, Colson forced Kyle's legs straight up his chest and over his shoulders.

Muttering, "So flexible. Nice," Colson took Kyle's mouth with his, moving into an ever-yielding kiss in which the two shared the residual cum Colson had deposited in Kyle's mouth. Colson's fingers went to Kyle's ass, invading and working Kyle's channel, as, lost to overpowering man, Kyle moaned and groaned. Colson stroked Kyle's cock with his other hand as he rocked back and forth on Kyle's body— maintaining the pressure and stroking until Kyle had come for him.

"Please, please," Kyle murmured. "Put it in me, please."

Colson rolled off to the side and sat on the end of the bed for a moment, looking down into Kyle's eyes lustfully. It was obvious they weren't finished. Kyle looked back, his own eyes full of want and admiration. Colson was dominating him; he was doing everything right.

"Are you sure you are ready for it?" the older man ask.

"Yes, please. Shaft me."

The banker went down on his knees between Kyle's legs, draped over the end of the bed, grasped Kyle's ankles and wishboned the legs straight out and up as his mouth went to Kyle's hole. The younger man arched his back and moaned at the assault of the mouth and teeth and the penetration of the tongue. The assault was fierce and Kyle opened right up for it.

Standing up between Kyle's legs, still holding them outstretched, Colson said in a low, commanding voice, "There next to you, that case. Open it. Do it yourself." Kyle opened the case to find packets of condoms and a tube of lube. Showing his flexibility, he managed to raise his torso to Colson's chest and bury his lips in the man's chest hair, as his hands rolled a condom on Colson's cock. He followed with lubing up his entrance and Colson's cock, jacking up the older man's cock to hard by stroking the shaft with the lubed hands.

Here it comes, Kyle thought, as he arched his torso back, waiting for Colson to enter him. But that wasn't what he did just then. He pulled Kyle up from the bed, once more exhibiting his power, carried him over to the window, where there was a wide ledge running the entire length of that wall, and set Kyle down, moving his legs into the splits along the ledge.

"I want to take advantage of your flexibility," Colson said. "Your body is magnificent. Young, pliable, flawless."

"Just don't make me wait for it," Kyle murmured. He leaned forward, the palms of his hands on the cold window, a cheek there too, his eyes looking out across the treetops of the gentrified Fan District and the lightly following snow.

He winced as the thick cock worked itself into his ass, mercifully well open from the finger play to receive it and sighed as the bigger man brought his arms around, putting him into an enveloping bear hug, his hairiness making Kyle feel like he was covered in a fur coat—a fur coat with a ramrod up his ass.

Kyle opened his mouth to gasp as the cock moved up, deeper inside him.

"I love your flexibility," the voice at his ear whispered. "I am an expert in the Kama Sutra. This is the 'elevated splits.' I love that you can do it. Not many can. I will pay you to allow me to put you through all of the positions."

"You don't have to pay me," Kyle reiterated. He groaned as Colson fucked him in this demanding position. The term "Kama Sutra" had jumped out at him, and, yes, he wanted to explore that. He loved the thought of the variety and demand of it; he needed spice in his sex life. But more than this term, he latched onto the word "love." He so much wanted love. Despite all of his talents and activities—maybe because of them—he felt he was held out, isolated, by others. This bear of a man had used the word "love." Kyle already felt that he was falling in love.

"The afternoon delight," Colson murmured, as he changed the position to where Kyle was backed to the window, the heels of his hands reversed and digging into the ledge, and his body suspended over the carpet, his knees hooked on Colson's hips and Colson's hands palming Kyle's buttocks, supporting the young man's body in midair as he fucked him deep.

After what Colson termed "bent spoons" on the bed, with Colson on his back, knees bent, and Kyle's back on his chest, with Colson holding Kyle's legs raised and spread wide with a hand grip under the young man's knees, Colson's cock pistoning Kyle's hole, the two men both released their last ejaculations of the night.

They went to sleep with Kyle, sighing and purring, in Colson's bear-hug, furry arms.

When Kyle woke up in the morning, he was alone in the bed—and in the room. Still purring, he stretched, the word "love" pouring forth in his mind. He had loved the inventive, demanding fucking—demanding, yet respectful; velvet-covered steel. The steel hardness of the man's cock inside him. He loved the charisma of the big bear of a man who was Derek Colson. He loved.

When he rose from the bed, he found the twelve fifty-dollar bills on the dresser. He'd not only been paid for, but he'd been tipped, as well. Just a rent-boy, prostituted to the needs of the recreation center. That certainly took the edge off of the thought of "love."

* * * *

The lounge areas of the Rainbow Connection recreation center had needed replacing for a couple of years. What was there was broken or the upholstery slashed and could only give someone a bad impression of the men coming there. Now, thanks to a donation from the philanthropist, Derek Colson, it all was new, replaced with highly durable furniture that should last longer than the original set had. The furnishings were dedicated in a ceremony attended by the center's board members and any of the clients that could be mustered up on a Friday afternoon—and, of course, by the philanthropist himself, Derek Colson.

As a member of the board, Kyle Kendricks was there—trying to look calm, but trembling inside because Colson was there. It had been two weeks since Colson had fucked him royally in the Jefferson Hotel room. Kyle was aching for the man. As board treasurer, Trent Taylor gave a speech and shepherded the guest of honor around. While everyone was mingling and other board members were fawning over Colson, Trent came over to Kyle.

"He wants to talk to you before either of you leave."

"He?"

"Derek Colson, of course. The furniture cost $20,000, by the way. We're still beholding to him for $10,000 of that. I thought you should know."

Why should I know, Kyle wondered. He wasn't the money man around here. That was for Trent to worry about. But then he saw Derek ask where the men's room was and excuse himself. As he turned, Colson gave Kyle a pointed look. It was the most attention the man had given Kyle yet that day.

Trent came back to Kyle and hissed, "Follow him. He's made clear that he gave the money because of you."

Right. For the good of the recreation center, Kyle thought. But, as naturally as he could seem, he followed Colson down the hall to the men's room.

Colson was at a urinal when Kyle came in. He had his dick out and was pissing into the urinal. Kyle sidled up beside him and unzipped. He didn't bother to pull his shaft out, though, because he knew that wasn't what they were doing there. Colson finished peeing, gave his meaty cock a couple of shakes, cupped it, and half turned it to Kyle, making sure that Kyle saw it. It was half hard. Kyle stared at it and took a deep breath.

"I've meant to ask if you enjoyed this the other night at the Jefferson. I had to leave before you woke up," Colson said in a low, but strong voice.

"Yes. Of course I enjoyed it." It's been two weeks; I'm in agony for it, is what Kyle wanted to say, despite making me feel like a whore. But he didn't say that. It was embarrassing for him to be this in thrall to an older man like this. He could have almost any top going through this facility. They were always after him. It's just that this big, hairy bear of a man pushed all of Kyle's buttons. "But the money. You didn't have to leave the—"

"Most flexible body I've ever had. Sweetest hole. I loved doing you. Worth every penny. I want to see you again. I'll give you $500 for another session in the sack."

Out of that, "loved" and "see you again" is what resonated with Kyle. "When? But you know you don't have to—"

58

"Today. This afternoon. Now. I'll call and get a hotel room. I want to tie you in knots, lay you out, and spike you to the floor. I'm that hot for you. Haven't thought about anything else for days—just putting you in a complete submissive position and fucking the shit out of you."

Kyle moaned. Colson was hard—hugely hard. Kyle was hard too. If Colson took him into one the stalls right here and fucked him over the toilet, Kyle would be happy to take the risk. Not much of a risk though. This was a gay center. Lots of guys had probably been fucked over the toilets in this john.

"I can't stand it. Put it back for now," he squeaked. Colson laughed and stuffed his shaft back into his fly. "No need for a hotel room," Kyle continued. "I live just over on Grove. Alone. I can fix you dinner . . . unless you have to get home."

"I'm not even here," Colson said with a laugh. "I'm in New York City at this moment. Shhh, don't tell anyone. I don't get back to Richmond until tomorrow afternoon."

"So, my place is OK?"

"Love it." That "love" word again. Kyle zeroed right into that.

"You can cook too?" Colson said in surprise. "Is there anything you can't do?"

"I don't know. Try me."

"Is there anything you won't do for me?"

"No."

Colson smiled. That had been the right answer.

* * * *

"It's called a 'bully' and you're handling it great," Colson whispered into Kyle's ear just inside the door to Kyle's apartment, their clothes scattered about on the foyer floor. "I've been dreaming of taking you in this position for days."

Colson was standing, crouched down a bit in the center of the foyer. Kyle was draped on the front of him, facing away, Colson's crowned cock deep up into Kyle's channel. Colson had Kyle in a full Nelson from behind, the palms of his hands pressed into the sides of Kyle's head. Kyle's legs were wrapped around Colson's thighs, and Colson was bouncing the smaller, lighter man's body up and down on his cock. "Love how you take the 'bully,'" Colson muttered.

Love. It was love for Kyle too. He was becoming increasingly aware that he loved a bully—and not a sexual position with that name.

Kyle served up a steak and potatoes dinner that Colson said he loved.

For dessert, Kyle knelt on the dining room table, his torso arched back into Colson's chest, one of his arms slung back, the hand cupping the back of Colson's neck, his other hand jacking his cock, as Colson covered and fucked him from behind, his hands gripping Kyle's waist. Colson said that this was 'elevated bodyguard' position.

They did the 'crab' in bed, Colson on his back and Kyle elevated over his body, looking up at the ceiling, supporting himself over Colson on the hands and feet of bent arms and legs, as Colson fucked up into his ass. It was taxing for both of them and they then slept much of the night. It was a 'deep Impact' wakeup the next morning, with Kyle on his back, butt at the end of the bed, his legs bent up into his body and Colson holding his feet together, while he stood at the end of the bed and mined Kyle's ass deep to a mutual ejaculation.

"Loved it," Colson said as he was dressing. "Next week again?"

"I loved it too," Kyle said. What he was thinking, though, was, I love you. He just was too scared to say it out loud. "Sure anytime next week you can get away. Any time you can get away. Any time at all."

Once more, there were twelve fifty-dollar bills on the dresser when Colson left.

Kyle put that money with the $600 he'd been given earlier without asking for it. He'd buy something nice for Derek, maybe on their month or two-month anniversary of having met. This wasn't about the money.

* * * *

"I wanted to make sure you were here," Trent said as he came away from the podium in welcoming the addition of a nurse practitioner position to the Rainbow Connection free clinic. He whispered that while Derek Colson was at the podium saying how honored he was to be donating the money for that.

"I'm glad I'm here too," Kyle answered, although it was for a far different reason than he supposed. Summer was drawing to a close. Derek's wife was in a flurry of packing and monopolizing his time before she shoved off to Paris for the fall. Kyle hadn't seen Derek for three weeks and he was afraid that the banker's interest in him was waning. That would break Kyle's heart. He was smitten.

But, no such thing. When Colson was able to get close enough to Kyle to talk to him in private, he got right to the point. "It's been too long. I'm celebrating Margret's trip to Europe by taking some politicos out on my boat. Would you like to come along? The day Margaret leaves and the night I fuck your lights out, of course."

"You own a boat?"

"Yeah, I keep it down in Hampton. It comes in handy in closing business deals. It would be good to have you along for the ride."

"Sure, why not?"

"Terrific," Colson said. As he turned away, he added, "This should cover it for all," as he slipped $1,000 in fifties in Kyle's pocket. But Kyle didn't hear that and didn't find the money until later. His initial thought on that was that he'd taken the $1,200 he'd already been given out of the case at the back of his bottom drawer and just had forgotten he'd done so. But when he got home, he forgot to put the money in the case, so he didn't discover that the original $1,200 was still there.

Maybe Kyle should have thought harder before saying "why not?" The three guys Colson was taking out beyond the three-mile limit to fish were all members of the Virginia

House of Delegates. They were on the fence in a bill Colson was interested in spiking. It was a real party, with far more drinking and drugging than any attempt to fish. All five men pranced around the boat—which was more of a small yacht than what Kyle had imagined—in Speedos. Kyle looked great in his. Colson and one of the delegates, an early-thirties well-gymed guy looked fine. The two older, rather tubby politicians shouldn't have made the attempt.

They were all there for the fun, though, they all were closet randy tops knowing exactly what ride they were being bribed to go on, and all enjoyed having Kyle along. They started with the beer, with Kyle keeping up with them on that. He was the first one to start to fade when the hard liquor came out. Colson kept him on the side of consciousness, though, by monitoring his intake. That didn't mean that Kyle, half blotto, didn't try out a joint for the first time—or, eventually, a line of coke when that came out.

The ceiling was spinning when Kyle, on his back on one of the bunks below, realized there was a cock in his ass and a fat man between his legs, huffing and puffing, as he pumped Kyle. It took the penetration of the second one for Kyle to fully realize that neither one of them was Colson. The younger, gymed guy was more athletic, vigorous, and longer lasting in his fuck, but Kyle was mostly gone by then and let himself be manipulated like a rag doll. He had no idea if Colson had fucked him or not.

His head throbbing and his world still spinning a bit, Kyle was silent and sullen on the drive back to Richmond late that night. Colson did notice that there was frost in the air and that Kyle was upset about something, but Colson saw no reason to care. The whore had been well paid. Colson was doing a happy dance. He—or maybe Kyle—had managed to get all three votes in his pocket.

Kyle had no complaint to give. He'd been paid $1,000 for the outing. The whore didn't have any reason to have his nose out of joint.

"I might as well give the check to you," he said as the limousine cruised west on I-64. He held an envelope out to Kyle. Kyle opened it; it contained a check for $30,000.

"The check?" Kyle asked, his face wincing at the effort to speak with the hammers beating on his head.

"The donation for the nurse practitioner, yeah. That's for the center. You got $1,000 already. You did very good, Kyle. I loved how you took care of us. You and me in the sling. That was heaven. You've got a great ass."

Kyle groaned. He'd seen the sling below in the yacht. He had no memory of having been in it.

"Has Trent talked to you about the party next Saturday?" Colson asked.

"No. What party?"

"I said I'd build a shelter addition if he supplied the men for a party I'm having Saturday night. He said that you and he would take care of it. You'll be there, of course. You did A-1 work with the politicians."

"Of course," Kyle said, turning his face toward the forest they were driving through so that Derek couldn't see the shock he couldn't hide.

* * * *

"He's not a philanthropist; he's a john soliciting men to fuck. He thinks I'm a whore."

"He's a *high-paying* john, Kyle. And, where he's concerned, you *are* a whore and have been. He's paid you and paid you well to let him fuck you. He's told me what he paid you. We're making a whole lot of money off him. It works out for everyone."

Yeah, right. Everyone. Everyone but me, Kyle wanted to scream. He wanted to cry out that he'd thought he loved the big lug—that they were in a relationship. It turned out, though, that he was just the guy's whore.

"But I was just the guy's whore, Trent."

"You were his *high-priced* whore," Trent repeated. "You let men fuck you before I introduced you to this the gold mine that is Derek Colson. You gave it away for free before. You were underselling yourself. Colson pays you well and pays the center even better. Now, do you want to help

63

me recruit other guys from those coming to the shelter to be at the party, or don't you?"

"I'll get back to you on that," Kyle said. Of course he didn't plan on doing that, but he didn't know what was what here yet. Somebody was going to have to pay for this, but he wasn't sure who or how. Until then he best keep his powder dry. "Are all the guys going to be there to be fucked by Derek's guests?"

"He wants us to provide the caterers and servers too. Again, guys from the rec center. They'll be paid—and well. Look how you've been paid if you include his donations to the center—$10,000 a fuck. All to a good cause. This isn't the first party we've done for him. We have a squad I call 'don't see; don't hear; don't talk.' They get paid and they get to watch. But they get to keep their mouths shut."

"Who's on the squad?" Kyle asked.

Trent told him.

"You'll be hearing from me," Kyle said. He went back to his office at the nearby Virginia Commonwealth University and tried to calm himself. He'd been such a fool. He had thought he loved the big lug and that Colson maybe loved him in return. He'd just been a whore to Colson. He was just a whore to the rec center too.

Maybe it was time to leave Richmond. There was that offer from San Francisco. He sifted through the papers on his desk. Yes, the offer was still good. He sat and thought and thought and thought. The first thing he had to do was to erase from his mind this fantasy he had built about loving Derek Colson and being loved in return. It was all business— solicitation and pimping. That done, he was free to think more on what to do about it.

He'd have to erase from his mind too that Trent was his friend and looked out for his welfare. That was an easier thought to give up.

At length, he called Trent back and in a hard voice said, "OK, I'll play."

* * * *

"So, Eddie," Kyle said, coming out of the shower room in the gym at Rainbow Connection with just a towel around his waist and calling out to the towel attendant. "I hear you are going to be a waiter at a party this Saturday night."

"Yeah, for the rich dude, Colson," Eddie said, giving Kyle the eye. Both of them knew that Eddie had been hard for Kyle for months. "You going to be there?" Eddie asked.

"Yeah, Colson wants to have guys who will give his guests blow jobs and good fucks. You going to be doing any of that?"

"I doubt that. I'll be busy waitering, and the guests at those parties are usually just tops. I'm a top too."

"Ooo, you are? I didn't know that. Interesting," Kyle said as if this was totally news to him and made a difference in how he'd been playing hard to get for Eddie. He came up to Eddie and reached down and rubbed his crotch with a hand. "Good thing I'm in the mood for a top right now." He let his towel drop, took Eddie's hand, and put it where Eddie had been wanting to put it for some time.

Kyle let Eddie fuck him in the shower, up against the tiles. When they were done, Kyle told Eddie what a good cocksman he was and that he'd like to have Eddie again—but maybe Eddie could do something for him if they were going to get it on again.

Of course Eddie would do something for him.

The party went just as Derek Colson would want it to, and much of the time he and Kyle were upstairs on Derek's bed or up against his bureau or on his floor or just doing a standing fuck in the middle of the room.

The next morning, Kyle called on Colson at the bank—the first time he'd visited him there. Colson wasn't too delighted to see him, but he did. Kyle took along his laptop and showed Colson the great videos Eddie had taken for him at the party the previous night.

"Your receptionist was good enough to give me the address where your wife is staying in Paris," Kyle said. "I'll bet she'd like to see coverage of your party last night."

"You wouldn't," Colson said, his voice quite strained. An attempt to stare Kyle down, though, convinced him otherwise.

"I'm going to give you a chance to be a philanthropist for real, Derek. You don't know what you had in me. I wasn't letting you fuck me for money. You could have had me for free. I told you repeatedly that you didn't have to pay for it. Now I want you to pay for not having it. I'd like you to make a check out for $100,000 and then I just won't show these videos to anyone."

"Make it out to you, I suppose."

"No, not to me. And not to Rainbow Connection either. I don't want you writing another check to Trent Taylor. I want you to cut him off and influence your friends to do so to until they replace him on the board there. No, I want you to make the check out to the women's shelter out on the West End. I want to help you to be a real philanthropist. There are no strings attached to real philanthropy, Derek."

"Done," Colson said. "But you know, Trent told me you went with the deal. The money isn't anything to me. You are. I've never had anyone as flexible as you to fuck. I loved every minute of it."

That is the trouble, Kyle thought. You loved the act; you didn't love the guy you were doing it with. And to you I was just a whore. But, dumb as I was, I loved you.

"Can we go back to square one, you and me, Kyle?"

Kyle hesitated, but then he said, "Sure, we can try it again."

"Wednesday night? I can come to your place? About 8:00 p.m.?"

"Sure, that's fine," Kyle said breezily. "I'll take that check on out to the women's shelter now, if you don't mind. Until Wednesday. It will cost you $500, though."

Colson agreed instantly and made out another check for Kyle.

Wednesday would be just fine with Kyle. He was getting on a plane to move to San Francisco on Monday.

66

Never Mentioned Again

"Shit, the way this snow is falling, I'm not getting my rocks off tonight."

"Steady as she goes, Chuck. Lucky for us there are bars close to the ship. Let's try this one."

Naval Petty Officer Three Ryan Stevens pushed open the door of the bar and ushered Naval Petty Officer Two Chuck Adams into a dimly lit bar, filled with smoke and with muted and fuzzy Country Western music coming through the sound system. The light was brightest at the long bar. Two men were sitting at this end of the bar and a gaggle of three bar girls held down the other. The tables to the left, in more darkness, were occupied by a mixed bag of mixed-colored and mixed-gender blue-class patrons. The whites took up the center, with the Hispanics in the front corner of the room and the blacks, in the deeper corners, in the back corner. B-girls were working the floor. One was taking a sailor through a beaded-curtain door at the back of the room, and two more here draped on guys—a mechanic, by the look of him, and a sailor—on the small dance floor.

This was probably as busy as this bar got. It was a Saturday night near the Philadelphia docks where a naval repair facility was located. More sailors than was usual with most naval ports were on leave, as they were in resting mode when their ships were in for repair or refitting.

Ryan and Chuck were bosom buddies—but not in the sense, they insisted to each other, as were some sailors who were young, virile, and randy but stuck out at sea for long periods of time with no one to hook up with but each other. They were from the same area of Florida—Ryan from Tampa and Chuck from St. Petersburg—and were much the same age, their mid twenties now. They were from different spectrums of the social divide, but they'd been together from training to ship assignment, and went everywhere as a pair, each watching the back of the other.

They were so close that there had been speculation about them from the other sailors, but, if they'd heard it, Ryan and Chuck had pretended they didn't. And it didn't prevent them from sharing a woman when it came down to stripping and getting it down, although, in these rare instances, they stuck to using separate entrances at the same time.

Ryan, a redhead descended from the Irish, was from a wealthy family. He'd gone to private schools but hadn't done more than scrape by academically, and his family saw the Navy as a chance for him to grow up. It was working; he was ahead of the curve in moving up the enlisted ranks. That probably was because just getting by in a private school still imparted more accumulated smarts and sense of leadership than graduating from a public high school in Florida. Chuck, a Nordic blond, whose male family members worked the oil rigs in the gulf and female members dressed hair, had made it through public high school, but barely. Both had been on their respective football teams in high school, but hadn't been stars. It was a bond between them, though—talking football like they were a part of it. Both were fine looking, trimmed out, and muscular. Working on a ship helped ensure the trimmed out and muscular aspects.

Both had come in on a ship that had been in the Persian Gulf for four months and had docked in Philadelphia the previous day for refitting. And both were randy as hell when they showed up for shore leave, despite the start of the snow, and made it only as far as Cleo's Bar, nearly within sight of their ship.

They bellied up to the bar and ordered Buds from the hefty bartender, who had a friendly look for them but who obviously was capable of a mean look and doubled as the bar's bouncer. He had an anchor tattooed on his bicep and the three fell into a comfortable chat comparing service records.

"Speaking of service," Ryan said. "Any action around here tonight?"

The barkeep inclined his head toward the other end of the bar without looking there. "Take your pick. $20 on the bar top gets you beyond the beaded curtains there with one of them with me looking the other way and whistling and then it's up to you and them. If you pay more than $20 for a BJ or $50 for a ride, you've been taken. And you should know—"

He didn't finish that sentence as the guys at the front end of the bar had suddenly discovered a thirst that had to be service right now, and *that*, after all, was what the bartender was here for.

While he was gone, Ryan and Chuck took a look around, but the only free dollies were those three at the back end of the bar. Two of them were talking to each other across the one in the middle. She caught Chuck's eye, though, and rose off her stool and sauntered on up the bar to the two sailors.

"Two hunks like you shouldn't be in here all by your lonesomes," she said as she got to them. "Buy a girl a drink for some company? You two in the Navy?"

Ryan rolled his eyes. They were in winter service uniforms—black sailor jumpers over black trousers, with the thirteen-button, squared-off fly—and their naval insignia on their sleeves. And they could almost see the naval vessels in dry-dock from where they were sitting. Of course they were in the Navy. But then his eyes were rolling for another reason. The woman had her hand on his crotch.

"Sure, I'm Popeye One and he's Popeye Two," Chuck answered for them, moving over a stool so that she could perch between them.

"A drink for the lady. Another one of whatever she was drinking," Ryan croaked to the bartender, who appeared with a frozen daiquiri within a few minutes, as both men leaned into their elbows on the bar top and gave their full attention to the B-Girl. Each of them had a hand low on her hip on either side. She didn't bat an eyelash.

She had eyelashes to bat too. She was a mix of white and black, which on her had arrived at high cheek bones, a smooth light-chocolate skin tone, a lovely oval face, and long, silky black hair. She kept her hands moving above the bar top and touching each of the guys here and there to make them want to hyperventilate. The long, scarlet fingernails matched the color on her lips. Her eye shadow was a luminous deep violet, with sparkles in it, which brought out the same color and quality of her pupils.

"You two stick together like glue?" she asked. It was evident to all three of them that she was fishing on whether this was leading up to something in sequence or a threesome.

"Usually," Chuck answered. "Do you mind?"

"Not really," she answered, "but maybe one's enough for starters."

When he delivered the drink, the bartender said, "This here's Tracy. I think you should—"

But whatever he might have said was cut off by Tracy cupping Chuck's chin, lightly brushing the tips of her fingernails at the soft tissue of his throat, while she came in for a kiss. A rumbling sound came up from the depths of his belly, and his hand went down to her plump butt cheek and squeezed. Ryan's did the same when Tracy turned her head and gave him a kiss, giving them equal time.

"Guess this is my lucky day," she said when she came up for air. "Two sailor hunks out on a snowy night like this."

"Speaking of snow . . ." Ryan said.

"The night's for partying," Chuck continued. "We're new in Philly. You know where we can get some? To share, of course."

"Of course," Tracy said, drawing their attention to three black thugs sitting at a table in the back corner of the bar. "A couple of Franklins should get enough to give you two courage to handle little ole me. I can do the deal."

"Don't need no courage to take you on girl," Chuck said.

"But it would make it more fun," Ryan added.

They watched as Tracy went to the back corner of the bar and came back with five packets of white powder.

Ryan and Chuck each had already taken out an extra twenty over what would be needed for the drinks and a generous tip and laid the bills on the bar top.

"Who's first, or were you still thinkin'—?"

"Ryan can be first," Chuck said, with a smile. "Rank takes privilege and smaller to larger."

"Fuck you," Ryan said. But he was smiling—they bantered like this often, and truth was truth anyway—and didn't turn down the offer. He eagerly followed Tracy through the beaded curtain, a hand cupping one of her butt cheeks.

* * * *

Ryan was sitting, Jumper off, on a vinyl loveseat in a small room behind the bar. There was a single bed against the other wall, in case they needed that. His legs were spread and Tracy had turned up his heat by dragging her scarlet fingernails over his nipples and complimenting him on his hard-bodied torso. She knelt then between his legs, facing a coffee table. She lowered her head and sniffed up a line of the coke set out in rows on a sheet of white paper. One row already was gone, up Ryan's nose.

He leaned over and put his arms around her, finding that her halter top unhooked between her breasts. She sighed as he pulled her top aside, cupped her pert breasts, and thumbed her nipples. Taking one hand away briefly to brush the hair off the side of her face and bury his mouth in the hollow of her neck before returning it to squeeze and work her breast, he eagerly took her mouth in his for a deep kiss as she turned her face to him.

71

Coming out of the kiss, Tracy briefly put her hands over his on her breasts and moaned deeply before leaning over the coffee table and taking in another line of the coke. After sniffing it up and brushing her nose with long, scarlet-tipped fingers, she swiveled around, facing him, still kneeling between his thighs. Her face turned up and his down into another kiss as, slowly, methodically, she unbuttoned the thirteen anchor-on-black-back buttons of his square cut codpiece and pulled his cock out of the fly of his regulation briefs.

He was big, erect, hard. She groaned, to denote she respected the size of him, and his cock did a little lurch in appreciation for how she rubbed it between her soft hands, ran her fingernails down the sides of it, and brushed it against her cheek before opening her red lips over it and taking it deep into her throat. It was Ryan's turn to groan. She hummed with it in her throat, pulling a gasp out of him at the vibrations thus caused.

If his banter with his buddy was suggesting that Ryan was the smaller of the two, she knew she was in for quite a ride later. The big blond did have this hunk of a guy in bulk.

She supplied and applied the condom and said that she wanted it in the ass. Standing and leaning over the coffee table to snort another line, she lifted the back of her miniskirt and wiggled her buttocks, encouraging Ryan to pull the thread of her G-string out of her crack and to the side, which he did before burying his face between her butt cheeks.

She was riding his cock, facing away from him and crouched over his lap, and taking him deep in long strokes when Ryan moved his hands down from her breasts to her crotch and inside the waistband of her G-string.

He froze, let out a explicative, and then jerked, making to rise, when Tracy gripped his forearms with her hands, and said, with a gasp. "No, might as well keep it up. We're almost done here, and you paid to get it off."

* * * *

72

Ryan came stumbling out from behind the beaded curtain and might have said something, but Chuck was right there, ready for his turn. Tracy's arm came through the curtain, her hand lassoing Chuck's arm and pulling him into the darkness beyond.

Ryan shrugged and walked, none too straight, back to the bar.

"Here, you probably need this," the bartender said, plunking down a fresh Bud, giving Ryan a sharp, "Are you going to make trouble?" look and then going to the window end of the bar to jaw with the guys there when Ryan, still shell shocked and in a haze from the two lines he'd snorted, showed he was subdued.

Twenty minutes later, Chuck came out of the back and saddled up to the bar. The two men looked at each other in the mirror behind the bar, not facing off directly. The bartender came over and plopped a Bud down in front of Chuck.

"Well, hell," Ryan said, at length.

"Yep," Chuck answered. Both took several swigs from the beer before either spoke again.

"It was a he, not a she," Ryan said in a small voice and in such a way that maybe Chuck didn't know and was just now getting the word.

"Yep, a real good fuck, though," Chuck said.

This time Ryan turned to look at Chuck, face to face. "You knew and fucked him anyway—whatever they're called?"

"Yep. The high-falutin' term is transvestite. Tranny, shemale, ladyboy. Whatever. They've all got holes and can be fun. This one Tracy—was great. Don't tell me you didn't know before you went back there with her."

Ryan gave him a confused look.

Chuck laughed. "Well, fuck."

"You fuck men?" Ryan asked, his voice as ghastly as the expression on his face.

"Any port in the storm, good buddy," Chuck said before taking a deep swig of his beer. "A hole is a hole and, as you knew when we came in here, I had a raging hard on."

"But . . ."

"Which wasn't being satisfied by anyone else." Chuck hit Ryan with a meaningful look.

"I didn't know," Ryan said in a quiet voice. "If I had . . ."

"Hey, look, Ryan. Did you think I was hanging around you so close because you didn't drop the football each and every time it was slung to you? We didn't go to the same schools, but guys in football programs talk to each other—especially guys you are spiking. Did you think your past would forever be kept a secret?"

Ryan didn't answer. He looked down at his lap rather than directly at Chuck or even at Chuck in the mirror. Chuck put a hand on Ryan's thigh and Ryan didn't shrug it off.

"Been waitin' for you, bro," Chuck whispered. "You gonna keep me waitin'? I'm still, you know, way horny enough."

"I . . . I . . . didn't know. I wonder if there are any cheap hotels around here," Ryan said, in almost a whisper.

"There'd better be, good buddy. There fuckin' well better be."

"But, one thing, Chuck," Ryan said. "This Tracy thing. I really don't want this ever mentioned again."

"Lips are sealed, good buddy," Chuck said, with a smile. "Let it never be mentioned again. Now come on out into the snow and let's find us that small hotel."

Home Alone

"So, you didn't have any trouble finding it." Aaron opened the front door to his house, figuring it was Chuck who was there. There was a porch light, but he didn't turn it on even though darkness had fallen. He did, though, poke his head out of the door to look up and down the street before standing aside and letting Chuck walk in past him. As he turned and watched, Chuck walked all the way back to the kitchen and then back, pausing at where stairs went up and down in the split-level house. Seeing that the other two levels were dark, he walked back to the foyer and stood at the door into the dimly lit living room. He gave Aaron an expectant look.

Chuck was in gym shorts, a muscle T, and gym shoes, without socks. He cut an imposing, not-to-be-ignored figure despite pushing forty—blond, built to body-builder specifications, tall, and walking cocky. His hair was in a Marine buzz cut either because there was a receding bald spot on top he didn't want to draw attention to or because he'd been a Marine, which was entirely possible, given his physique and the confident way he carried himself. That hair otherwise wasn't his problem, though, as was shown by the perpetual five-o'clock shadow he sported on his face and the curly blond hair that peeked up from the neckline V of the T-shirt and covered his forearms and calves. He had a barbed-wire crown tattoo around his left, bulging bicep, and there was evidence of a more colorful tattoo coming up from his right pectoral muscle and pulling over his right shoulder and down his right arm to his wrist.

In contrast to the square-jawed muscleman appearance of Chuck, Aaron, dark, trim, a good six inches shorter, fifteen years younger, and office professional looking and with more refined, delicate features than Chuck, looked like he was from another world altogether.

"So, where's this ship carving collection you say you have?"

"Downstairs. You want a beer, though, before we go down?" Aaron shut the front door but remained there, leaning back into as if he was reconsidering having let Chuck in.

Chuck smiled a little smile at the reference to go down, but he answered, "Sure, why not?" He took a good look at Aaron's tight little buns as he walked past him and to the kitchen at the back of the house.

Aaron returned with the beers. He did a little double-take as Chuck had slipped his athletic T off and dropped it on a chair in the foyer next to the front door. His torso was, of course, magnificent. With a shaky hand, Aaron handed one of the beers Chuck and said, "Let's sit in the living room." He gestured to a sofa and, after Chuck sat at one end, Aaron sat down at the other.

The two had just come from an after-work workout at the gym they both went to. At least it was after Aaron's office-job work. He'd never asked if or where Chuck worked. Chuck always seemed to be at Phil's Gym, and his body looked like he spent all of his time there. The last couple of weeks Chuck had been helping Aaron with his workouts and had been his spotter on Tuesday and Thursday evenings. Chuck had remarked that Aaron was bulking up well with his help, and Aaron could feel the improvement himself, although he didn't seek to be muscle bound and probably never would be. Still, Aaron liked what he saw in the mirror of himself and so, he thought, with good reason, did Chuck.

"So, you said you were married," Chuck said after he'd taken a swig of his beer.

"Yes. My wife, Rachel. And we have two kids."

"Where are they?"

"My wife and kids?"

"Yeah, your wife and kids. We seem to be alone. Where are you wife and kids? Not hiding in the dark upstairs, I hope."

"They're in New York. The Bronx. Visiting her parents."

"Ah."

"Whenever the kids are out of school for an extended time, Rachel takes them up there. Her parents run a jewelry store, but they dote on the kids. They rarely are able to get away to come down here to visit us."

"Ah, I see."

"You see what?" Aaron didn't mean it to sound defensive, but when he looked up and into Chuck's face, the smirk he saw made him feel defensive. Chuck no longer was at the other end of the sofa. He'd narrowed the distance between them. His right arm was resting on the top of the sofa and, for the first time, Aaron realized that Chuck was touching his shoulder with the fingers of his hand and rubbing little circles on top of Aaron's thin T-shirt material there. Aaron was aroused by the riot of colors in the tattoo covering Chuck's right chest and arm.

"How long has your wife not been enough for you, Aaron?" The voice was low, calm. Chuck's eyes were boring into Aaron's face. Aaron blushed.

"I . . . I don't know what you mean," Aaron said, his voice sounding mousey even to himself.

"I think you do, Aaron. Phil told me you had asked about me. You didn't really think he wouldn't tell me you had, did you? Phil's my partner at the gym. He tells me everything."

Ah, so that's what he does and why he's at the gym all the time, Aaron thought. He's one of the owners. But then he realized he was avoiding the issue. Why the fuck *did* it matter where Chuck worked? That's not what he was baldly suggesting here. "I don't really see where my marriage—"

"Give it up, Aaron. Why the fuck did you ask me here? Why are we alone here? I know. I've known for a few weeks. You've let me touch you—Intimately—when we work out. And you go hard when I do. Are you living in some sort of fantasy world of convenient denial? You haven't said anything. But that speaks for itself right there. I'm here, in your house, while your family is away. You asked me to come here on some flimsy excuse. Don't tell me you don't know what I mean or that you don't know why you asked me to come here."

The hand that had been at Aaron's shoulder suddenly was under Aaron's right thigh, twisting Aaron's body around to where his back was against the arm of the shoulder and, now, his right leg was raised and bent, and trapped against the back cushion of the sofa by Chuck's left torso. Aaron's left leg was dangling off the sofa, his foot on the floor in front of the sofa. His legs were spread. His crotch was exposed, vulnerable. Chuck's right hand then went to the back of Aaron's neck, pulling the younger man's head forward. Chuck cupped Aaron's chin in his left hand. His face dipped down to Aaron's and he took Aaron's mouth into a possessive kiss.

Aaron struggled against the kiss—at first—using his left arm to try to push Chuck's chest away. His right arm was trapped between his body and the back cushion of the sofa. Chuck was too strong for him and held the kiss, becoming more brutal with it, getting his tongue in Aaron's mouth and swabbing Aaron's inner cheeks until he felt Aaron's body go limp and Aaron's left hand stop trying to push him away. His fingers had pushed into the matting of curly blond hair on Chuck's exposed chest, and he was tugging on the hair. As he surrendered more in the kiss, his hand grabbed Chuck's right bicep and pulled Chuck into him rather than trying to push him away. His mouth relaxed, went soft, returned Chuck's kiss with passion.

When he felt he'd established some control, Chuck pulled out of the kiss, but he continued to dominate Aaron's body. Still gripping the hair at the back of Aaron's head, he held their faces close. Aaron tried to look away, but Chuck cruelly jerked his head back, staring him down, until Aaron's eyes couldn't hold contact anymore and, with a sigh, he dipped them in surrender.

"I didn't mean for this . . ." Aaron whimper. "I think you need to leave."

"You *did* mean for this. Just maybe not this fast," Chuck said. "You don't want your wife just now, do you? You want me."

Aaron started to demur, but Chuck took him into a kiss again, which progressively was more actively returned by Aaron. Chuck's right hand released Aaron's chin and went to the young man's crotch. Aaron jerked when Chuck grasped his balls and the root of his cock through the material of his gym shorts and squeezed them rhythmically, causing Aaron's cock to engorge even more than it already had and Aaron to moan deeply, but Chuck didn't release him from the kiss. When Chuck stopped squeezing his jewels, the tension once again went out of Aaron's body and his side of the kiss became more passionate. Chuck pulled the waistband of Aaron's gym shorts, and his jock pouch as well, to below his balls, grasped Aaron's cock, and slow stroked it. He'd pulled the foreskin down off Aaron's uncut cock and was bringing precum up by rubbing the young man's piss slit. Aaron was moaning within the confines of the kiss.

"You're hard for me," Chuck murmured when they came out of the kiss.

"Yes," Aaron admitted. "You're driving me crazy down there. We should stop, or—"

"I'm hard for you too. We're not going to stop."

As if needing confirmation of Chuck's hard on, Aaron's left hand went to Chuck's crotch and then, finding that Chuck hadn't lied, Aaron's hand went in through one of the leg holes of the older man's gym shorts and, after digging fingers into the curly pubic hair and tugging on it to feel Chuck flinch and suck in air, established a handhold on the hardening cock. "God, it's huge," he whispered.

"And you want it," Chuck responded, his voice low and hoarse from lust. "Shit, I've got to get inside you."

Aaron whimpered but said nothing.

The middle finger of Chuck's right hand went to Aaron's asshole, and he penetrated it in an exploratory slide that took the pad of his finger to Aaron's prostate. Aaron flinched and gasped. Chuck gave a low laugh, as, although Aaron continued to groan, the passage opened for the finger. "Men have fucked you before, haven't they?"

"Not for a long time. Not since college. I wanted . . . I wanted life to be simple."

I don't think it's been that long, Chuck thought, but we all have our secrets. You can have yours as long as you let me in. "It's not. Life's not simple," he said. "Urges can't be denied. I'm going to fuck you. You want me to fuck you."

Aaron didn't answer beyond the low panting he was doing. He didn't have to. He had let his body relax. His right arm was dangling down off the front edge of the sofa now. He was open to Chuck. He was giving both his crotch and his ass up to the man, and Chuck was working them masterfully. He even jutted his pelvis up more to further accommodate the finger buried up his ass. Chuck laughed, but he extracted his finger and pulled Aaron's T-shirt over his head and his gym shorts and jock down off his legs with that hand. Aaron didn't help him, but he didn't resist him. Chuck's hand glided down Aaron's body, slowly, and down into his bush, grasping his cock again.

"Am I bigger than any you've had before?" he asked.

"Yes," Aaron answered. "I don't know if I can—"

"Oh, you can and will." Chuck liked Aaron's answer, though. He didn't even care if it was true or not. He moved his right hand back to Aaron's ass. Aaron rolled his pelvis up to him again, and two fingers went up his ass. Once again he flinched and moaned, but the passage opened wider.

"You have a fine body, a fuckable body," Chuck whispered.

"Not as fine as yours," Aaron answered. His free hand went to Chuck's chest, caressing the massive bulging of the man's pectorals, digging his fingers into the curly chest hair and tugging at it to hear Chuck, growl. Chuck growled.

"Tell me you want it," Chuck said. Then, "I'm gonna fuck you so bad," as he growled again at Aaron's play in his chest hair.

"I want it," Aaron answered. It came out almost in a sob, though.

Chuck repositioned his body, moving down Aaron's torso with his mouth and tongue. He ever so briefly took Aaron's cock in his mouth, and then his balls, but then he grasped the backs of Aaron's thighs and pushed them up and onto Aaron's chest. Aaron moaned, as Chuck's mouth went to his asshole, and a good five minutes were devoted to eating Aaron's ass out and opening the passage even further.

Then Chuck was moving up Aaron's body again, grasping his right leg and hooking that on Chuck's shoulder, until he was hovering over Aaron and frotting their cocks together.

"Are you ready for it?" he growled.

"Upstairs. Protection." Aaron made like he was going to roll out from underneath Chuck's body, but the heavier man didn't let him.

"I've got rubbers right here, in my gym bag," Chuck said, leaning over and unzipping his bag without losing position on top of Aaron's body. "If you really want it, though, you'll have to crown me." He split the packet and handed the disk to Aaron. Using both hands, Aaron reached down and expertly rolled the Magnum Trojan on Chuck's erection just from the feel of what he was doing.

Not fucked for some time, my eye, Chuck thought. He gave another low laugh. But he was nearly home. He wouldn't belabor that point.

Chuck spent several seconds teasing Aaron, slapping his sheathed cock on Aaron's belly and pressing it down into the crack of Aaron's rolled-up pelvis but only brushing Aaron's rim in passing.

"Now," Aaron sobbed, clutching at Chuck's meaty buttocks.

"Now," Chuck agreed, as Aaron cried out, arched his back, and dug his fingernails into Chuck's ass. Chuck had shucked his gym shorts and jock and was as naked now as

Aaron was. Chuck initially gave him no more than an inch beyond his cut bulb, though. He held there as Aaron panted and moaned, waiting for Aaron to take him. The younger man was blossoming open to him. Aaron's passage walls were gripping Chuck's cock, rippling over it, and pulling him inside. The passage opened right up and Chuck went with the long, deep slide, as Aaron babbled "Yes, yes, All of it. Oh, god, oh shit."

Chuck was meeting that with, "Relax, open even more to me baby. Take me. Yes, like that. Oh, baby! We are going downtown."

Aaron took him all. Chuck pulled back and then slid in again. Pulled back, slid in—repeatedly, picking up speed and thrust. Aaron started to go with him, sighing and moaning and whimpering, "Deep, deep. Take me deep."

Chuck complied. Soon there was no talking, just the mutually fed rhythm of the fuck, as Chuck moved his hips fast, dug deeper. Faster and faster. Aaron was clutching the man's shoulder blades now, moving his pelvis to take the cock hard and deep. As he approached his own ejaculation, Aaron was crying out, "Yes, yes! You're the best! You're huge. Fuck me hard!" His hand went to his cock and he stroked himself to the rhythm of the fuck, coming in three bursts of cum up into the curly hair on Chuck's flat belly. Then he went limp, his arms dropping away, his head flopping over the side, purring and humming as Chuck fucked on for another ten minutes of vigorous thrusting.

The older man tensed up, pulled out of Aaron's ass, and he scrambled up Aaron's body on his knees, as he jerked the condom off his cock. "On the face, on the face," he commanded, and Aaron turned his head forward to take the ejaculation on his cheek. Chuck betrayed him, though. He grabbed Aaron's head by the hair, forced his cock into Aaron's mouth, and came in the younger man's gagging throat. Then, before Aaron could react, Chuck had dipped down, taken Aaron's mouth in his and kissed him in a cum-sharing possessive kiss.

When he pulled away, Aaron, his eyes big as saucers, muttered a "God damn."

"Haven't been fucked in a while? Don't god damn lie to me," Chuck said. "You fuck men like a bunny in heat."

"You liked it," Aaron retorted. "You liked thinking you were seducing me."

"Yeah, I liked it," Chuck said, pulling off Aaron's body, sitting back at the other end of the sofa, and taking another swig of his beer. "Shit, it's warm. The goddamn beer isn't cold anymore."

"I'll get you another one," Aaron said, as he rolled off the sofa and padded, naked, into the kitchen.

"Do you even *have* a ship carving collection?" Chuck called out to the absent Aaron.

Aaron walked back into the room, carrying two beers. Giving one to Chuck, he said. "Yes, I do, but there isn't time to see it now. You'll have to see it next time."

"Why not now? And you want there to be a next time? Next time would be rougher than this time was."

"Yes, of course I want you again. I wasn't lying. You have one of the biggest cocks I've had. And you know how to use it."

"Do you really have a wife and children?"

"Yes. They're gone for another week and a half. To the Bronx, as I said. And I'd like to keep them out of this, thank you very much."

"Why do you want me to leave before seeing this supposed ship collection?"

"The Nelsons, next door. They have choir rehearsal on Thursday nights. They'll be home in another half an hour or so. I don't want them to see your Jeep in the driveway. How about Tuesday evening? They have some sort of supper group thing they go to on Tuesdays."

"Can't Tuesday," Chuck said. "I'll be fucking Chad, the black guy who comes to the gym, on Tuesday. A regular date. I'll have to do you on Thursday again."

"At least you're honest about it," Aaron said. "I get enough of the love crap from Rachel. At least neither one of us has to pretend this is anything but a biological urge, the need to get our rocks off."

Oh, you love it, all of what goes with men fucking, not just the ejaculation. Don't try to pretend otherwise, but I try to be honest, yes, unlike you, Chuck thought. But what he said was, "My Jeep's not in your driveway. I parked it down the street. And I'm not done with you. Unless you think you're strong enough to toss me out, I'm going to fuck the shit out of you. You want to show me the bedrooms?"

"The guest bedroom," Aaron said, a clutch in his voice. He gestured to the set of stairs that led up to an upper level. "I don't want to do it in the master bedroom. You understand, I'm sure. In fact, I'm not sure it's a good idea at all."

"I don't give a fuck whether or not you think it's a good idea. You *want* me to dominate you."

Aaron gave a shudder and a little smile as Chuck stood, picked the smaller man up, slung Aaron over his shoulder, and headed for the stairs to the bedrooms.

"I don't have to be anywhere until noon tomorrow," Chuck said as he mounted the stairs.

A Question of Restraint

"What do you see, Varick? Where are you going?"

I put out a restraining hand as the Baron von Richthoven brushed past me and out into the corridor of the first-class carriage of the train. I followed him as he moved toward the steps down to the platform of the Heidelberg rail station. The train had stopped here en route from where we started in Berlin—leaving hurriedly—and where we were headed in Munich. It was a time of retreat, and Varick had chosen his secret hunting chalet near Füssen, the Bavarian Alps, as his place of hiding—and hunting—at least for now. I had accompanied him to try to protect him from himself and because I didn't have any other choice.

"I wouldn't suggest leaving the train, Varick," I called out to him as he was doing just that, his black silk cape billowing around his tall, trim body. "We have no idea how long the train will stand at this station." I was speaking to his back, as he moved along the platform, his attention riveted over to the shadows of an iron column three tracks down that was helping to hold up the canopy over the concourse separating the end of the tracks from the station building. His gold lion-headed walking stick provided a staccato beat to his progress. He was an imposing man, dark and hawk-like while still being uncannily handsome. He still was in his forties—or so at least it appeared—although looking somewhat younger, and, as I well knew, he clearly was charismatic.

Neither that nor his title had kept him out of trouble in Berlin, however.

Suddenly he stopped dead in his tracks and I almost ran into him. "There. Over there. See him, Otto?" He was pointing with his stick toward where his attention had been focused ever since he stood in our train compartment and gazed out of the window.

"No, Varick. You promised restraint. No more at least until we reach Füssen. You will have more free rein there to do as you wish, as you need."

The young man—I knew it was the young man who Varick was focused on—was beautiful. His smile was radiant as he looked up into the face of his companion who had pulled him close into an embrace—obviously a farewell embrace. The young man's curly blond hair was tussled and, in the beams of light filtering through the translucent glass canopy onto the platform, it looked like his head was swathed in a halo. He wasn't tall, but he was perfectly formed. His clothes were those of a student, albeit an affluent one. Heidelberg was the home of a major university. It was at the end of a term, and it could be reasonably speculated that he was a student returning home and bidding farewell to a lover.

It didn't take much to assess the lover judgment. Before Varick had pulled up, the two men had been kissing there in the shadows. The taller man was cupping the young blond god's buttocks with his hands, squeezing them, and, briefly, the blond had raised a leg to hook his knee on the taller man's hip. If they could have done so without causing a scandal, they would have been fucking.

"Only if he is taking this train," Varick murmured to me. "That will be a sign that I can have him."

"You've had rather too many signs of late, Varick," I responded. "That is why we are on this train."

"You presume too much," Varick said, suddenly turning to me, his expression changed. Seeing the other Varick in him, I shrank away from him, but he reached out, his hand suddenly clawlike, and pulled me back to him. "You chose to come with me in this exile. You chose to share this with me. Only if he rides the train. Only if he wants it."

Varick pulled me back to the train and we stood on the platform by the door up into the area separating first-class from second, positioning ourselves on the platform as if we were stretching our legs to break the journey.

My heart both sank and doubled its beat as the young blond man approached. He was taking this train. As he approached, his eyes locked onto those of Varick's and I groaned in the knowledge that that was all it took. Varick was of a mesmerizing stock, his piercing violet-hued eyes able to capture, disrobe, and ravish the susceptible at will. The young blond's answering radiant smile marked that he could be possessed. When he turned and mounted the stairs into the train, Varick followed the blond closely from behind. I followed as well, no less a captive of Varick's stare than anyone else with my proclivities.

At the top of the stairs, the young man turned as to enter the second-class compartment, but Varick laid a hand on his arm and said, in low, melodic voice, "Perhaps you would join us off to the right here. We are in the first-class carriage. You would be more comfortable and there is plenty of room in our compartment. We would enjoy the companionship." His hand then went to the young man's buttocks, squeezing one of the well-rounded, firm orbs, and steering him to the right.

The student smiled at Varick, and with a quiet, "*Danke*"—thanks—"I would appreciate that," and without so much as a flinch for the hand still palming his buttocks, turned to the right. With that, I knew he was lost. It probably would have been better in the long run if I had accepted that and capitulated to the inevitability of it.

Few of the first-class compartments were occupied— none in proximity to ours. The young man sat in the seat facing the one that Varick and I occupied, and we said little until the conductor had been through, Varick had smoothly paid the difference in the ticket price for the student, and the train had started on its onward journey.

It wasn't lost on the young man that he was being paid for.

"Perhaps you can pull the curtains to the corridor, Otto, and give us more privacy."

Varick wasn't looking at me. His eyes were holding the blue eyes of the beautiful young student with his. The young man didn't stand a chance. He wasn't even fighting it—pure innocence and openness. He knew. He just didn't know the all of it—not by a long shot. After pulling the blinds down on the windows looking out into the corridor, I shrank back in the corner of the seat and watched it all unfold, both horrified and fascinated.

The conversation started with minor chitchat. Varick—the Baron von Richthoven—who had been residing in Berlin, was heading for a vacation at his hunting lodge in the Bavarian Alps. I, Otto Gensler, his lawyer, friend, and, I suppose, his protector, was accompanying him. All so natural and benign. All true, but not nearly as benign as it sounded. "Vacationing" was more like retreating three steps ahead of the mob bearing pitchforks, and the hunting lodge rather than the Castle in Mecklenberg being the goal more because of its remoteness and secrecy than anything else—Varick could have his way longer and with complete privacy in at the remote hunting lodge in Füssen than in Mecklenberg.

"So, you are a student at Heidelberg?" Varick asked.

"Yes," Stefan Heinz answered, for that was what we'd ascertained was his name. "I am Austrian. My family lives in Saltzburg. That is where I go now. The school term is over."

"And you are studying art at the university?"

"Yes," Stefan answered Varick, in surprise. "But how did you—?"

"You are carrying art supplies. I would bet you even model for the classes, don't you?"

"For extra money, yes. But, again—?"

"You are a beautiful young man. I can't conceive that your teachers would not take advantage of that—and of you."

I have no idea how Varick was able to do it—to so quickly strip a young man down with words like this, with the stripping to continue to the emotions and then the physical.

But it was his gift—or his curse. I continued to struggle with which one it was. In any event, the young man was walking right into his web.

"Yes, well . . ."

"I'm sure that your teachers take full advantage of you," Varick honed in.

"I'm not sure what you mean," Stefan answered, but his blush conveyed otherwise—and the saucy expression he gave indicated that he wouldn't shrink from the ever-stripping discussion. In my imagination—soon to be reality, I knew—every phrase Varick's soothing voice caressed the young man with stripped off an article of the man's emotional shield and then his clothing until the young man was naked, open, and vulnerable. legs spread and bent, pelvis raised to receive the thrust, head turned to the side, throat exposed, vein throbbing. Inevitably, Varick would be inside him, both emotionally and physically.

Why don't you rise and run? I wondered, the warning screaming through my brain so loud that I'm surprised he didn't hear it. But of course he didn't do that. He already was captured in the web. Already the mesmerizing and impossibly handsome, dark and mysterious, baron sitting beside me had his legs open in a wide stance and a hand stroking his crotch, exhibiting a clearly discernible line of his extraordinarily long and thick cock down the inner surface of his thigh. The young man, sitting across from him couldn't miss that. In fact, his eyes, when they were able to tear away from Varick's had been flitting to Varick's crotch even before Varick laid a hand there.

"You lay under men, don't you? Probably for money to augment your family's allowance. But I suppose you lay under your art teacher for some thought of love or something like that. I, we"—I lurched a bit at being brought into this scene by him; I had been trying to play the pure voyeur—"saw you in the shadows on the Heidelberg station platform. That was your art teacher, wasn't it?"

"Yes," Stefan said. He tried momentarily to look away, and I even saw his muscles—his very nicely formed muscles—tense as if to rise and flee, but he didn't flee, and he couldn't keep his eyes from returning to ogling Varick's crotch. All forms of subterfuge discarded, the baron had his cock out now, slowly stroking it as he spoke in calm, smooth, mesmerizing tones in stark contrast to his angry, upcurved, thick, and long erection.

"You are paid to model in the nude, are you not?"

"Yes," Stefan answered, his voice breathless.

"And men pay you to cover you."

A slight pause, and then, almost a whisper, "Yes."

"But your art teacher doesn't pay, does he? With your art teacher it's love."

Stefan didn't answer, but his eyes were locked on Varick's stiff, oversized cock.

"I would not ask for love, Stefan. I will pay. All you have to do is say 'yes.'"

"Varick," I muttered.

"All you have to do is say yes." He ignored both my utterance and my restraining hand on his forearm. "For a start, five marks to see you as the art students see you, in the nude. Say yes to that, Stefan."

"Yes," Stefan said, standing and slowly, sensually disrobing. There was no chance of misunderstanding that the student knew where this was leading. Varick wasn't the only one who sucked in his breath, gave a little gasp, and murmured a "beautiful," when Stefan was standing there for us, in the nude. I was equally as moved. And it didn't go unnoticed that the young man was in erection, albeit one that couldn't compete with Varick's.

I was in erection too. I wanted him as much as Varick could want him.

"Ten marks to service me and twenty-five to let me fully possess you. Say 'yes,' Stefan."

"Varick," I muttered again, once more laying a hand on his forearm. "You promised. Restraint at least until safely at the lodge."

"Shut up, Otto. You want him too. He will agree to it. He wants it," Varick retorted as he shook my hand off, already metamorphosing from the man into the monster. "Say 'yes,' Stefan." The voice was hard, commanding.

"Yes," Stefan whispered as he sank between Varick's spread legs and took the throbbing cock into his mouth.

I don't know why I bothered to struggle with it. The young man was lost from the moment the baron's eyes captured his outside the train. He had offered no hint of desired resistance from that point. He turned right rather than left. He didn't shrink from Varick's possessive hand on his buttocks. He turned right, fully knowing where it would lead him, already having said "yes" in his mind. He didn't even flinch when Varick freed his staff and stroked it. He would have done it without the money.

I shouldn't have cared about—for—him, but I did.

As Stefan's mouth came off the cock, Varick was holding a silver flask out to him. "Here. Drink from this. It will help you sheath the shaft."

Varick wasn't even pretending that the flask didn't contain a drug. As he swallowed from the flask, the young man's eyes latched onto Varick's with a worshipping expression, Stefan didn't even pretend that he wasn't going to be penetrated, violated, fully possessed.

While I watched, scrunched down in the seat, my own cock freed and in my hand, Varick fucked the young man in the seat directly across from me. In the first taking there wasn't much to see. Stefan, sitting, was pressed into the back of the seat, his finely muscled, alabaster legs spread and raised, hugging the baron's waist, as Varick, his cape covering the two torsos otherwise, hunched between Stefan's thighs. All other connection was underneath the cape. The undulating of the material of the cape and Stefan's groans, small cries, and moans provided the evidence that Varick was fucking the young man. Stefan's toes curled and then released in the rhythm of the fuck. His eyelids fluttered and he grimaced, and he cried out with each thrust. Knowing Varick's cock, I knew the young man was taking it hard and deep. I also knew that Stefan had a great familiarity with men's cocks to be able to take it like this at all.

As I watched, Varick's right hand rose up from inside the cape, cupped the back of Stefan's head, and pulled the young man's face in for a deep kiss on the lips. After a breathless eternity of this connection, Varick pulled his face away. The eyes of the two were locked—Stefan's in dreamy surrender and, I have no doubt, Varick's in victory. Varick's hand pulled Stefan's head into the young man's left shoulder. Without a skip in the rhythm of the fuck, as evidenced by the undulating of the cape, Varick's tongue went to the exposed and stretched throat. The tongue momentarily licked at the flesh and protruding vein there and then Varick opened his mouth, showed his fangs, and sank them into the young man's throat.

Stefan gave a little cry and struggled ineffectively and weakly but settled down quickly to low moans and the gentle sound of suckling as Varick fucked and fed.

"Varick," I called out softly after a few moments where only the sounds of feeding and sighing could be heard. "Enough. No evidence on the train that would point south." I wanted to say more. I wanted to say that this one was special—special to me, for reasons I couldn't verbalize. But I knew that, with the baron, it had to be about him—about his preservation.

He didn't answer, and he didn't completely comply, but he changed positions. He switched so that he sat in the seat and Stefan was in his lap, facing me. His legs streamed behind Varick's hips on either side, his knees pressed into where the seat met the lower back, his calves running up the back of the seat. He was leaning forward, the heels of his hands on Varick's knees, telling me that he hadn't lost all strength in his body . . . yet. Varick was holding the young man's waist and pulling his passage up and down on the cock. Stefan's face was an exhibition of dreamy ecstasy.

I saw no harm in Varick just fucking the young man and having a taste, so I settled back in my seat and watched, my own cock in my hand, my thoughts vicariously of me being in Varick's position in the fuck.

Varick stopped manipulating the young man's body when Stefan took over the rise and fall on his own. One of Varick's hands palmed Stefan's chest and pulled the young man back into Varick's chest. The other cupped his chin and turned Stefan's face to his for a kiss.

I almost missed that Varick had gone back to feeding at the young man's throat—and I would have missed it if I hadn't noticed that Stefan was losing his strength. His hands had slipped off Varick's knees and he was just hanging there. I could barely see the pupils of his eyes for the whites. The expression of ecstasy was still there, but the look was glazed, fading. I knew it was just a matter of time now.

But I waited for Varick to have his moment, his release, coming in a little cry of his own, a jerk of both his and Stefan's bodies, a gasp from Stefan and look of wonder floating across the young man's face. I knew it wouldn't just be a coming; it would be a warm flood of complete possession and an afterglow of peace—eternal peace for some.

Not for Stefan, though, I hoped.

"More than enough, Varick," I called out. "Not here. Not now. How would we evade discovery?"

"Oh, I'm so sorry, Otto," the baron side, icily as he took his mouth away from Stefan's throat. But the important thing is that he *had* taken his mouth away. "I am being piggish again, aren't I? Here, you may have a taste. Enjoy."

He pulled Stefan off him and laid the young man down along the seat, as he rose, readjusted his clothing and returned and sat next to me on the seat. "I said enjoy yourself," he said, turning to me, his eyes flashing and the tone of his voice one of irritation. I knew it wasn't a polite offer or a request—that it was a goad and command, that he was reminding me that I was no better, no different, than he was.

"I just think—" I started to say, not really knowing what I thought—or why I thought it.

"No, no. You are quite right. This one is worthy of taking home with us. But taste. By all means taste."

I moved across the carriage and gathered Stefan up in my arms as I sat in the seat. I was cooing to him and whispering sweet nothings. I had no idea why I was doing that. I had no realization that I was as lost to Stefan as Stefan now was to Varick. I rocked him back and forth as he continued to moan softly. As he rebuilt strength, he raised his arms, embracing my neck. Our faces were close together and the kiss came naturally. His hand going to my still-exposed cock also seemed natural.

"Take me. I want you to fuck me too," he murmured.

How could I refuse? I turned his body on the seat so that he was lying on his back, his head and shoulders raised on the thick pillows provided with the compartment. Winding an arm under his waist, I lifted his pelvis and, positioned myself, kneeling, between his thighs, I slid easily inside him. He gave a little jerk, but took me easily. He was still dilated from Varick's thick shaft, wet deep inside from Varick's cum. It was all natural, easy. I pumped him slowly. In, out; in, out. I luxuriated in how easily and fully he opened to me, taking me deep inside his soft, sweet core.

We continued kissing until I turned his head, exposing and stretching his neck. All very natural, as was my licking his throat and finding the throbbing vein, sinking my fangs into it, and beginning to feed.

I understood restraint, though. I released my seed quickly and immediately stopped suckling at his neck. I only gave myself a taste of him. In that taste, though, I was even more lost to him than I had been before. He was a sweet fuck. He opened completely, trustingly, to me, and I took him tenderly, appreciatively, but fully, steely hard and throbbing skin rubbing against tender channel walls, giving and receiving loving attention. As open as he was, he pulled me in deep—in keeping with our kind, I was nearly as hugely endowed as Varick was. His passage muscles caressed and undulated over my shaft, denying me nothing in girth or length. I indeed, was horse hung. Still, Varick was a monster to my merely especially gifted. If he accepted Varick like this and Varick was in one of his moods, I knew he'd tear the young man asunder with the massiveness of his endowment. Varick, in fact, was given to such moods, which was a primary reason we were escaping south. I couldn't help feeling protective of the young beauty.

From across the carriage, Varick emitted a wicked laugh. "Weren't you the one who told me not to finish him, Otto?"

That's all it took, but I'm not sure what I would have done if Varick hadn't mocked me so. I pulled off Stefan my body and arranged him carefully on the seat. He was smiling a beatific smile, all drugged innocence and naivety.

"Come," Varick commanded, and I turned and stood in front of him at the other side of the compartment as he unbuckled my belt and dropped my trousers and underdrawers. He took my balls in his hand and squeezed and distended them as he run his tongue down one side of my shaft and up the other before taking me in his mouth. I took his head in my hands, surrendered all to him, and groaned.

He laid me on my back on the seat and pushed his knees under my buttocks. I grunted and groaned as he entered me and began to pump me, deep, deep in the soft core of me. He took my mouth in his and invaded with his tongue. When we disengaged, I turned my head and stretched my throat for him and he fed. He didn't feed for long. It was more a reaffirmation of master and submissive relationship. I had grown too old to provide the sweetness and freshness of blood he craved.

And I was too important to him alive—at least I'd always thought so. But he also needed me under his control, and he knew how to achieve that. Unbuttoning my shirt, he brushed the sides open and found a nipple with his thumb and forefinger, teasing it hard. He moved his mouth down to the nipple, sliced his teeth in at either side of the aureole, and began to suckle blood. His cock pumped on inside me, deeper, harder, faster. I knew that the feeding would—must—stop with his quickly approaching ejaculation. Still I felt myself fading away—into a land of not caring, one of pure, sensual pleasure. Someday I would cross over—and I would not care. His flow came in a flood of peace, matching my own. He continued to feed.

He clearly was irritated that his pleasure with Stefan had been interrupted. He understood why it had been and had to be, but it still angered him and he had to take it out on someone. This wasn't the first time that it had been me.

I felt myself weakening, my ears buzzing. Clearly still angry with me, Varick was taking me beyond the normal limits. I should have been alarmed, but such was the effect of the feeding that I just didn't care, that I set the rhythm of my ebbing life to suckling sensation of his feeding. I was in a haze when he left me. I watched, interested but no longer concerned, as he moved back to Stefan and lay on top of him on the opposite bench. Stefan spread his legs and hooked his heels on Varick's thighs, welcoming him in. The young man sighed, his hands going to Varick's shoulder blades, his head lolling over to one side to accept Varick's dripping fangs, as Varick's buttocks once more started undulating into the rhythm of the fuck.

* * * *

Munich to Füssen

I lay on a padded, but still uncomfortable table, Dr. Pilser standing over me wearing a white coat. He was looking furtively behind him beyond where a white curtain was half pulled between my table and the other side, where someone else was lying on another table. Varick was standing beyond that table. Pilser obviously thought I was still out, because he had one of my legs bent, and he was fingering my ass, the finger being up inside my channel. He was fondling my cock and balls with his other hand.

I was naked and a needle at the end of tube lead was inserted into the crook of one of my arms, with blood dripping into me from a bag hanging on a stand next to the bed. It's the first time I had required a transfusion. We'd been here before, in Dr. Pilser's surgery in Füssen, for other young men Varick wanted to spin out a little longer when we were staying at the hunting lodge. But this was the first time I was here to receive a transfusion myself. Varick had never gone as far with me as he had done on the train from Heidelberg to Munich. It didn't escape me that our relationship was entering dangerous ground. I could no longer be sure that his need for my support would restrain him.

When we'd left the train in Munich Varick had barely been able to help both Stefan and me onto the platform.

Seeing us struggling, a conductor had blown his whistle and porters had come running. So had Pietr, the lodge's driver and, fortunately for him, too old and grizzled to be of special interest to Varick, who jumped down from the carriage and hobbled to us.

"No, no, just a bit of motion sickness, both of them," the baron had said, his voice commanding enough to bring the panic to an end. "Just help get them to the carriage. They will be fine."

I was more fine than Stefan was, although the sloppy smile on his face seemed to calm the concern that he was in pain. Neither one of us was in pain, really. Both of us had ceased our journey just this side of paradise, thanks to Varick's expert cocking. Both of us would have willingly crossed over for just that little extra slice of paradise. I remember muttering. "Stefan. To the hospital. Here in Munich," and Varick agreeing with me as we both were handed up into the carriage.

But of course Varick didn't have the carriage go to the hospital in Munich. He told Pietr to drive on to Füssen. Varick had a doctor in Füssen, Dr. Pilser, who could keep his secrets and who was expert in the new technique of blood transfusions. We had used him before. He was happy as long as Varick paid him well—and not just in money. He was given sexual access to those he was transfusing. I had never before thought that this would include me—but the doctor's probing fingers up my ass and hand on my cock told me that it did.

The baron had fucked Stefan again en route from Munich to Füssen. He had restrained himself from taking any more of the young man's blood, but that didn't stop him from crouching between Stefan's raised and spread legs, the young man's knees hooked on Varick's hips and his hands clutching the baron's biceps, his fists opening and closing to the rhythm of the thrusts. The young man obviously was aware enough to enjoy the cock working deep inside his ass. Varick's cape covered their torsos and undulated with the fuck. Stefan's head was turned and he was watching me, his eyes seeming to gleam in the darkness of the carriage, his gaze one of ecstasy and triumph that it was him and not me that Varick was fucking.

The young man wasn't unaware of the dynamics playing here. He was accepting the dire risk he was taking. Still, I don't think he was fully aware where this was headed. Like most young men his age, he believed himself indestructible—and he placed a high value on personal pleasure. To him, this was high adventure and never-before-experienced ecstasy. He wouldn't be the first young man to learn that it went terminally beyond that.

I lay across the opposite seat, barely conscious, my mind in a swirling haze, straining to feel the next breath that came to me in a low pant. Unlike Stefan, I knew where this ultimately was headed.

The baron must have realized he had taken Stefan to the brink again, because when we reached Füssen and Dr. Pilser had been raised to return to his surgery and give transfusions to both Stefan and me, it was me who Varick obviously had told Pilser he could fuck to partially cover the bill. I realized that Stefan was the one lying on the other table, beyond the half-pulled curtain. I groaned as the doctor lifted and bent my other leg, spreading them apart. He realized then that I had come around from the anesthetic he'd given me before hooking me up to the transfusion bag. I saw that the bag held a full unit of blood, which I had assumed I didn't need, although Stefan probably did.

I found out then, though, why I was given a full unit. Pilser came up on the table, placed a thick pillow under the small of my back to raise my pelvis, and penetrated me with his cock, holding just inside me until I had adjusted to him and then moving deeper. He was thick and throbbing. I groaned with mixed feelings—fear of yet another taxing stretch inside me that night and wanting the cock moving inside me, challenging my channel walls to take him. He was a well-built man with a strong cock. He, in fact, was built too large to be a mere mortal. Varick, in his jealousy, rarely shared me—certainly not with another like us.

Pilser moved his torso over mine, stiff arming me on either side of my chest. As he sank inside me and started to pump me with his cock, he grabbed the hair on my head with one hand, pulled my head to the side, and stretched out my neck. I saw the flash of his fangs as he lowered his mouth to my neck, pierced the vein, and started to feed.

It came as a shock and surprise, but there was no reason why it should have. My body was just a way station now for the blood pumping from the bag into my arm. It should have worried and depressed me, but it didn't. I felt alive, electric, and, arching my back and raising my pelvis to him, began to move with him in the dance of the ultimate fuck. Sex with another one such as us was pleasure on a much higher plane than in coupling with a mere mortal.

I moved with Pilser in the fuck, taking him deep and soft and open, my deep channel walls going spongy and shimmering. Both he and I were concentrating on gauging the thrusts of his cock—and my counterthrusts—with the pulse of the feeding at my throat. We came together in a mutual cry and release.

"Otto here will be fine in a couple of hours," I heard Pilser telling Varick as I was dressing. "The other young man should rest from it for a few days. Three days, I recommend. That is unless—"

"Thank you, Herr Doctor," Varick said, handing over cash, and then we were on our way.

* * * *

"You aren't going to end it with Stefan?" I asked. "You wouldn't have had him given a transfusion if you were going to end it—at least anytime soon."

"He has captivated me," the baron answered. We were sitting in the dining room of the hunting lodge, a chalet pressed into the mountainside high up the mountain, at the tree line, and made out of huge logs. We were smoking and drinking brandy. Varick had put Stefan in his bed, and Stefan had immediately plunged into sleep. Erik, a new servant, young, blond, and more pretty than handsome, had served us and departed back to the kitchen. From the looks Varick gave him, I knew Erik wouldn't be working here for long—not that he'd be fired or quit—which was a pity, because the young man was giving me looks of unmistakable want. I would have to tell the butler to start looking for Erik's replacement immediately. I did not pity the butler, though. He had selected Erik knowing that such a lad would soon need to be replaced.

"I don't understand how I can keep him and use him at the same time," Varick said.

"We're talking about Stefan now?" I asked. Erik had just left the room and Varick's eyes were still on the door through which the young man had exited.

"Yes, Stefan. I have no such quandaries about the new servant. He is pretty but not worth a transfusion, I don't think. He is one evening's pleasure at best—just an hour or more of sport. I will use and discard him. If you want him, use him soon, use him gently, and don't spoil my sport with him."

"There is only one way to preserve Stefan through the next three days," I said, changing a discussion that I found distasteful. We weren't all as callous and self-centered as Varick was. Some of us answered the question of restraint with more humanity. "And I'm sure you know what the way is of preserving Stefan. I know you can't keep away from him. He's in your bed now. But you can give him time to recover."

"You mean the mask, don't you?"

"Yes," I answered. "You can fuck him without the need to drain him. Is he worth the discomfort of the mask?" I held my breath. I couldn't tell Varick I had feelings for Stefan as well and was trying to do what I could to keep him alive. Saving him would have to be Varick's idea.

"Yes. The mask is in my office. You will hold the key for the next three nights?"

"Yes," I said. And longer than that, if I am able.

"I will go get it. I am satiated for tonight, and I don't need it every night. But that third night . . ."

"I will see to that," I answered.

"You are none too ready for it again, either," he said.

I was touched that he cared even that much. The last time had been touch and go. I wasn't sure how much longer he could maintain restraint even with me.

"I have another idea," I said.

Before he went up to bed, we had fashioned the leather mask over his face that had a lock on it. I kept the key. The mask allowed him to breathe, but he could not bring his fangs to a position to draw blood.

He went up to bed and I stayed, waiting for Erik to come clear the table. When he did, I returned the look of want that he gave me. I peeked into Varick's bed chamber as I was going to my own. Stefan was awake and on his back, his legs bent and spread, his hands clutching Varick's bare buttocks, as the baron lay between the young blond student's thighs and fucked him in long strokes. Stefan turned his face toward the door and gave me a look of triumph. Varick was wearing the mask.

If only you knew, Stefan, what I am trying to do for you. If only you knew.

Erik came to me later in the night. I was too tired to take him properly, but I did want to have him before Varick got to him. I lay on my back, with Erik straddling my hips and riding my cock. When I felt myself close, I raised my chest to his, embraced him, took him into a kiss. I ran my fingers into his curly black hair and pulled his head to the side. I was feeding on him—but just a taste—when I bathed him deep with my cum. He was delicate and had swooned already. But he was still in usable condition. And he had been taken across that divide. The feeding and the fully possessing size of me had given him pleasures such as he'd never experienced before. He would be open to more of the same now.

I held him close to me through the night and felt strong enough in the morning to put him on all fours and fuck him hard, but I didn't feed. He hadn't remembered all that had happened earlier in the night other than that there were higher-plane pleasures to be had from taking a man who was inhumanly big and who suckled at the throat.

Varick was irritable the next day, but manageable. Stefan did not leave Varick's bed. For me, it was only a matter of keeping Varick from returning to his bed chamber during the day, while he was free of the mask.

The following night when Erik came to me— voluntarily—I fucked him royally and feasted on his blood. He now was aware of what was happening to him and fully made the connection of the fucking and feeding as necessary to attain the pleasure he now had to have. I had slowly brought him into it, so that, fearlessly now, he was seeking rather than shrinking away from the sensual act of giving me more than his channel. Becoming a willing blood giver was a conditioning process that enticed with incredible sexual pleasure. Man will take almost any risk to be sexually satiated in a way and to a degree he never has been before. And, like any submissive, he delighted in being able to sheath a cock of mammoth proportions.

The act of sucking blood while fucking a man with an oversized cock brought the man into a realm of euphoria and sensuality that was an elixir to him, leaving him wanting more and more intense sucking and fucking. Erik had no idea how draining it could be, and I maintained restraint, not leaving him much weakened, and whatever weakness he felt was taken as a glorious pleasure brought on by the act. But after that first feeding he still came to me—just as knowing the dangers I willing went to Varick. He would want more and more of it before any realization set in of what it was taking away from him. The big-cocked sex that accompanied it was more intense than anything he would have experienced before. And even once he knew all, he would no longer care.

I knew all of this, as I was trapped by it myself, saved only by Varick's willingness to show restraint with me. Once we were locked together, with him suckling at my neck and his monster cock moving inside me, I was lost to him. I was one with him, willing to melt into him and disappear altogether. He could go as far as he wanted, and I would welcome it and seek new heights in the experience even to the end. The coordinated rhythm of the suckling and draining at the throat—or crook of the arm or armpit, or, as Varick's favorite with me, at the nipple—and the deep pump of the all-possessing cock merged into an enveloping symphony that was unlike any other sensation or pleasure.

As I had found, it enhanced the experience for the taker to rise into the same realm. The infusion of the blood was electric and powering. The senses and vitality soared. One's cock thickened and lengthened to almost unmanageable proportions. Stamina was heightened. The coordinated rhythm of the suck and fuck was like composing a symphony. One's orgasm rolled on and on, the cum produced and released was more prodigious. One felt more alive and sensual than ever before. The same unity of the two bodies and the melting of the giver into the taker that was experienced by the giver was also experienced by the taker, who wanted to possess and completely subsume his prey. One had to fight for restraint. Varick was the master in all realms but this—the more drawn into the need of this special world, the less restraint he was able to command. It was why we had had to leave Berlin.

The next morning I took the mask off Varick again. He was in a foul mood, as was, I thought, natural and stomped around in high dungeon all day. Stefan didn't appear outside Varick's bed chamber. Erik took his meals to him. I thought that was wise. Varick was fucking Stefan and he hadn't recovered all of his strength yet. I shuddered at the thought of what Varick would do with him once the young man had fully recovered.

Varick was pacing back and forth by supper time, roaring at everything and everyone. I had thought to wait on my plan for as long as possible, but this seemed to be as long as he would hold off. More than once he told me he was going up to his bed chamber but that he didn't want to wear the mask. Each time I found a diversion for him. I knew that such a trip would be the end for Stefan.

The last diversion was Erik. When he delivered the after-supper smokes and brandy, I drew Varick's attention to the young man as he was departing.

"You won't need the mask when you sleep with Stefan tonight if you are fully satiated for the night," I said. "I

103

have had Erik already. His blood is sweet. His channel is sweet as well. He is expendable, and you can take him the distance. I really recommend—"

"Call him in," Varick growled.

"Let us finish our smokes and brandy first," I said. "Then I will fetch him and leave you two alone. I suggest one of the bed chambers on the first floor." I didn't want Varick going anywhere near his own bed chamber and Stefan when he was in this condition.

I waited for several minutes after sending Erik into Varick. When I checked to see if they were gone from the dining room, they weren't. Varick was fucking him right there on the dining table. Erik was bent over the table, hands pressed into the surface of the table. Varick was covering him from behind, one arm embracing the young man's waist and the other hand cupping Erik's chin. Varick was taking him in long strokes from behind. I watched until I saw Varick pull Erik's head to the side to stretch his neck, and sink his fangs into the young servant's throat. Erik emitted a long, drawn-out sigh as Varick commenced to feed.

Some minutes later, I checked again. Erik was no longer supporting himself. Varick was holding his body up. Erik's head was turned toward me. There was a look of serenity and ecstasy on his face. Varick was still fucking him and feeding on him. The sucking sounds were long, fierce, draining. Erik's supreme pleasure was evident not only from the angelic expression on his face but also from his deep moans and mewings. Weak as he was, he still was able to raise an arm, the fingers of his hand running through Varick's luxurious black curls, and holding Varick's head into his throat. I regretted the waste, of course. But the young man had been brought across the divide. He submitted to this willingly. He would never have known the pleasure he was receiving now if he had lived a long life, and, having gotten a taste of it from me, he would not ever have been fully satisfied in a long life without being used by Varick. He was fully satisfied in this moment.

Sometime later, I checked again. Erik was on his back on the table, one leg dangling down toward the floor and the other one being held raised and spread by Varick. The baron, nearly lying on top of Erik was still stroking with his cock and feeding on one of Erik's nipples. The young man looked drained. His eyes were open but glazed. A beatific smile still was formed on his lips.

When I next checked, Varick was gone, presumably to bed, with Stefan, but his blood lust fully satiated. I took up the drained body of Erik, slight and light in death, which had sunk under the dining table, and took it to the servants' wing, laying him in his bed. I closed his eyes with a brush of my hand, whispered an apology, and went to bed.

Everything was fine through the next day with Varick, although I spent the entire day trying to figure out how to keep him from declaring Stefan fit and then not being able to control himself with the young man. Varick seemed to be able to practice less restraint with each passing day.

In the end, I did what I had to do. Right after supper, I enticed him to my room and into fucking and feeding on me. In truth I needed it myself from him. But, as I half feared, as he had done in the train carriage, he was passing the normal limits of our coupling and I was growing very weak. I only narrowly managed to roll out from underneath him and to lock him in my room for the night.

The next day, he wasn't happy, but he recognized that he was losing control. He agreed to wear the mask again.

I sat for hours that night before going up to my bed. I was worried about the baron and his increased lack of restraint. I also was worried about Stefan. I schemed on how to get him out of this situation. I realized that now I would never have him, but that was secondary to finding a way to save him.

Thankfully, the night went well in Varick's bed chamber and the glimmer of a hope for Stefan came the next day. He was well enough to be up and about, and I took him into Füssen with me to shop for clothes for him. I sent him back to the lodge with Pietr, the carriage driver, who was to return later for me as I went in to the offices of the law firm that I was connected with when I was in Füssen.

I was checking the news services for word on Berlin and whether the furor over the baron's activities there had been settling down, when a young man, another lawyer, I was told, by the name of Dieter Speidel, was shown in to see me. He was a beautiful young man, not yet thirty, a good five years younger than I was. Blond and blue-eyed, he had a strikingly handsome face even when it was set in a look of concern, as it was now. Still, when our eyes first met, he was able to give me a radiant smile of mutual understanding, mutual interest. My eyes slid down his expensively clothed, fine torso to his crotch. He clearly was gifted there. I would want to lie under him rather than on him.

"Yes, I understand you asked for me?" I said, surprised. Who here would be asking for me?

"Yes, I work in Saltzburg, Austria," the man said. "I have been trying to trace a missing son of the family Heinz that resides there. His name is Stefan. He is a student at Heidelberg University, but he hasn't returned home from the end of the school year yet. He was last seen getting off the train in Munich. He was in the company of Baron Varick von Richthoven. I understand you represent the baron."

My blood—such as I still had—ran cold. "Yes, I represent the baron, but I haven't seen him in—"

"A Doctor Pilser here in Füssen says he saw the baron a couple of days ago. And the young man who was with him fits the description of Stefan Heinz. In fact, I have been told that a young man of Stefan's description was seen in the stores here with you earlier in the day."

He moved closer to me and put a hand on my forearm. I felt it burning there, but I could not acknowledge it—or my strong attraction to him. I couldn't withstand the hold of his eyes on mine either and looked away.

"I was helping my nephew dress for the university this afternoon, and I believe the baron is in Munich," I said. "I will, of course, contact him immediately and see if I can shed some light on this. Where are you staying in Füssen?"

As he gave me his contact information, my mind was racing on what I needed to do. I kept pushing the need to strangle Doctor Pilser into the background as not of the highest priority.

"Ah, well, it must have been some other young man then," Speidel said. "Speaking of my hotel, though, there is a café there and I haven't had afternoon tea yet. Have you had yours? Perhaps you would care to join me. I find you . . . interesting."

I thought it was perhaps too easy to deflect him, and, that proved to be true.

I was upright, but kneeling on the bed in Dieter's hotel room. He was embracing me from behind, an arm around my waist, a hand cupping my chin. I could feel his heart beating against my back—the rhythm was fast, but in synch with the rhythm of my own. He had a fine cock. It was deep up inside me and exploring, caressing the walls of my passage deep in the soft core of me. My passage was responding, the muscles of the walls undulating over the thick, long shaft.

We came out of a kiss, and I cried out in passionate welcome—wanting—as the hand cupping my chin pulled my head over to the side and he sank his fangs into my throat. The cock inside me expanded and lengthened as he fed.

My sensations exploded into a new world of pleasure and want. My channel walls grasped his cock, pulling it deeper inside me as his feeding enhanced his size and length and milked it to an orgasm that started in a gush and then just rolled on and on, as my flow started as well. I felt the throbbing suckling at my throat and the continued expanding of his cock inside me, making new demands in opening my passage, which responded immediately. He started to pump me, demanding and deep, cum spinning out of him and deep up into my intestines, matching the thrusts to the suck at my neck. Even as I felt myself weakening, I was melting into him, becoming one with him, wanting to disappeared into his body. I was gripping his head with one hand, pressing it into my throat, and working my cock with the other.

He was a master. I had thought there was only one—Varick. But this man was Varick's equal. I was one with him. I could deny him nothing.

Colored lights flashed before my eyes, my focus of attention raced between what was churning inside me and what was sucking at my neck. My strength was flowing out of me and I collapsed within his embrace, fully open and giving to Dieter, fully dependent on him for support—for very life itself. I cried out in ultimate pleasure as his ejaculation increased in strength, triggering mine to do so as well, both of them rolling on and on into an eternity of ecstasy, the mixing of our fluids flowing out of me and puddling on and soaking into the bedspread.

I should have known from the beginning, from the first look we exchanged, from the size of his cock snaking down his thigh inside his tight trousers. Dieter was one of us.

He murmured into my ear as we cooled down, holding position, and I answered I know not what. Buzzing was still pounding in my ears. My heart was racing and I was gauging it coming back into a realm of safety, not being sure that it ever would, not caring if it didn't. I was weak and just collapsed on the bed when he released my body and rose back onto his feet. In my weakness I drifted off to a fretful sleep. When I woke, feeling the strength returning to me— knowing he had used restraint and left me in functional condition—he was gone from the hotel room.

I don't know what I told him. I didn't want to think of what I might have told him. But I knew that Varick was in danger—that we needed to move on, and we needed to do so quickly. His match was nearby and was seeking Stefan.

I spent a couple of hours making arrangements for getting the three of us—Varick, Stefan, and me—away and heading to somewhere safe. The complication was that somewhere safe for Stefan wasn't with Varick and me. I had to make separate arrangements to pull him away from the baron without Varick suspecting I was doing so—and Stefan as well, for that matter—and getting him delivered to his lawyer, Speidel, without him being able to trace it back to me or the baron.

But would he, in fact, be safe with Speidel? Did Speidel even represent Stefan's family, or was he another, competing Varick, who had sniffed the air, realized what a prize Stefan was, and wanted the young man for himself. Speidel was one of us. The attraction of Stefan for Speidel couldn't be any less than it had been for the baron or for me. And Stefan couldn't be trusted now, either. Now that he'd had Varick and me, he would crave what Speidel could give him. I couldn't deal with that question now. There was too much need to separate the young man from Varick and get Varick to a place of safety and at a distance from Stefan's siren charms.

I succeeded in making the arrangements that needed to be made, called Pietr in from the biergarten he'd been waiting in, and had him take me up to the hunting lodge.

Dieter Speidel's body was on the staircase, his trousers ripped off him, his body drained of blood. So, in the end, he was no match for Varick. I rushed on up the stairs to Varick's bed chamber. He was on top of Stefan on the bed, his cock buried inside Stefan, his fangs dripping in blood. Stefan was laying under him, arms and legs akimbo; mouth slack open, although in a smile; eyes glazed over. He clearly was gone.

I lost control of myself. Everything I had done, had tried to do, had gone for naught. There were lit candles in the chamber. I grabbed one up in my hands and stumbled around the room, lighting the curtains on the windows and the drapes on the poster bed. Varick lay there, embracing Stefan's body and looking at me with dull eyes. He was drunk on the blood of two men. If he had moved at all, it would have had to be sluggishly. But he was in a stupor of ultimate pleasure. He grinned at me, fangs dripping in blood, oblivious to the flames engulfing the room.

Exiting the chamber, I grabbed the key out of the lock, slammed the door shut, and locked Varick in the burning room. I ran down the staircase, yelling "Fire! Get out of the house now!" and cleared all of the servants out of the lodge. We stood there, well away from the log chalet, and watched it burn to the ground. Ashes to ashes.

* * * *

A week later, having settled the baron's estate as best as I could—with the understanding that a cousin of his, Ludwig, would take over the title and assets, I was sitting in a first-class carriage of a train leaving Munich en route to Berlin. I had not been connected to Varick's activities that had caused him to escape Berlin, I had ascertained. So, it was clear for me to return to the city.

I turned toward the door into the carriage to see that there was a young man, a beautiful blond young man standing there.

"Excuse me," he said. "I was told I should come to this compartment. But if—"

"No, that's quite all right," I said. "Please come in. And perhaps lower the shades to the corridor. We'll have more privacy that way." He was delectable. He also was smiling at me in the way that I understood indicated a special interest. I was ready for a cleansing of the palate, a new beginning, a making my own way.

"How far are you going?" I asked.

"To Heidelberg," he said. "My name is Alfred. I am a student at the university there. Forgive me for saying it, but you are a strikingly handsome man. You remind me of one of my professors. My professor and I are very close. Very." He was smiling the special smile at me from the seat across from me. This compartment was narrower than the one on the train had been coming here. Our knees were touching. He used his to spread my thighs a bit. One of his hands dropped to his crotch. All of these were signs I well recognized.

"Excuse me, but I don't actually have a ticket for the train—and I don't have the money for the fare. Perhaps—"

"I am happy to cover the cost," I answered, "in exchange for the companionship."

"I feel that this is going to be a very interesting trip," he said.

I readily agreed with him. His eyes were on my crotch. They had gone large as he realization of how big I was built.

I was crouched over him in his seat, with the carriage rocking gently back and forth in its movement on the tracks, helping to set the rhythm of the fuck. His bare knees were hooked on my hips, his trousers and underdrawers puddled on the floor between the seats, and his hands were cupping my buttocks, as, under my black cape covering our bodies, I fucked him. At first, he was panting hard and moaning deeply, fighting to accommodate my expanding cock, but once my fangs had sliced into his throat, he slowly quieted down and his channel went soft and slack, yielding to my thickening and lengthening. The slight sucking noise of my cock working inside him coincided with the sound of me gently feeding at his throat. He was sighing in the deep pleasure I was bringing him.

I had just set into coordinating the rhythm of the suck and fuck when the door to the corridor, which I was sure I had locked, slid open and there, standing in the doorway was . . . Varick.

"I believe it will be a very interesting trip indeed," he said, as he entered the compartment, slid the door closed behind him, and shot home the lock again. "May I join you two? My name is Ludwig—now—Baron von Richthoven. I met Alfred here on the platform. He said he would lay under you and me on the trip to Heidelberg for twenty marks apiece. I see you have settled in ahead of me. No problem. Use him gently. I will be the finisher."

He turned and looked at me. But of course I was speechless. His smile showed that he had distended his fangs.

"But first perhaps we should talk about the burning of my hunting lodge."

He settled in behind and on top of me, gently coaxed my head over to the side, and sank his fangs into my throat. I felt him push my cape up my back and, with a sigh of resignation, I raised my pelvis to accord his cock entry into my channel.

111

Five-Year Reunion

I almost had to laugh at the incongruity of it. Hardy had patiently waited for me to neatly fold my clothes and had even brushed the dust off a stack of mats in the exercise room behind the Porterville High School gym before he'd wrestled me to a mat and incapacitated me while he got his dick inside me. It was all so unnecessary, him having me belly over a medicine ball with his body covering mine from behind and above while his beefy arms trapped my arms in a full Nelson hold. I didn't fight him. I wanted him to power fuck me. I didn't intend to lower the boom on him until after he'd done so. When he wasn't expecting it and when he was forced to realize there was no way out for him.

It had been the same five years earlier, on graduation night, when Coach Hardy—my track and tennis coach, but also the wrestling and assistant football coach in this rural county high school—had taken my virginity. Making doubly sure I was of age—demanding to see my driver's license and all—he'd gotten me drunk (or so he thought) then and bound me and fucked me in the bed of his pickup truck down by Bass Lake. But I wasn't that drunk. I had anticipated, wanted, and prepared for what he did. All he would have had to do was ask me if I wanted him to fuck me—to initiate me in what a man, twice my age and with the body of a god, could do to a younger, naïve, but willing, young man.

But if he wanted it this way, incapacitating my body, covering me from above, and pistoning my ass with his thick cock, I'd let him have it. I wanted it this way from him. It wouldn't happen again.

It was part of the reason I'd come to my Porterville High School five-year reunion. A more acknowledged reason was the publicity angle, pushed by my talent agent, Scott, who was sitting at a table in the school cafeteria while Coach Hardy fucked me in a tiled weight-lifting room dimly lit from parking lot lighting coming in through high clerestory windows and that smelled like old gym socks—with Scott fully knowing where I was and what I was doing.

I was one of those phenomena frequently happening in high school—the guy few in his class could remember who had become a celebrity within five years of leaving school. In my case, it had been going to New York rather than college and falling into juicy stage—and more recently movie—parts that made everyone in my high school class dig into their memories to convince themselves and others that they'd been my best friend in school. Scott's idea had been for a movie magazine to do a "returning to his roots" spread on me. The coverage on that had been collected this afternoon. and the magazine people were gone, leaving Scott and me to pay our dues for the high school's cooperation by attending the alumni dinner.

It had all been touch-and-go on getting this set up with the high school because I had recently come out as gay. The intersection of my having an agent and juicy stage and movie roles was just what I was doing now—being fucked by someone who wanted me and who could do something for me.

In Hardy's case, it had been about special attention and favorable placement on teams that led to trophies. In Scott's and various producer's and director's cases it was access in exchange for favoritism. Most of my roles had me type cast as a vulnerable young man taken advantage of by an older man. The major movie I starred in and that had just come out was linked with my coming out in public. The older leading actor in the movie hadn't been exactly pleased by that—movie goers were suddenly looking at the film as a glimpse of reality rather than acting, which pulled the older actor into an uncomfortable position, even though he was a randy old homo himself. He'd never come out publicly, however, although I'd let him fuck me off the set to be happy with me being cast in the part. Scott had said coming out would boost my box office standing and visibility, and it sure as hell did.

Coming out gay also smoothed the extra reasons I had for coming back to this five-year reunion.

Hardy fucked me hard and deep just as he had done on graduation night in the bed of his truck under the stars. And this time I fully participated in the ride to the extent that he let me. I had been fucked a lot and learned a lot from some very important and expert men since that first coupling with the coach. I moved my pelvis with him, I pulled him inside me, and I set my muscles working on his cock, milking him dry so that his moans and groans overrode mine.

And then, as I was dressing and he was looking at me in a whole new way, I lowered the boom on him and returned to the cafeteria, the two of us taking separate routes, and slipped into my seat next to Scott. The lights were out in the audience and I hadn't seemed to have been missed. Speeches and entertainment still were spotlighted on the raised platform at one end of the cafeteria.

Scott nodded to me as I returned to my seat, a quizzical look on his face. I nodded back and then I caught the eye of my high school drama coach, Evan Norton, across the table and gave him a smile, which he returned.

You're next, ran through my mind.

* * * *

"Everything OK?" Scott asked sotto voce out of the side of his mouth while doing his best to pretend he was listening to the vice principal introducing a girls' singing quartet on the platform.

"Everything's great," I answered. I smiled at my former drama coach, Norton, again. He opened his mouth as if to say something, but the music began, slightly off key, and he settled back into his chair and turned his gaze to the platform.

One of the waiters for the evening, a member of the high school football team, and a particularly hunky one, came by the table and I made him lean in real close to me to ask him for another cup of punch. I prolonged our exchange, which the football player didn't seem to mind a bit, and made sure that Hardy, uncomfortably seated across the hall with his wife and at the coaches' table, saw me talking to Ron, the football player.

I almost regretted that I wasn't going to be spending more time here. Ron must have known what I liked—I'd just very publicly come out. It was almost like he was coming on to me—like maybe what he liked yin and yanged with what I liked. He was quite a hunk. I gave a sigh when I'd let him go.

Earlier in the evening—before Hardy had gotten me alone—I'd seen the coach's eyes follow this particular player around the room. If he wasn't playing Ron now, I knew that he intended to do so soon. So this made me wonder again— was Ron a top, and thus of possible interest to me, or a bottom, of little use to me? I wanted Hardy to see that I spoke to the young man, though. I wanted him to think I gave the football player a warning and possibly someone to call if he wanted to.

What I'd told Hardy after he fucked me was that his days of taking privileges with student athletes were numbered—that if I heard even so much as a hint that he was fucking other students, like he'd fucked me, I'd manage to give a national interview of how and where I'd lost my virginity to a man and enough of an ID on who did it that everyone in this county would know it was Hardy. I didn't care if he was careful to ensure the guy was of age. I could muster enough of a national audience to nail his ass to the wall. I'd also been asked about my first time. It would be easy to answer that in a national tabloid.

He hadn't taken my lowering the boom on him all that well. He'd bluffed until he realized I could easily have a platform to talk about it and then he'd shown me how much he thought of himself.

"Hey, if it's more of me you want, just come back and I'll take care of you anytime you want."

"No, it's not more of you I want, Coach Hardy. I can get better than you right there in Hollywood."

After he'd gotten over that rejection, he offered me money to keep quiet. I laughed at that, of course, being able to say that I made more money in ten minutes in front of a camera than he made in a month.

I left him with the impression that I'd do it—that I already had written out a mock interview and my agent had it. He just didn't know when I'd do it. Maybe not for a very, very long time if I didn't hear of any other students being manhandled by him.

"Is it time that we can start a merciful retreat then?" Scott asked, leaning in to me and putting his hand on my thigh and squeezing.

"We're in a high school cafeteria, Scott," I whispered.

"Oh, fine, then," he responded with some exasperation. "Can we start our escape?"

"No, not yet," I said. "I'm not finished here."

I half rose from my seat and moved around the table to where I was sitting next to Evan Norton. Most of the eyes in the room followed me. They had been watching me since I'd returned from my tryst with Hardy. It didn't really matter what was going on on stage. I was the visiting celebrity who, just five years ago, was one of them—and, they'd already determined, not exactly someone who stood out in my yearbook or who was predicted to take the world by storm. I was visible proof that there was hope for each of them. If almost nobody Randy Worth could turn into movie star Tyler Hill in five short years, so could they. And they all were watching me as if the secret to how I did it could be read on my shirt sleeve and could be replicated by them.

Little did they know that it had more to do with taking my shirt off—and my pants and briefs as well.

Evan Norton began to tremble with pleasure and anticipation as I rounded the table to the seat next to him and leaned in to talk to him. All the school was now watching him as well.

I'd forgotten how good looking he was and how elegantly he dressed. I could remember the fluid, dancing movement when he walked and the precise way he had of talking, making full use of his rich, baritone voice. I'd forgotten how I'd mimicked him and later received favorable comments on how I carried myself.

He'd been on the stage himself, of course, before giving it up because the parts didn't meet his expectations and turning to teach drama to high school students. I'd been his "find." He'd given up New York quickly, and thus wasn't much more than six years my senior when I took drama from him. All of the girls had swooned over him. No doubt they still did.

I didn't realize until after Hardy had taken me for the first time on graduation night that I too had swooned over Norton too. I just hadn't known why. I knew why the evening Hardy fucked me. Earlier I saw the drama coach in the shadows backstage at graduation, kissing a young man, a guy who had graduated from the school a couple of years earlier, who Norton had brought in as a stagehand for the graduation ceremony in the school auditorium. I suddenly realized why Norton had been so magnetic. I also did some review of the previous year and I realized why he had spent so much time and effort on me. He was interested in me too.

There just was nothing that had been consummated. He left on vacation as soon as graduation was over—probably with the young man he'd brought in as a stage hand—and I'd escaped town as soon afterward as I could as well, ashamed that I had given it away to Coach Hardy and that I had enjoyed doing it.

But I realized that it had all started with him—not with Hardy, really.

"Mr. Norton—Ed," I whispered to him. "Earlier in the evening you were telling me that the backstage had been upgraded considerably since I was here. You, know, I'd like to see that."

"You would?" he asked, both surprised and pleased. "When would you—?"

"Right now, if that would be OK with you. My agent says we'll have to be leaving soon. I'd hate to go without seeing that—and spending a little more time with you."

* * * *

Trembling with pleasure and excitement and maybe with something a bit more, Norton showed me around the backstage area of the school's auditorium. I showed interest—I indeed found that I was interested and was surfacing the pleasures of the stage productions I'd been in here and Norton's enthusiasm for them—and his hard work at instilling the basics of an actor's skills in me. On this end—the professional success end—of the art, I could fully appreciate the fundamentals I had been given and how, through Norton, we had used limited resources, now augmented, not the least because of the fame I'd brought to the school's drama program, to weave magic. I lodged in my brain the intent to write a check for the school's drama department as soon as I got back to California.

He had instilled much more of both affection and interest in me than just for stage work, I now realized. And, unlike Hardy, he had held off, kept himself in check.

We had moved to the back, dimly lit corner of the area, where folded scrims—painted curtains—for some completed production or other were folded and stacked.

"And over here is—"

Drawing close to him, I cupped the back of his neck with a hand and brought his face into mine for a kiss. His eyes went large in surprise and panic, but I didn't release him. My other hand went to his crotch, hunting for and finding his cock through the material of his trousers. He was hard—hard for me. I knew he would be. He slowly melted to my kiss and his hands went to my waist.

"Randy," he said, elongating the word and drawing it out into a hiss of escaped tension when our lips parted.

"Yes, right, Randy," I whispered. "I'm Randy. I'm randy for you. I want you to fuck me. You've heard that I've come out, haven't you—that is OK—that you wouldn't be taking any anything from me?"

"I didn't . . . I didn't know," he responded. "Well, I didn't know then, not for sure. But, yes, I've read about you. And, yes, I knew you inclinations back in high school. I just never expected . . . well, you know."

With him still holding me to him with his hands on my waist, I unbuttoned his shirt and then mine, flaring the sides open, and rubbing my smooth chest against his well-muscled, slightly hirsute one. He didn't object, nor did he object when I took his mouth again with mine, opening my lips to his tongue, encouraging him to lead. I unzipped him and then me, and held our cocks together, slowly frotting them. He was as long and thick as I had always imagined him to be.

"Randy. Randy. I don't know what to say," he murmured. His fingers were playing with one of my nipples—maybe inadvertently, but maybe because he sensed I'd find that highly arousing, which I did.

"You don't have to say anything. I know you wanted me five years ago when I was your student. I wanted you too. I came—to this reunion—mostly for you. You were the good part of coming back. Not just because you held off, waited. But mostly because you helped me understand what it is that I wanted, what direction I wanted to go in."

He gave a low moan as we both heard his trousers rustle to the rough wooden planks of the flooring, the belt buckle making a metallic sound as it hit. Then the sound of the falling of my trousers as well.

"I don't know," he whispered. "I don't know if I can . . . with you. You are a movie star now."

"Thanks largely to you," I murmured. "You don't have to do anything if you don't want to. Just lie back on this pile of material here. I'll do it all."

Saddled on his pelvis, hovering over him and looking down into his eyes to take in the pleasure he was experiencing, I held his upward bent arms to the material with my hands on his upper arms above his elbow and rode his cock languidly. When he no longer could hold himself in check, he rolled me over to the side, putting my arms in the same position, slid his knees under my buttocks to raise them to his thrust, which I met with a hissed "Yes" and an upward thrust of my own, and pumped me increasingly hard and deep to a mutual ejaculation.

All the time his eyes were looking down into mine as I had done with him, and I did nothing to mask the pleasure he was giving me—the pleasure we were sharing.

He was reaching down into the core of me, and both of us could feel me totally surrendering to him, my shimmering walls giving way, the muscles of the channel undulating over his plunging shaft. I let all of the tension drain out of my body and lay there completely open to him, my head turning to the side, my tongue hanging out, groaning deeply, with full satisfaction, as he fucked on.

* * * *

"You were gone a long time. I don't think this reunion crap will never end. You got what you wanted, I see." Scott's expression was one triangulated on boredom, amusement, and slight panic at being trapped in a middle America scene.

I had let Norton return to his chair before I came into the room. I figured it would go unnoticed that we were gone together then. As I thought, there was a murmur across the cafeteria and all eyes flashed to me as I moved to my seat. I took only a glance at Evan Norton to ensure that he was OK, and I could see that he was more than OK. I made a vow to visit this town more often, if only to drop in on him—he had proven to be a master cocksman—and not the high school. Maybe I'd bring him out to Hollywood and help him with networking there.

"Yes, everything is great," I said back to Scott, forcing my eyes and smile to scan the room instead in greeting to all those who were watching me. Thankfully, the principal was on the platform giving what sounded like—and I'm sure

120

everyone in the room hoped—were the final remarks of the evening.

"Exchanged briefs too?" He asked. I turned and looked at Scott, who had a sardonic expression on his face.

"Excuse me?" I said, in surprise.

"You two came back wearing each other's ties," he said. "Are you wearing each other's briefs too?"

"Could be," I said, with a sloppy grin. "I guess we should stay well away from each other as we leave," I added, "so no one else notices."

"Do you want to go home with him?" Scott asked.

I looked hard at him. The remark had been delivered lightly, but somehow I didn't think it was given lightly.

"Yes and No, Scott." I answered. "If you weren't here, I'd be happy to go home with him. But you are here. I want to go back to your hotel room and have you fuck the stuffing out of me."

Putting Hardy in his place and at last getting it on with Evan Norton had been very satisfying. But that was my past. Scott was my future in a cutthroat business. A five-year high school reunion didn't even register on a priority scale with the future of my career.

We left the cafeteria together, but as we got out to the parking lot, our attention was arrested by lights pointed at us and flashing from an old jalopy of a convertible in the lot. The lights went off and, in the light from the lot poles overhead, I could see that the football team hunk, Ron, was sitting in the driver's seat, his eyes honed on me, a questioning expression on his face.

"I think that guy wants to get your attention," Scott said. The car lights flashed again.

"Yeah, maybe," I answered.

"I think he wants you. Do you want him too?"

"Yeah, I guess so." I was in the mood for someone young and virile.

"Go ahead. Relive your high school days for a few more hours. Find the bank of a lake and let him screw you silly. You'll enjoy yourself and he'll have something to remember forever, even if there aren't many he can tell about it. There's always time for us. I'll be back at the hotel when you're finished."

"Thanks, Scott. Thanks for understanding." As I walked toward Ron's car, my mind was trying to remember the directions to Bass Lake.

Slap of Realization

I looked over at the table under the window of my studio apartment in Spinnaker Bay looking out over Baltimore's inner harbor, and last night's fight came back to me. The potted rose bush I'd gotten for him today to take to my mother on our trip to Dover, Delaware, was still there. He hadn't touched it. He'd told me that he might open the window and toss it out.

He must have gotten over his snit. It wasn't just the survival of the rose bush that told me that. Trent was below me, under the covers. I had wakened with my legs hooked on his shoulders and watching the covers moving and listening to them rustling and to the sound and sensation of his mouth working my cock, encouraging me to an erection. I didn't require that much encouragement.

"Why would I take your mother a potted plant?" he'd asked, incredulity written all over his face and seeping from the tone of his voice.

"It's just what's done. It's what is expected among her friends the first time any of their sons brings a friend home for the weekend."

"Yeah, well, I think you're taking this trip entirely too seriously. We've been together for, what? seven months now and this is the first time you take me to meet your people? And all the points of etiquette you've slapped on me? What, you've never taken a boyfriend home before?" He gave me a sharp look. "You haven't, have you? You've never told them that you were actively gay, have you? That you like to pound men's asses."

"Shhh," I said. "The boyfriend stuff. We'd agreed we wouldn't go into that. It's too soon."

"Seven months is too soon? And is this a conversation we should be having when you have your dick inside me?"

He had a point there. He was on his belly on the bed, and I was mounted on him. He'd just then turned his head toward the window and seen the potted rose bush, so I only then was able to tell him that it was a gift from him. The studio apartment just begged for us to be fucking whenever we were here. The bed took up most of the room. Half my salary as a loan officer at First Mariner Bank went to this view of the Inner Harbor, which we'd positioned the bed to enjoy. It was worth it, though. Trent didn't contribute to the rent. He contributed in other ways. His job as a bartender in a Fells Point gay dive didn't permit him to weigh in on the rent of a 550-square-foot palace like this.

"Take your dick out of me, and tell me how I need to take a gift to your mother when you never took one to mine."

He had a point, but it had seemed natural not to take one to his mother, a hotel maid in a downtown Baltimore fleabag. It would have had to be a bottle of gin to impress her, and Trent had said not to bother because the smell of available booze would have attracted his father to pay a visit.

I hadn't had any trouble with Trent's mother or her uptown apartment, though. She was comfortable to be with—easy to talk to and quick with the smart joke. That didn't mean Trent wouldn't have trouble in a rural farmhouse in Dover, Delaware, inhabited by my mother and her sister, and my own maiden sister, who worked in a library. That was an entirely different world than we lived in here. Being called on it was a slap of realization, though.

My inability to answer Trent's question had led to a dual pouting session and a night turned from each other in the bed.

All must be forgotten this morning, though. He was working his way up my body with his tongue. He reached my lips with his. I could feel his buttocks rubbing against the front of my thighs as I bent my legs, pressing my feet into the mattress. I wondered if . . . because sometimes we just didn't get to it in the frenzy of the moment . . . but, yes, he was smoothing a condom down on my cock with one hand, as he cupped my head in the crook of his other arm and opened his lips for my tongue to work itself in.

Trent pulled off my mouth long enough to look directly into my eyes and whisper, "Good morning, Marty. We have time for a trip to heaven?"

"Always," I answered. "So, you're not mad at me?"

"How could I be mad at you?"

Oh, about a hundred ways, I thought. We spent a third of our time mad at each other for some reason. Two very different worlds. There was no reason we should get along. The odd couple. But somehow . . . "Shit. Holy shit. Yesss!"

We spent two-thirds of our time in ecstasy like this.

Holding my erect cock elevated with one hand, he was descending on it. I didn't quite feel my balls nestle up into the curve of his buttocks, though, or the feel of his bush hair mingling with mine—we both groomed, but not much.

"Fuck me. You do it. I want you to make love to me," he murmured.

Using the leverage of my feet, I started a rhythm of upward thrusts, pulling my own buttocks off the bed as I fucked up into his channel and then letting them come back down on the sheets.

"Oh, fuck, yes! Nail me!" he cried out.

And I did. Again and again and again. We came nearly together. We'd been practicing that and had come close to perfecting it. It would be perfect when we could sense the other one about to blow rather than having to announce it in breathy monosyllables.

He showered first and then moved about the room, filling a duffle bag with clothes and whatever else he needed for the weekend. He moved naked, and it was several minutes before I could take my eyes off his beautiful body—still in wonder at having a young man so beautiful in my bed—and focused on what he was packing and what he had laid out to wear: black chino skinny jeans and a black muscle T.

"You're not taking those clothes and wearing that, are you?" I asked—in a voice that I should have known better than use.

"Why? Why not?" Trent asked, turning on me. "It's what I wore the last time we visited *my* mother."

We're not visiting your mother, I almost blurted. God, it was good I didn't say that, though. I knew he'd take it wrong when, in fact, it was a compliment to his mother. "Remember that we're not declaring. How about you look in my closet to see if there's something you can wear and take that won't make me want to jump your bones."

"Like you jumped my bones last time we were at my mother's—fucking me on her bed—with her snoring and drunk as a skunk in the other room?"

Yeah, like that, I thought. But again I couldn't say it. "It's going to be a rough weekend, Trent. I've been putting it off. It isn't you, really. And it certainly isn't *your* mother. It's *my* mother, aunt, and sister. They live in another world. Maybe we should just not—"

"Fine," he said, clipping and punching the word. "I'll look in your closet. Anything you don't want—?"

"Take anything you want," I said, suddenly contrite and scared this would lead to another fight. "I packed yesterday. Oh, and maybe cut down on the jewelry. Just for this weekend." Was I pushing my luck?

"The jewelry."

"Yes. Just what shows. The eyebrow ring and the earring. You know, just so it doesn't . . . scream so."

"Fine." It was even more clipped than the first time, if that was possible.

At the door, as we were leaving and he already was in the outer corridor, I said, "Aren't you going to take the potted rose for my mother?"

126

"Fine," he said again, walking deliberately over to the window, picking the plant up, and giving me a venomous stare down as he passed me at the door.

Oh, yes, this was going to be one hell of a weekend.

* * * *

"She'll just naturally put us up in separate bedrooms. She won't even think of doing otherwise."

"Fine."

We were barreling up I-95 from Baltimore toward the cutoff over to downstate Delaware. I checked the cars around me and then looked over at Trent in the passenger seat. He was pressed up against the passenger door, but the distance he was putting between us had to be just symbolic in this Camaro coupe. I didn't like the sound of the "fine." It didn't sound so much an exasperated acknowledgment that we wouldn't be sleeping together this weekend at my mother's house as it sounded like he didn't care if he'd be sleeping with me at all.

"It's just that they are quite traditional. Dover hasn't really made it into the twenty-first century, and my women folk haven't made it beyond Dover."

"I said it's fine."

"It's just that it's a big step for me, even bringing you home. I hope you won't go all sarcastic on me. I'm trying not to cut you out of my life. I'm trying to move up slowly on everything. This is important to us. I'm trying to show commitment here."

"How noble of you not to want to cut me out of your life. Do you think they'll be OK with me French kissing you at the breakfast table? Not your cock, of course. Just on the lips."

"Come on, Trent. I'm trying to be serious here. I'm trying to let you in on a full life. Gradually. If this isn't going to work out—"

"I said fine. It was just a joke. Loosen up, Marty. And maybe we should stop talking about it. The rose bush might tattle on us."

And that was pretty much it for the rest of the drive down Route 13 to Dover—a smaller town, Leipsic, really, not quite as far as Dover. In fact that had been the extent of our conversation in the car until right before we turned off 13 to go over toward the Delaware Bay to Leipsic. Then Trent dropped the bombshell.

"This is the visit it will be, Marty. This is when you tell your mother and the others that we're a couple. Now or never. And I don't stick around for never."

It was just a few more minutes to the old farmhouse my mother had been born and raised in and had inherited and refused to live anywhere else when she'd married my dad, now long gone. I hyperventilated the rest of the way.

* * * *

"Land, it's good to see you. Expected you an hour ago, but we've kept lunch ready. Judith said we should fix something that would keep and could just be taken out, and she was right. You look like you need fed, Martin. And this, this must be Todd. I've heard so much about you and it was so nice that Martin could give you a ride out to the stock car races."

Trent gave me an amused look. I hadn't told him that I told her he was along because he had a ticket to the stock car raises in Dover Sunday night, and I'd volunteered to drive him to that to meet up with friends. He knew I'd been living with Todd before him, though.

"It's Trent, Mother," I said, cringing. Why did she have to butcher his name as Todd. Todd and I had been a number before Trent. Mother of course had never heard that—but Trent had. I was starting out behind the eight ball here. I looked at Trent again. His expression had turned to the sardonic.

"Let me take you up to the bedroom first so you can drop your bags before lunch is on. Don't stand in the way, gawking like that, Sarah. Maybe you can go on into the kitchen and tell Judith she can start serving up."

Sarah, my younger sister, who had gone to junior college in Dover, gotten a librarian certificate and a job in the library there, had never explored further than Delaware and the Eastern Shore, and lived at home, indeed was gawking. She was gawking at Trent, who was probably the most beautiful and exotic-looking young man she'd ever seen. He was to me too, but Sarah couldn't hope that Trent would ever be to her what he was to me.

Trent gave her a sunny smile and winked, and I could see her shudder and blush before she moved from between us and the bottom of the staircase in the foyer and flitted down the hall into the kitchen.

"I hope you don't mind. You'll both be sleeping in Martin's old room. It has twin beds."

With that, Mother gestured toward the staircase.

Trent smiled at me and it was my turn to shudder and blush. Of course we'd both be in my room in the twin beds. There wasn't any other bedroom in the house available to us. Why hadn't I thought about that and avoided the "separate beds" discussion altogether? I'd lost points I hadn't had to.

"And, my, what is that you're carrying, To— . . . Trent?" she asked as she put a foot on the first stair tread and turned and looked at us.

"Roses. A pot of roses, Mrs. Hammond. I brought them for you." Trent was all smiles and disarming politeness. "Marty told me that your name was Rose and that pink was your favorite color."

Oh, lord, laying it on a little thick there, Trent, I thought. I didn't remember telling him my mother's first name, but I must have. But I certainly didn't tell him her favorite color was pink. I'd picked the roses out at random.

"My, how thoughtful of you," my mother gushed. "Fancy that Martin knew pink was my favorite color—and how gentlemanly of you not only to bring me a present but to make such connections."

She clearly was pleased, and I saw a more girlish step in her carriage as she preceded us up the stairs. For my part, I was stunned. Trent was scoring a homerun with my mother—right after drawing god worship from my sister—

and all on his own. There only remained the formidable Judith. We referred to her as Aunt Judith and she was quite a nut to crack. Often scowling, nearly always judgmental, and more manly than most men in the Dover region. She wasn't really my aunt, but she and my mother had been that close and she had moved in here shortly after her husband ran off and left her—coincidentally the same time my own father had hit the road solo.

In the bedroom, after Mother had told us where the bathroom was where we could freshen up before lunch, which would be ready when we were—house layout directions that I hardly needed, but Mother already was lost to giving Trent her full, near-giggly attention—she left us. I gathered Trent into my chest and gave him a deep kiss. He didn't resist me. It was like a warm, sunny day here in my mother's house, after the iciness in the car on the way from Baltimore.

"So, we can sleep together after all," I said, "or at least fuck before we go to our own comfortable beds."

"How convenient for you," Trent said.

"The turn with the roses was brilliant," I said.

"And I didn't bite the heads off the buds as we came upstairs. Fancy that," he responded, his voice icy, his eyes flashing. "Your mother and sister are nice," he added in a less tense voice.

"You haven't met Aunt Judith yet."

"When are you going to tell her—your mother—that we're lovers, a couple—that we live together?" Trent said. "Or were you planning not to at all—that bit about me just catching a ride to the Dover International Speedway."

"I will. I promise. Right after lunch."

"Good, because I don't know if I can sustain the role of 'just a thoughtful friend' for the weekend."

"You won't have to, I promise." I pulled him in for another kiss.

A ship's bell range in the near distance.

"What the shit?"

"It's a call to a meal, Trent," I said. "A tradition in the house. There are a lot of traditions in the house. But that

130

'shit,' Trent. Can you watch the language? Something else not used in this house."

"Fine," he said. Clipped off and icy again.

It would be a miracle if we made it through lunch. We hadn't even encountered Aunt Judith yet.

* * * *

When I returned to the dining room with the freshly iced chocolate cake, Trent and Aunt Judith were having a raucous discussion of the people they'd seen drunk on their tails in bars. One would think that Trent, a bartender, would have the award-winning stories, but Judith was meeting him story for story and using salty language, which, thankfully, Trent was studiously avoiding as I had requested—at least through most of the meal. Where he was laughing, Judith was snorting. Sister Sarah was watching in fascination tinged with horror—not by any means at anything Trent was saying. Trent had acted the perfect, smooth-talking gentleman most of the meal and had given much appreciated attention to all three women in turn.

Some of the swear words had come creeping back in toward the end, but I couldn't expect Trent to hold it in forever, and most of the blue language was Judith's, inevitably loosening him up and pulling him in. In any event, it wasn't as noticeable or grating as I feared it would be.

At the end of the meal of cold fried chicken, German potato salad, coleslaw, and hot biscuits and homemade strawberry preserves, Mother had announced that there was chocolate cake for dessert, but we had to wait for it to be iced.

I went into the kitchen with her and sat and we talked about our separate lives while she spread fudge icing on the German chocolate cake. All the time we talked, I had it on the tip of my tongue to tell her what Trent was to me, but it just wouldn't come out. Perhaps if she pressed me about him, but, to her, he was just a guy I knew who was I giving a ride to meet up with friends at the car races on Sunday.

We almost got there. "I really like your friend, Trent," she said. "He's a real gentleman and a breath of fresh air in this old, stale house."

"Mother—" I started after a pause, but then she spoke again.

"There. The cake's done. We mustn't keep them waiting longer. Judith is enjoying herself with Trent entirely too much. You take the cake, please, and I'll bring the plates and dessert forks."

And then we were back in the dining room, where the first thing I saw was Judith dabbing her eyes with a napkin and with a broad grin on her face. Never had I seen anyone win over and transform "Sergeant" Judith as quickly and completely as Trent had.

While Judith reviewed for my mother some of the funniest exchanges she and Trent had had—which was unnecessary, as we could hear it all from the kitchen, but Mother was too patient and considerate to cut off—Trent turned to me.

In sotto voce, he asked, "Did you tell your mom about us while you were in the kitchen so long?"

"I tried, but—"

He didn't stay with me to hear whatever lame excuse I would be able to come up with on such notice. His attention went to Sarah, while the two older women were chattering with each other, and Sarah almost melted on the spot as he complimented her on her dress.

"You two go on into the parlor and make yourselves comfortable," Mother said after we had devoured the cake, the icing still warm to the last, "while we women clean up this mess."

"If it's OK with you, Mrs. Hammond, maybe Marty and I could find somewhere to walk to keep the pounds that went into this delicious meal from settling around our waistline." Trent had stood up from the table.

"That sounds like a great idea, although I just can't imagine you having a pound of anything gathered anywhere." The compliment came from my mother, although, in watching Sarah across the table, I could see that she was thinking far more prurient thoughts about Trent than that.

"Take him down to the end of Grace Street, Martin," Mother continued. "That dead ends into the entrance of a park by the river now that has a very nice walking trail. We'll be right here when you get back."

Trent walked along, head downcast, kicking rocks from the pathway as we walked down Grace and then into the park. They'd done a nice job with it. The path ran down toward the lake. There was a grassy area on the left rising up to a stand of mature pine trees with heavy boughs sweeping down to the ground. Without saying anything, Trent started walking up the grassy hillside and into the trees.

"Looking for privacy?" I said as I followed him into the trees along a narrow path between the drooping boughs.

"You know what I like to look for from you, Marty," he said. It came out almost as a growl.

Indeed I knew what Trent like to get from me. "Where? Where did you go?" I asked, not being able to see him as I looked around.

A hand came out of the cover of a pine tree and pulled me inside, to the trunk of the tree. Boughs of broad, green pine needles spread out around us, obliterating the view of anything but the sweet-smelling interior of the tree. I laughed and then moaned low, as Trent turned my back to the trunk of the tree and came in for a kiss and a feel of my crotch through the material of my trousers.

We kissed and fondled, building up hot desire. He unzipped me and stroked my cock as we kissed. He went down on his knees between my legs and took me to heaven with his soft mouth. It was only then, as the steel ball ran up and down the vein in the underside of my cock that I realized that he hadn't taken his tongue piercing out. Why hadn't I noticed that? Had the women seen it? Surely they had. None of them had said anything about it. I wasn't going to think about it now. He was going to take me to heaven with a blow job.

"Trent? What?" I murmured as I felt him rolling a condom on my cock.

"Yes, here, now," he whispered, moving my hands to his belt buckle. "Fuck me." I unbuckled and unzipped him, and pushed his trousers and briefs off his hips, where they fell to the matting of brown needles under the tree from last year's molting.

We kissed deeply and, embracing his torso in my arms after unbuttoning and spreading his shirt, I moved my lips down his throat to his nipples. I felt, more than observed, the weighing down of the pine limbs as Trent lifted his legs to hook onto boughs on either side of my hips, using his hand to position his hole on my erect cock and then impale himself on my shaft.

I held him, but I let him do most of the work of fucking himself on my cock until, with separate cries and a shared long sigh, we both ejaculated.

We held for several more moments, kissing and fondling each other, and then he let his legs down and I heard him pulling his briefs and trousers back up.

"That was nice. Very nice," I murmured.

"Yes, it was," Trent agreed. "I'll always remember it. Good-bye, Marty," he said, and then he turned and melted away from the tree.

In a mellow mood, I zipped up, came out of the tree myself and walked down to the side of the stream babbling through the park, expecting Trent to join me at my side from wherever he had disappeared to. When I realized he wasn't going to, I walked home, entering the kitchen door from whence we had departed, as Grace was the next street over from the back yard of my mother's house.

My mother was alone in the kitchen. The lovemaking with Trent had shamed me, making me realize how important he'd been to me. I owed it to him to be honest with my family, and it probably was now or never.

"Mother—" I started after clearing of my throat.

"You and Trent haven't had some sort of falling out, have you?" she said. She turned her face to me and I could see the look of concern in her expression.

"No, of course not."

"Good, because he's a keeper, Marty. It's time you got some stability in your life."

"Keeper? Stability? You mean you know? About Trent and me? About me?"

"I've known about you for years, Marty. I've been waiting for you to bring a young man home. I knew that would mean you finally were serious."

"And you aren't angry? Disappointed?"

"No, of course not. Why would I judge you or disapprove of anything you'd chosen for yourself? I accept you any way you are. And you've never judged Judith and me."

"Judith and you."

She gave me a sharp look and then a horse laugh. "You didn't see it, did you? All these years. Of course not. You were in college—and then on your own. And we haven't flaunted it. Yes, Judith and me. You thought both of our husbands taking off at the same time and Judith moving in here was some sort of coincidence? It wasn't any coincidence. It was my life coming back into the balance of what was meant to be. It was me gaining happiness—and gaining courage, although that was mostly Judith." She laughed again, but then her expression became serious. "You aren't too observant, are you Martin? Maybe not observant enough."

"What do you mean?"

"I'll ask you again. Did you and Trent have some sort of falling out? And I'll repeat that it seems to me he's the best thing that's happened to you. And, no, I'm not fooled by how he's tried to tone himself down just for us. It tells me how much he wants you too."

"Why are you asking me this."

"He's standing out front now, waiting for a taxi. He came back from your walk without you and said he discovered that his ticket for the Dover races started this evening and he'd decided he should go on over there. The Dover International Speedway is the biggest thing going on in this town, Martin. There aren't any races there this weekend. Judith and I knew as soon as you phoned and told us you were giving a young man a ride to go there that you were bringing someone home you couldn't—or wouldn't—tell us about. Dammit, Martin, do you know how hard Judith has tried not to screw this weekend up for you and Trent? And now Trent's out there waiting for a taxi to leave you. You just best thank your lucky stars that I called the cab company back and told them we wouldn't be needing one. Now get on out there and stop this mistake from happening."

The double-dose slap of realization woke me with a jolt. I got on out there, calling out to Trent as I moved, "It's OK. They know, Trent. It's great. Everything is great."

The look Trent gave me when he turned around told me that everything wasn't great—at least not yet. And I guess I didn't deserve for it to be that easy. But I'd try to make it great and just keep on trying until it worked. Mother was right. Trent was a keeper.

Taken Hiking

Noah Young was an angel. With a flawlessly handsome face, a beatific, innocent smile and blond curls haloing his head, and a perfectly formed, somewhat diminutive body, he was frequently described as angelic. The high tenor voice he graced the Shenandoah Conservatory's Chamber Choir with—not frequently risen to in one's freshman year at Shenandoah University in Winchester, Virginia—was angelic. His inspired artwork on theater backdrops for the conservatory's theater program was considered to be inspired by heaven. He even stood out as a graceful angel in his dance classes.

He hadn't realized he was gay until he entered the music program at Shenandoah University. He had suspected he was just neither this nor that and had been content with the oft-expressed projection that his angelic nature and musical gift was leading him toward a life of celibacy in the priesthood.

There wasn't much in the way of gay life in Gatlinburg, Tennessee, where he came from, in the shadow of the Great Smokies—at least anywhere Noah was looking. Noah didn't do much looking on his own. He was lost in his music and art and his love of hiking up into the Great Smokies, an activity that helped keep him trim and fit. There had been girls attracted to him—and even some boys. Who wouldn't be attracted to an angel? But he'd been so immersed in his own interests that he hadn't even noticed their interest.

Winchester, Virginia, was a bit more "of this world," though, and Noah certainly did notice the interest that a bass from the chamber choir, a senior with considerable stature both in the college social whirl and physically, celebrated a successful choir Christmas concert by trapping Noah in the backseat of his car on the side of a remote forested lane when coming home from an after-concert party, covering Noah with kisses and his considerably larger body, and missionary fucking Noah's virginity away.

They had both been high on the concert success and drunk on Christmas punch, and the bass apologized profusely, but Noah, more confused and embarrassed at having felt touched as never before by the experience, was ambivalent in his response, so the bass doggie fucked him again in the backseat of his car the night before they all went home for the Christmas break.

In Gatlinburg, at New Year's, Noah finally became aware that his high school vocal coach's interest hadn't only been for his talent.

"You have come home changed in some way, Noah," Mr. Connor had said when they met at the punchbowl after a New Year's Eve concert and found a table together in the corner of the hall.

"Yes, being up in northern Virginia and everything that has been happening at the conservatory has really opened my eyes."

"You have gained experience outside of music and art? If so, that's wonderful. I was so afraid you wouldn't discover there is more than that to life—and that your experiences with life can only enhance your music and art." Connor put a hand on Noah's thigh. Noah didn't flinch.

Noah looked into Connor's eyes and said, "I've opened my eyes to so much more than I knew existed. If I had known when I was still here—"

"Have you discovered woman at last at that university of yours?" Connor asked.

"No, not that."

"Men?" the former vocal coach asked. He squeezed Noah's thigh. This time Noah did shudder—and he covered Connor's hand with his, but quite obviously not to brush it away.

"I have some new compositions on my piano at home, Noah. Would you like to come to my place and hear them?"

"Yes, I'd like that."

Connor fucked Noah on a bearskin rug beside Connor's baby grand piano in a cramped living room. It was all so romantic, with candles and everything that Connor had moved around the room to provide atmospheric lighting as soon as they had entered the log cabin perched on the side of a mountain. There was a fireplace with a fire going as well. The scene was fit for an angel. It would have been a perfect setting in which to lose one's virginity if Noah's hadn't already been taken from him.

But it was Noah's first prolonged, languid fuck, lying on his back, his legs bent, with Mr. Connor crouched between his legs, first giving Noah his first cock suck and then hovering over him, leaning his face down to Noah's for a kiss, while he positioned his cock and entered, entered, entered Noah's channel. The penetration caused channel walls to stretch and shimmer and Noah to arch his back, claw at Connor's shoulder blades with his hands, pant and moan, and, when Connor began stroking, deep in the core of the young angel, to open and close his clutching at the older man's back to the rhythm of the fuck.

Connor thrust again and again, each time deeper, each time with less of an interval between thrusts. He was embracing Noah close at the chest, and Noah could feel the quickening of both of their heartbeats.

"Yes, yes, fuck me!" he cried out, and instinctively, naturally, he set his own pelvis in motion, moving with Connor's thrusts, pulling the long cock deeper, deeper. Noah's hand went between their bellies and found his own cock. They rocked and beat against each other for several minutes, no sound coming out of them but the animalistic groaning and snorting of two lovers in uncontrolled heat . . .

until, with a cry, Noah exploded. Connor followed soon after, pulling out of Noah and releasing on his belly.

They lay there, in continued embrace, panting, their eyes locked together in satiated lust. But not completely satiated, no. Connor turned Noah belly to rug, ran an arm under the young man's waist to lift his buttocks, mounted him, thrust his cock inside the hole again, and started the pumping all over again.

It wasn't until the next morning, the start of a new year, that Noah was to hear Connor play his new compositions on the piano.

This was a whole new world for Noah, and he went back to college resigned to the knowledge that he not only was gay, but also that he was a submissive and enjoyed the sex. For the next four months he sought, but didn't achieve, the same exhilaration he had felt on that bear rug in Connor's apartment, with the long, long cock of the vocal coach caressing his channel walls deep at his core. What he did find, though, was the more vigorous, fast exploding cock of the bass waiting for him and new experiences of giving and receiving furtive hand and blow jobs.

As spring approached, one of Noah's old loves, mountain hiking, began to press on him increasingly. He had grown up in the shadow of the Great Smokies and walking sections of the Appalachian Trail. Here he was several hundred miles north, but the mountain chain—this time the Blue Ridge—could clearly be seen off to the east as he went about his way on the university campus. The Appalachian Trail also crossed the ridge of these mountains. The more frustrated he became at not finding a lover here to equal Mr. Connor in Gatlinburg, the more frustrated he became that he wasn't hiking the mountains. He'd brought all of his gear.

* * * *

The problem with going hiking on the Skyline Drive, which rode the ridge of the Blue Ridge up from the pass between Waynesboro and Charlottesville to the nearby town of Front Royal, a distance of 105 miles, was that provisions were expensive and hiking the Appalachian Trail was something you didn't want to do alone. There were too many opportunities to injure yourself or to get hopelessly lost on your own. Noah had already decided he'd do it during his spring break. He just hadn't found anyone else at the school who would do it with him or who he felt certain enough would be a useful companion.

"Why don't you advertise on something like Craig's List," his roommate, Mason, said one day. "There's got to be other guys out there looking for someone to hike with."

Mason was a second-year business major. His family owned a string of drycleaners in the Washington, D.C., area, and Mason was barely making it academic wise. He would have liked to have gone to a bigger university, playing football. He'd been a fullback in high school and had done well at that, but not well enough to be recruited when taken into account that his grades weren't good enough to make it into UVa or Virginia Tech. His parents wanted him to go to a Virginia school, and it didn't matter where he got a business degree from, really. He had a family business to go straight to from college. Thus, he was able to major in drinking and carousing at Shenandoah.

He would have liked to carouse with Noah, but Noah hadn't seen him as anything but a roommate who, thankfully, usually was off somewhere else.

Noah thought the Craig's List idea was fine. And within minutes he'd brought up this:

Be taken hiking the AT on Skyline Drive from Rockfish Gap north to FR. Looking for willing fit, male companion. All expenses paid. Send photo.

Noah sent a photo and noted the dates he was interested in hiking—during his spring break. He figured the hike would take six days. The next day he got a response.

Cute. Dates OK. Would meet up the evening before in Waynesboro, the Lion's Den. If interested, submissive, and like it big, send nude photo.

Attached had been the nude photo of a young, hung, muscular dark-haired guy who probably was in his mid twenties.

"So, that's what this was about," Mason said, looking over Noah's shoulder. "You could try again. There's got to be other hikers out there looking for a hookup."

"*This* looks like a hookup," Noah said. "He looks hot."

Mason sucked in air. He'd heard that Noah did hand and blow jobs, although there'd never been a hint of doing it with him. But he didn't know that Noah could so calmly entertain a proposal like this. And as far as being hot, the guy in the photo wasn't any hotter—or more hung—than Mason was, to his mind. And they were similarly dark haired and slightly hirsute.

"Only one problem," Noah said.

"Oh, what?" Mason asked. He put his hands on Noah's shoulder and Noah didn't shrink away from him. He normally could think of more than one problem with this proposition. But he was suddenly learning more about Noah than he'd hoped to think he could. Noah was the angel; he couldn't be expected to even think about going hiking with another guy proposing this.

"How am I to get to Waynesboro to start the hike and then get from Front Royal to here? I know, I could ask on Craig's List. Maybe exchange a blow job or something for the trips."

"You don't have to ask on Craig's List," Mason said, his voice a little shaky.

"I can hardly post it to the student union board," Noah said.

"You don't have to do that either. I have a car. I'll take you to Waynesboro in exchange for a blow job and back from Front Royal for another."

"You?"

"Yes. Tonight?"

Of course it didn't end with a blow job that night. After Noah sucked Mason, with Mason sitting on the side of his bed, Mason sucked off Noah. Mason didn't let Noah complete the blow job—which should have been an indication right there that Mason would want more. Mason did, though, make Noah come with his mouth as he knelt between Noah's thighs. But then, pressing on the blond angel's belly, Mason made Noah recline back, put the palms of his hands under Noah's buttocks, raising his pelvis, and ate out Noah's ass to the point that Noah was begging for a fuck.

Mason gave him a fuck. Holding Noah's legs spread and raised, Mason crouched between Noah's thighs and pounded away on him in a deep missionary. Noah lay there, inert, his head lolled to the side, panting and moaning, as Mason gave him everything he'd wanted to give him since September.

It didn't end there. In the night Noah felt the weight of Mason come down on his back, and his hips being coaxed to raise up, and Mason did him again doggie style.

Noah offered no resistance. It wasn't his dream fucking, but it was better than the bass in the chamber choir did and it didn't have to be furtive. They were roommates. No one questioned what happened during the night in their locked room. In fact, several who knew Mason or Noah assumed that it had been going on for months.

Mason's attentions were exhausting. Noah gave up the chamber choir bass who was moving on to fresher meat anyway. But Mason made good, and the second week of April he drove Noah down to Waynesboro on a Friday night and left him and his hiking equipment in front of a dive outside town with the sign "Lion's Den" on it.

✳ ✳ ✳

Noah walked into the tavern, which obviously was a gay bar based on observation of the clientele. All eyes went to him when he entered. It wasn't every day that an angel walked into the Lion's Den. He recognized the guy who had sent him the proposition and the photo immediately. He was leaning over the bar, talking to the bartender. They stopped talking and watched, somewhat incredulously, Noah's approach to the bar.

"You came," the man, whose name had been given as John, said. He wasn't quite as good looking as his photo promised, but close enough for Noah. He mostly was just a hiking companion. The fuck buddy part of it would be OK as long as he was paying for all the provisions—and, Noah assumed, for the accommodations for the night.

"Yes, are you John?"

"I didn't think you'd come. You looked too good to be doing more than teasing. And the photo really was you, wasn't it? Not some movie star."

"Yes, it was me," Noah said, with a little laugh. "Hope you aren't disappointed."

"Now that depends. Let's get it straight right off the bat. You gonna take cock during this hike?"

"Yes, if you're going to provide all the provisions and will put me up tonight."

"You know I won't go all the way up to the trail without making sure you're what I want, don't you?"

"Yes, I can understand that."

"There are cabins out back here. I've rented one. Let's go."

"Don't we have time for a drink first?"

"Sure. Good idea. Maybe more than one. Wouldn't want you to get skittish."

It was far more than one drink, with more being pressed on Noah than John was having. John spent some of the time off on a cell phone.

At the door to the bar, Noah somewhat sluggishly pointed to his heavy backpack. "My stuff for the hike is here. Can you, like . . . ?"

"Sure I'll carry it back to the cabin for you. Steady on there, sport." He was cupping and squeezing Noah's buttocks. Noah didn't resist.

"Where's *your* stuff?" Noah asked.

"In the truck." John vaguely gestured toward a line of trucks parked haphazardly in front of the cabins in back. A few of the trucks had guys sitting in the driver's seat and

144

smoking, watching John guiding a weaving Noah toward the cabins, with slitted eyes and knowing smiles.

At the cabin door, John dropped the backpack, pulled Noah to him, and went into a tonsil-swabbing kiss. Noah didn't resist at the beginning and was fully invested in it at the conclusion. John laughed, lifted Noah's body with one arm under his pits and the other under his knees, said, "Might as well do this right," kicked open the cabin door, and propelled the two of them into a small room dominated by a double bed.

Another guy, Tom, kicked the door back shut from inside the room. A third guy, James, walked in from the bathroom. Both were hulking construction workers wearing just briefs and construction boots.

Noah was quickly stripped and John was fucking him missionary style at the end of the bed. Tom was on one side holding Noah's right leg up and out. James was on the other side holding up the left. Both had lost their briefs. Both had made Noah grasp and stroke their cocks to erection while John pounded his ass. Noah lay, inert, on the bed, his back arched, his head buzzing from the liquor, and not really minding the cock working inside him. John wasn't sheathed, which was a new sensation for Noah. Tom wasn't sheathed when he took his turn next. Nor James. Nor were Keith and Scott, the two guys who had been waiting outside in their trucks, when they entered the room. Keith and Scott had turned Noah and were taking him doggie style.

This wasn't lovemaking. This was pure animal-need fucking, throbbing cock sliding in channel, coaxing the walls to stretch for it, pistoning every faster, deeper, seeking release and, finding it, being replaced by yet another cock. This wasn't personal. Noah was just providing a sheath. He could endure this. Even as buzzed as he was, he was able to analyze it, to consider each cock separately, each man's technique even in a straightforward pumping like this. In the months since he'd become sexually active, he'd studied the cocking of each man who had taken him—the chamber choir bass, Mr. Connor, Mason. Not a long list. But each one different. If he concentrated on the differences of these cocks, he could get some enjoyment and instruction out of this gang bang. He'd wondered about the life of a male prostitute. He'd even wondered if it might be a life for him. There were so many gay men at the conservatory—and there was talk of only being able to make it in one of the music capitals of the world if you took tricks to augment your income. Could he? This would help him decide.

He wasn't fighting them. He was going with it. That probably was why they weren't manhandling him, beating him. It may help him to come out of this alive.

They came to the top of the order again, with John on his back on the bed and Noah on his back on top of John, with John fucking him from below. James appeared at Noah's head straddling his chest and offering his cock, which Noah dutifully took in his mouth. James also had a bottle of poppers, which he waved under Noah's nose, making Noah more mellow and relaxing his channel more.

"You'll want this," was all James said before Tom saddled up between Noah's and John's legs and began to work his cock into Noah's hole on top of John's.

Noah groaned and moaned, but he took them. None of them other than John were especially hung. None of them were as presentable as John either, which was why, Noah supposed, only John's photo was sent. Just a bunch of country hick bad boys, Noah thought. He was managing. This was all new experience for him.

Keith and Scott doubled him standing up with Noah wedged between them.

They let him shower and then took him back to the Lion's Den for a steak dinner. They all sat close around him, watching for signs that he'd break for the door or yell for help. But he could see that the Lion's Den wasn't the sort of place that would offer him any help. There was more beer. They were keeping him buzzed. He was sore, yes, but it was an experience. All of these men wanting him.

After dinner they all had him again in the cabin. Men drifted in and out. They weren't always the same group he'd started with. They were all men, though, and they all here holding erections as they approached either his ass or his mouth.

He slept between John and Tom, with James on top of him, and then between Tom and James with John on top of him, and so forth, until he zoned out and went to sleep with a cock still churning in him.

When he woke, he was in the cabin alone. All of the men were gone, although there was the smell of stale smoke and musky cum in the air, and his channel was gaping open and running with the cum of countless men. His backpack was there, seemingly untouched, and there was $124 in assorted bills sitting on the dresser. At least they'd paid him.

So, this was what it was like to be a rent-boy. He could do this if he had to. He struggled to the bathroom and the thin stream of water that came out of a groaning shower head, but the pain and soreness retreated the longer he stood under the lukewarm water. He could do this.

When he came out of the shower, the bartender from the Lion's Den was standing in the open door, two twenties in his hand. He fucked Noah in a side split on the bed, giving him attention with his lips—on his cock and nipples as well as his mouth. His was closer to lovemaking than any that had gone on the night before, and his dick was thicker too—and more interesting to take. He had an off-rhythm thrust that made Noah hold his breath for the end to the longer intervals, and his bulb paid extra attention to Noah's prostrate, giving the younger man a prodigious wad when he came. The bartender was sheathed, but he gave Noah a facial when he was finishing.

"Nice lay. The guys were right. There's breakfast on the house over at the Lion's Den, if you want it," the man said as he pulled up his trousers and headed for the door.

Noah the male prostitute, Noah thought, as he rolled off the bed and walked off to the shower again.

There were no trucks in front of the cabin, although there were a few in front of the Lion's Den. Time for him to see if the Lion's Den served a breakfast that made up for all the energy he'd been drained of and then, he guessed, to put in a call to Mason to come get him. It was obvious that John hadn't really been advertising for a hiking buddy.

* * * *

"You going up on the trail too?" Noah turned to see a man in his forties, in hiking gear, and with a weighty backpack at his feet. There were two men standing with him—another older man, but muscular and with a Marine buzz cut like the first. And then there was a short, young redhead, pretty much the same cut of young man as Noah was except for the coloring.

"I had hoped to, but my hiking partner didn't show. It's not good to try to hike in the mountains alone."

"You going north on the Skyline Drive or south on the Blue Ridge Parkway? I'm Dale, by the way. In banking in Washington, D.C. I try to do the trail regularly to keep in shape." There was no doubt that Dale was in shape.

"I was going to go north on to Front Royal. I'm a student at Shenandoah University. Freshman. Name's Noah."

"We're going north too," Dale said. "Would be happy for you to go along. This here's Howard, he's got a construction company in Alexandria. And Kyle. He's a student too. George Mason. He's along for the company. You got your gear in order?"

"Not the provisions, sorry," Noah said. "The other guy was supposed to bring those—and pay for the park pass."

"Would love to have you along. I can take care of everything. You could just keep us good company, if you're willing. Uh, how old are you, by the way?"

"If I'm willing?" Noah asked.

"He means if you'll take our cocks—Dale's and mine," Howard spoke up for the first time. "That's what Kyle's along for. We heard guys talkin' about you inside."

Noah shouldn't have been surprised, and he wasn't really. They were standing on the porch into of a gay tavern. The three had probably stayed in one of the cabins in back.

148

They might have been quite aware of what was happening in Noah's cabin.

"I'm over eighteen," Noah answered.

"Sorry that Howard was so bald about it," Dale said, "but the bartender said you took cock—that you were abandoned here. That you take a lot of cock. I see the taxi pulling up to take me up to the park entrance. You want to come or not?"

They didn't fuck him the first night. They made good time—the other three were in excellent shape and Noah managed. Dale and Howard saw that he wasn't toned up for the hiking yet, though, so when they reached the Dundo Group Camp facilities and set up tents far enough from any of the other hikers to not draw attention, they took care of supper and then let Noah rest. Each of them, in turn, though, went into Kyle's tent, and the shimmering of the tent wall and the sound of grunts in two different tones each time made clear to Noah that Kyle was being fucked.

The next night they stopped some twenty miles further on, at the Lewis Mountain camping grounds. This time they overshot the camp by a quarter of a mile and camped in a glen well off the trail. Howard fucked Kyle while he sat on a log and Kyle sat on his cock facing him, while Dale fixed dinner of noodles and Snickers bars. Noah sat to the side and watched, with both of the older men watching him to see if he'd bolt. He didn't. Kyle's wrists were tied behind his back with a leather strap—a favorite fetish of Howard's, Noah was to learn—and fucked himself on Howard's cock using the leverage of his feet. Both men were naked and both had beautiful bodies for their ages. Dale was just in briefs himself and Noah could clearly see that he was in erection.

"Come to my tent with me," Dale said to Noah after they'd finished eating. Howard and Kyle, who had finished the fuck late, were still eating. Howard was still sitting on the log and Kyle was sitting on the ground between Howard's thighs.

Noah stood to follow Dale into his tent, but Kyle arrested their movement. "Pay him, Dale."

"He's being provisioned," Dale answered.

"Don't be cheap, Dale. And don't give it away so cheaply, Noah. I get $25 a fuck and you provide my provisions too. Don't shortchange him."

"OK, OK," Dale said. "I'll give it to him in the tent."

Noah turned to thank Kyle, but he already had his head turned and was sucking on Howard's cock.

Dale gave it to Noah in the tent. He was a lover, like Mr. Connor was, not just a fucker. They lay stretched out on a sleeping bag on top of an air mattress in the close confines of the tent. Dale prepared Noah, embracing him and kissing him on the lips, throat, and nipples while he divested Noah of his T-shirt, shorts, and briefs. He nudged Noah into a 69 position that Noah finally figured out, and the two men sucked each other off, neither going to ejaculation. Then Dale was embracing Noah chest to chest again, holding him close and stroking his cock—not allowing Noah to handle his and not letting up on the stroking despite Noah's begging until Noah had come.

Then, still holding Noah in the embrace and kissing him, Dale moved his hand lower, working first one finger and then another and another, up to the knuckle, into Noah's hole and nearly fist fucking him. Noah writhed and moaned and begged for the cock until Dale rolled over on top of him, between his legs; pulled his pelvis up with an arm under his waist; penetrated him with a hard, thick, long cock; and fucked him in ever-increasing pace for a good fifteen minutes before he came.

Noah lay there, panting and exhausted—and satiated in a way he hadn't been since lying under Mr. Connor. He wasn't given time to rest, though. As soon as Dale was gone from the tent, Howard was there. He was a no play sort of guy, rolling Noah on his stomach, pinning his wrists behind his back and tying them off with the leather strap after strapping Noah's buttocks a couple of times to hear him suck his breath in and cry out, and then slid in hard and deep and fucked the shit out of Noah.

Dale carried Noah back to his own tent and then the two went back to sharing Kyle.

The next night, camping off the trail just short of the Thornton Gap entrance to the park was nearly a repeat, although Noah had toughened up and moved up in experience enough to take more of the initiative. It was his turn, on his own initiative to ride Howard's cock while the man sat on a log and Dale and Kyle prepared the dinner and then, later, he walked to Dale's tent first, with Dale following him, and Dale lay on his back with his arms over his head and Noah grasping the man's arms while he straddled Dale's hips and rode his cock.

Noah was learning to do more than just submit to a man. And on this night, he was $100 richer than when he'd come on the trail and had earned nearly $125 before. This hiking was proving to be profitable—which gave Noah pause for thought.

At the Matthews Arms campground—or, rather, a quarter mile beyond it and off the trail—the men didn't have the complete privacy they may have expected. Two other men entered camp as they were setting up and started setting up camp themselves.

If Noah thought Dale and Howard would be upset at the intrusion, he was wrong. The two sets of men knew each other. "This is Charles from Leesburg and Malcolm, also from Leesburg," Dale said, introducing the two to Noah. "Malcolm's an Orthopedist."

"He's a stunner," Malcolm said, giving Noah an appreciating look. "I'll give him—"

"I'll pay him $200 to fuck him right now," Charles broke in to say.

He was another lover, covering Noah with kisses in his tent while stripping him and putting him into a 69 positions. Noah thought that maybe he and Dale went to the same school of debaucher. Between sucking and stroking him, the man had Noah begging for mercy, and when the cock penetrated him, it caressed every inch of Noah's shimmering, expanding walls, as it invaded to the quick of him and played him deep in his soft core like a violin concerto.

"You were lovely—are lovely, because I'm not finished," Charles whispered after the first fuck. Noah groaned, but he got a little jolt of pleasure too, knowing this wasn't over. "I want to see you after this hike. I'll leave you my card. You will come over to Leesburg."

"I'm at school in Winchester. I have no transportation to get to Leesburg. Oh shit. Oh fuck." Charles was finger fucking him, with three fingers. The index finger had found Noah's prostate. He was breathing hard, opening his legs, giving the man fuller access. The hand was in to the knuckles. If nothing else, Noah had been reamed wide over the past few days. Both Dale and Charles took advantage of that.

"I own a car dealership in Fairfax," Charles said. "I'll give you a car. It won't be a new one, but it will be a nice one. But then you'll have to be available to me when I want you."

"Oh FUCK!" Noah cried out. The knuckles had breached his hole. Charles didn't make him suffer, though. He rolled over on top of him, extracted his hand, inserted his dick, and started to pump.

The fisting had been useful to Noah. That night the doctor—Malcolm—and Howard sandwiched him in a double fuck. Howard tied his wrists behind his back again and he was saddled on Howard's cock, Howard on his back and holding Noah's waist in his hands, while the doctor fucked him from behind, sliding his cock along the top of Howard's buried staff. His thought on that, forcing his mind through the pain of having two cocks inside him at once, was that it was fortunate he'd been doubled twice in Waynesboro, that much of Charles' fist had been up there earlier, and that he was earning $50 rather than $25 in a single taking.

By the time they got to Front Royal, Noah had the cards of four men who wanted to pay him for sex, plus entry into a hiking club for men who hiked the Appalachian Trail as a cover for taking young men out into the woods and fucking them silly. All for pay. He'd come back to school with almost $500 more than he'd gone up into the mountains with. And against this he was bowlegged sore for several days, but toughening up, had some memories of pain overtaken

152

with pleasure, gained quite a lot of experience in having sex with men, and had a plan for turning a profit for several more years.

He also had a very nice Mustang to drive—used, but a classic in good running order.

Two months later, when one of Noah's classmates asked him if he had a summer job lined up, Noah just smiled and said he did. He didn't tell the classmate what it was, though. The same classmate asked him if he was going to continue with his theater arts study.

"I think there's a glut of trained talent going into New York," the classmate said. "And that's the only place you can even start making a living as chorus in plays. And even there—"

"Yes, I think I'm headed to New York when this degree is finished," Noah broke in. "And I think I can earn a living there OK."

"Maybe so," the classmate said. He was a little dubious, but if anyone could, Noah probably could. He was an angel, and probably the best singer, artist, and dancer in his class. The classmate didn't have a clue how Noah planned to earn his keep in New York—indeed what was proving to be profitable right here in Virginia, sitting next to the Blue Ridge Mountains and the Appalachian Trail.

A Funeral and a Wedding

"It was good of you to come."

"I was surprised that your father wanted me here." I was sitting in the courtyard of a restored traditional Turkish home on Efeler Street, three blocks up the hill from the old walled harbor of Kyrenia, in Turkish-held Cyprus. Zeki Ceren, the son of Serhan, was looking a bit uncomfortable but also quite handsome. There was quite a bit in him of his father. I think he would have been more comfortable in this setting in a Turkish robe than in the white, almost diaphanous, cotton shirt, riding jodhpurs, and high-top black leather boots. He'd said he' been out riding before I had appeared at his doorstep. The shirt was billowy, showing his deep-tanned skin underneath, including ring piercings in his nipples, which gave me a pause in thought. The riding pants were tighter than I would think was comfortable, but they certainly left little to the imagination.

I wondered if he knew of the actual relationship between his father and me. Would we be sitting here in this lush courtyard beside a burbling fountain and drinking tea if he did? He crossed his legs slowly enough for me to think he wanted me to see the rearrangement of thigh and calve muscles—and the length and line of the bulge at the crotch. He couldn't know about my relationship with his father, and not be interested himself, to be teasing me like this. I had to hold myself in check—to wonder if I was engaging in

154

dangerous wishful thinking. He could just be naturally sexy, oblivious to his father's proclivities, and violently opposed to who, privately, his father was.

"My father spoke of you often, affectionately. He hoped that you would visit him here. And now you're here."

"Yes, now I'm here, although I wish it would be under happier circumstances. The ceremony will be when, exactly?"

"Two days hence, 4:00 p.m., at Saint Andrews at the foot of this street. He'll be buried in the courtyard there. I assume you realize that he followed the British ways—those of his mother—rather than his Turkish father, or he would have had to be buried within a day of his death."

"And you wish me to have a part in the ceremony?"

"Father wished it. And it's all arranged. Saint Andrews is a small, informal church despite its very-English trappings." He gave me a flutter of his dark eyelashes over the top of his tea cup. I wondered once again what he knew and if this was a signal that he liked this situation—me being here. His father had been a professor of Middle Eastern affairs at Georgetown for two terms when I was there. We'd had an affair. I never forgot him after he returned here to northern Cyprus. It had never occurred to me that he wouldn't have forgotten about me either.

At the door, Zeki put a hand on my arm and gave me a sad smile—one nonetheless that reflected a face that, like his father's, was achingly handsome in a dark, sultry way. "I do very much appreciate your coming. I know my father was extremely fond of you. I'm glad to have met you at last. I'm sorry I received you on an occasion such as this, seemingly frivolously in riding clothes—I was quite fond of my father and I am devastated by his death. Please plan to come back to this house after the burial. My father wanted to pass on something to you."

I could hardly criticize him for not dressing more somberly when we met. He looked downright arousing in the riding clothes. I, on the other hand, was dressed like the American tourist I was. When he'd called to ask me to come see him, I'd already driven my motorbike up to the village of

Bellapais to visit the ruins of the abbey there and to sit and luxuriate at the tavern on the city square next to the abbey entrance. Sitting on the outside terrace of the Tree of Idleness. I was in a T-shirt, cargo shorts, and sandals—certainly in keeping with the other younger men there. The older men were covered head and foot, though, in cloths that had to be hot this time of year.

When I left the Efeler Street house it was late in the evening. Darkness came late to the Mediterranean island of Cyprus at this time of year, and it was just falling. I could have gotten on the motor scooter I was renting and driven up the road toward the mountain artists' village of Bellapais, hanging on the southern side of the Kyrenia Mountain range, where I was checked into the Olive Tree Villas complex, but the ancient Kyrenia harbor lured me down to the water. I could hear the music from here. I parked the motor scooter, which gave me an ominous belch when I turned it off, next to the Harbor Club. The establishment was a British-style pub sitting at the bottom of a steep cobble-stoned street and in the shadow of the hulking Kyrenia harbor castle that held down the eastern end of the harbor.

The small harbor itself was an oval, with a ring of docks and waterside open-air restaurants on the southern and western curve, the castle to the east, and a long breakwater across the northern side. A stone jetty pierced the center of the harbor, showing the original harbor had been even smaller than this one. An ancient lighthouse—really just a stone pillar supporting a basin to light a fire—rose from the end of the jetty.

Even at this time of the evening, dinner was only now starting to be served, but the harbor-side tables already were occupied with boisterous Turks and tourists. The area was strewn with multicolored fairy lights along the harbor wall, which illuminated various sizes of sailboats, skiffs, and yachts bobbing up and down just beyond where the edges of the tables ended. Stone building, once merchant businesses and houses rimmed the harbor, parting only a few places to give steep-slope access to the streets above. Originally, the storage and merchant floor were at ground level, facing the harbor, and the merchant's residences were in the stories above, facing back onto a higher street curving around the harbor. The attached row of houses formed the upper town's first protective wall. Now restaurants and gift shops operated out of these original ground-floor storage rooms. The tables were jammed together on the dock during warm weather, which, in Cyprus, was most of the seasons of the year, and were taken back indoors for the winter months of service.

There didn't seem to be any tables appropriate for a single diner. I circled around the harbor and then back again toward the castle without finding someplace appropriate for me to wedge myself in. On the walk back, though, a strong hand reached out, took my wrist, and arrested my progress.

"Have you lost your party, or are you looking for tablemates?"

The voice was deep, heavily accented. I looked around and sucked air in. He was a magnificent brute. Not Turkish; no, definitely not Turkish. He was from somewhere in Scandinavia, and the same with the other men, all tall, muscular, and of military bearing. They weren't from the officer ranks; they were much rougher and unpolished looking than that—not much more than a step above the thuggish—but all sunny smiles. Serious grunt soldiers out on leave. There was danger—and a lot of possibilities—there.

"I thought to have dinner in the harbor, but there doesn't seem to be any room," I answered.

"Then you aren't looking for someone you're dining with?"

"No, I'm all alone."

"I can hardly believe a handsome man can be here alone. There's room right here, if you don't mind a bit of a rough and randy crowd."

I certainly didn't mind this crowd. They were all smiles, welcoming, and giving me the eye.

"Names Magnus," the blond hunk said. "We're Norwegian, from the UN contingent patrolling the Green Line." Cyprus was divided between the Greeks in the south and the Turks in the north, and although they were starting to get along better than they did when the Turks invaded the island and occupied the north in the mid seventies, a UN force dividing them was still needed. So these were soldiers. They certainly were blond gods—heavenly fit.

"Ross Tagert here," I answered. "From Philadelphia, in the United States."

"Ah, the city of brotherly love. How great is that?" Magnus answered. His expression was a questioning one. I gave him a little smile and a dip of my eyes, the universal signal of a willing submissive—if that's what he was looking for.

Smiling a bit more broadly and a hand going to the small of my back, Magnus introduced me to the two nearest to where I sat, Filip and Oscar. Both were all grins. Magnus was all touchy feely from that point. I made no effort to fend him off. Seeing the spitting image of my old lover, Serhan Ceren, in his son, Zeki, just a few years younger than I was, had brought up my juices of arousal. I actually wasn't here in Cyprus just to have a part in Serhan's funeral. I also was escaping myself in the States, where I increasingly was finding it difficult to keep the expression of my preferences separate from my professional life. There were times when I almost felt like exploding. I'd come to the Mediterranean for what I planned to be an extensive vacation to free myself from the bonds of responsibility, if only for a short time.

We got into enough of a conversation for them to ascertain that I was American, in my late twenties—as they all were—and staying at a bungalow holiday complex called the Olive Tree on the Mustafa Catagay Road up the side of the mountains toward Bellapais—and that my preferred means of transport was a motorcycle. Their questions were suggestive enough, as well, not causing me to blush or rankle, for them to pin down my preferences—which obviously matched theirs, although I got the impression that their leanings could go either way as long as they were satisfied. Magnus placed his hand where there could be no doubt, and I let it rest there, rhythmically squeezing and releasing my package, encouraging me to engorge.

They were on a two-day furlough from their Green Line base in the western sector of the divided capital of

Nicosia, in the center of the island. They'd been deployed "too long" and hadn't "had any" for "too long." I gauged their virility to mean they hadn't had any since earlier that afternoon. They were staying right here at the western end of the harbor in the old Dome Hotel. They'd spent the day roaming the Turkish side of the island on their motorbikes as far away as the ancient city of Salamis on the eastern coast. They were thirsty as hell and obviously were doing something about that. They got off onto sports in their discussions and didn't delve any more into my background while we were at dinner, which was just fine to me.

After dinner, we went up to the upper-story bar at the Harbor Club and lined up across the bar. I was next to the far wall, with Magnus on the stool next to me. He gave me dreamy looks while we drank beer and I gave them back. He had a hand on the small of my back, and when I leaned in to him to ask him how long they were deployed in Cyprus, which was for another six months, my hand went to the small of his back too. The muscle was hard even there. He had the build of a bodybuilder and was a good five inches taller than I was.

"Isn't that guy cute who just walked into the bar?" he leaned over and said into my ear, speaking over the noise of the patrons in the crowded, raucous bar. His hand went to my buttocks. I neither did anything to move his hand away or showed any concern that he was telling me a man in the bar was cute.

"You're cute too," he said as he leaned in again. "Gotta ask. Are you just going with the flow here or are you a serious player?"

"A what?" I asked, both of us moving our heads so I could talk in his ear. My lips had brushed something on his face as we both moved. It sent a chill up my spine.

"A serious player. You get it on with men; you don't just tease talk?" This time when we were switching ears and mouths, Magnus arrested the movement when our mouths were close, and he kissed me a brushing kiss on the lips. Time stood still and our eyes met. I leaned in for a deeper kiss.

"I guess that answers that," he said, with a laugh. He took one of my hands and moved it between his thighs. He was hung and hard. "The only question that remains is whether you take cock or give it. Are you going to let me in? Let me fuck you?"

"It's late," I said, giving him a smile but not answering his question. "I think I need to get back up the mountain while I'm not too drunk. I just hope I'm not too drunk to remember that my rental motorbike has a red seat on it."

"Will you be in the harbor tomorrow?" he asked.

"Maybe. I have an appointment in the morning, but I could be here sometime in the afternoon."

"You didn't answer my question."

"Yes," I answered. "Both. I might be in the harbor tomorrow and I take cock."

He smiled. "If you are in the harbor tomorrow, I'll take you somewhere and show you a good time," Magnus said.

"That sounds like a good possibility. I'll have to think about it. Right now, though, I've got to take a piss. Do you have any idea where . . . ah, yes, thanks." He waved me in the direction of the men's room.

When I came out, he wasn't at the bar. But he was downstairs by the bike rack when I got down there.

"Well, it was good meeting you," I said, hopping on the rental bike with the red seat. "Maybe tomorrow. I'll think about it."

"I'll treat you right," he said and then he was asking, "Something wrong with your bike?"

"Yeah, it doesn't do anything but sputter. Did this when it stopped last. It seems I'm stranded."

"You don't have to be. My bike's here. I can give you a ride up to the Olive Tree."

At the door of my cabana unit, he pulled me to him and we went into a deep kiss. "I've come all the way up here. We could pretend it's tomorrow," he said. "You gonna invite me in? You gonna take my cock?"

"Would you like to come in?" I asked with a smile.

160

The unit was compact. A kitchenette unit on the wall to the right where we entered and the side wall of a bathroom to the left. This opened to one room, a sofa and chair to the left and a small table and two straight chairs to the right. The queen-size bed was beyond and beyond that a wall of glass, with sliding glass doors out onto a small patio. A bit of lawn area and the terrace surrounded the communal pool beyond that.

I barely had the lights on in the living-dining area when he was pulling me to him and pressing on my shoulders, signaling that I was to go on my knees in front of him. He unzipped himself, pulled out his cock, and grabbed the back of my head between his hands. Just like that I was giving him head. His cock was huge and hard. He obviously was aching for it.

He was so ready for it that he started fucking me before I was fully ready for him. There was a short strip scene, and an interlude with me on my back at the foot of the bed, heels on his shoulders, and him eating my ass out and sucking my cock. But quickly, all too quickly, we were at the wall of glass, him standing and crouched a bit, palming and spreading my buttocks to give him maximum passage spread, and me with my fists locked behind his neck, as he bounced me up and down on his cock. In short order he had switched this to the more demanding position of turning me, facing away from him, but still holding me off the ground, my feet hooked on the meat of his calves, and my arms flung up, fists locked behind his neck, while he grabbed my waist and pulled my passage on and off his cock.

It was while I was in this position that I looked out into the pool area and saw two men, muscular but lithe, younger than I was, fucking on a lounge bed. One was lying on his back and the other one was crouched over his pelvis, feet on the ground, and rising and falling on the other guy's cock. I wasn't surprised. I'd picked the place because it was listed in gay travel directories. What was arresting was that both of them had their heads turned to my unit, where, obviously with the light on in my living-dining area, they were getting a full view of the hulking and towering Magnus suspending me in front of him and fucking me. I was too far gone in the fuck to worry what they could see. They were doing it too.

When Magnus tired of these bullying positions, he sat on the bed, leaning back, and I squatted on his lap, facing away from the bed, gripping his raised and spread knees, the heels of his feet dug into the bottom edge of the mattress, and I fucked myself on his cock.

It was an athletic fuck we both enjoyed. There was no coyness. It was clear he wanted to fuck me and I was equally clear that I wanted him to fuck me—a straightforward, primeval, athletic fuck, with no reservations, complexity, conditions, or commitments. He came when he had me with my weight on my shoulders on the carpet at bottom of the bed, with my spine running up the rise of the foot of the bed and my legs jackknifed so that my toes were pressed into the carpet next to my head. He was standing over me and fucking down into my hole in reverse.

He slept the night with me in my bed, pulling me to him periodically, when he'd hardened again, and fucking me in demanding positions. I perhaps should have felt guilty at being such a slut about it—signaling as I did at the Harbor Club that he could have me, something that a man in my position in the States could not do, but I didn't. I wasn't in the States. Unconsciously, at least, I'd come here precisely to be able to do this without guilt.

"This means nothing but getting off," he declared as we reached the decision point of him leaving or staying the night. "Any expectations or entanglements and I'm out of here."

He'd already fucked me—gotten his rocks off good—so he had little to lose in just walking out.

"No expectations other than that you fuck me again during the night if you stay," I answered. He fucked me twice again.

I'd enjoyed it so much that the next morning, when he sheepishly stood there holding up the spark plug he'd taken out of my motorbike the night before, I laughed with him.

162

"If you want, I'll be happy to go back to the harbor and fix your bike. My mates, Filip and Oscar, can help me bring it back to you."

"That's fine with me."

"It's fine with you that I bring my buddies back?"

"Yes, of course."

"You are no innocent, are you?" he asked. "You took it like a champ."

"No, I'm no innocent," I replied. "You gave it like a champ."

"Filip and Oscar have great bodies." He wasn't really changing the subject.

"I noticed," I answered.

"If they take the time and effort to bring the bike back up . . . and I feel sort of bad that I got my rocks off so great and they—"

"Yes, they can fuck me. Together, if that's what gets them off. I can handle DP." Already I felt so much freer than I was able to be in the States.

The two other Norwegian studs were more conventional than Magnus had been. Filip fucked me in a straight-on missionary, lying between my spread and raised legs and plowing me deep, and Oscar preferred the doggie fuck, me on all fours on the bed and him mounting and fucking me from behind and above. I can't say I minded being under any of them. I was somewhat disappointed they hadn't DPed me.

The three were leaving my unit, as I caught the eye of a great, sultry-looking young Turkish guy clipping a hedge. The look he gave me told me in no uncertain terms that he'd been one of the guys watching Magnus fucking me at the window the previous night while he and other guy were having at it by the pool.

* * * *

As I was turning back from waving the three hunky and grinning Norwegian UN contingent soldiers away on their bikes, the young Turkish guy lowered his hedge clippers

163

and walked over to me. He too was wearing a grin—and nothing else but low-riding jeans and sandals without socks. I was wearing less—just low-riding cargo shorts.

"Excuse me, you're a guest here, aren't you?" he asked in heavily accented English.

"Yes. This is my room," I answered. The answer was a bit idiotic, but then so was the question. Why wouldn't he think I was checked into this room? I felt sort of tongue-tied, though, because I was quite sure that this was one of the guys who had watched me being bully fucked at my window the previous night. But then I didn't really want to let him go. He was a sultry hunk and a half himself. Dark-skinned, slim but well muscled, swarthy, mean-boy aspect with back hair, piercing black eyes, perpetual five-o'clock shadow, hirsute chest, and a knowing—and interested—look in his eyes.

The UN soldiers had let me know in no uncertain terms that as much as they'd enjoyed fucking me, they would be going back to their unit and they weren't interested in any entanglements—that we'd just had recreational, one-time fucks. And I'd let them know that that was perfectly fine with me. I hadn't come to Cyprus for commitment or drama.

"My name is Erol," the dark stud standing in front of me said. "I work here. My uncle is the manager. One of my jobs is to make guests happy. This is your first visit to Girne, isn't it?" Girne was the Turkish word for Kyrenia.

"Yes, my first visit," I answered.

"Maybe you would like someone to show you around. Maybe take you on a boat ride in the Mediterranean. Maybe show you the best places to swim—places where you can get an all-over tan? Maybe show you a good time." He turned his head to look at the backs of the three UN soldiers, still visible, motoring the curvy road down into Kyrenia. He'd known what they were doing here.

"Maybe," I answered, giving him a smile.

He turned his face back to me, a look of interest and lust in his eyes that I couldn't have misinterpreted even if I had wanted to. "I have a friend, Onur. He works here too. We could show you a good time." Before I could say anything, he whistled loudly and called something out in

Turkish in which I discerned "Onur" had been included. Around the side of the line of rooms trotted another young hunk, undoubtedly the other guy I'd seen fucking on the bed lounger by the pool the previous night. A big grin exploded on his face when he saw me. He was as lithe and well-muscled, and great looking as Erol was, but without the five-o'clock shadow and hirsute chest.

"Me and Onur show you a good time today? Yes?"

"Maybe yes, but not this morning. I have to go out this morning. I have an appointment down in Ky— . . . down in Girne."

"We show you a real good time, both of us," Erol repeated. Onur was wagging his head in agreement.

"Both of you? Together."

"If you like," Erol said. "We'd like," he added.

"We saw you with the big blond men in your room this morning," Onur interjected. "Three of them. Were they all on you at the same time? You like that? Erol and me can—"

"We'll see," I interjected. "Yes, maybe." I, indeed, was a little disappointed the UN guys hadn't doubled me.

But, lordy, he didn't have to tell me that, I thought. I pretty much figured what he was trying to convey to me already. It might have been a bit of blackmail in case I stood them up, but I got a bit of my own back on them twenty minutes later when I was dressed and coming out of the unit to my bike, which the UN soldiers had quickly brought to rights, down into the town.

They were both standing there, waiting to see me off. Their eyes bugged out when they saw me, though. I was in my work uniform—black shirt and trousers and a clerical collar. I was going to Kyrenia to meet with the rector of Saint Andrews Anglican church to coordinate on the funeral ceremony for Serhan Ceren—one priest to another.

Learning that I was a cleric—an Episcopal priest—didn't deter the two young Turks from showing me the good time they had in mind, but it put another bee in their bonnet.

* * * *

165

It was all sort of hazy in my mind and I was feeling mellow.
Actually I couldn't feel anything at all. Serhan was just getting off me,
having been heavily between my legs, trapping me under him on the
studio couch in his university office, and having just pulled out of me. He
had a dick that was thick and long enough to tax a man, something that
would be impossible not to feel. This is what told me I was in a dream.
For some reason Serhan Ceren being long out of my life and dead didn't
seem to clue me into being in a fantasy. He smiled at me and I smiled
back. There had been a time when guilt was mixed in with my longing
in coming to Serhan's office, as one of his students, to lie under him and
to let him possess me as he did—for not, not for a good grade—but I
obviously was long past this in this dream. When he rose from me, he
turned to stand beside me, his cock in his hand. He rubbed the cock,
slick from his cum, on my cheek, and I turned my head and took it in
my mouth.

I opened my eyes, squinting because of the glare of
the unrelenting sun off the waters of the Mediterranean. Erol
was kneeling beside me, rubbing his cock on my cheek. I
opened my mouth to it, sucked it in, and gave him head. This
wasn't like the dream with Serhan, though—with a Turk, to
be sure, but one older and chunkier than this young stud.
With Erol, this was a preliminary to anal sex, not a follow up.
When he was hard, he moved to the center of the boat and
coaxed my thighs open and motioned for me to drape my
legs over the sides of the small rowboat we were in. My
shoulders were wedged into where the boat curved into the
bow, and my arms were draped over the sides there. Onur
was at the stern of the boat, watching us and grinning, as he
rowed. Erol ran his knees under my buttocks, elevating my
pelvis. Leaning over me, he groaned and I moaned as he
penetrated me with his cock, worked to force it deep inside
me, and began the rhythm of the fuck.

I had already fucked Onur. The two had come to my
door after I'd had lunch with the rector of St. Andrews and
returned to the Olive Tree. They wanted to show me more of
the island. Cyprus had great beaches and the clear, blue
waters of the Mediterranean. There were private beaches

nearby, very private. We rode there on one motor bike, Onur nestled in behind Erol and I behind Onur as we took the beach road to the east of Kyrenia.

They were right. There were pristine beaches that we could have all to ourselves—beaches that were ringed for privacy by rock cliffs that marched right out into the water. The one we stopped at had water deep enough beyond its rock walls that we could safely dive off the tops of the cliffs into the water. We did it again and again, laughing and touching and prodding each other as we climbed the rock. And increasingly we took our time coming back onto the beach from the water, the three of us cavorting and wrestling with each other in the surf just off the beach—embracing, kissing, and fondling.

They fucked me first there, in the water, going straight for the double. Erol stood. facing the beach, in chest-high water, when he crouched a bit, and I was draped in front of him. My chest was floating on the surface of the water, my arms outstretched and my hands moving to keep the current under me. My feet were hooked on the meaty back of Erol's thighs, and he grasped my waist between his hands and pulled me on and off his cock. Onur swam out to us, pushing my chest up, my back into Erol's chest, pulling my legs forward, and wrapped them around his waist. While he was kissing me and I was clutching his shoulder blades with my hands, he entered me on top of Erol's cock to the sounds of my moans and panting, and they moved me forward and back in the water, first Erol deep and then Onur.

Erol had asked me if I'd like to take a boat out into the Mediterranean—that he knew of one he could borrow just up the road from this beach. I would be very happy to be able to look back at the island from a boat, I answered, and to test out his claim that the waters of the Mediterranean were so pure here that I could clearly see the bottom even in twenty feet of water.

Would Onur and I be OK without him for a half hour or so?

Surely, we could find something to do while he was gone, I'd answered. I fucked Onur on a towel on the beach, lying on top of him with the heels of his feet rubbing the backs of my calves and his fingers lightly running across my shoulder blades as I slid in and out in his sweet channel to the tune of my light grunts and his deep sighs.

And then it was my turn to be fucked by Erol again in the boat when we'd gotten out into the sea, under the rowing power of Onur, sitting in the stern of the boat and grinning at us while Erol fucked me.

"Is it really true you are a priest?" Erol asked as we sat, our legs entwined, on towels on the beach near the rowboat we'd pulled up onto the sand.

"Yes, it's true," I answered. "I'm an Episcopal priest. I'm an elder, though, I'm not a monk. I've taken no pledge of celibacy. And my preferences are known by my bishop."

"I believe you've known many men," Erol said, giving me a sharp, sideways look.

"Probably more than I should have," I answered. I gave a laugh to soften that, but it was a dry laugh. I wasn't proud of my weakness.

"But as a priest you can perform weddings?" Onur spoke up for the first time.

"Yes, I can," I said.

The two looked at each other and Erol nodded his head. "Erol and I wish to be married. Our friends enjoy having wedding parties. We wish to do that too. We need someone to marry us—to perform a ceremony—though. Would you marry us?"

"Marry you?" I asked, trying to hide my shock. "You're Turkish. Aren't you Muslims?"

"Yes, we are. We want our friends to know we are joined as much as they are to their wives. We know it will just be for show, but it will mean something to our friends and us. And we don't want to miss having the wedding party."

"But marriage is a commitment," I said. "Just here today, I've fucked you and Erol and you have fucked me. That isn't—"

"You haven't been in Kibris long, have you?" Erol asked, with a laugh. "Being married doesn't stop either the

168

husband or the wife from fucking other people here. In Kibris we live to love and to enjoy ourselves to the fullest."

He had me there. You didn't have to be here in Cyprus—or Kibris, when you used the Turkish word for the island—to toss fidelity out the window for the sheer pleasure of it. There was quite enough of that going around in the States too. And what harm would it be to be part of their party? Everyone involved would know and accept that there was no religious sanction involved.

"I'll think about it. I don't know how long I'll be here on the island."

"We could put a party together fast," Onur said. He was looking at me with such hopefulness in his eyes and that I almost agreed on the spot. He had been such a sweet fuck.

"I'll think about it," I repeated. "Perhaps we should go back now."

"I don't think so. I don't think we go back yet," Erol said. His voice was low, thick, dripping in lust. His eyes read lust too.

We fucked in a chain. Onur was on all fours on the towels. I was crouched over him, my arms laced in to his chest, clutching his pecs, and fucking him like a dog. And Erol, in turn was standing behind me, grabbing my hips with his hands, and fucking me from the rear. Eventually, Erol readjusted his stance to where both he and I were shafting Onur's ass together. I had had two men inside me as recently as earlier in the day; this was my first time to share a man with another, and it was a memorable sensation. We repeated the three-way progression in my room when we returned to the Olive Tree. I told them to let me know how soon they could put a wedding party together, but that I couldn't stay in Cyprus forever.

* * * *

Serhan Ceren had been a very private man and had spent much of his life outside of Cyprus, teaching at universities. Thus, there were very few people in attendance at his funeral at Saint Andrews and his internment in the church yard afterward. There were expatriate retirees and businessmen in Kyrenia who had known him, a few educated academics of mixed Turkish and European lineage, as he was, who taught at the university near Salamis on the east coast, and, of course, his house servants, who had been given the next few days off, his son told me, to have time to grieve and celebrate their employer's life.

And there was his son, Zeki, who came in a cream-colored suit that fit him like a glove.

"My father didn't like mourning or the color black," he said to me as we had a few words in the narthex before the service. "He always said he preferred the colors of life even in situations of death."

"I also recall that about him," I said. "Unfortunately, as an Episcopal priest, I am stuck with the color black and a white collar for services such as this."

"Oh, I'm quite pleased you are in clerical garb," Zeki said, as he took his hand from mine and walked up the aisle in the small stone church to take his place in front of the closed coffin. Leaning over, he whispered in my ear, "It makes my thoughts of what we might become involved in all the more arousing."

He moved away from me then, but not before squeezing one of my butt cheeks. If I ever thought I had fooled him in the level of my interest in him, I was the one who was the fool.

Seeing him in this setting made my heart ache and, I must admit, had an effect on other parts of my anatomy as well. He was so much like his father, in sensual looks and in his arousing smile, and even in the gait with which he walked, wide stanced, as if he had something unusually large between his thighs. I knew that, if he was anything like his father, he did. He was wearing a diaphanous white cotton shirt again today, and, with the deep natural tan of his three-quarters Turkish skin, his torso, hirsute, with black curly hair, and his prominent nipples, with rings in them, were easily discerned.

Halfway up the aisle, Zeki hesitated, stopped, turned, and walked back to where I was standing with the rector of Saint Andrew's.

"You do remember that you're coming back to my father's house afterward—that he left something he wanted to give to you? The house is just down the street here."

"Yes, I remember." And I certainly did. I had been wondering what Serhan could have left me. "I will be delayed, though, I'm afraid. There is more that is official that has to be done here after the internment."

"That will be perfect," he said.

I did a double take when I arrived and knocked on the double wooden doors of the traditional Turkish house. Leading straight back from the entrance door was an open-air tunnel that led back to the house's courtyard, which was faced on two sides by the L-shaped house proper—two stories, with a balconied verandah all around overlooking the courtyard. The courtyard was floored with flagstones, with lush tropical-plant gardens and a fountain. Divans with backs sat by the fountain, a sitting area with rattan armchairs was off to one side, and a patio table set was off the other.

This is where Zeki guided me. It's where we had been sitting, in the rattan armchairs, when I had previously visited. This time he guided me to one of the divans, though, and sat beside me. What had made me do a double take at the entrance was that he had changed after coming back to the house. He now was wearing just some sort of billowy skirt affair. His torso, tanned, muscular, cut, and hirsute was bare. He was magnificent and I went hard.

He was moving fast. I was so aroused by him that I wouldn't be applying any brakes.

"I hope I'm not being too forward, but my father told me what you were to him at Georgetown University. I was surprised—but also interested, and, I must say, aroused—when I learned you were a priest."

"It doesn't disturb you that your father and I had a relationship? I would think that the son of a Muslim who was covering a priest would have concerns. Of course, I wasn't a priest at the time. I'm not even sure I intended to become one then. And your father was Muslim. I don't think it really occurred to either of us that—"

"No, it doesn't disturb me that my father fucked you. Let's call it what it is—he fucked you. You may call it a relationship, if you like, but the raw truth is that he dominated you. He made you his fuck toy, and you did for him whatever he demanded of you. And you wanted him to fuck you, didn't you?"

"Yes," I answered honestly.

"And to bind you."

"Yes."

"And, when he was in the mood, to whip and flog you."

"Yes."

"I want to fuck you too. Surely I have made that clear. I might wish to bind and whip you too. The thought of seducing a priest arouses me and has had me nearly hyperventilating ever since I heard you were a priest. Of course, you are way beyond being seduced, but we can pretend. You want me inside you, don't you?"

The baldness of that hit me like a ton of bricks. I shuddered and he took my hand in his, intertwining the fingers and leaving the middle finger free to rub the palm of my hand. A chill went up my spine. He was sitting very close to me.

"I'm sorry," he continued. "Am I being too forward? Have I misjudged you? Your responses to me told me you were attracted to me. My father told me that you easily went under him and other men—that you enjoyed it. Am I misreading you?"

"No, you aren't misjudging me," I answered, my voice not much more than a croak. I moaned as one of his arms went around me and tipped me back as his lips came in to capture mine. His other hand went to my crotch, unzipped me, possessed my already-hard cock, and gently stroked it. I found that freeing his cock was just a matter of moving my hands in the folds of his diaphanous Turkish skirt. Gentle pressure on the back of my neck brought my face down to his lap, and I took the cock in my mouth and gave him head while he stroked me off.

"As I wish, I will fuck you," he murmured.

172

"Yes," I responded.

"And, if it pleases me, bind and whip you."

"Yes."

When I sat back up, I moved to take off my collar and then would have taken off my clerical shirt, as well, but he reached out and stayed my hand. "No, I want to take you as a priest," he whispered.

He fucked me on the divan, with me three-quarters turned on my left side, with my right leg bent and flung across my body and Zeki stretched behind me, his thick, long cock working my channel and his right hand stroking my cock while my head rested in the crook of his left arm and he pulled my face around for his kisses.

He was an expert, knowing to pay attention to my prostate to heighten my arousal but also to mine my ass deep, reaching into the core of me and pulling the maximum passion out of me. He was as thick and long as his father had been—thicker than nearly every other man I had had inside me.

Afterward we lay there, not moving, Zeki not withdrawing from me, both of us knowing that it was just a momentary rest until we had both regained our strength and ardor to move with each other like we were long-time lovers—just as I had moved with his father, Serhan.

"Was this what your father had to give to me?" I asked in a whisper. "His son? If it is, there could have been no finer gift to me. You are a god in your own right, but you remind me so much of your father that I want to cry."

"We could cry together for my father," Zeki murmured. "He was a romantic. He would appreciate that. He also would appreciate your calling me his gift. I appreciate that too. I'm so glad I've seduced you. I am sorry I said you were beyond that."

"It didn't take much," I said, with a laugh.

"No, it didn't take much," he said. He reached up, undid my collar and removed it, pulled my shirt over my head, and moved his lips to one of my nipples as a hand clasped my cock in a loose grip, inviting me to move inside the sheathed fingers, which, moving my hips languidly, I did.

"After what we just did—what you did in response—I don't want to think of you as a priest anymore. My father said it wouldn't take much—that you enjoyed sex immensely."

"Your father was my first. I moved deeper into it—with more men, indiscriminately—after him."

"Obviously," he said, and laughed again. "But no, that's not his gift to you. His gift is this house, and a stipend to maintain it. He hoped that you would keep the house servants on until they wished to leave."

"This house?" I exclaimed, pulling away from him and sitting up. But he just pulled me back down into his embrace with a low laugh. "We're not finished here," he growled.

It was a good thing I'd given in to him so easily and quickly. He was a powerful man. I'm sure he could just take what he wanted whether or not it was granted to him. Not a problem with me. I would give him anything he wanted. "It's a grand house. Surely you are the one who should have it."

Zeki laughed again. "I have houses of my own and all the financial means I require. It will mean more to me that you come here from time to time—and that, when you do, you lie under me and let me have my way with you."

"I could deny you nothing," I answered.

"You will perhaps stay then? If you stay, I will test you."

"At least for the foreseeable future," I said. "Life has become more complicated than I really want to face in the States, and, perhaps more important, I find I have a wedding to perform here, and I don't have a date for that yet. But if you aren't going to be here, in this house—"

Zeki smiled down into my face, kissed me, and showed that we were about to float up to heaven again. Which we did after he spoke again. "I said I had other houses, not that I had to sleep in them rather than here—and one of them is just across the wall from this one."

Martin's Hundred

March, 1622
Wolstenholme Towne, Virginia

The unseasonable warmth that early March brought James West to the holding pool of the stream leading down to the river. James was a young settler in the royal grant English Virginia Company's Martin's Hundred holding on the Virginia peninsula east of Jamestown. As far as he knew, he was the only one who knew about this pool in the cascade of the stream as it came down a wall of rock that was tucked away in a forest. The pool was nearly a half hour's walk from Wolstenholme Towne, the seat of Martin's Hundred—"hundred" being an English word for "county." That he was coming there on this particularly warm day was because this was where he liked to come in privacy to wash himself and his clothes. It had been some time since he'd been able to do that. Between times he availed himself of the more limited resources in the stockaded town.

That wasn't the only reason for coming here that day, though. He wasn't coming alone. He had told his special friend, Charles Stephens, of the isolated pool and of the benefits of cleanliness in seeking it out. Without words, though, he had gotten across the privacy of the idyllic setting. Increasingly the two had wanted to seek out privacy. Increasingly they had been apprising each other with special interest, one in the other, through signaling of looks and choices of words and touching. They had an understanding of mutual need and desire without having directly vocalized it. They'd also established that James was the dominant one of the pair and the slimmer, more lithe and timid, Charles the submissive.

The pool, half way down the rock face of an escarpment, the upper lip of which was bounded by large boulders with curved tops, was closely hedged by dense tree cover. A pathway that James had taken as natural—and probably shouldn't have—wound its way from the creek bed, up along the side of the pool, and then up to the top of the escarpment, where the waterfall commenced its plunge to the stream bed below.

Almost shyly, but with great anticipation, each peeking at the other, each in full erection, the two young men stripped off the clothes they were wearing—billowy white cotton shirts; tight breeches, with laced-up codpieces; and woolen socks with leather boots—added them to the pile of other clothes that had been saved back for washing, and crouched down near each other beside the stream. First things first, they wanted to get their clothes washed. While they were doing that in the altogether, though, they could ogle each other and build a lust and a bravery to carry through with their intentions. Before washing themselves in the pool, they climbed up to the top of the escarpment. Each claimed a boulder on either side of the stream and laid his clothes out to dry.

In the stream, at the top of the escarpment, James came to Charles as he was crossing the stream, and their bodies and lips came together. James held Charles close. They had kissed thusly before, but never in nakedness, and both were trembling—not just from the nip in the air and the coldness of the water their feet were in, but more so in the passion of being together, at last, alone, and the anticipation of what they intended to do here.

Breaking from the embrace and knowing how deep the pool was at the waterfall end, James turned and dove head first into the pool below. Charles more gingerly worked his way down the path and waded, teeth chattering, as he slowly got acclimated to the cold water, into the shallow end of the pool. James had laid clumps of moss at the water's edge, and the two now came close together and stood, in knee-deep water, scrubbing each other's bodies. Their scrubbing became intimate and was accompanied by deep kissing. James held their cocks together, frotting them. Then, when desire and lust overtook them, Charles climbed James' body, hooking his legs on the sturdy Englishman's hips, and grabbed James' biceps to hold himself in place. After positioning his cock and penetrating Charles' channel a couple of inches, accompanied by cries of passion at the taking from Charles, James grabbed Charles' waist in his hands and commenced pulling the smaller man on and off his cock.

They had drifted farther into the pool in this process, so that the water come to under their taut nipples. But any onlooker—and there was one, a young savage of the Powhatan tribe was standing, concealed, within the trees rimming the pool and watching, his own cock in hand—would have no trouble knowing what they were doing.

After ejaculating, the two cavorted in the pool until they were wanting it and randy again, which was not long in transpiring, as both were healthy, virile young men. They came out of the water and James chased Charles to the top of the escarpment. Charles lay out on his belly, arms outstretched, hugging the curve of the boulder on top of his drying clothes. James mounted his hips, drove his hard cock inside Charles' passage, and fucked him again.

The sun was below the treetops after James had taken Charles for a third time in a doggie position on top of the boulder before they were finished and their clothes were dry. Laughing and exhilarated by their first taste of a fully completed tryst in the privacy—or so they thought—of the primeval forest of the virgin Virginia peninsula, the two dressed, gathered up their other washed and dried clothes, and kissed in departure.

James let Charles go on ahead so that the two would arrive at the Wolstenholme Towne stockade separately. He went down on his haunches on a rock beside the pool to think on and savor the at-last completed coupling with the other young man. His peripheral vision registered movement off at the edge of the trees on the other side of the pool, and he turned his attention there. But he saw nothing.

It was just the rustling of the departure of the young Powhatan tribe savage, melting back into the forest after having left his seed on the ground on the other side of the pool.

* * * *

The relationship with Charles was short-lived. He was called to go to the nearby settlement of Jamestown the day after he and James at last were able to consummate their mating. James promised to visit him there when he could. It wasn't a great distance, but increasingly it wasn't a safe journey to take, as the English settlers traversed back and forth between the two communities often and the danger of an encounter with savages was on the increase. Relatively good relations had been established with the chief of the Powhatans, ties that had been solidified when Chief Wahunsenacawh's daughter, Pocahontas, married the English settler John Rolfe, in 1614. But Wahunsenacawh had died four years earlier, in 1618, while visiting England, and the tribe had come under his brother, Opechancanough, under whose rule relations had increasingly become belligerent.

Thus, it was with concern and wariness that Richard Martin, head of the settlement came out of the stockade at Wolstenholme Towne, on March 15th, to receive the unexpected visit of a delegation from the Powhatans. James came to the stockade gate to watch the uneasy meeting and, while lurking there, became aware of particular attention an especially handsome and well-formed young savage of the delegation was paying him. The young savage looked upon James with a steady gaze and a small smile. James found him alluring but wondered why he was being picked out for the attention.

The meeting didn't go well. Voices were raised and knuckles whitened in clutching weapons, holding them at the ready. But neither side pushed the issues, and the Powhatans withdrew.

Martin was talking with another man as they returned to the stockade.

"I wonder what this visit was really about," Martin was saying. "No demands were made; only insults given. I wonder what they were up to."

"Some of them were looking the stockade over," the man answered. James hoped the man hadn't noticed the young savage looking him over. "Methinks they are scouting our defenses. I suggest that we tighten our surveillance and ensure everyone is inside the stockade by dark."

"Yea, I can see the wisdom of that," Martin responded, as the two passed James by and he lost contact with what they were saying.

James was left with the clutchy feeling he'd be trapped in the stockade until the unrest settled. He had always been separate from these people—other than Charles—and continually had the worry they would find out about his preference and make life miserable for him. He handled this by being as separate as he could. This feeling, plus the continued unseasonably warm weather, called him back to the pool below the escarpment again. There had been no sign of savages in that direction. The pool was remote. Surely the dangers would be along the trails between the English settlements up and down the river.

He took the chance two days later, taking clothes to wash with him that he hadn't taken when he went with Charles, as he had known that cleaning clothes was not what he'd be wanting to take up most of his time that day.

As he approached the pool, though, he realized he wasn't the only one there that day. He arrested his approach and crouched down at the tree line. The young savage who had given him the eye at the stockade earlier was standing in the shallow end of the pool. He was bathing himself. His nakedness made James' cock lurch and harden. The young savage was beautiful—lithe but muscular, not an ounce of fat on him. His legs were long and shapely, his body was hairless and of a darker tone than the skin of the Englishmen, even when they were burnt by the sun—more reddish gold than tan. His long, straight, black hair, which he was scrubbing, descended down his back to his shoulder blades. There were tufts of black hair in his armpits and at his crotch.

As James watched and almost moaned, the young savage took his half-hard cock in his hand and stroked it to ejaculation. Then he neatly dove into the deep end of the pool and swam laps. When he came out of the water, whipping his hair about his head to drive the water drops out of it, it was almost like he was posing for James—as if he knew James was watching him from the tree line and stroking his own cock—which, indeed, was the case.

Moving like a dancer or a panther, the savage pulled himself up the steep pathway to the boulders at the top of the escarpment and lay on his back on the curve of one of the boulders, arms and legs spread, offering his beautiful body to the sun to dry. The savage's cock stood up, proud and thick from his body.

James sucked in air and gave a little gasp when the savage produced a carved and polished cylinder of wood—in the shape of a phallus, and, turning, bending over the curved boulder, and spreading his legs so that James was looking directly into his passage, erect cock, and drooping balls, worked the wooden phallus into his passage and fucked himself with it.

But then the savage turned again and sat on the boulder, pelvis rolled up and legs spread and bent at the knees with his toes gripping the rock, the phallus still being held inside himself with one hand and looked directly at where James was hidden—or had believed himself to have been hidden. It became quite obvious that the savage knew James was there and that he had wanted James to be there. He smiled a sensuous smile, gestured at James, and looked down at the end of the phallus sticking out of his ass.

Quick as a rabbit, and operating entirely on instinct and lust, James was up the path in a flash, tearing at and discarding his shirt, unlacing his codpiece, kneeling between

180

the savage's thighs, raising the young man's pelvis with palms clutching the savages buttocks, pulling the wooden phallus out to be replaced by his cock, and began fucking the young man hard.

The savage received him with open arms and a thrusting pelvis. The two rolled around on top of the boulder, thrusting and counterthrusting, reaching for and achieving a rhythm of the fuck. They roughly and brutally took and gave everything they had—two healthy, virile, randy young men lost in the fuck.

They exhausted each other—or at least the savage exhausted James. After repeated fuckings, where desire and lust were the only means they had to converse and connect with each other and where it seemed the savage was sheathing and milking James' cock for all he was worth, but where the communication of desire was more than enough, the two, panting and their chests heaving from the exertion, fell away from each other, lying side by side, face up to the sun.

James was totally exhausted, but the savage was not. He rolled over on top of James, gripped James' cock in his channel, and rode James to one last mutual exhaustion as, balls aching, James moaned his surrender. When they had ejaculated, the savage, with James going flaccid inside him, lay on top of the English settler, chest to chest, and both dozed off.

When James woke the young savage was gone. The young settler almost could believe he had dreamed it all, but it had been too vivid for a dream and his balls ached too much from the milking. All the same, he immediately wanted to be inside the savage again, and he remained by the pool almost to dusk, slowly washing and drying the clothes he'd brought with him, in the hope that the savage would return to him. But he didn't.

James didn't make it back to the stockade until after dark. The gate was closed tight, and James was afraid he'd be mistaken for a savage and shot if he pounded on the gate. He went around the corner, on the river side of the stockade, and pulled up to and crouched at the base of the stockade wall on the lip of the trench that had been dug around the stockade.

He drifted off to sleep in a crouched position, and this time, when he felt the presence of another man, breathing slowly, he initially did think he was dreaming. He had no weapons. He'd been foolish to leave the stockade without a musket or so much as a knife.

And his heart leapt into his mouth when he realized that the other man was a savage. But it wasn't just any savage. It was *his* savage—the young man he had fucked at the pool. The savage was crouching beside him, working the laces of James' codpiece, freeing his cock, and taking it into his mouth. Both breathing heavily. but both trying not to make a sound that would raise someone in the stockade, the savage sat in James' lap, facing him, skewered himself on James' cock, and rose and fell on the staff until the two men had come again. The savage was wearing just deerskin leggings, with a codpiece that, when opened pulled all the way to the back and tucked into his waistband, allowing James full access to his passage with his cock. The savage unlaced James' shirt and flared it, so they would melt into each other, lips to lips nipples to nipples, as the savage rose and fell on the cock. They could feel their hearts beating together as one—the beat the same, not one beat for the Englishman and another, different one, for the savage.

After they had come and kissed one last time, the savage evaporated into the darkness.

* * * *

The cold arrived the next morning. James couldn't break away that day as he was needed to help shore up one of the stockade walls, but on the 17th, he pulled away and ran to the pool. But the savage wasn't there. There was no question of swimming in the pool. When the cold had come on, it was with a vengeance. On succeeding days, James was needed in the vegetable patch, plowing up the earth in preparation for planting, and helping to extend the stockade wall around that piece of ground. Richard Martin had expressed the fear that anyone working in the patch was in danger of being picked off by the savages with an arrow, so the men were back at felling small trees, splitting them, and building at least enough of a visual screen around the field that workers in the garden could not be seen from the edge of the forest.

During these days, James maintained a vigil on that forest edge, and thus he was sure that it was only he who, on the morning of March 22nd, saw the savage—*his* young savage—expose himself enough to catch James' attention and signal that the young settler should follow him. There was an air of concern and immediacy about the savage's gestures, so James dropped his hoe and walked, as unobtrusively as he could, to the forest edge and then beyond, into the forest, keeping sight of the savage's disappearing figure, dressed now in deerskin vest as well as breeches, deeper into the forest.

He led James back, by a route he hadn't used before, to the pool—their pool—in the heart of the forest.

Still, there were no words communicated between the two, nor need for words. Their immediate need for sex—for James to be inside the savage and for the native to have James there—was all the language they needed to share.

There was no question of going into the pool or even disrobing. The savage backed James up against the trunk of an old oak tree just out of view of both the pathway and the pool, knelt in front of him, unlaced his codpiece, and took James' stiff cock in his mouth. Holding the savage's head in his hands and running his fingers into the native's silky, straight, black hair, James helped move his head as it bobbed on his cock. The savage didn't take James to completion, nor did James want him to. Pushing the native away from him when he needed to interrupt the sucking or he would come, James lifted his lover up and turned his back to the tree. Fully understanding James' intention, which matched his want, the savage unlaced his codpiece as James turned him, climbed James' hips with his knees, wrapped his arms around the young settler's neck, took James' mouth with his, and the two groaned and grunted in unison—a universal shared language—as James pushed the torso of the savage up the tree trunk and then let him descend, only to push him up again with the strength of the thrusts of James' cock up inside his passage. After an eternity of sweaty, deep-thrusting fuck, the two lovers came together.

They held there, kissing and fondling each other with their hands, neither of them showing any need to break away and leave this place. Both of them knew they weren't finished with each other. They found a depression in the ground, under the protective low-sweeping branches of a fir tree, out of the chilling wind and the possibility of discovery by any wandering Englishman or savage.

James fucked the savage twice more, the savage on his back and James lying on him between his legs in the first taking and then taking him from the side the second time, with a rest between until, like the previous tryst, James was exhausted into sleep. And, once again, when he woke, he was alone.

He heard the wailing before he came in sight of Wolstenholme Towne and almost simultaneously saw the tongues of fire leaping over the treetops. Running for all he was worth, he came upon a site of devastation and massacre. All told, the Powhatan war party had murdered some fifty of the settlers, both men and women, more of the latter, as they were more defenseless against the attack. Most of the stockade walls were down and all of the buildings were aflame.

No one asked James where he'd been during the raid. No one cared. No one knew he hadn't been there. All the shocked survivors knew was that it was the middle of the afternoon, they were now defenseless to a renewed attack, and there were some fifty of their fellows who needed to be put under the ground before they left seeking safety—most like in Jamestown, if it was not in the same condition.

When they reached Jamestown, they found that it had been spared but that many other separate dwellings and small communities had also been raided that day, on March 22nd. There now were more settlers congregating in Jamestown than the fort there could sustain. Fortuitously, two ships were in the river that were ready to return to England for resupply. They had not been intended to carry passengers, but now they would. They would take enough to reduce the population in Jamestown to a sustainable number. They would take volunteers, settlers who, after the horrors of the day, had had enough of this new world. Barring enough of those, they would conduct a lottery.

James was reunited with Charles in Jamestown. They even managed to find enough privacy between boxes in a storage shed for James to fuck Charles against a wall. Their lust, mutual joy that the other one was alive, and need for each other ignited and flared immediately, and they pledged, given the horror they both had escaped, to remain together. Charles drew a "leave" in the lottery. James thought long and hard, but life in the new world just didn't measure up now with the possibility of life with Charles. So he volunteered to leave on the same ship Charles was assigned to.

It wasn't until they were in a small boat rowing out to the vessel that was to take them home to England and to a life with the only certainty being that they would be together, that it occurred to James why he had not been at Wolstenholme Towne for the massacre there. Looking back at the shore, he caught a glimpse of a young savage—his savage—standing half hidden in trees running down to the bank of the river. The savage smiled, laid a hand on his heart, then to his lips, and then extended toward James.

James gestured back his appreciation and love. Now he knew why the savage had insistently lured him away from Wolstenholme Towne on the morning of the March 22nd.

Edge Teetering

Brian knew he'd been impetuous. Unfortunately, it was a little late for realizing that. He turned his head from the window of the Cyprus Air plane as it cleared the French coast above Marseilles and sailed out over the Mediterranean. He looked over at the two young men sitting across the aisle from him in first class, aching for them—either one of them. It was obvious they were a couple. They unabashedly were holding hands now. They'd come on with tennis rackets—a couple a piece. They were both in great shape—and young. That was the kicker. They had to be no older than their mid twenties. And they were traveling first class and were well groomed. Brian made them out to be pro tennis players. They certainly didn't seem to mind anyone knowing they were a couple.

Brian wondered which one of them topped—and what he did with the other. Was he a rough lover, Brian wondered. One of them was taller and more muscular than the other. He was Mediterranean in appearance to the sandy-hued hair of the other—deeply tanned, black hair, a curl of hair sprouting above the neckline of his T-shirt, molded to firm pectorals. He looked a little rugged and he leaned over the other guy like he dominated the sandy-haired one.

He must be the dominant one, the top. Was he hung? In the daydream Brian went into, yes he was hung, and rough and a bit cruel.

He embraced Brian from behind as Brian leaned over the bed, his fists buried in the mattress if the Larnaka hotel Brian was headed to. Somehow they had lost Sandy and it was just him, Brian, and Constandinos now. Brian thought of him as Constandinos—Cypriot Greek. Constandinos was palming his belly with one hand and cupping his chin with the other, pulling the back of Brian's head back to the black, curly matting between his pectorals. Brian grunted as Constandinos penetrated him with the thick cock, and, although he had the sensation of being filled and stretched, in his daydream there was no pain. He moaned as the young man began to pump him hard.

The young man. Brian snapped out of the daydream and turned his face back to the window, staring down at the blue Mediterranean, dotted with sea craft. A young man—a man like Travis. Like Travis, who had walked out on him saying he'd gotten too old. The timing couldn't have been worse. It was a week before Brian turned fifty and just a day after Josh had called to cancel the modeling job, saying they needed a younger, trimmer guy. Brian wasn't fat. He spent two thirds of his life, it felt like, staying in trim for the cameras. The cameras always put extra weight on a man—especially when it was underwear he was modeling.

"But they'd said—"

"Yes, they said they wanted a mature model," Josh had said. "But it turns out that to them early forties was mature."

It had been bad enough that the gig had been marked for a mature man, Brian thought, resisting the urge to bang his head against the airplane window. But then to learn that he was going to be ten years older the next week than what the client considered mature. He'd lost it and sunk into a funk. He'd turned his phone off, not taking calls from Josh, his agent, and certainly not returning Travis' calls to set a time when he and his thirtysomething new sugar daddy could come for the rest of his things.

Brian had turned on the TV set. He never watched TV. He was looking at a travelogue, and by the end of the week he'd bought a restored stone village house somewhere on the island of Cyprus—one that came with a vineyard. Yay him. It took hooking up with a travel agency—the one he used for international travel, the gay-friendly one that set him up with everything gay friendly—to even find out where his new home was. It was in the southern part of the island, which Brian found out was divided into a Turkish zone in the north and a Greek zone in the south. The village was called Phini, it apparently was an old mountain village being gentrified by British ex-patriots mainly, and it was on the southern slope of Mount Olympus in the Troodos mountain range.

"I thought Mount Olympus was in Greece," Brian had said.

"The tallest mountain in any Greek area is named Mount Olympus," the travel agency had said.

"So, this Phini is on the Greek side of the island," Brian had responded.

"Yes, of course."

That's the first time in this midlife crisis foolishness of his that Brian had realized that he was going off the rails in his response to being on the edge of what he thought of as over-the-hill old age. He'd thought he'd bought on the Turkish side of the island. He'd been fucked by two young, hung, fun-loving Turkish brothers on a deserted Turkish beach once and was looking forward to something like that again. It had been the first time he'd accepted double penetration, and it had certainly been memorable.

Brian stared at the sea through the window of the plane, drifting off, remembering.

Both of them had been stocky, muscular, and hirsute, covered with black, curly hair, more than willing, and all smiles. And they'd both fit inside him at once. They had played him like an amusement park ride, one plunging as the other pulled back, sandwiching him between them, on a beach on the Turkish coast when he was doing a photo shoot in whatever ancient ruined city that was. One brother under him, on his back, Brian on his back on top of him, the Turk palming his pecs and snuffling in his ear, talking dirty in broken English and in what was probably Turkish. His

Turkish words sexier than the English ones—rougher, dirtier, more moving.

His cock held steady inside Brian's channel at first, while the other brother covered him from above, hovering over him, fists buried in the sand beside Brian's shoulders, doing pushups on him, pumping him, sliding his cock against the other Turk's inside Brian's channel. The brother below him starting to move his hips as well then, Brian moaning, barely able to take them, but taking them, one diving, the other withdrawing, the other diving and the first one withdrawing. Barebacking him, but he didn't care, him coming in his excitement before they came, almost simultaneously, inside him. Pulling out together then, only to plunge again, into the slickness of their deposited cum, making Brian shudder and come again in the squeezing hand of one of the brothers.

He had no idea if they really were brothers. They had said they were brothers. But they'd said it in broken English, with smiles wrapped around their faces, as they touched him here and there, brushing his hand away from his cock and taking over the stroking, each providing a hand, sharing in the hand job as they later would share in the fuck. Maybe they weren't brothers; maybe they were just teasing him. He, of course, spoke no Turkish. Maybe they'd said they were brothers to heighten the arousal of the encounter. It certainly had done that for him. It may have been the difference in letting them take him together.

He'd just been lying on his towel after coming out of the sea to the then-deserted beach, his bathing suit off and laying beside him, languidly stroking his cock. He had watched them stride down the beach, arm in arm, grins on their faces when they'd seen him, walking like they owned the ocean. He couldn't have claimed they didn't. They both were in skimpy bathing suits, both muscular and hirsute, both visibly going hard as they approached him. They'd gone down on their haunches on either side of him, asked him what he wanted, touched him here and there. They'd asked him straightforward if he wanted them to fuck him—had acted delighted when he said yes, heated up by their smiles and their bodies and their touches. They asked him what he'd take and then he took and took and took. He had had no idea they would both fuck him at the same time. But they did. For all he knew, they'd asked him if he'd take double and he's said yes.

They rose and continued their sauntering journey down the beach, arm in arm, merrily jabbering of their victory in Turkish, leaving him vanquished, moaning, legs bent and spread, spent, sore, stretched, throbbing—wantonly satisfied.

Of course, he'd been younger then—in his early thirties. They had been in their twenties, though. They probably hadn't known he was ten years older than they were. He'd always taken good care of himself, starting to lose the battle only of late. Brian had only gone with younger men—and power tops. He'd never felt too old to attract younger men before. And he never paid for it.

Turkish. Muscular and hirsute. Black curly hair. The release brought him out of his daydream. He realized he had been rubbing his basket and had come in his trousers, a wet spot showing at his crotch. He wondered if the hunk in the other seat would fuck him if he showed the young man that he had come in his seat just thinking of young hunks like him, working Brian's body—if Brian could rise from his seat and wedge himself over the dark hunk across the aisle, unzipping the young man and handling his cock, making it thicken, and then riding it, facing him, while the other young man touched him here and there, egging him on.

He looked over at the couple across the aisle again. The dark hunk was smiling. Brian thought it was for him. But then the stewardess leaned over in the aisle between the seats, and Brian realized that the smile had been for her and the bottles of beer the young men had ordered—probably more for the beer bottles than the stewardess. The young men. Brian turned his face toward the window again. There was an island down there. It wasn't Cyprus, but he could hardly wait until it was. He moved his hand to his basket again and rubbed.

* * * *

The agent that would take him to his house and see that he was settled in didn't meet him at the airport. Brian now almost wished he had. He'd been the one to opt out of being met today. He was arriving in the early afternoon. He wanted time to rest and gather himself before driving up to the village house he'd bought off the Internet nearly sight unseen and no longer wanted. Now he just felt foolish and trapped.

He also felt invisible. The couple across the aisle from him bounded out into the aisle before he could get there and they had eyes only for each other. Not even a grunt from the Constandinos who had fucked Brian in his daydream. Constandinos. He laughed. That was the name of the travel agency guy who would be picking him up the next day and driving him up to Phini. Brian had rented a car through the agency and it already was up at the mountain house. Brian had somehow matched up the names. He'd used this agency before and he'd always been met by a young escort who serviced him too. He wondered how young this Constandinos was.

The airport was a dump, hardly worthy of being called an international airport. But he'd been told that it was just temporary and had been temporary for over forty years, the former international airport being locked in no-man's-land between the Greeks and Turks outside of Nicosia, the capital city in the center of the island. Even after all this time the Greek Cypriots refused to upgrade the international airport on the southern coast of the island because they didn't want to accept the division of the island as permanent.

The taxi driver who took him to the nearby Larnaka seafront was young and handsome and had dark, curly hair. He barely looked at his fare, though. The hotel wasn't just gay friendly, it seemed to Brian in surveying the lobby that it was gay insistent—couples were hanging off each other. All good-looking, young men. None paying any attention to Brian, however. The bellhop who took him to his room was also young and was quite open about being available for a fuck. But he wanted a hefty price and obviously was a bottom.

Even if there was something Brian could do with him—and he now was a little frantic for some sort of attention—he had never paid for a fuck before and didn't intend to start doing that now.

They compromised. For a cut fee, Brian lay on the bed, fully clothed, feet on the floor, thighs spread, and the bellhop knelt between his legs, unzipped him, fished his cock out, and gave him a blow job. Feeling distant from it at first, Brian warmed to the suck as he hardened and his juices started to build. He reached down and took the young man's head in his hands and, starting to move his own pelvis, helped guide the mouth rubbing his bulb against an inner cheek here, pushing deeper into the throat there. Pulling off the shaft, the bellhop queried whether Brian now wanted him to sit on his cock as Brian lay there on his back and ride him for a lesser fee than originally cited. But still Brian demurred. He was a bottom too—and for power tops. And he didn't pay for fucks.

Apparently, now, he did pay for getting his cock sucked off.

The young man took the cock in his mouth again, taking it deep this time, applying pressure to the side of the shaft, and Brian moaned in pleasure. The stroking took on a rhythm, with a deep penetration on each third beat. Brian demanded in a strangled voice, and the bellhop worked his fingers through the folds of material of Brian's trousers and briefs and found and penetrated Brian's ass, reaching for and rubbing his prostate. Brian threw an arm over his face, dreamed he was being done by the Constandinos in the airplane, and managed to come more prodigiously than he had thought he could under these circumstances. It did relieve the tension a bit.

After a quick, unsatisfying nap as he fought jet lag, Brian pulled on a Speedo, turning this way and that in front of the mirror on the back of the door and telling himself he didn't look a day over thirty-nine and he was handsome and as trim and well-formed as ever, and went out onto the beach that stretched between Larnaka's seafront hotels and restaurants and the harbor.

The Larnaka seafront was constructed in the old south-of-France style, the hill and city rising behind a solid bank of gaily painted restaurants, with hotels above, a wide terrace accommodating outdoor cafés, bordered by the palm tree-lined road. Across that ran a broad promenade, bordering the sand at the top of the beach, the line of tall palm trees marking the boundary. Then a shale beach running down to the harbor and the fringe of swimming beach. Two arms of rock embraced the harbor to the west and east, an ancient stone light house at the west and a Byzantine fortress to the east.

There was more promenading and displaying going on on the sand than swimming in the sea. It was a beach for ogling and being ogled, not for swimming. Brian lay on the beach, just to the sea side of the shadows cast by the palm trees, and posed to be ogled, but he didn't attract the attention of any young men. Well, he did, but they all mentioned money. The only man who didn't was almost as old as Brian was, by his looks. OK, he was muscular, Greek, and good-looking, but he was nearly bald and the thatch of hair on his chest was salt and pepper and Brian had always gone with much younger men. The man had smacked his lips, popped his tongue in his cheek, and given Brian's body the up and down "eye," as he crouched and grasped Brian's ankle in a strong grip.

"You an American? I like Americans. You want suck and fuck?" he'd asked in a surprisingly refined British accent, yet using somewhat broken English. "I big-cock fuck you good. I know a deserted beach. I do you good on the beach. I got best cock in Larnaka. No pay. I fuck you; we both like."

Strangely, considering the man wasn't young, Brian warmed and felt himself going hard, but still he demurred. Later in the evening he thought back on this and tried to remember the man as being younger and him having said yes.

It wasn't any better that evening. The agency had given him a list of restaurants and bars where he'd be comfortable. He picked out what was a half village-décor indoor tavern and half outdoor café two blocks up from the seafront. The name of the place was Adonis, and several of the young men there fit that description, but they already were paired off. Brian settled at a table by himself in the outside area. There was a beautiful, dark-haired young man sitting on a stool in the corner and playing Spanish guitar tunes. His voice was as easy to listen to as he was to watch. He kept looking over in Brian's direction, and Brian spent far more time at the tavern—alone—picking his way through a meze dinner and nursing brandy sours than he intended to because he was tired from the jet lag and imagining a sulky Spanish guitarist between his thighs was better than having nothing to imagine at all.

It took him more than an hour to realize that the guitar player was smiling past him at an older Greek man at a table behind Brian. The man was older than the guitar player, but he was more what that cancelling client had referred to as mature than Brian's mature. He also was a hunk and a half.

A waiter kept buzzing around Brian, though. He said his name was Nicos. He was tall and thin, with a mop of curly blond hair and pale blue eyes. He made quite clear that he was available—for a price—and would go each way. It wasn't what Brian wanted and he never paid for sex—or at least for a fuck, he now had to say, as he'd paid the bellhop for a blow job earlier in the day. Nicos was young—not much over twenty—and, although thin, he had big feet and big hands.

Money laying on the dresser in Brian's hotel room, Brian lay on his back in the center of the bed, legs spread, buttocks elevated on pillows, as big-cocked Nicos, having given Brian a feel at the restaurant and said the right words to close the deal, hovered above him, fists buried in the mattress on either side of Brian's shoulders, knees bent between Brian's thighs, and shaft mining Brian's channel deep. There was no passion or inventiveness in the fuck, which was just as well, as Brian was tired from the flight to Cyprus from London, which had closely followed the flight from New York to London.

But Brian had a big cock inside him—a young man's cock. He shut his eyes and dreamed of Constandinos from the plane and of the Turks on the beach while he stroked himself to an ejaculation. No affection was involved; no

moans and groans or dirty words from Nicos, and few from
Brian either. It was just business for Nicos and animal need
of release for Brian. Nicos wasn't touching him anywhere
except inside his channel. Both were concentrating on getting
off. But Brian felt filled and stretched, and Nicos knew to
give his prostate attention. Brian set his pelvis in motion,
going with the fuck, matching the rhythm, taking the cock
deeper. Nicos was young, vigorous; his cock was long and
hard. Taking him deeper yet. Emptying his mind out, thinking
not that he'd had to pay and that other young men had
looked past him during the day, but concentrating on having
a young, hard, long cock, deep inside him, stroking, rubbing
across his prostate.

Nicos was still filling and pumping his channel when
Brian drifted off to sleep after having come. When he woke,
it was in the middle of the night—it would take him days to
adjust to the change in time. He checked, but although the
money on the dresser—which he'd pretend he hadn't put
there because he'd never had to pay for a fuck and by god he
wouldn't do it when he settled in Phini—was gone, nothing
else was missing, including a big wad of bills in his wallet.

He'd been told that Cypriot Greeks were honest.
Thank god that had borne out as true. Before he went back
to sleep, Brian nursed a bit of regret that he'd paid for the
fuck. There wasn't even anything romantic about it. In
addition to Constandinos from the plane, he'd had to think
about the Spanish guitarist at the restaurant—and had to
think of both of them as intense, rough lovers—to get
himself off properly. The biggest regret had been to have
been forced to pay for it to get it from a young guy. If he'd
been willing to compromise, there was the forty-something
Greek on the beach who seemed interested in doing him. But
then he thought about the times he'd paid a travel agency and
a young escort had been included. And it was always a guy
who had banged him good. He'd paid for that in his travel
package now that he thought about it. The escort had always
been careful to give the impression that he found Brian
arousing and wanted to bang him. But this rationalization
only depressed him. He felt he had to either hold the line or

jump over that edge to "not getting any" old age. It was sort of pathetic, he thought, to be teetering on the edge of aging out.

He had to remember that his original idea on coming to Cyprus was to go cold turkey and give in to old age without his friends and colleagues in New York seeing that happen—and either pitying him or laughing at him behind his back. He didn't like to think about it, but he'd been catty a time or two when a male model colleague had aged and faded out. That was coming back to bite him in the ass.

* * * *

"Are you Mr. Brady? I'm Constandinos. But you should call me just Dinos."

Brian had seen him when he'd descended the stairs to the lobby. This wasn't the sort of hotel that had an elevator. The man had drawn his attention because for a few seconds he thought he was the older man from the beach the previous day—the one who had hit on him, promising him the best fuck to be had in the town. Then this guy had taken his hat off and he still had hair. There was a flutter of regret at not having taken the man on the beach up on his offer but then the dampening closedown again that the man was too old for what Brian wanted—for the struggle he was having with himself of being on the edge of entering a new, sexless phase of his life. He was on the edge of avoiding being old and having to beg or pay for it, or settle in to getting half the satisfaction with other men trying to fight being too old for it.

The disappointment flooded in that the gay escort he was paying for to settle him into his remote mountain village home wasn't young. He was just another old fart, like Brian. He wasn't going to keep Brian from teetering over the edge into old age, if only for a brief moment. That was unfair, of course. This Constandinos didn't look to be quite as old as Brian and he was a solidly built, muscular, beautiful man, with an outgoing smile. But he also had graying sideburns and his wavy hair was salt and pepper. At least he had hair.

196

"Yes. You were sent to take me to my new house in Phini? If I'm to call you Dinos, you should call me Brian."

"Yes I am your guide and here to service your every need," Dinos said. "I'm told you've used our travel agency before and know of the extent of our services," he continued, leaving little doubt on how extensive the contract of services was. He held out an elegantly manicured hand, gently grasped Brian's arm, and turned him toward the reception desk. "If you'll check out, I'll drive you up to Phini. Your house is livable and stocked. It will take a bit more than an hour. The container you had shipped is there now. Have you had lunch? We could stop at a café I know of overlooking the sea near Limassol before starting up into the mountains."

Dinos was driving an old Mercedes sports convertible that was in pristine condition. He drove fast, wearing leather driving gloves, but he concentrated on the road and drove expertly.

Drove expertly, Brian thought, wondering how well he drove in sex. He couldn't help not thinking of the sexual issue even though he was fighting the age issue. Brian couldn't help it, he was highly sexed. Of course this flew in the face of feeling old and being forced to give it all up, teetering on the edge of old age, but being conflicted was just that. He couldn't do anything about it. Dinos dressed expensively and elegantly. His white shirt and linen trousers were well tailored and fit him like a glove. Either the trousers were tailored to push his genitals up and forward or he was hung. Brian couldn't help himself from checking that out, even if he had no intention of going there. Despite knowing he didn't want to be, Brian was drawn to and aroused by the man.

It didn't help that on the terrace of the café overlooking the sea, Dinos did as other Mediterranean men did at the end of the meal, over ouzo and coffee—stripped off his shirt and laid back in his chair, taking in the sun beating down on the edge of the azure sea. He left little doubt that he'd done it to give Brian a good look at his musculature, which was impressive. As was the man on the beach of comparable age, Dinos' chest hair, swirling around his pectorals and down his sternum onto his nearly flat belly, was salt and pepper. His chest was beefy, but hard and muscular. Brian neither took off his shirt nor gawked at Dinos—he gawked much more at young, shirtless men sitting near them. And if he went hard over lunch, it was in thinking of these young men and fantasizing laying under them.

Or at least that was what he still was telling himself. Though of course he checked out Dinos' bare torso.

The man's voice was low, smooth, enhanced by the British accent when he spoke English. "Have you bought the house for holidays—for an escape? You look like a movie star. Are you hiding from fans?"

"I suppose you could say I'm retreating, but permanently," Brian answered. "I plan to live here, and if I'm escaping anything, it's life. I'm a painter."

It wasn't a lie. Brian did paint, and he sold what he painted. He intended it to be his new life. He didn't intend being told ever again that he was too old for a modeling job—especially one that had specified that the model be mature. He was beginning a new life here, an autumn of his life phase. Or was it winter? This life would be as a painter. He had saved and invested well. He didn't have to be anything, if he didn't want to be. But he didn't want to just wait around for death. He'd be a painter in this phase of his life.

"Ah, a painter. The travel service said you were a male model, and I'm sure I have seen you in magazine ads."

"I was that in the States as well as an artist. Leaving that is one reason I am moving here."

"And escaping from life? You look too much alive to be escaping from life. A bad love relationship, perhaps?"

"Yes, that's part of it. He wanted someone younger."

"Ah, younger. Youth is wasted on the young. I've found that expertise requires maturity. Don't you believe that to really be expert in something you need to have a great deal of experience, Brian?"

"I suppose," Brian answered, his voice dubious, his attention half on a couple of young, luscious men rising from their lunch and departing the café.

"Ah, sexy young men, aren't they?" Dinos asked, following Brian's gaze. "They no doubt are on their way to fuck. We have siesta in Cyprus, just like most Mediterranean countries do—withdrawing from the sun to sleep the hotter hours so that we can party late into the night. But Cyprus is a sensual island. Most elsewhere in the Mediterranean sleep during siesta. In Cyprus we fuck. But look at those two young men. Do you think they will fuck as well as a mature, experienced man could fuck them? I think not. In Cyprus men age on the surface, but as long as they fuck often they can stay hard into old age. And they can give a young man a better, more experienced, fuck then a younger man can. So, I say that youth is wasted on the young, and the pursuit of youth is a waste also. What is needed is an older man, with a hard cock and good technique."

He looked expectantly at Brian, who only was able to mumble a, "Yes, I suppose," followed by an "Ah, here is the bill." Dinos didn't fight him for the check.

While they were waiting for the change to come back and after Dinos had pulled his shirt back on, he leaned over and touched Brian on his arm. "I don't think you answered me, so I have to ask again: You are aware of the extent of the service in your contract with my travel agency, are you not?"

"Yes," Brian answered, "but I need not press you on those services."

"I want you to," Dinos said. "It has nothing to do with the services contracted. I find you very attractive." Then he looked up and smiled at the waiter who brought back the change. "Hello, Antony. You are looking very well."

"Thank you, Dinos," the waiter answered. "It is good to see you again."

"Tell our friend here, if you will, how good I fuck."

"Dinos fucks very, very good," Antony said to Brian, with hardly a pause at the forwardness of the question, giving him a smile. "You are very lucky if he is going to fuck you." And then he turned and was gone.

The road up into the mountains narrowed and became more rutted, but Dinos drove just as fast and just as well as he had on flatter ground. They just didn't converse much. They were still rising, driving on curves, though, when Dinos commanded in a gruff voice, "Unzip me. Stroke my cock."

The domination mode grabbed Brian, who melted at being commanded this way. Without thinking further or going through his agonizing litany of either of them being too old, he reached over, unzipped Dinos, and took out the Cypriot's half-hard cock. Brian himself had been hard ever since Dinos' monologue on the relative experience of older men at the seaside café.

At the house, without so much as a look either way, Brian not taking in either his rental car, a Fiat 500, or the small walk-in steel container at the other side of the entrance or how close the stone facing of the village house was to the road, barely leaving room between the stone and the road for the vehicles to park, Dinos hustled Brian straight through the house and out onto a stone-floored terrace balcony. He was stripping Brian as they walked, himself losing only his shirt, but with his dick protruding from his fly, long, thick, hard, and slightly upturned. He hadn't let Brian stop stroking him as they approached the villa. He was thick and long, but there was no evidence he was close to coming.

On the terrace, he sat in a patio chair and pulled Brian onto his lap, facing him. Holding his cock erect with one hand, he maneuvered Brian in place, straddling his lap, feet on the stone floor on either side of the chair, worked the bulb of his cock into place, and then, grasping, squeezing, and parting Brian's butt cheeks, he forced Brian's channel down. Forcing it to take four inches of the cock in one go. Brian grabbed Dinos' shoulders with his hands, arched his back, and cried out at the raw penetration of the cock.

"Keep your feet on the stones, hold yourself up, give me room to fuck," Dinos growled, and as Brian obeyed, Dinos gave him three more inches of the cock and started his hips moving, jabbing up into Brian's channel, as Brian tightened his grip on Dinos' shoulders. After a few minutes, Brian started to rise and fall too, taking his share of responsibility for the fuck, joining the rhythm of Dinos' fuck.

He pulled one hand down into his lap and stroked his cock, coming before Dinos did inside him.

Brian collapsed into Dinos' lap, threw his arms around Dinos' neck, and the two went into a series of deep kisses until Dinos' cock came back to life and they fucked once more, this time more languidly, taking longer and deeper penetrations of the cock up into Brian's channel. When they'd come a second time and were cooling down, not changing position, Dinos' shaft still buried up inside Brian, going flaccid, Dinos whispered, "Do older men do it better than younger?"

"Yes," Brian answered in a murmur, "at least you do."

"I think all older men with experience and who can still get hard can, Brian. And they will be more grateful to you than a younger man would be. Don't judge a man by his age, his wrinkles, or that he is losing the battle to keep in shape. Judge him by the hardness and staying power of his cock and what he can do with it. Now, do you want to see your new house?"

"Yes," Brian whispered, "especially the bedroom."

As he pulled off Dinos' lap and turned, he saw that the back of the house sloped down the side of the mountain. The land—his plot of land—was terraced and covered with grape vines tied to wooden fences. An old man, squat and gnarled, was standing two terraces down, looking up. He had been watching them fuck.

* * * *

The layout of the house was straightforward. It had been restored on the inside with clean, modern lines, while the quaint village aged-stone style of it had been preserved on the outside. The entire mountain village was like this. Dinos said it was in the covenant of the place when the government had permitted foreigners to restore houses here for their use.

"I'm afraid it looks a bit like one of your pristine theme parks to a Cypriot. But you may view it anyway you like. You have to have money to live here. If it's young men you want, they will be attracted by knowing you live here."

If this was supposed to make Brian feel wanted by young men, it didn't. He wasn't really interested in being some young man's sugar daddy—not again. He'd done that and was done with that—if he could maintain his resolve. He had pulled on his trousers—but not his briefs—for the tour of the house. They both moved around shirtless and barefooted. Both of them knew that Dinos would fuck Brian again before he departed.

Where they had entered was essentially an open front porch notched out of the middle of the front of the two-room deep house. To the left upon entering the great room was a kitchen, separated from the great room by a counter. To the right was the master bedroom suite, with a full bath next to the entry porch and the master bedroom projecting out to the back of the house. The bathroom facilities were as modern as anything Brian had seen in the States. If anything, they were more stylish, in keeping with European tastes. The shower stall door, of course, was clear glass and the back wall of the stall also was glass, looking out onto a small rock-walled garden niche set in the side of the house.

"The bath is perfect for fucking, don't you think?" Dinos asked, giving Brian a sexy smile.

"Yes," Brian answered, more than half wanting Dinos to fuck him under cascading water from the shower head there and then—to press Brian's back against the rock wall at the foot of the shower and growl for Brian to climb his hips with his knees. They were both hard again, and Dinos was guiding Brian around with a grip on his buttocks.

But Dinos escorted Brian out of the master bedroom and back into the great room. To the left of the great room were two rooms, a bedroom and bath on the street side and an enclosed porch, with windows wrapping around two sides on the back side of the house. The deep balcony terrace, looking down the terraced mountainside and to the next mountain, ran the entire length of the back. The house had come fully furnished, just awaiting Brian's personal touches. Soon a walker and then a wheel chair, he thought bitterly, feeling a bit sorry for himself. How much longer, he wondered, could he stay as hard as he was for Dinos now—as hard as Dinos was staying for him?

"This will be perfect for my painting studio," Brian said, when he was shown the sun porch.

"Ah, yes, your painting," Dinos said. "Are you going to show me your paintings?"

"They should be in the container out front. When I've had them out, you certainly can see them."

"I'll help you unload the container then, shall I?"

"Surely that's not included in the service I've paid for," Brian said, with a little laugh.

"I am curious enough about your paintings that I'll be happy to do it. But, speaking of the service, I would like to show you the master bedroom again."

"You are very flexible. I do not think you should talk about being old again," Dinos whispered in Brian's ear as he fucked him from behind against the wall of the bedroom beside the doorway into the great room. Both Brian's feet and hands were pressed to the wall, his trousers on the floor under him, his buttocks projecting out from the wall, as Dinos stood behind him, one arm around his waist and the other running up his chest, his hand cupping Brian's chin, as he fucked up into Brian's channel.

Brian sensed movement at the door and looked around to see that the old man he'd previously seen in the vineyard was standing there, looking at them. He was several inches shorter than either Brian or Dinos, even if he weren't hunched over a bit, and was stocky. He was ugly as a gargoyle. He looked to be at least sixty. He stood there only for a couple of seconds and then withdrew.

"Who the fuck?" Brian exclaimed.

"That's Leonidas. You'll be calling him Leo."

"Why the fuck would I be calling him anything?" Brian said, breathless from the exertion of bearing back as Dinos thrust forward and up in the fuck.

"He works for you. He takes care of your vineyard. You won't have to do anything but drink the wine. He works the other vineyards on this hill too. And, in turn, he lives in your basement."

"My basement?"

"Yes, underneath us, opening to the hillside under the terrace. In old times it was where they sheltered their livestock. There's a flat down there now, and a wine cellar."

"I didn't see stairs."

"There are none inside the house. You have to go down and around."

"It didn't keep him out of the house."

"No, it didn't. He's here to help unload the container and set up whatever you brought with you. He'll have the run of the house. Incidentally, he has the thickest cock in the village, and he can keep it hard for hours."

"But he looks as old as the hills," Brian muttered.

"He has the thickest cock in the village and can keep it hard for hours," Dinos repeated. "Remember what I told you earlier. You need to give what I said about age and experience more thought."

There was no thinking then, just animal rutting as Dinos finished the fuck and let Brian slip to the floor in a puddle of satiation.

"Shall we do it in the shower now?" Dinos asked in a matter-of-fact voice. It was too soon for Dinos to be hard again, but, in the shower and whispering, "Experience is the master," in Brian's ear, he demonstrated how he could bring Brian to and past release again with his hand.

When the two finally emerged from the house, Leonidas was standing outside, beside the container, and helped unload it without a single word said on what he saw or a judgmental look or leer being directed by him at Brian.

"These paintings are magnificent," Dinos said as they were being moved to the sun porch. "Do you have a dealer set up here in Cyprus to handle them?"

"No, not yet," Brian answered, please that the Cypriot had praised his work.

"Our offices are down in Limassol. There are galleries there—good ones. We can help you get displayed there."

"As part of the travel agency services?" Brian asked. "Isn't that stretching the agency's services a bit far?"

"I like to see how far I can stretch . . . services," Dinos answered, giving Brian a meaningful look and causing Brian to blush despite his age and look to where Leonidas was to see if he heard and understood. He was close enough to have heard, but he gave no discernible reaction. "And my services continue as long as I am getting pleasure out of them," Dinos added. "My whole life isn't spent on the travel agency's clock. This is Cyprus. Personal pleasure has priority."

* * * *

"You want him. You want to fuck him, don't you?"

"I do fantasize him fucking me," Brian answered, turning his attention from the beautiful young guitarist back to Dinos. They were on the patio of a taverna in Phini, strung with fairy lights that kept traveling up into the deep blue night sky, the air crisp and clear in the mountains. The guitarist, setting in the corner of the patio on a barstool, a light shining on his tumbling black curls from above, was much the same as the guitarist from the previous night, the one who had looked past Brian with a smile for another man. This guitarist had a smile for everyone on the patio, though, including Brian. He was smarter than the guitarist from the night before. He understood what produced tips. "But that's not going to happen."

"What isn't that going to happen?" Dinos asked.

"I'm old; he's young. He has a young lover—male or female, I don't know—or an established sugar daddy. But he looks too content not to have a lover."

"He's a whore," Dinos says. "He makes more money from fucking—yes, either man or woman—than he does from playing his guitar here. You aren't too old for him—you could only be too poor for him, which you aren't. You are still a handsome man with a great body. He would fuck you and enjoy it. All you have to do is to slip a fifty euro note in his tip bucket and smile at him. Then wait until his evening is finished. He will follow you home and fuck you. And he will be pleased to do you. He would do that three or four times a week for as long as you wanted, just as long as you had money to give him. That would answer your concern, wouldn't it? You can afford him."

"I don't pay for fucking, and I am too old for young men."

"I told you you were very flexible this afternoon. I meant it. It's flexibility and attitude and conditioning, not physical age, that count. And why not pay for it if you want it? Why deny yourself pleasure if you have the money? You are an American—and a rich one. We ran your credit rating before taking your business. You want him inside you, don't you? Marcos has a very nice cock. I have fucked men with him before."

"You've fucked men with him before?"

"Yes. You have been with two men at once before, haven't you?"

"Yes—but when I was younger."

"Pay him. We will fuck you together. You are only as old as you want to be. You have the money, you have the desire, and I've told you that you are attractive enough for him to enjoying fucking you. Why begrudge him the money if he needs it? You have paid me, and I've fucked you repeatedly today. Did you not enjoy it? Do you doubt that I enjoyed it? And, still, I won't turn down my salary from the travel agency to be here with you. Don't be old. Be satisfied."

Brian hesitated, but after a few minutes he rose. Why the hell not, he thought, teetering again on that edge, but what was on the other side of the fence not looking as bleak and threatening and defeating as before. What if he got a look of rejection when he dropped the money in the bucket, though? He'd be crushed. He'd fall off the edge.

He walked over to the tip bucket beside the guitarist and dropped a fifty-euro note in it. He looked up into Marcos' eyes and received a smile and a tip of the head in return. There was no sign of distaste or reluctance.

Marcos lay on his back at the end of the bed, his feet flat on the floor. Brian was straddling the young guitarist's pelvis, facing him, leveraging on his bent knees as he rose and fell on the hard shaft. Dinos had been right. Marcos had a very nice cock. Marcos, his curly black hair fanned out around his head, was holding Brian's waist between his hands and watching the expressions on Brian's face with dreamy eyes. His mouth was set in a sensual smile. Brian was scrutinizing Marcos' face just as closely, looking for any sign of distaste or boredom. He found none. And when he dipped his face down to Marcos' for a kiss, he was met with open, welcoming lips, and a sweet, deep kiss.

There was nothing to be discerned in Marcos' demeanor to indicate that he was getting anything but complete pleasure out of the fuck.

Dinos slid in from the shadows of the corner of the room where he'd been watching Brian riding Marcos' cock. He was as naked as they were. All three of them had beautiful bodies—Dinos' and Brian's bodies were just more solid, more mature, the form of a Zeus to Marcos' Adonis. Dinos moved in close behind Brian. He cupped Brian's chin and turned the American's head to the side, taking his mouth in a kiss. Marcos reached down, cupped Brian's cock, and began to stroke it. One of Dinos' arms went around Brian's chest; his other hand went to his own cock.

Brian began to struggle within Dinos' embrace and to try to break out of the kiss as Dinos worked his cock inside Brian's passage on top of Marcos' already-buried staff. Fully sheathed, Dinos held for a moment and then began to pump Brian's channel. Feeling the rub of Dinos' cock, Marcos began to stroke as well. Dinos let loose of Brian and Brian bent over Marcos, fists buried in the bedspread at either side of Marcos' arms, panting hard to fight off hyperventilation, moaning and groaning in response to the play of two cocks inside him, building up to an explosion—an explosion of cum the likes of Vesuvius.

His mind went back, with pleasure, to a beach and two hunky Turkish men walking toward him.

* * * *

207

Brian had the entire next day to himself. Neither Dinos nor Marcos were there. It had taken him no time at all to unpack and make the house his. The afternoon was free to set up a canvas in his sunroom and begin to paint. Naturally enough, he painted the terraced vineyard descending from the back of his house. And also naturally enough the scene included a bent-over old Cypriot working in the field. Leonidas.

What Dinos had said about Leonidas and his attributes kept running through Brian's mind. There had been so much to absorb over the past two days, though. Too much, really. All of his pouts and life-ending decisions had been exploded in his face. Well, most of them. Dinos was younger than he was. Not by much, but younger. He still was settled on having younger men or nothing. Dinos getting him over the hurdle of paying for it had opened the sunshine over his life, though. That wouldn't be bad—as long as young men didn't laugh at him even when he offered them money for sex. He'd spent time in front of the mirror again this morning. It would be years, he figured, before he was the gargoyle that Leonidas, out working in the vineyard, was. There was no reason why he should ever be as work-worn as Leonidas was.

That night he went back to the taverna for a late supper—late for him, quite obviously not late for the Cypriots, who were just starting to show up when he was finishing. Marcos wasn't there. He wasn't playing that night. Brian was almost relieved. He'd been drawn to Marcos, like a moth to the flame, but he knew he couldn't have him every night. It was just the residual panic that he was running out of time—that he wouldn't be desirable to a young man for long even if he paid for it. He fantasized about the young man not being able to get it up for him—him not being able to make a young man hard. And then he kept telling himself that he wasn't teetering on that edge anymore, that that edge was still a distance away and that he should stop agonizing over it.

He went home, took a long shower, and climbed, naked, into his bed. It was almost a relief to have the bed all to himself.

He had no idea what time it was when he woke. He just knew it was pitch dark and someone was grasping his ankles and pulling him down toward the foot of the bed. He opened his mouth to call down.

"Don't cry out. I will fuck you good." The voice was heavily accented, but he'd heard it before. Leonidas.

He was turned on the bed, urged up to his hands and knees, seized from behind, and then he did cry out and squirm, briefly trying to pull away, but the man was much too strong for him. Leonidas was working his cock inside Brian's passage. The cock was as thick if not thicker than Dino's and Marcos' together. It was all Brian could do to concentrate on opening for the man, stretching, and taking him in. Brian was panting hard and groaning. Leonidas was grunting at getting it all inside Brian, He reached around and grasped Brian's balls and the root of his cock in a strong, heavily calloused hand. He squeezed, making Brian's eyes water and his mouth jabber, begging for mercy. None was to come, and Brian was turned to sobbing jelly as Leonidas began to pump him.

And to pump him and pump him. Each time Brian was ready to blow, Leonidas sensed this and stopped, dead, holding Brian close, not permitting him to move a muscle, holding them both in suspension, teetering on the edge of coming, until the need for release had passed. Then he resumed a steady pumping and the rolling and squeezing of Brian's balls, as well as the squeezing of the base of his cock.

Panting, panting, panting, groaning and moaning, whining for release, begging for mercy, for completion, Brian felt himself ready to ejaculate again. But again, the masterful, experienced cocksman held him in abeyance, whispering that he didn't have permission to come yet. Then, when the need had passed, Brian's balls aching, the pumping resumed. He was taken to the edge and held off, taken to the edge and held off, until he was exhausted, putty in Leonidas' hands, completely conquered.

He let out a whimper and a sigh and was permitted to collapse on the bed, completely taken, totally spent, when Leonidas allowed him to come, and, a master at the fuck, came himself simultaneously.

Brian's murmur of "I . . . have . . . never . . . been taken so fully before" got choked off by the realization that Leonidas had come, but he was still hard.

"Oh fuck, oh shit," Brian murmured, as the old man clamped his arm around Brian's waist, pulling him back up on all fours, and began to pump him again.

All of Brian's "never again will" declarations were dispelled. He no longer was teetering on the edge of anything. He was soaring out over the edge into a new life.

And he didn't give a shit.

Business Cruise

"I don't think you'll find it that easy. I think . . . oh, here they are."

Randy broke off his sentence and went into a pose at the semicircular banquette seat in the dimly lit hotel bar. He'd drawn attention to the entrance of the bar, where three men were standing, about to enter. I knew one of them, of course—Angelo, my pimp. He was Randy's and my pimp to be more exact. The other two evidently were the two businessmen he'd lined Randy and me up to service. This was their hotel. Some sort of car parts manufacturing convention was going on here at this Baltimore hotel.

One of the men looked like he'd attend this sort of auto parts convention—big boned and big bodied, a blustery sort of guy, with a crooked nose, borderline ugly, florid face, and balding. He wore his suit uncomfortably, like he was more accustomed to be in coveralls on the assembly line. Looks were deceiving, I knew, though. I wouldn't blow him off as being the lesser of the two for a big tip. He didn't look like he did this regularly—more like the guilty feeling it would give him would loosen up his wallet for a good tip.

The other guy looked like he worked out a lot and would give a guy a good workout—like he'd expect good service without expectation of a guilt tip. He looked like he thought a lot of himself and spent a lot of time to make sure that others thought a lot of him too—muscular, walking on the balls of his feet, wavy, well-groomed hair, a carefully groomed permanent five-o'clock shadow look popular with male models. The first guy looked to be in his late forties, the "looker" appearing to be late thirties, but probably five years older than he looked.

Angelo? Well, he was thin and wiry, sneaky looking—sneaky more than in looks, though—appearing to be every bit the slimy two-bit hood that he was. Alligator shoes, sharkskin suit—reptilian in every way.

As they approached, both johns looking Randy and me over well, I wondered, as I always did when I went out on a job with another rent-boy, how the two would make their pick. Randy and I were much the same in appearance—both bottle blonds, with good faces and bodies. But where Randy was a bit boyish and undersized, I was more solid, a bit taller and more muscular. I'd been told we had the same, welcoming smile, but my eyes were hazel and Randy's a watery blue. Of the two, I think Randy would give the impression of submitting to be manhandled, overwhelmed, quickly surrendering, whereas I'd provide more exercise and sass.

This being the case, I guess I wasn't surprised that the older guy slid in beside Randy and the younger athlete beside me. Angelo sat on a stool at the open end of the banquette. "John and John," he said, indicating the two johns. Neither Randy nor I were surprised they both were named John—or so we were told. I quickly thought of my guy as John 1 and Randy's as John 2. "Steve and Mike," he then said, pointing to me as Steve and Randy as Mike. Not our real names either. John 2 repeated our names and John 1 just nodded knowingly, once again indicating that John 2 was a neophyte at this and John 1 wasn't.

Angelo stayed around for one drink and until the two Johns signaled they were satisfied and each passed him $200. Randy and I'd each get $75 of that. If we didn't like the split, that was just tough. Early on I'd complained about that and the split I got was a lip.

The four of us had another drink and some nervous small talk. The older guy wanted a third drink and was ordering, when John 1 said, "I've had enough drink. Want to see my room, Steve?"

"Sure," I said, and we left Randy and John 2 in the bar. I didn't really think they'd last the third drink, though. Randy wanted to get on with it and move on to doing something else tonight. He had his hand on John 2's basket under the cocktail table, and I could see that the old guy was heating up.

John 1 was as athletic, demanding, and impersonal as I'd thought he would be. He was just there for the exercise and to get off. He had a good body and a fine cock. I didn't have any trouble performing for him. After we were naked with some standing in a clutch, undressing each other, and frotting our cocks hard while kissing, he sat down at the foot of the bed, spread his legs, pressed me down to a kneeling position, and held my head in position while I sucked his cock.

We then went through a see-saw progression of him lifting me and settling me on his cock in his lap, facing him, and me bouncing on his shaft until he growled for me to reach back for the carpet. I arched back, with my head and hands pressed to the floor and him pulling me off and on his cock with a strong hand grip on my hips. At his command, I raised my torso, he lay back on the bed, and I rode the shaft for a while. Then, on command, I arched back to the floor for him to take over the fuck for a while. Eventually, he told me to come and I did, and then he came inside me in his condom.

This was where the surprise came in, though. As I was building up to come, I heard a card key in the door, and John 2 entered the room. He had trousers and a shirt on but not for long. As John 1 finished me, John 2 was getting naked and pulling on his cock. The two of them were pulling a two-fer. John 1 pushed me off onto the floor, got up and pulled on his trousers and shirt and went out the door—to go do Randy, I gathered.

I gathered that, because John 2 then did me. He wasn't either the athlete or the looker that John 1 was, and he had a paunch on him. But he also had the thicker, longer cock, and he made the most of it. He was all business and in it for a quick and efficient ejaculation. He hauled me up from the floor, bent me over, belly to bed, mounted and penetrated me, and took me hard in a fast, deep pump as he grasped my hips with his hands.

I thought that was going to be it, but it wasn't. John 2 wanted his blow job after the fuck, and then he wanted another fuck, this time pushing me onto the bed at the foot on my back, slapping my legs apart, and taking me in a swift missionary position.

He gave me a good tip afterward—even considering they'd taken a two-fer—and gruffly told me in one breath that I'd been a good lay and in the next to dress and get out of his room.

I went back down to the hotel bar, where Angelo was waiting for us. Randy wasn't there. I wasn't surprised. Whereas John 2 was a "bang-bang, thanks and get out" kind of client, John 1 got his exercise in a fuck. But I was wrong. Randy had already come down to the bar and left the hotel. I knew this because of what Angelo said next.

"Randy tells me you plan on cutting loose and going back to Philadelphia."

"Thinking about it, yeah," I answered guardedly. I knew he wouldn't take it well, which is why I hadn't said anything to him about it yet. I hadn't planned to tell him at all; I'd planned just to split and disappear. I had been a fool to mention it to Randy. Earlier in the evening was the first time I'd mentioned it to anyone. "There's a Chippendales show forming there at a club and I've been offered a place on the line," I offered.

"Here, come with me a minute," Angelo said, rising from his seat at the bar. I already was standing or maybe I wouldn't have been so easy for him to move out of the bar and to the men's room. In the men's room, he sucker punched me—one to the solar plexus when I wasn't expecting it and an upper cut to my chin as I was going down. He hauled me by my hair, pushed me into a stall, locked it behind us, slammed my head into the porcelain tank top a couple of times to daze me further, jerked my trousers down, mounted me, and fucked me hard.

After he'd come, he grabbed my hair again, his other hand gripping one of my wrists and pulling my arm high and painfully up my back, slammed my head into the toilet tank again, and muttered, "You'll leave when I tell you you can go. Not before. Got that?"

Yeah, I got that message.

It wasn't as bad as it might seem. The beating wasn't to my liking, but Angelo fucked just fine. I was whining for it while he was fucking me. It was his cocking more than anything else that kept me with him.

* * * *

"Get in the car. You're going on a cruise."

I had been walking down the street out of the Fells Point area toward the inner harbor. It was still morning, but I wanted to get into the Fourth of July mood in the inner harbor early and keep in the mood through the fireworks over Fort McHenry, the origin of the national anthem, across the inner harbor from the promenade. The old, red Cadillac convertible, Angelo in the driver's seat, top down—both the convertible and Angelo—had pulled up beside me.

"Day off. It's a holiday, Angelo. I want to see the fireworks."

"You get a holiday when I say you do," Angelo said. "And if you want to see fireworks, I'll show you fireworks. Get in the car. You've got a gig. Six guys in a fishing boat—all for you. Good pay. Get in the fuckin' car," he commanded once more.

I opened the passenger door, slid in, and closed the door behind me.

"This is about last night, isn't it?" I said. "About me telling Randy I was going to leave. I was just kidding him, Angelo." I wasn't, of course, but my ears were still ringing from where they'd hit the porcelain in the hotel restroom. I was reconsidering my options. I shouldn't have told him where I was planning to go. If I went there now, he could find me.

"Maybe, maybe not," Angelo answered. "Either way, this is a gig you're not going to forget."

He was right.

We didn't talk. He was driving fast and we were in a convertible, buffeted by wind and making more of its "I'm too old to be handled like this" structural sounds. He got on the Baltimore beltway and then off on 173, exiting into the Stony Point area and to a marina on the Patapsco River that leads into the Chesapeake Bay. There wasn't much activity at the marina because most of the holiday voters had already shoved off and either had sailed up into the inner harbor to join in the festivities there or down into the Chesapeake Bay for the day. Only one yacht was being prepared to be taken out, and it obviously was the one I was going on. There were six thuggish, beefy guys milling around either doing something awkwardly enough to indicate they weren't sailors or standing with cigars in their mouths, watching the others doing something.

My heart skipped a beat. Even though we weren't real close to them, thuggish had entered my mind mainly because, although all were just in shorts and were hairy, beefy guys ranging from their late twenties into the forties, all had shoulder holsters on with guns at their armpits. If any guys looked like mafia, these were them.

As Angelo pulled up to the end of the dock, two guys peeled off from the pier beside the yacht and walked back to us. One guy was tall and heavy, beefy and hairy. He was mean looking, his nose looking like it had met a few too many fists, but the look of him making me think that whoever had hit him had gotten the worst of the beating. The other guy was muscular, but not fat. He also was a lot better looking. Still, he looked Italian—Sicilian even—and ready to win a fight. He too was matted with hair, but on him it looked stylish and sexy—black and curly, not so thick that you couldn't see the hard body, and puffed up nipples, under it. Mean Looking went around to Angelo's side of the car; Better Looking came around to my side.

216

Better Looking opened the passenger door and I stepped out, while Angelo said something to Mean Looking. I was looking into the eyes of Better Looking, wondering if he was going to top me, thinking from the way he was looking at me that he was, and if he was hung when his eyes opened wide, staring past me, and I heard to the two pops. Mean Looking's gun must have had a silencer on it, because I didn't immediately identify the pops with gunshots. I felt something sticky on my arm, though. I looked down. It was red—blood. Looking around, I saw Angelo slump over toward the passenger seat, his eyes open and dead looking. Mean Looking was standing there with his gun out.

I doubled over and wretched next to the passenger door, after which Better Looking grabbed me by the arms and started to hustle me onto the dock and toward the yacht. "Why'd you fuckin' do that, Salvo," he yelled as he herded me.

"He demanded twice what Tony said we were paying for the whore," Mean Looking answered, like that justified his reaction.

I was in shock and too drained to move on my own. Better Looking, who was addressed as Nick as I was being manhandled onto the yacht, was doing all of the moving. In short order I was pushed below, into the bowels of the yacht, and to a small cabin, where I was dropped on a bunk that took up most of the space. Nick withdrew from the cabin, but as he did, Mean Looking—Salvo—pushed his way inside. He was still brandishing his gun and there was a wild-eyed look in his eyes. There was something else there too—something that was like satisfaction and lust from a kill. I knew this man liked killing things.

Pointing the gun at me, he commanded, "Strip down," in a growl. Fumbling and numb, I did so. He had a cock out of his fly in no time flat. He was hard. Killing a man had made him hard.

After reaching down, grasping my ankles, and jerking my legs apart, he lay on top of me, his good two hundred and fifty pounds pinning me to the bed. His knees pressed between mine, keeping my legs spread apart. One of his hands gripped my throat and the other one held his gun, pointed to my head. I yelped and groaned as he entered me, dry and raw. He fucked me hard, settling down to a rhythm and losing some of his animal lust as he pounded me. He didn't lose the gun he was holding to my head, though.

"Show me you want it. Fuck yourself on it," he demanded, and went up on his knees, his cock withdrawing from me with just the bulb inside me. "Show me I don't want to do you. Fuck me good." Trembling and moaning from fright as much as anything, I bent my knees, put my feet flat on the bed, and started fucking myself on his hard shaft. He was thick, and as I moved my pelvis and opened to him, my rhythm became more steady and my moans were more about the cock inside me than my fear. I turned my cheek to the bed, lifted my arms for the first time, and grasped the back of his head, running my fingers into his greasy hair. I had half a notion to go for the gun, but I knew there was little chance of surviving that. And a part of me wanted him to come inside me too—to finish me raw and make me come as well. It was an exciting feeling for a man to come inside me if the decision wasn't mine—if I wasn't given any chance to weigh in on the safety of it.

He laughed. "Yeah, I knew you wanted it," he muttered.

"Fuck me," I murmured.

"What was that? Say it louder. Yell it."

"Fuck me! Screw me to the bed! Fuck my lights out! Give me your cum!" I cried out, arching my back. With another laugh, he placed his free hand on the small of my back, pressing my butt up to his crotch, and took over the fuck. Now that he was inside me and taking over the fuck, fucking me good, I concentrated on that more than on the danger I was in.

This was why I was a rent-boy—because I liked having men inside me, plowing me. And some of the tension drained out of me—not all, not by any means—and I settled into the fuck, moving with him, responding to the raw intimacy of the barebacking, which I preferred and felt no guilt over under these circumstances. He felt it too—I could tell. He was groaning in harmony with me and loosening his grip on me, reaching for my cock and stroking me off as he fucked, knowingly giving me pleasure too. But just as he was loosening up on me to the point of me wondering again if I should make a grab for the gun, he came in a flood of cum and pressed the barrel of the gun to my temple.

Better Looking—Nick—appeared at the door. "Knock it off, Salvo, and leave him be."

"He saw. He's a witness, Nick."

"He's also the guy we bought to service Tony. What'll you say if Tony asks for his lay and you have to say you splattered his brains all over the cabin wall? Where we gonna get another lay for Tony before we have to cast off? Leave him be for now."

Salvo climbed off me, backed out of the cabin, and closed the door, locking me in. I lay there, working at not hyperventilating, trying to calm myself. When the ringing stopped in my ears, I realized that the yacht was moving.

* * * *

The cabin door opened. I felt a flood of relief that it was Nick rather than Salvo.

"If you can hold yourself together and do what you have to do, you can come topside," he growled, not smiling. "You're here to service Tony. He's the one with the cigar. If you can't behave, I'll move you to Tony's cabin and he'll deal with you later. You won't like the result."

"I can manage," I said. I almost added, "If you can keep that Salvo animal away from me," but I didn't think Nick would see the point of that. I'd yelled how good Salvo was fucking me while he was doing it loud enough for everyone on the ship to hear me.

"OK, then. Put this on." He tossed a white thong bikini swimsuit to me—just a pouch in front and a string running up the crack behind. He was wearing just a Speedo himself, and he was looking in great shape.

He watched me as I put it on, his eyes plastered to my crotch. I brushed past him but then stood in the narrow corridor, close to him, feeling the heat of his body, seeing that he was hard, and letting him go up the ladder to the yacht deck in front of me. We paused briefly, long enough for him to grab a kiss and a grope. I knew he wanted to fuck me. I'd do what I could to play on that.

Topside, the five other guys were lined up at the railing with fishing poles. Only the oldest of them, nearly bald, with salt-and-pepper hair all over him everywhere else, was sitting in a chair bolted to the deck. He was short and pot-bellied and was smoking a cigar, so I knew he was Tony. The boat was anchored in deep water. I could barely see a coastline to the west. We couldn't have gotten any farther than the Chesapeake Bay, but, for all I knew, we were still in the Patapsco River.

"Come here, you little fucker. Give me luck," Tony called out. He was gesturing at me with a meaty paw. I went over to him, and he pulled me in between his legs, facing the water, letting me perch a bit on his raised-seat chair. His crotch was pressed against my virtually bare buttocks. He wasn't going hard, which I thought should be the effect if I was here for him to fuck. I wondered if he'd need drugs to get it up.

The six guys already were talking business, their business seeming to have something to do with a rival gang in Jersey, across the river from New York City. There seemed to be a problem of a turf war. They talked about rubbing this guy and that guy out—either that they had already done so and were discussing the possible fallout from that or they were weighing the merits of doing so and discussing the possible fallout of that. This wasn't good for me—that they were so openly discussing this in my presence.

Other than riding herd on the discussion, not making suggestions but either taking them under advisement or shooting them down with his reasons, Tony was interested in the fishing. He wanted to land a big one. I came in for third in his attention. He clearly was interested in me, though. I could feel him going hard inside his shorts now—he just took a while to go hard, which relieved me on the drug need question—and he was pawing me. But he did so absentmindedly, as if I didn't rank high in his list of priorities. Since he obviously was the big cheese here, I needed him to need me, so I let my hands wander and he showed a little more interest.

Someone down the line—a guy named Mario, who appeared to be Tony's lieutenant and was in his late thirties, in pretty good condition, but as hairy and thuggish as the rest, caught a fish. That turned their conversation off business and all were intent on catching something. Salvo caught a fish and then a young guy, thinner than the rest, not yet fully thuggish, caught one. This seemed to make Tony a bit mad—that the thug in training had caught a fish and he hadn't. He pushed me off his lap, ready to concentrate more seriously on catching a fish.

"You ain't bringing me no luck," he said. "Go sun yourself or something."

"Up on top," Nick said. "On top of the bridge." He pointed to where there was a ladder ascending the side of the bridge house above the main salon.

So, I went up there. Nick handed me a towel and gave me a wink as I passed him. I hadn't been stretched out on my back on the towel for long, before he joined me. He stretched his body out alongside mine, cupped my neck with one hand, bringing my mouth to his for a deep kiss, and ran the other hand down my body. I shuddered, still keyed up over the danger I was in, but wanting him. He took one of my hands and ran it under the waistband of his Speedo. He was hard and huge—both long and thick. He pulled the waistband of the Speedo down under his balls, and we continued to kiss as I stroked his cock.

He groaned and rolled over on top of me. As he did so, I spread my legs, rolled up my pelvis, hooked my ankles on his calves and, pushing my hands underneath his Speedo in back, pushed the suit to below his buttocks and palmed his meaty butt cheeks. He had no trouble moving the string of the bikini out of my crack and slowly pushed himself inside me. He held deep inside me, waiting for me to heat up and beg for him, which I did.

"You're a stud," I whimpered. "Move it inside me. Fuck me."

We rocked against each other as he slow fucked me.

I arched my back and opened my mouth to cry out as he ejaculated—almost simultaneously with me doing so—but he pressed his hand over my mouth to stifle my voice. His ejaculation went on for several seconds, coming in waves, each wave sending me higher over the moon. Like Salvo before him, he was barebacking me. Like with Salvo, it was much more exciting and satisfying for me to feel his releases inside me.

Without taking his hand away from my mouth, he lowered his lips to my ear and whispered, "Be quiet. Don't let them know I'm here. I'll get you out of this. Trust me. I'm a cop. I'll get you out of this somehow. I'm on top of you because someone could look up here and this is a better excuse then admitting what I've told you."

"I hoped you were on top of me—inside me— because you wanted to be," I murmured.

"That too," he answered.

I lay there, under him, in his firm embrace, absorbing what he said, hope flooding in. I felt him going hard again, and when he moved his mouth to mine this time, I opened entirely to him, taking his tongue inside sucking on it, as I felt him engorging.

"Fuck me. Fuck me again," I whispered when we came out of the kiss. "It'll be better, easier knowing you aren't one of them."

He gave a low laugh. "You *are* a needy little whore, aren't you?" And then, when I didn't answer, he said, "You. Fuck yourself. Ride it yourself."

He pulled away from me and turned on his back. I straddled his pelvis, facing his bent legs, grasping his knees, and rode his cock. After a few minutes of this, he pushed me down onto my belly, twisted around without dislodging his cock, and fucked down into my hole from the reverse, him grasping my ankles and me grasping his. He finished me with him on his back and me on top of him, looking up at the sky, while he held my arms trapped in a full Nelson and laced his legs around mine, spreading and lifting them as he fucked up into my channel.

At dinner, the six of them huddled over a coffee table in the salon, eating pizza the apprentice thug had cooked, and talking once again about who they needed to whack off to feel safe in doing their rackets in Jersey. I perched at the bar, still concerned that they were freely discussing all of this in front of me.

There was more posturing and arguing that night than there had been out on deck in the afternoon. That afternoon when they got close to a boiling point, someone got a strike on his fishing pole and the argument was stifled. There was no fishing pause this evening. The apparent lieutenant, Mario, was arguing for whacking the whole rival family, including women and children. Tony argued that this would bring unknown extended family over from New York and they'd be in a full-scale war then. Mario countered with, "And we'll blow them all away too."

Nick stepped in to suggest they all simmer down and talk about it again in the morning, before sailing on up the Delaware Canal to New Jersey. No one mentioned taking the yacht—or me—back to Baltimore, and I was getting the impression that they'd stolen the yacht and had no intention of going back to where Angelo was slumped over in the front seat of his vintage Cadillac convertible with two bullet holes in his head. He undoubtedly had been found by now anyway, although the fireworks in the inner harbor would not have started yet.

"I think tomorrow is a good time to resume this discussion," Tony said, standing, giving an evil-eye look at Mario and another look at Salvo, which no one present seemed to miss. "Time for sleep," he said. He motioned to me when he'd said that.

"Sleep?" the apprentice thug blurted out, which got him a dirty look too, but not the menacing look Tony had given. The other men in the room couldn't help sniggering, and Tony's gaze swept the gathering. I sensed that there was some sort of power struggle going on here—but I didn't want to think about the dynamics in this gang any more than I had to. I meekly followed Tony down to the lower level and into the largest of the bedroom cabins. It was well appointed and dominated by a free-standing queen-sized bed.

The bed pretty much filled the space. I understood what it was for and why we were here. I knelt between Tony's legs as he sat, dressed only in his cigar and his gun holster, and sucked his cock. He was small, almost unseeable in the thick salt-and-pepper thatch of his pubic hair when flaccid, but he thickened and lengthened a bit as I took the cock in my mouth, rolled it around, got the balls in there too, and gave him a hummer.

I rode him, facing him, then, thankfully without having a cigar in the way, when I dipped down to kiss him and then further down to dig his nipples out of this chest thatch with my tongue and give them suck. His grunts and groans told me he was having a good time. When he came, barebacking as the others had, I rolled off him and he gathered me into his side in an embrace that had my head tucked into his neck. He was snoring almost immediately. I could have reached over and taken his gun, I suppose, but a strap was secured over it. I didn't know what to do with a gun, and I was quite sure he did. I realized it would be crazy to try anything. Maybe I would have felt differently before Nick told me he was a cop and would get me out of this. I had stopped looking for escape routes after he'd done that. I hadn't even given another look at the small motorboat hanging off the stern of the yacht. I wouldn't know how to drive a motorboat either. If I got out of this mess, I told myself there were some things I would have to learn in life. I'd known that prostitution was a dangerous occupation before I'd gotten myself into this mess.

Tony woke, turned me away from him onto my side, pulled me close and presented his cock, hard again in my butt crack. I rolled up my buttocks to him and reached back, held him in position, and took him inside me. He was long enough to rub against my prostate, so it was good enough for me to give him the response he wanted. He reached around with a beefy paw and stroked my cock. I moved against the cock enough to give him the friction he needed to come again and he went back to sleep, going flaccid, and thus virtually disappearing, inside me.

The gun shot temporarily deafened me. It had hit right behind my head—into Tony's head. Blood spurted all over the place. With a scream, I instinctive rolled away from Tony's body. Mario was standing on the other side of the bed, the smoking gun in his hand. The thug apprentice, the sixth guy whose name I never heard, and Nick poured into the cabin.

"Throw him over the side," Mario growled, and the apprentice and Noname came to the bed and hustled up Tony's body between them. Nick stood in the doorway, looking now at Mario and then at me, indecisive. But then he turned and followed the other two, lugging the body, out into the corridor.

Mario, giving me an evil smile—the blood lust expression on his face no different from the one that had been on Salvo's face after he'd shot Angelo, stalked around the bed and toward me, where I was plastered, naked, against the bulkhead. He was holding his gun at the ready, pointed down rather than at me, but only a minor adjustment would be required to raise it.

"No, no, please," I whimpered. "I won't tell anyone." That was a nonsensical answer, I knew, but I could think of nothing else to plead my case. I sank to the deck of the cabin, making myself as small a target as I could, knowing even then that that too was just silliness.

I closed my eyes, half wondering if I'd even hear the next gunshot. But a few seconds went by without a change. So I opened my eyes. He was standing there, smiling, his dick out now. He was stroking it. He dropped the gun on the bed and moved to me, needing only a step and a half to be there. He reached down, pulled me up, pressed me up to the wall, and insinuated his pelvis into my crotch. He felt his hard on pressing at my lower belly.

"What was Tony's is now mine," he muttered. "Straddle my hips."

Whimpering, but realizing that I had a few more moments to live, I climbed his hips with my legs, and locked my fists behind his neck. Reaching down, he positioned his cock and then cruelly thrust up inside me, as I arched my back and cried out.

He fucked him hard, fast, deep, vigorously, and, like a dog in heat, I opened to him, took the full measure of him, and moved my pelvis with his. When he took my mouth in his and brutally kissed me, I opened to him and sucked on his tongue. When he released my mouth, I moved my face down to his chest, teased his nipples out of his chest hair, and sucked on them. He banged me hard and I came for him. And then he came in me and let me sink to the floor.

He laughed, took one step away to reach for the gun that he'd dropped on the bed. "No hard feelings, guy. You're a great lay, but you know what I gotta do."

Yes, of course I knew. It's just that none of this could be real. None of this could be happening to me.

Nick, standing in the door of the cabin, blew him away with three shots. Mario gave a look of surprise and dropped like a rock on the deck beside me. He lifeless eyes looked into mine, seemingly forming the questions, "What?" and "Why?"

Giving me a nod, Nick disappeared from the doorway. I heard a flurry of shots and then there he was again. I watched as he picked up a lighter from next to the cigar sitting in a tray on the built-in dresser and lit up the bedspread and the curtains on the portholes.

"Come with me," he commanded, and I sluggishly stood and followed him out of the door. He dipped into two other cabins to light up material and then we were on the deck.

The bodies of Salvo, the apprentice thug, and Noname were lying about on the deck. I stood, numb and unable to take it all in as Nick winched down the motorboat at the stern of the yacht and the flames built up strength in the superstructure behind me.

* * * *

226

"What? We've run out of gas?" I asked stupidly. The motor had stopped and we were wallowing a good distance away from the burning yacht, but not close to shore yet.

"No. We can continue in a bit. But I'm hard for you. I can't resist you."

I looked into his eyes. The flames from the yacht lit the area up enough that I could see his expression. Blood lust. The same sexual high from killing men that I'd seen in Salvo's eyes and then Mario's.

Nick reached out for me, and turned me away from him. We both were on our knees in the center of the motorboat. He embraced me around the belly with one arm and his other hand cupped my chin and pulled my head back him so that we were cheek to cheek. He had placed his gun on the deck in front of me. He ran his fingers into my hair and pulled my face around to his, his grip painful enough for me that I grimaced as he took my mouth with his. His dick was hard, thick, and long, pressing into and running up the small of my back. I raised my buttocks so that the shaft descended and moved into position. It was not so much that he entered me as that I pulled him inside me.

But then he cruelly thrust upward inside me, burying himself deep. I pulled away from the kiss and cried out. He gripped me close, painfully, though, and fucked me hard, brutally. He pulled my head to the side painfully with a yank of my hair and buried his teeth into the side of my throat. He was drawing blood and sucking it out of me.

He was fucking me hard. He released his hold on my throat, but not on my hair. He pushed me down onto all fours on the deck, my hands down as well as my knees, and he mounted my ass at a higher angle, crouching over me now on his feet, thrusting harder, deeper. His hand was buried in my hair, cruelly bowing my torso back to him. I was staring at the burning yacht and crying out for mercy, while not really wanting it. I was getting the fuck of my life.

My hand touched the hand grip of his gun.

Was he really a cop, saving me? Or was he just another thug, feeding me a line, and preparing to plug me and toss me overboard when he was done with me?

A cop or a thug? The lady or the tiger? I moved my hand over the pistol grip.

Decisions, decisions.

I could feel him coming close to exploding. I certainly was going to jack off any second now.

Decisions, decisions.

Iran in USA

"It isn't over until it's over, fucker." Chris bumped my shoulder as he passed me, almost dumping me in the pool at the Natatorium. I'd say his expression was a mix of disappointment, determination, and more than a bit of a sneer. I said nothing, and I didn't respond to the aggression. I'm not sure I would have felt or reacted differently if I'd been just below the cut-off line and he'd been just above it.

It's not that I didn't think I deserved my place on the U.S. Olympic men's diving team. I thought I was the best diver in the United States, and I'd had stats from Stanford that made that at least arguable. But the trials here in Indianapolis hadn't been the greatest for me, whereas Chris Fair had outdone himself. By my accounting, we'd come out equal in the trials stats—both on the cusp of being selected or not. The judges must have weighed in past performances, as I think was right, and they picked me over Chris.

I didn't take Chris' warning lightly that it wasn't over yet, though. He'd been named an alternate when we'd met one last time in Indianapolis for the Olympic squad to start jelling, to get our training schedule, and to do a few dives for the coaches to look at and critique. And he'd been here, breathing down my neck as the guy who would be going to Rio if something happened and I didn't make it. That brought a whole new meaning to him nudging me toward the side of the pool when he'd brushed by me.

He could have pinned his hopes on any of the other team members not making it, but he seemed extra resentful that I was on the team and he wasn't. If there was going to be a "convenient" accident that worked in Chris' favor, I was pretty sure it was going to be mine.

Chris had been a collegiate competitor of mine for three years, and we both felt the competition, and neither one of us had any love to give the other. I thought Chris was devious, and I—and others—were careful around him in competition. None of the guys put it past him to give us that nudge in passing that would make us slip, fall, and break something. I was sure, though, that, if it was going to happen, it would be me.

He certainly was still competing today. While we were going through some dives, Coach Wood had left the pool. I wanted to ask him something and sought him out in the office and locker room area of the Natatorium. I found him, but I pulled back from entering the office where I saw him on his back on a desk and Chris straddling his pelvis and riding his cock. I was shocked, but not surprised, by either of them. I knew Chris would do whatever he had to to get what he wanted, and Warren Wood had given me broad hints before that he wanted to fuck me. We too had a long history of being at the same meets, and he had heard that I was gay—which wasn't all that uncommon among male divers—and that, if I liked a guy, I'd let him fuck me.

Wood of course couldn't opening declare as gay, but swimmers knew it well enough to try to use it to get on his team. He put together championship teams. That's why he was the U.S. Olympic swim team coach for Rio.

I didn't particularly like Coach Wood. He had a good body for his age, but he was an arrogant son of a bitch, and those guys who did let him fuck them said he was rough and only cared about his own pleasure. And I'd never thought of going with Chris. He obviously was a bottom, like me, and he was a little shit. I'd do anything I had to to get to Rio and do well there, though, so I knew I had to reassess what I'd do for Coach Wood if he demanded it of me.

I'd returned to the pool, and it was then, after a while, that Chris had come out and declared that he was still fighting for position.

I looked for Chris as the team was gathering at the Miami airport three weeks later to fly down to Rio for the opening of the summer Olympics, but he wasn't there. There was no reason why he should have been there; alternates didn't travel with the team as long as the team was intact. But I wouldn't have put it past Chris to somehow have worked his way into the trip—just to be there and handy when something "accidentally" happened to a team member. I breathed a sigh of relief when we got on board the charter plane taking us and the men's gymnastics team to Brazil and settled in to meeting some of the really hot guys on the gymnastics team. I quickly zeroed in on Pedro Gonzalez, a dark-complexioned hunk with great musculature.

But I shouldn't have breathed that sigh of relief and I should have been on my guard rather than making eyes with Pedro after the third time he'd passed by my seat on the way back to his and had brushed my arm with his hand. I was still sharing meaningful mating looks with Pedro when Coach Wood came back, sat down in the seat facing mine, and reached over to put both of his hands on the seat arms on either side of me, essentially trapping me in place.

"I've been looking for you, Jason," he said. "I think you and I have some business."

"Business, I asked?" Even then I assumed he was talking about some sort of discussion of my diving.

"You know it was a close call on putting you on the team."

"Yeah, Coach, I didn't have the greatest trials, but I think my competition history stands up well."

"There isn't much distance between you and the alternates. If something were to happen to you—or if you became a discipline problem—I wouldn't have any trouble at all changing you out for an alternate."

"What you are saying, Coach?" I asked.

"I think you know what I'm saying, Jason. You need to continually earn your place on this team. You need to stop playing at teasing and avoiding me and decide you need to be a team player—a player on my team. I'm going forward to the head now. I think you will decide you need to go to the head in a minute or two yourself."

I didn't have any trouble understanding what he meant. I had already thought about what I'd do if Coach Wood made demands. It was inevitable what I'd be willing to do. It's not like I didn't give out willingly and casually, wanting it, when it suited me.

I sat on the toilet in the closet-like airplane head, while Coach Wood hovered over me, his hands palmed against the bulkhead behind me, and I gave him a blow job to the point that he was engorged. Hard, he pulled me off the toilet and turned me to the bulkhead, with my hands replacing his on the bulkhead. His hands were busy fingering my ass and squeezing and separating my butt cheeks.

"Nice," he muttered. "I've been looking forward to this."

I heard the snap of a rubber being pulled on and adjusted and then he forced his way inside me with his hard cock, giving me little time to adjust to him and laughing at my objecting groans. Saddled on my ass, his hands went back to the bulkhead in front of me, covering and trapping mine, and he cruelly fucked my ass to an ejaculation. I was no virgin, but neither was I accustomed to being taken this roughly, impersonally, and without a great deal of preparation.

Still, I told myself that I'd foreseen being in this position, and I settled down to taking what pleasure I could from the encounter. I relaxed and opened to him, and we settled down to the natural rhythm of the fuck.

Before we left the head, he said, "Athletes double up in the Olympic village, but coaches get singles. Your roommate isn't going to be seeing much of you at night, Jason. If you want to hold your place on the team, you'll be spending most of the nights in my bed."

When I didn't answer, he banged my head on the bulkhead and said, "I didn't hear you say yes." He banged my head again. "Oh, did that hurt? Maybe I need to give Chris Fair a call?"

232

"No, Coach, you don't need to call Chris."

"So, you're going to be my fuck toy in Rio? Say it. Thank me for the opportunity."

"Yes, thank you, Coach."

It wasn't that I was traumatized or anything. I fucked around, liked to be fucked, and was fucked a lot. It was mostly that I wasn't attracted to Coach and his reputation was just what I had found—rough and banging his lay's head against the wall a lot. I planned on getting what cock I could in Rio. That was as much a draw for going to the Olympics for me as was medaling. I just hadn't planned on it being Coach's cock I was getting.

* * * *

One of the perks of being on an Olympic team—and not one I'd thought about beforehand—was the pampering the athletes got for their bodies. I suppose professional athletes were used to it, but it certainly wasn't what collegiate diving teams usually got.

The masseur's name was Diego Cielo. He was Brazilian. The U.S. Olympic team didn't go so far as to pay to bring an American down to give massages to its divers—it hired locally. Diego was one magnificent hunk. I was going hard lying on my belly on his massage table with just a skimpy towel over my buttocks before he even touched me with those sensuous and sensual greased-up hands.

He started off with just tight athletic shorts on, his bronzed, muscular torso and bulging biceps, with ropy veins running down his arms being oh so sexy even without taking into account the colorful, swirling sleeve tattoo that came down to embrace and cup his left pectoral muscle. Sensing early, though, that I went hard for him and would take his cock if he wanted to give me a full-body massage, the athletic shorts didn't stay on for very long.

Before we got to the main event, and while I was still on my belly and the towel was still covering my butt, even though his hands had already been under the towel and on my hard cock and his lubed fingers had already been inside me, rubbing my prostate and giving me my first ejaculation, an attendant had come in and put a cardboard box on a counter within my view.

"Ah, good, now the games can truly begin," I heard Diego mutter in that great South American accent of his.

"What do you mean? What's in the box?" I asked.

In answer, he went over and opened the box. He took out a handful of condom disks in wrappers and dropped them on the massage table at my eye level. Each of the wrappers had the Olympic rings embossed on it.

"Rubbers," I said.

"Yes, as you say, rubbers," he answered. "For some, the coinage of the Olympics. I'm told that more are used at the games while they are in session than the whole world uses in a month. I believe it. You aren't uncomfortable with me saying it, are you, Mr. Malloy?"

"No, that doesn't make me uncomfortable. I makes me . . ."

"Horny?" Diego filled in.

"Yes, horny," I answered.

"Ah, I thought so. You got hard for me quickly. You take men's cocks, if I'm not mistaken. When I penetrated you, my finger was drawn right in and you opened for it."

"Yes, I take men's cocks," I answered.

"Is that what you would like from me? Would you like me to fuck you?"

"Yes," I whispered.

"Turn over, and turn your head toward me," he said.

When I'd done so, I found that he'd lost the athletic shorts and was in full, up-curved erection. He was presenting his cock to me and I opened my mouth to it. As I sucked on his cock, he stroked mine with a hand. Tentatively, I moved my right hand to his chest, running my fingers up his rib cage, stopping to trace the definition of each one, feeling him shudder at my touch. I ran the fingers over the swirls of color on his left breast, worshipping the perfection of him, and he flexed for me with a low groan, his pectoral muscle bulging out. His nipple puffed up at my touch. He reacted with a slight jerk when I pinched the nipple. I increased the pressure of the inside of my cheeks on his throbbing cock and he began to move it in a slow fucking motion. He had such slim hips and waist, rising to a bulging chest. He was a beautiful young man—years older than I was, but beautiful, hard bodied, berry brown, smooth skinned—even his groin and balls had been shaved. There was a tattoo of a red rose above and to the right of the base of his cock.

I arched my back and moved my left hand to cover his hand on my cock, urging him to squeeze harder, but he pulled the hand out from underneath mine, leaving me to stroke as he took my ball sack in his hand and squeezed and rolled my balls, which was just fine with me too. He reached over me and picked up one of the condom packets.

"I'm going to fuck you, am I not?" he murmured.

"Yes, please," I answered.

He held up the condom packet for me to see. "Do you want me to open this?"

"Yes," I answered, expelling his cock from my mouth, but only to teeth down one side of it and to suck in his ball sack.

He slit the packet open, took the condom disk out, and asked, "Do you want us to use this, you and I? Or do you want me to bareback you? I'm clean. We're tested regularly."

"I'm not," I answered, with genuine regret.

"And you've been with men indiscriminately?"

"Oh, yes. Does that bother you?"

"Not in the least. We will use the condom."

I almost laughed as he placed the center of the disk on his bulb and rolled the rubber down the length of his shaft. The condom had the rings of the Olympic symbol embossed on the shaft.

"Turn back over," he commanded, in a low, guttural voice. I moaned and trembled as I did so. He came up on the table, palmed my belly, and pulled me up to my knees. Then he thrust inside me, my channel already open from the attention his lubed fingers had given it, and fucked me like a dog. He was good, very good.

I was being fucked by the Olympic rings.

"You are loose, and you open up easily to the fingers. You have taken the fist before . . . and more than one man at once?"

"Occasionally. But you are big. I can feel you. You are bigger than most." I knew he'd like to hear that. It was true nonetheless. And I knew he'd like that my voice sounded belabored when I answered him while he was stroking inside me.

"After I finish fucking you, you will take the hand? It will give you a good jack off. You've taken the fist before?"

"If you want to do that. Yes, it makes me come big."

When he'd shot off, I was throbbing but only had come that once. He went up on his knees beside me on the table, pushing me down on my side. His left arm went around me, his hand clasping and squeezing the root of my cock, as he concentrated on how many of the lubed fingers of his other hand he could get in my ass.

"You want this, yes?" he asked.

"Yes, oh yes," I answered, breathless. This was the Olympics. I'd come here to get it all.

Throwing my arms over my head and grasping the edge of the table as he got one, two, three, and then four fingers inside me, up to the knuckles, I groaned and moaned at the full penetration and stretching. He knew his bodies well; he knew I was well used and could take it.

"You'd be surprised how many Olympians like to be fisted," he murmured.

At the moment I couldn't give a shit what anyone else but me liked or was getting, and I yelped as his knuckles were sucked inside my sphincter ring. Mission complete—certainly as far as I was concerned—and I let him know that. Some guys could take it up to the forearm, but I wasn't some guys. He stopped there, momentarily, giving me time to adjust to having a fist in my ass, as I panted and whimpered. Happily, his hands were not broad at the knuckles.

"God, I'm fucked," I whispered.

"Yes, you are all mine now," he murmured. "I have you by my fist. You're doing fine. You're beautiful and fine."

236

When my trembling came under control, he set about massaging my prostate—making a comment about internal massage being as important as external—with his buried fingers and squeezing the base of my cock with the other hand until, with a cry, I shot my second load over the side of the table.

To give him greater access, I had raised and bent my right leg and set the foot down on the other side of his slim hips and he'd turned his pelvis toward me. When I had come, he withdrew his fingers and penetrated me again with his cock, sheathed in a second Olympic rings condom. I panted and moved my pelvis with the rhythm of the second fuck as he fucked me deeper and more slowly.

"Fuck me, fuck me, fuck me," I murmured, breathing in shallow little bursts, clutching at the edges of the massage table, concentrating all of my attention on the thick shaft moving inside me, expertly finding and rubbing my prostate and then kissing the walls as it slowly penetrated deeper. Turning my face into his chest, I found his nipple, and sucked hard on it. He gasped, and I gasped as he quickly pulled his shaft back and then gasped again when he plunged in. Again and again and again. The master, moving methodically to his second ejaculation, announced with a "Shit, that's good!"

This was a massage the likes of which I'd never had before.

"You like to be fucked, don't you?"

"Yes," I whispered, wondering if he'd do it a third time. Ready for him if he did.

"You'll do well here at the Olympics," he said. "Prime meat, randy and cocky. And for you, many narcissistic men, in love with their own bodies and those of other men. And you have a great body and a dynamite face. You are flexible and can take a big cock. You'll get all of the attention you can handle in the village. The only ones who won't be interested are those limiting themselves to women and those who doped themselves into being eunuchs. They will be weeded out soon enough, though. Just don't forget me. When you go to schedule another massage, remember the name Diego Cielo.

I'll give you more Olympic condoms then. You'll need more by then."

"Yes, of course I'll ask for you." I reached for his cock, but he already was climbing down from the table. A glance at the clock told me our session was over. In one fluid move from the table, Diego was pulling his shorts back on and sending the two condoms, bloated like slugs with his cum, in a perfect arc and into a nearby wastebasket. Just another Olympic guy massage session for him?

Gotta say it was memorable for me. They say about sex and Olympic athletes, "What plays at the Olympics, stays at the Olympics," but I wanted to shout the cocking skills of this Diego guy to the treetops.

As I was leaving, he opened the box and scooped up a handful of condoms. Handing them to me, he said, "These are like gold in the Olympic Village. I think you will need these and even more. You are a highly sexed—and sexy— young man." I glowed in the compliment. I wanted to say that he was nifty as could be at fucking to, but I'm sure he already knew that.

* * * *

The supply of condoms Diego gave me did last until the next time he massaged—and rode—me, but only because most of the men I went with provided their own. Diego had been right. As seriously as the athletes took their turn at sports competition, just as seriously did they take their sex orgies and in putting as many notches involving different nationalities on their gym bags as they could during the two weeks of the Olympics.

I saw so many Olympic rings condoms being rolled onto cocks before the cocks disappeared inside me or whatever guy was beside me at a party and being fucked at the same time that after a few days I couldn't see the symbol anywhere without thinking of rubbers and hard shafts. News traveled fast in the Olympic Village and no news moved faster than information on who would take cock—and how well they took it. I must have established a good reputation

238

for taking it, because I took a lot of it. There must have been hetero fuck fests going on all over the Olympic village, but I had my hands so full with randy guys sniffing for it from other guys that I didn't stumble into any of them.

I had to bunk with a roommate, but that was taken care of for me. The dark-complexioned, hunky-bodied U.S. gymnast Pedro Gonzalez had gotten to whoever did the room scheduling and got me put in his room. Ten minutes after we had been shown to the room, he was mounted on my ass, fucking me. That was when we still had a supply of rubbers we'd brought with us. They didn't last long. He was athletic, flexible, inventive, and demanding. I was flexible and game to have my body manipulated in this or that demanding position, as long as he could get his cock in my ass or my mouth. His very first position after the initial, wild, needy doggie fuck was what he called a flying eagle, with him sitting on the foot of the bed, feet on the floor, hands gripping my wrists, as, facing away from him, my body was cantilevered out over his knees, my legs streaming back around his hips, and Pedro pulling me on and off his cock.

I wasn't there most nights—I was in Coach Wood's bed—receiving rough but fairly standard fucking most of the nights. But we didn't practice or compete all that many hours of the day, and there was time almost every day for Pedro to show me a new, demanding move.

He wasn't possessive. He had grown friendly with an Israeli gymnast, with black curly hair, one who didn't shave his body as most gymnast did and therefore stood out a bit more than most of them as a sexy man. Pedro and Moshe fucked me together, usually with Moshe under me, his dick buried up in my ass and Pedro taking various flexible poses above and behind me, stroking inside me on top of Moshe's cock.

Apparently there weren't that many men at the Olympics who would take doubles because my dance card quickly filled up with requests for this specialty. The same when it got around that I could—and would—take fisting.

And then there were the hours in which it rained and all of the outdoor competitions were suspended. I would lay on my bed, on my back, with my legs bent and spread, and a succession of hung, cut athletes would come and go from our room, going between my legs and coming in my channel—and then arcing those condoms emblazoned with the Olympic rings expertly into the waste bin. I got a country pin from every one of them and had, I'll bet, one of the most complete collections in the village.

Everyone was keyed up at the Olympics. Everyone wanted to release tension. Many were virile and oversexed. Many of the men athletes were narcissists and worshipped not only their own bodies but also those of other men. Most men were macho tops. Not that many were willing, seeking bottoms. When it rained in Rio, I could count on spending a lot of time on my back, with my legs open, and my channel filled with a thrusting cock sheathed in a condom with the Olympic rings emblazoned along the shaft. I wouldn't be surprised if I left Rio with the shape of the rings transferred to my inner passage walls.

These rainy-day events—and I don't want to claim that it rained all that often during the day at the Rio Olympics—led to a challenge game between Pedro and me. We didn't have room maid service in the Olympic Village. Fresh sheets and towels would be left by our door every third day, there were cleaning implements and a sweeper in a hall closet if we needed them, and we were responsible for emptying our own trash cans down a chute at the end of the hall. Pedro and I designated one of our trash cans for condom discarding and nothing else and we didn't empty that can until the end of our stay. I bet Pedro I could fill the trash can just from condoms used with me and he bet I couldn't. Even though he did what he could to fill it, he won the bet—but not by much. I didn't quite get the trash can filled. Granted, it was a pretty big can.

Even with all those men, though, I wasn't being overtaxed. My goal was to find one who stretched me to the point of splitting, who held me, panting heavily completely in his filling possession, and who I'd remember for a week as I hobbled around bowlegged. Surely among all these hunky Olympians I could find the god of the cock.

Pedro and I grew close. I had graduated that year at Stanford. He had graduated the year before from Michigan State and had taken an advertising job with an athletic sports gear company in Denver. I'd received an offer from the same company. We started talking about me taking that job and the two of us rooming together in Denver. The opportunity was looking good. Pedro had a beautiful body and he was hung. He also was liberal about partying but was good about cleaning up afterward. Neither of us were slobs or clean nuts to an irritating degree. We got on well together.

Our events weren't scheduled on top of each other's. He got me tickets to the gymnastics and I got him tickets to the diving competitions.

It was while I was watching the first night of Pedro's competitions that I first saw Ari Askami. He was sitting next to my masseur, Diego Cielo, across the gymnastics arena. It was Askami, in fact, who first caught my attention. First was his height. I couldn't tell if the guy was standing up or sitting down over there he was so tall. And then it was the breadth of him, his chest and bulging shoulders causing him to impinge into the space of the guys sitting on either side of him. It was just this first impression of massive size, because my gaze drifted off to the right of him, where I saw Diego. Diego had seen me too, and was waving. My attention then went to the floor exercises, where Pedro was performing—and doing very nicely.

When I looked back to Diego, he was in conversation with the massive guy sitting beside him. They were looking over toward me rather than down on the floor at the action. I then saw that the massive guy was old—maybe in his forties—and ugly as sin, with a displaced nose. He was bald. No interest there, so my attention went back to the great bodies on the gymnasts as they performed on the bars and the floor, the vault and the horse.

Next thing I knew, Diego was lowering himself into the empty seat beside me.

"See that guy across the way, the one who was sitting with me?" he asked.

"Yeah," I answered, neutrally, not wanting to indicate any interest, because I had none in the guy.

"He's big stuff here. He's coach of the Iranian Greco-Roman wrestling team now, but he's a four-time gold winner himself. Three golds—Greco-Roman, shot put, and javelin—in 1996 and Greco-Roman in 2000. Heavy weight."

"I could tell the heavy weight part," I answered. "1996. That was Atlanta, wasn't it? The year of the bomb?" That's what I said, but the year 1996 was more significantly telling me the guy was at least forty. He stood up now, as he'd been watching Diego talking to me, and he pointed at us from across the area. The guy must be closer to seven feet tall than six and closer to three hundred pounds than two hundred. He had a rounded, but slight, beer belly on him, and, although he was bald, his tattooed shoulders showing in his athletic T were hairy and hair cascaded over the V neckline of the T. Pretty gross, I thought, among all of these young cut bodies in the arena—in the stands as well as on the floor.

"His name is Ari Askami," Diego continued. "He has a problem and I've been telling him about you—about what you'll take. There aren't many who can take him, but he's horny. He wants to fuck you."

"I don't think so, Diego, thanks. But he doesn't look like anything I would be interested in. And I'm having no trouble getting it here in Rio."

"I'm not surprised—but I think you'd be surprised by him. Here, he gave me a ticket to give you for the Greco-Roman events whether or not you're interested. I think you'd be interested. There are some real hunks in that event." And, with that—after handing me the ticket—Diego left me and my attention went back to the floor. Pedro was on the vault, and, once again, did a magnificent job of it.

He was so euphoric that night that he fucked me good in various athletic positions, including a variation of his spread eagle specialty, where I was pitched out over the foot of the bed like a ski jumper in flight, standing on my toes on the floor, legs spread, and he grasped my wrists, bowing my torso back to him, the two of us kissing, as he crouched between my spread legs and pistoned my channel with his cock. What Pedro lacked in length and thickness, he made up for in inventive technique. I had a platform dive that launched in a similar position to this and thereafter I thought of Pedro fucking me when I took off into that dive.

Diego was right about an interest in watching the Greco-Roman gladiators going at each other, so I used the ticket he gave me to attend a Greco-Roman wrestling event. Not surprisingly, the Iranian team was contesting and Ari Askami, their coach, was strutting up and down the sidelines as they wrestled. He saw me as soon as I entered the small venue and added some "chest up" to his strut. It didn't help much. More impressive were his wrestlers, in their strange and revealing one-piece suits with the scoop back and front and the droop in front that leaves nothing to the imagination about their genital equipment. I looked back at Askami. He had even more of a droop at the crotch than either of his wrestlers did. Diego had told me he was super hung. That was enticing, but the rest of the package wasn't.

The Iranians were very well equipped and I honed into watching two in the 84–96 KG class, the one just below the heavyweight class that Askami had competed in in his Olympics. Given what Diego had told me about Askami's "problem" and what I might be in a position to do for him, I was somewhat curious what he'd look like in one of those wrestling costumes with the drooping genital sack, but the rest of him just grabbed my interest away.

According to the program, the two wrestlers who turned me on were Shahrokh Heshemi and Kuonarie Shahnazi, both with dark, curly hair, thuggish, but handsome faces, and hairy barrel chests that their costumes didn't even begin to hide. They both won each round of their matches during the two-hour competition, and both advanced to the next round. Both also looked up at where I was sitting and smiled when Ari Askami pointed me out in the stands. They stood—more like crouched—in a semicircle pointed toward me, leaning into each other, Askami in the middle, arms around each other's shoulders, baskets pronounced and pulling down on the wrestler's costumes and Askami's athletic shorts. Askami, the coach, was probably giving his boys wrestling pointers, but all three of them took time to pick me out in the stands with their eyes, to mumble to each other as they looked at me, and to smile knowingly and snigger. I went hard at thinking of the possibilities in a foursome.

I stood to give the two wrestlers a good look at me. I did what I could to erase the coach in my mind. I wouldn't have thrown either of the young wrestlers out of bed—even if it weren't obvious that once they'd come into my bed, both their size and their wrestling skills would dictate that they could have whatever they wanted.

I would have happily given them anything they wanted.

My thoughts kept going back to those two in the next two days as I practiced from the opening of my own competition. On the first day of my dive qualifications, Shahrokh and Kuonarie were in the stands, watching, and obviously cheering me on. I hadn't given them tickets and the place was packed. They had to have gone out of their way to get tickets. I did very well that day and advanced to the next round. The two Iranians waited around for me to shower and dress and leave and were standing at the entrance to the venue when I walked out. There were no real preliminaries.

"You dive well," Kuonarie said after they introduced themselves. "You have great body."

"Thanks. You two have great bodies too. I saw you wrestle."

"We know," Shahrokh chimed in. Then right to the reason they'd stayed around. "We saw you watch us and we both wanted to fuck you. We hear you take cock. Two men's cock at once sometimes. As much an orgy that Rio Olympics are, we find it hard to find lays we can share."

"We like to share men," Kuonarie interjected. "We have good cocks."

"We fuck you good, yes?" Shahrokh took his turn.

"The two of us together, yes? You come with us now. We fuck you good. We fuck you now?"

244

They looked like puppy dogs, panting with their tongues hanging out, wagging their tails. What could I say?

"Yes, OK," is what I said.

They didn't lie. They fucked me together in their shared room in the village—and they both had good cocks. Not great cocks, but good enough, ideal for double penetration, long but not appreciably thick. And they were experienced in taking a man together. They fucked me standing up in the middle of their room, between the two single beds, me sandwiched between them, with my knees hooked on Shahrokh's hips. One of the beds intrigued me a bit. They'd rigged restraints coming down from the ceiling over the bed at the corners, but not directly over the bed—spaced out a good two feet on each side.

After some preliminary frotting and sucking with me sandwiched between the two tall, hunky Iranians, me facing Shahrokh and Kuonarie embracing me from behind—both playing me with their hands and eventually both finding my hole with greased fingers and working together to open me up, Shahrokh, in a guttural voice, instructed me to climb his hips with my legs. I did this, and Kuonarie, from in back, helped guide Shahrokh's cock, sheathed with the omnipresent Olympic rings rubber, to and into my hole. When he was in deep and had bounced me on his cock for a minute or two to get us going, Kuonarie penetrated me from behind with his own Olympic rings-sheathed cock and we were off to the races, the two of them working together expertly to ensure that I had one cock thrusting up into me as the other withdrew and then the reverse.

It was as good a DP as I'd ever gotten. These two had had a lot of practice at it.

I came quickly, after which I found that the restraints over the bed were exactly for what I thought they might be for. In just a few swift moves, they had me trussed up, lying on my back on the bed, both my arms and my legs raised and spread, trapped by the restraints hanging from the ceiling. My buttocks was thrust up by a vinyl-covered angle pillow. The room was equipped to support just what they were going to do with me.

For the next hour they had their way with me, individually and, in the end, together again. While one was fucking me in the ass, the other was face fucking me. And, eventually, for a grand finale, Kuonarie worked his way under me and entered my ass with his cock from below, while Shahrokh crouched over me and fucked me from above.

They were both hunks, full of humor and smiles, enjoying themselves but making sure I was enjoying myself as well. And I did. I enjoyed myself—right up to the point where they were dressing but hadn't released me, and the door opened and Ari Askami walked in, flicking a godawful long and thick rubber dildo on his forearm.

He also brought in a ball gag and had it on me before I knew what was happening. Now all I could do was strain at the restraints, produce muffled screams through the ball gag, and bite into the rubber ball. I did plenty of that before he exhausted me, almost hyperventilating when he stripped, his body still pudgy, hairy, and past its prime and his face still thuggish ugly, but revealing the longest, thickest cock I'd ever seen. It was as thick as a man's wrist and stood out straight nearly a foot, red, angry, from his pubic thatch, pushing out under the undercurve of his beer belly. I looked at the thick, long dildo and then at the thicker, longer erection of the man, and prayed that he'd use the dildo on me first—thinking that the wrestlers together hadn't opened me up enough.

He did use the dildo on me—cruelly—and I writhed and panted and objected unsuccessfully through the ball gag. Eventually, exhausted, open to the dildo so that I was taking its greased slide without effort and with a good deal of pleasure, I settled down, moving my pelvis with it, meeting it thrust for thrust, waiting for the cock I knew was to follow.

But that wasn't the next act. He crouched over me, capturing my eyes with his, muttering that he wanted to see my response, bringing his ugly face to mine for the garlic on his breath to nearly knock me out. Just when I thought he'd thrust his cock inside me, something else entered me. His heavily greased fingers. He grabbed my chin with his free hand and held my face still, looking into his, giving him every change of my expression as, slowly, he added more greased fingers. My eyes popped open and I bit down on the ball gag as his knuckles breached the sphincter muscle. And I writhed under him and gave him muffled screams as he went in up to the wrist—and almost passed out when he opened his fist and spread his fingers inside me.

I'd been fist fucked before, but not to his depth and thickness—never before with the whole hand up to the wrist inside me. But I was now. He was inside me, I was well greased up, and, miraculously, I was opening to him as I'd never known would be possible.

He started to fist fuck me. My passage slowly stretched open and accommodated him. I'd never experienced this before. The pain overshadowed the pleasure—especially the emotional high that I was taking it—but there was enough pleasure that he was lifting me up to the clouds, and, when he released my chin, moved his hand down my torso, and grasped my cock, I gave him an explosion of an ejaculation. This was new, unexplored territory for me. This is what I'd dreamed about in coming to Rio—well, beyond competing for a medal. I'd heard the stories of the sex in the Olympic Village and how it added to one's experience and capabilities. Couldn't add much more exotic experience than this. I was collecting the gold medal of "taking it."

My ejaculation was his signal to remove his fist and replace it with his impossibly long and thick cock. The fist had expanded my walls for the first five inches, but he wasn't much more than half way inside me with the cock when he reached that mark—and he kept on sinking, his bulb pressing and making me yield him a wider passage as he sank into me. He grabbed my butt cheeks and pulled my buttocks up off the surface of the bed and spread the cheeks, giving him as much access as possible. I also spread my legs as much as I could to take it.

I felt his belly pressing at mine, his coarse pubic hair mingling with mine, as he bottomed inside me and held. He held and held as we both felt my inner passage walls open to him, caressing his cock, my muscles undulating over his throbbing and veined monster cock. And then he began to pump me and I lost all contact with anything in this world but concentration on where that monster shaft was and what it was doing. I'd been panting before, but I panted more heavily now, and whimpered, and groaned and moaned deeply as his stroking increased in intensity.

When he came, he collapsed on top of me, painfully pressing me into the bed. He pulled the ball gag out of my mouth, causing my moan to become more audible, and brought his face down to mine. I turned my head to the side to avoid his mouth coming into contact with mine, and sobbed. His lips went to the hollow of my throat, and he kissed and then nipped me there. At the same time his hands came up and put the ball gag in again.

At the moment I sobbed in relief that it was over and that I had survived it. In retrospect, I marveled that I had taken the dildo and the fist and then the monster shaft and that I had walked along the clouds as never before, given him a fuller and stronger ejaculation than I'd ever given a man before. Not, however, as full and strong as his. I had known from the explosive expansion of the condom bulb inside me when he had come and then was surprised by a second and third shudder and pressing on my inner walls. When he pulled the Olympic-rings-embossed condom off his cock after he'd stood up from me, I was amazed at how much cum it held.

Surprisingly—alarmingly—he was still monstrously erect. He came around to the side of the bed, removed the ball gag, and forced his cock in my mouth, making me suck him even larger. Then I moaned as I watched him roll another condom on and then he replaced the ball gag and was crouched over me again, entering me again, sliding deep inside me, my walls once more grudgingly giving way to him, and started to stroke. He came, removed the condom, made me suck him.

"The nuts too," he commanded, and, eyes watering, I swallowed and rolled, one after the other, his balls in my mouth. They were too big to ingest together.

When he was satisfied, he backed up, sat in a chair he reversed before sitting in it, and lit up a cigarette he took off

248

of one of the desk of one of the wrestlers. He sat there, naked, his flaccid cock nearly reaching the floor at the back of the chair, his ball sack hanging low, his eyes glued to me as I was bound to the bed, trussed up like a pig on a spit. He said nothing. He just sat there regaining his libido.

I lay there, my eyes darting around the room, looking for release, but always going back to him and to that long, thick cock of his. In awe that it had been inside me—all of it. Mentally checking myself for damage. My passage walls still throbbed and I was sore—from stretching and chafing, not splitting, thank god—but there was something else. I was proud to have taken the cock. There were moments coming back to me of being on a soaring high as the cock forced its consuming slide inside me. It was frightening and glorious all at the same time. Part of me wanted release and escape from this ogre. Part of me wanted him inside me again, reaming me larger, making me fit him for a mutually satisfying fuck.

After about five minutes and already on the second cigarette, he began working his cock up again with his hand. Massively erect once more after not much more than ten minutes since his last ejaculation, he stood from the chair; crushed out his third cigarette on the wood desk top; rolled on another condom; removed the ball gag, saying he wanted to hear my responses now; moved into position between my spread and trussed legs; and fucked me again.

I took him more easily this time, although with much babbling and crying out, both in terms of begging for mercy and begging for the fuck. There was less pain, more pleasure. I quickly went to a high, concentrating on the massive cock inside me, closing my eyes and thinking of the man attached to it as only a motor. Sighing, almost with regret, as the cock withdrew, holding my breath in anticipation, almost begging for it, as it held, and then screaming as it penetrated deep again, each time a new revelation of how thick, long, and possessing it was. Each time fearing it would split me, but when it didn't, soaring to the heights and dancing on the clouds—earning the gold medal of taking it. Taking him, managing him, listening to him groan in pleasure.

As he fucked me, I involuntarily, instinctively set my pelvis in motion, fucking him back. He laughed and grabbed my hips, pistoning me harder and thus moving me a step back in the pain department, having to adjust to his more vigorous fuck. Each time I adjusted more to him, he upped his game with me, always keeping me on the edge of breaking. I found being on the edge but not going over exhilarating, but I appreciated the danger of becoming addicted to that.

He fucked me a fourth time, with a fifteen-minute interval of sitting, smoking, staring at me, before he was finished with me. I was beyond exhaustion. I held my breath as he contemplated taking a fifth go at me. He tried, but he didn't manage it. He made an effort to harden his cock with his hand again, but his shaft had had enough. I knew that it was only reaching the point of his failure to get hard again that had made him stop. And I knew that would be the case as well if he ever got his hands on me again. He took it as a personal affront that he couldn't get it up a fifth time. I took it as a monstrous miracle that he had gotten it up four times.

While he tried to get it up, he moved around me. I closed my eyes tightly so that I couldn't see the grossness of his bloated body. He moved his hands all over my body, eventually arriving, with a well-greased hand, at my dick and balls. He squeezed and rolled my balls, and I moaned for him. He stroked my cock with the greased hand and I hardened for him. He released the pressure on the cock, and I involuntarily took over the stroking, thrusting and withdrawing my cock in the loose sheath of his fist. He laughed and I came for him. Ugly and as demanding as he was, I was his. We both knew it. But it hadn't made him hard. He slapped my cock with a snort and went back to straddling his chair, smoking a cigarette with one hand, and trying to harden himself with the other.

Unsuccessful, he snorted and stood up from his chair, and I breathed more easily, thinking the session had come to a close. He couldn't get it up again. But I could tell he was mad he couldn't get up again, and when he leaned over and came up with the can of lard, I began to hyperventilate, understanding that he wasn't finished with me after all. He made me look as he greased up his right hand, and then I writhed and objected from behind my ball gag to no avail as he leaned over me between my legs, grabbed me by the chin with one hand to hold my head in place for him to watch my facile expressions, and started to work his greased right hand into my channel. I took the fist fuck easier this time, having been opened up to the maximum by his earlier anal play.

His free hand went back to my cock. My balls were aching. I had no more cum to give him, but still he started stroking my cock, and, embarrassingly, I hardened. He set a rhythm of opening and closing his fist inside me in coordination with the stroking of my cock. Once more he let the hand on the cock go loose. Once more I moved my hips, taking over the stroking inside the loose sheath his fist provided. Once more he laughed at his control over me, his victory over my body.

I didn't have any more cum to give him—or at least thought I didn't—but he wasn't content with stopping until I was moving my hips in perfect rhythm to the opening and closing of his fist inside my passage and had given him a weak ejaculation. He wasn't the only one whose peter was petered out.

The wrestlers had fucked me for an hour and fifteen minutes. Ari Askami fucked me twice that long—for two and a half hours. Iran had invaded the USA for four hours. Iran had ravished the USA, and Iran had disengaged as the conqueror.

I couldn't walk when he let me off the bed. And I couldn't talk either. If I'd still had my tonsils, he would have face fucked them out of me.

"Good. It was very good," he said. "I will use you again. Diego was right that you could take it. I will test you more next time. We will see what the limits are to what you will take."

I was barely conscious and there was a ringing in my ears competing with the effort to hear what he said. But I heard and moaned deeply. I didn't answer him, though. He threw me over his shoulder and carried me out to the

251

common living room, where both of the younger Iranian wrestlers were waiting, playing with their cell phone.

"Take him back to his dorm," Askami growled and then left.

As they were lifting me up, Shahrokh smiled and said, "He fucked you good, didn't he?"

I was overcome, trying to figure out how to keep my legs spread and be able to walk a straight line at the same time. "Yes, he fucked me good," I managed with a hoarse voice.

I didn't walk back to my dorm, I was hustled back there, supported by a laughing and joking Iranian wrestler on either side of me. I was delighted that someone thought this was a lot of fun. Pedro was in the room when they carried me in and dropped me on my bed on my back. I slung my arm over my eyes to blot out the world, and raised and spread my legs.

"I'd leave him alone for a couple of days," Kuonarie said to Pedro before he left.

"You OK?" Pedro asked.

"No, I'm dead," I answered. "Can you soak a washcloth in cold water for me."

"Move your arm so I can put this on your head," he said when he came back with the washcloth.

"I don't want it on my head. Pull my shorts off. Put it on my ass."

"Holy shit, what have you had up there?" Pedro asked as he viewed the diameter of my asshole.

"An Iranian nuclear missile. A really fat one," I answered wearily. "I got invaded, occupied, and pillaged."

"Did you enjoy it?"

"Ask me next week, when I can walk and shit again."

* * * *

On the night of the finals in diving, I was there. I wasn't watching; I was competing in the finals. This was a minor miracle, I thought, and I only wished that Chris Fair could see that I was here—that I was here, the last American still in the competition. At the top of the platform on my first dive of the evening, I looked down at Coach Wood, standing just below me. I gave him the finger. It was while I was brushing my hand off on the hip of my Speedo and he probably didn't see it as giving him the finger—I certainly hoped no one else in the venue saw it. But I knew I'd done it. And he knew that I'd broken with him. I didn't need him anymore, and now I was the only one he had in the competition. I'd given him the finger for real the previous evening when the finalists were announced, and I'd refused to sleep in his bed that night. Fuck him now. Even if I came in tenth, it was better than anyone else on the U.S. team. And it was indisputably clear that I had earned this berth on the team—over Chris.

I'd slept with Pedro, celebrating with him his bronze star on the rings. I should have just slept and saved my energy for today, but I couldn't deny him his celebration. He fucked me in one of his favorite soaring eagle positions. I thought of that as I walked out to the edge of the platform. My first dive would start that way—pushing my chest forward, stiff-arming my arms straight back, taking flight off the platform. This was my worst dive. Not so today. I got very good marks. I was still in the hunt.

Others had come to watch. The Iranian wrestlers, Shahrokh and Kuonarie, were there in the eastern stands, cheering for me, laughing with each other. Shahrokh had a gold medal around his neck; Kuonarie a silver. Good for them. They had worked me over well. I'd thoroughly enjoyed them, and they were fully synchronized. They were right to want to share their men. If I wasn't leaving Rio tomorrow . . .

Pedro had come, his bronze medal around his neck. He was sitting in the western stands. He could have left the day before yesterday, but he'd stayed. He'd stayed to give me support. We already were talking about what sort of apartment in Denver would suit us both. He'd get a raise from the sporting goods firm for his bronze. It would be great if I could match that. But I was lucky to have made it thus far—not to have shot it all down with a bad soaring eagle dive.

Diego had come too. The massage sessions with him had been glorious fucks. I still had a good supply of Olympic-rings condoms. I could hand them out as party favors when I got home. We had exchanged addresses. I was content with moving in with Pedro, but we had an understanding. If Diego ever visited the States as he said he wanted to, I'd be getting one of those massages of his—and he could have whatever he wanted from me.

The second dive, the back one-and-a-half somersault tuck, had been the best dive I'd ever done in my life and it was scored accordingly. Miraculously, I was at the top of the leader board now, and just one more dive to go.

I looked up at the top of the stands, at the entrance on the north side, directly in front of me, when I'd climbed to the platform for my last dive. I was doing a handstand falling into a forward somersault pike. It was my best dive, my most impressive one visually. It was a dangerous dive; you had to push out far enough not to hit your head on the board in doing the forward somersault. It required total concentration and steady control. It was my last dive. It was all or nothing now, my last chance at gold.

When I looked at the top of the north stands I saw him, though. Ari Askami—looking massive and dumpy. Impressive, though, as he had his four gold medals from earlier Olympics around his neck. I was disconcerted. He'd come to watch me dive. But he'd worn his medals. He was making a statement. I wanted a medal. He had four and they all were gold. He was saying he owned me. He had had me. He had possessed me fully, fucked me totally, only letting me go when he was done with me.

He had sent a message via Diego that he wanted me again, but I hadn't responded.

I tried to tear my eyes away from him as I walked to the end of the platform, but he controlled me. He was smirking and I was trembling. Would I even be able to get up into a handstand without collapsing.

Later, standing on the second rung of the award blocks, I didn't care that they were playing the French national anthem, not the one for the United States. When the silver medal was placed around my neck, I kissed it and lifted it up for everyone to see. I hadn't come here for gold; I'd come here to be an Olympian—and, yes, because I'd heard the Olympics was a veritable fuck palace. I'd certainly verified that. My last dive had been near perfect. I had no regrets. I'd done is as well as I ever had. The French guy had just been a little better. Good for him. Others declared "gold or nothing." That wasn't me. I was delighted with a silver.

The awards finished, I felt keyed up, randy. I wanted to celebrate in a big way. people were leaving, but not everyone was moving. Coach Wood was standing by the pool, all puffed up. If he'd had cigars, I think he'd have been handing them out. He was looking directly at me. I knew exactly what he wanted—that he wanted to celebrate my silver too. He wanted to have his chance to tell me that he had made me.

Pedro was patiently standing in the west stands, smiling and looking at me proudly. He'd say nothing about his bronze medal against my silver. He'd just be happy for me.

In the east stands, Diego stood near the top. He'd told me he'd be happy to give me a massage after the diving competitions win or lose. I knew that he would massage all of the tension away from me and give me a divine celebratory fuck. Several rows below him, the Iranian wrestlers were pushing each other around and giving wolf whistles. They also were pointing down at me and applauding. They were celebrating with me already. They'd give me a good time, I knew, if I walked over to them.

And then I did start walking. I walked around the pool, barefoot and in a Speedo topped by an Athletic T-shirt, and up the aisle of the west stands, toward where Pedro Gonzalez was standing. As I walked, people parted for me, giving me a straight, unimpeded path. They smiled at me and whispered their congratulations. I was a minor god, if only for the moment. I took Pedro's hand when I reached him, both of us wanting me to lean in for a kiss, but there still being too many people milling around the venue, more than a few watching me, because I had a silver medal around my neck.

"Hi," I said.

"You did it."

"Yes, we did," I answered, gesturing to the bronze medal around his neck.

"Let's go back to the room and—"

"Tonight. Tonight we'll celebrate royally, Pedro," I said. "But for now, there's something I have to do—something I badly need."

He looked into my eyes and understood. We'd talked about it. "Are you sure?"

"Yes, I'm sure. This is the Olympics. I came here for an Olympian experience. It will be all right, I'm sure."

"Then do it."

I turned, descended the aisle to the pool, and then walked around to the north stands and up. Ari Askami was standing, one hand fondling his four gold medals, and the other one cupping his package. His eyes were boring into me, commanding me to come to him. When I reached him, he took my elbow in a vice grip.

"You will come with me to my room and you will take it all," he growled.

"Yes, I want it all," I said, lowering my eyes in willing, trembling in anticipation, submission.

The Horse Master

"This is Claude, Claude Barbier, Neal. He'll be living with us this summer. He's a concert pianist. French."

"I've heard interesting things about you, young man," the Frenchman said. "I'm looking forward to getting to know you better."

This was how I was greeted coming off the train in Gunzenhausen, an ancient Bavarian town on a large lake, Muhr am See, between Nürnberg, thirty-three miles to the northeast, and München, ninety miles to the southeast. I had landed in München five hours earlier from London and I was strung out. Gordon Haydon, the painter, had harassed me to come to him for the summer, but he hadn't bothered to drive to München to pick me up even though he was opening the boot of a perfectly fine Mercedes sedan at the Gunzenhausen station for me to hoist my bag into. And now he was telling me that we wouldn't be the only ones in his lakeside house this summer.

I wondered if the funny little old bald man Gordon had introduced me to as Claude Barbier would be demanding the same privileges Gordon would. Chances were good he would—not only from the way he smiled at me like he could eat me up alive but also because of how familiarly he was placing the surprisingly long and elegant fingers of one hand on the small of my back as we exited the Bahnhof.

I had resigned myself to one lecherous old man when I'd agreed to come model for Gordon "in nature, au natural," as he had put it, in exchange for help with my photography, room and board, and more money than I could have made doing anything else to bridge the school terms at Cambridge. Gordon had been my art professor there in my first year—before the scandal that had sent him into an exile retirement in Germany, but that, since I was of age and of little interest to anyone, hadn't swept me up as well.

At the car, the Frenchman, nearly salivating, held the door of the backseat open for me and probably would have followed me if Gordon hadn't said, "Ride up front with me, Claude."

Ever aware of my surroundings as a possible photo shoot, I avoided eye contact with Claude, who had turned in the front seat to look back at me and was babbling about what had brought him to Gunzenhausen for the summer himself—something about retreating from the busyness of the Paris whirl to perfect the music for a fall concert tour. I didn't listen too closely, and he seemed to be satisfied with an occasional grunt from me and to viewing my golden curls and blue eyes from profile as we curved around the east side of the Muhr am See, turning into ever-more-narrow and picturesque roads and bucolic scenery until the trees were meeting overhead.

I kept stroking my camera, anxious to be out and about and clicking off photos of this beautiful landscape. I also was fully aware that Claude had an arm extended into the backseat and was stroking my knee with long, elegant fingers—so incongruous on his short, rotund dwarfish body.

OK, so Gordon had told the Frenchman exactly what I would be doing for Gordon this summer, I thought with a sigh—and, I suppose, for the Frenchman too if I wanted to earn my keep. I was resigned to it, though. Gordon was paying me far more than he would without the understanding that I'd be lying under him. It's not like we hadn't done it before. He definitely knew his photography art, even though he personally preferred fine art. I couldn't pass up the opportunity for the instruction he could provide. I'd return to Cambridge far ahead of my peers.

And it was just sex—a renewable resource, as Gordon had continuously reminded me while he was banging me at Cambridge. It's a good thing I looked younger than my age, though, or he wouldn't have been banging me and I'd have missed out on the valuable instruction.

The car slowed, and I turned my head to the front windshield, only to drop my jaw in amazement. We were on a narrow lane, Gordon having told me that we were quite close to his lake house. In front of us, though, showing no indication he would move off the road, was a magnificently large gray draft horse, powerfully and beautifully, built, and riding on him was an equally magnificently constructed young man. He was naked to the waist, broad shoulders tapering down to a narrow waist. He was riding the horse nearly bareback, with just a red cloth for a saddle. His beefy legs hung down at the sides, there being no stirrups.

"Give him the horn," Claude said.

"I'd love to," Gordon answered, with a chuckle. "But I've already checked him out. He gives his horn; he doesn't take one, old chap. But, seriously, I don't want to spook the horse," Gordon continued. "He's wearing headphones and listening to music—maybe one of your piano pieces." He gave Claude an indulgent smile.

"Ah, in that case . . ." Claude responded, returning the smile and, thankfully, turning full frontal to the wind screen. "What a magnificent body," he said, giving a low whistle.

"The horse or Guido?" Gordon asked.

"Yes," Claude responded, and then he gave a low laugh.

"As I said, he's not for me—or for you, Claude."

"Pity," the Frenchman answered.

That told me all I needed to know about the preferred positions of all three men. "Open the sunroof," I said impulsively.

"Excuse me?" Gordon asked.

"Open the sunroof. I must photograph this."

"Good idea," Gordon said. He opened the sunroof, and I stood, coming out of the car up to my waist and started firing off shots of the horse and rider from the rear. I only stopped long enough to reach down to try to brush the Frenchman's hand away—unsuccessfully—from copping a feel of my crotch as I was hanging out of the top of the Mercedes.

Instinctively, the horse rider—who Gordon must know, as he called him Guido—sensed he was being followed, and he turned. The musculature of his chest, ornamented with curly black chest hair, was as magnificent as the view from the back had been. Our eyes met, and I fired off a couple of more shots. He didn't look particularly pleased at that, and, as he pulled the gray horse to the side of the road to give the Mercedes room to pass, he gave me a bit of a scowl. I photograph that too—he was just as breathtaking with a petulant scowl on his face.

I wasn't paying complete attention to him, though, as I had the Frenchman to worry about. He had turned full to toward the backseat, had unzipped me and pulled my trousers and briefs down onto my thighs, and, clutching my buttocks in his hands, had his face buried in my crotch. I was trapped in that position and, for the remainder of the drive to Gordon's house, I lay on the roof of the car; my arms extended; my buttocks being kneaded, with fingers exploring my anal entrance; and Claude expertly sucking me to an ejaculation. Giving in to him, I lay there, moaning, and moved my pelvis so that I was slow pumping his mouth cavity.

No, there was no question of the favors I would be expected to extend to the French gnome during the summer.

* * * *

The house was more than a bit of a surprise. It was set in a grove of trees, with the slope of a pasture behind it gently rolling down to the shore of the Muhr am See. At first it was hard to pick out the house at all. It was constructed of ancient, moss-covered stone slabs. The house rambled from left to right and was nestled into the trees and large boulders coming out of the ground, boulders which were of the same hue as the stones of the house. It was as if the building had sprouted from the ground there and had been there forever, formed at the same time as the topography around it.

Once inside, another surprise awaited me. The back of the house, facing the lake, was almost entirely of glass, and the house was laid out such that nearly every room opened to the glass-walled view of the pasture and the lake.

Despite the twelve hours of plane and rail travel punctuated by sit and run periods in airports and train stations I was also laid out immediately upon arriving at the house. Gordon, with Claude panting behind me, showed me to my room, at the end of a corridor off one side of the main house, showed me my bed, showed me his erection, showed me that he hadn't forgotten how to expertly undress a weary young man, and fucked me missionary style on my bed. Claude watched us, salivating, and took up Gordon's position between my legs as soon as the painter was done.

So, there was no uncertainty of what my role was to be here this summer.

Gordon was tall and gangly; his cock was short and stubby. Claude, who was short and roly-poly, had a long, thin cock. Both men were in their late fifties. Neither had much stamina. They both had fucked me and vacated the room, talking of cigars and scotch on the terrace, in less than a half hour. I rolled over, with a groan, and went to sleep immediately.

When I woke, the sun was setting over the lake. The view was magnificent and I immediately was figuring out exposures and camera stops to capture the sunset the next time it was this good. As I stared at the view, I noticed a feature I wished I could capture immediately, so I grabbed my camera and rushed, naked, to the glass wall, finding, thankfully, that I could push back a panel for an unobstructed shot.

There, in the meadow, were three horses—a heavy gray and two sleek thoroughbreds, a stallion and a slightly smaller mare. And standing there among them was the sturdy young hunk from the afternoon—Guido, Gordon had named him. The tableau was perfect set off by the setting sun. I clicked away with my camera.

The zoom lens gave me a shock. Guido was turned toward the house and I could swear that he was looking directly at me. He had his cock out and was masturbating himself. I was suddenly conscious that I was naked and in full view of him if the light was right. But then he didn't have a zoom lens. I did, and so I continued firing off photos of him stroking himself while the three horses stood by him, one of them nudging his shoulder with his nose.

I was able to handle the camera with one hand, and the other one went instinctively to my own hardening erection—both of the old men had fired off before I'd built up an ejaculation—and I pulled on my cock in rhythm with the young hunk. We came nearly simultaneously.

I was well versed in the knowledge of the play of light, so I was nearly positive that the horseman couldn't see me from where he was standing and with the light the way it was. But part of me wished that he had been able to see me and that we both knew we were jerking off together. I was resigned to a summer of lying under Gordon and Claude, but the man out there with the horses was everything the two of them weren't—young, muscular, virile, handsome, big cocked. In short, a horse in his own right. I hadn't had any men except for old ones, ones who had trouble getting it up and more trouble keeping it up long enough to give me pleasure. Ah, the thought of being ridden by that horse of a man.

* * * *

"No, don't move."

That's what I woke up to the next morning. Gordon's voice telling me not to move.

"I've got to piss," I said. I started to move an arm, but he hissed at me.

"I said don't move. You can piss in a couple of minutes." Your pose is just too luscious.

I opened an eye. He was sitting across the room behind an easel and obviously had been painting me while I slept. I slept in the nude, of course—he'd left me that way when he'd withdrawn. He hadn't fucked me, because he couldn't get it up more than once a day, I didn't think, and he'd already had his go at me when we'd arrived at the house. But he'd massaged me until I'd gotten it up and then had sucked me dry while finger fucking my ass.

He'd left me tangled in the sheets, with my buns protruding, and I'd gone to sleep that way and had been so exhausted from the trip here that I hadn't moved before I woke up.

"Sorry, I really have got to piss," I said, and, when he didn't object this time, I pushed myself up and out of the bed and padded to the bathroom off the corridor. I heard what I thought was a record of a piano piece, but it abruptly stopped, and I realized that it must be Claude Barbier practicing on the keys. I couldn't fault his piano playing.

When I came back, Gordon called me over to the easel and then pulled me into his side. He was just wearing shorts and his fly was open. He had an erection, possibly his only one for the day and I sighed, knowing he'd use it. I looked at his painting. It was near enough finished that he didn't need me to go back into the pose. And while Barbier was a master on the piano, Haydon was a master with the paint brush. As critical as I was of their sexual prowess, I had to be in awe of them both in their separate artistry. I was in the company of truly great artists, icons in their separate disciplines. I needed to appreciate that and be grateful I had been brought into their company. Someday I might find myself to be a footnote in one or both of their biographies.

I turned and threw my right leg over his thighs, reaching down to grasp his cock and holding it in place as I came down into his lap, skewering my ass channel on his shaft. Taking his head between my hands, I put our faces together and entered into a deep kiss. I moved my butt on his cock, bringing him to a quick ejaculation, ending in an appreciative sigh. Then, when he pressed the palm of a hand into my sternum, I arched back with my head and hands to the floor in front of the chair we were straddling and moaned for him as he stroked my cock off and I felt him going flaccid inside me. It satisfied him and it didn't do any damage to me. It was the least I could do for a man who could render me so sensually in oils and possibly give me a footnote in the history of art.

I came back up and took his mouth in mine again. His cock stirred inside me, but just couldn't manage another hardening—at least not then.

My camera was on a side table within reach and I pulled it over. "I want you to look at these shots," I said. "I think some of them are good. I'd like to pick out some and take them into town and have them blown up."

"We don't have to go into town for that—although I plan for us to do so for lunch anyway," he murmured. "I have all of the facilities here to process them. Pick out what you want and tell me how big you want them blown up."

He just smiled and did a couple of turns of the room later that morning, as I was hanging poster-size shots of the horse master on the walls of my bedroom, including a couple of sunset shots of him masturbating.

"You like him, I can tell," Gordon said. He hadn't made any comment of surprise that I had caught the hunk jacking himself off.

"Thus far he's the most striking subject I've seen—well, the horses as well. Somehow they go together."

"You mean he's horse hung."

"That too," I said, with a smile. "You gave him a name yesterday. Guido. So, do you know him?"

"I don't know him in quite the way you may mean," Gordon said. "I know that he's a top too. I unsuccessfully tried to buy him for myself. He was good-natured about it, though. He's Guido Marini, an Italian mother and an absent English father. He lives in a cottage in the woods down near the lake. His purpose in life seems to be those horses of his. I let him pasture them on the slope down to the lake. He has other pastures for them as well. He's part of the tourist industry here, as no doubt you'll learn later. Do you want him to fuck you?"

"I wouldn't turn him down," I answered, trying to sound noncommittal. I thought that was more politic than answering hell yes, I want him to fuck me.

Later, when we'd driven into Gunzenhausen and were seated in the outdoor café, the Vanilla Café, on Hensolt Strasse, I saw him again, and became even more interested in fucking him. He was across the street, near an old clock tower, astride his gray draft horse, wearing German lederhosen and posing for photographs for the tourists. I wanted to run over and photograph him too—and make lewd comments about how good he looked in tight leather shorts.

I didn't have to, though, as, spying us, he walked his horse over to us and spoke with Gordon and Claude in what I recognized as rudimentary French, which, nonetheless wasn't rudimentary enough for me to understand. I would have done better in Italian, and I sensed that Guido would have, as well. The conversation was brief. Although he was speaking with the two men, he was looking at me. I looked right back—looking up as he was still on his magnificent horse, both steed and man exuding power and sexuality.

When he saw a tourist group coming down the street, he moved back to his photo op position.

"What did he say?" I asked Gordon, barely able to contain myself.

"He asked who you were," Claude answered. "He knows who Gordon and I are."

"What did you tell him?"

"We told him you were Gordon's son, here on break from Cambridge. I don't think he believed me, and I didn't expect him to. Everyone around here knows we bring young men to the lake house and debauch them. He asked about you and the camera and we told him the truth—that you were studying photography. That seemed to satisfy him."

"Oh," I said, not knowing what I thought about that. I had been worried that they had said more—more about what I was doing beyond photography here. I had thought I didn't want him to know more about me, but now I realized that I wanted him to know more—to know it all.

"He asked if Claude and I fucked you," Gordon added, and I felt my blood turn to ice and then immediately boil. "I told him we did. He said he'd like to fuck you too. I said he'd have to ask you about that."

Oh. I felt myself blush and I turned my face away so that they couldn't see the mixed reaction I had to that.

On the way back to the house, I complimented Claude on his piano playing. He asked me if I played, and I said I'd taken lessons but wasn't very good at it. This led into him fucking me at the piano that afternoon when we returned to the house. He didn't have the problem that Gordon had about only being able to get it up once a day.

He told me he'd help me learn a simple rendering of the haunting tune I'd heard him play that morning. I knew it as "Elvira's Theme" from the movie soundtrack to *Scarface*, but he told me it was Mozart's Piano Concerto Number 21, the "Elvira Madigan Theme." He sat me on his lap, my legs spread over his thighs, and he took my hands in his, his fingers over mine, and guided me in the tune on the piano. We progressed from a simple one-handed version to two hands and then to chords. The tune was intoxicating and I felt myself melting into him, forgetting entirely his resemblance to a toad. His cock engorged up the small of my back, and I was panting when he unbuckled and unzipped my shorts—all that I was wearing—unzipped his own shorts—all that he was wearing—and, closing the lid over the piano keys, lifted and spread my legs so that my ankles were on the top of the grand piano case, lifted me with strong hands, and set my channel down on his erection.

He was longer—much longer—than Gordon was, and able to stay hard longer than Gordon could, and was strong enough to raise and lower me on his cock until we both had come. I stayed with him, feeling him go flaccid, and locking my fists behind his neck as we kissed and he rubbed my nipples. If I received instruction on the piano like this for the rest of the summer, I decided that being fucked by a toad wouldn't be half bad. I didn't even have to look at him in this position.

Still, my daydreams went to the horse master.

Later in the day, when I was posed in the nude on the low rock wall between the terrace and the grass of the pasture and Gordon was painting me, I turned my head at the sound of a neighing horse and looked into the pasture, where Guido's three horses were feeding—and Guido was standing among them and looking up at me.

"Turn your head back to where it's supposed to be," Gordon admonished.

Reluctantly I did so, but I was aching to be looking at Guido instead.

I only saw him one more time over the next month. We took an excursion south of Gunzenhausen to the larger and older town of Weissenburg. Gordon told me that he wanted to show me the reconstruction of the Limes in Weissenburg, one of a five-hundred-mile line of Roman fortresses that had been stretched along Germany to aid in Roman control of the unruly Germans two thousand years earlier.

I only found out why Gordon wanted to take me there after we had arrived. I had noticed that Guido and his horses had disappeared from the pasture area soon after I had arrived—too soon. I'd even ventured down to the lake and found his stone cottage, but it was locked up tight each time I went there. Gordon had told me that the horse master moved around the area with his horses and that he'd be back sometime during the summer. But after a month he hadn't returned.

But there he was, at the reconstructed gates of the Limes in Weissenburg, astride his thoroughbred stallion and dressed as a Roman cavalry officer. He was posing with tourists for photos. I found him to be achingly sexy, as I'm sure some of the tourists who rushed for photos did as well. He looked at me and gave me a little smile when we stood there briefly before Gordon and Claude pulled me away to an outdoor café, but it was just a look. He was too busy taking the tourists' money for photos to come to me, take me to a quiet corner of the fort, and fuck the shit out of me. For some reason I thought that's how he'd fuck—rough and a total taking. And after a month of the "maybe I can get it up" quick sex with Gordon and Claude, rough and total by a horse-hung muscular man was what I longed for.

"So, will you thank me for bringing you to see the horse master today?" Gordon asked, with a mischievous smile on his face.

"Aren't you afraid I'll run off with him?" I countered, a bit confused that he willingly was bringing forth competition—unfair competition at that.

"I want you two to fuck," Gordon said. "I want to see it so that I can paint it, though."

I didn't know what to think about that—so I shoved it out of my mind.

* * * *

I don't know how long I looked down at the lawn sloping down to the lake from the terrace that Thursday in the middle of July before I realized that Guido's three horses were grazing there. When I realized that they were, I rose from the chaise lounge where I'd been sunning myself in a Speedo and went into the house and straight to the kitchen. I threw together a basket of provisions, with cut-up pieces of cheese and French bread, and grabbed a bottle of Burgundy, which I uncorked and shoved the cork back in an inch, and two wine glasses. On my way out of the house, I took up a blanket, and then I marched down into the meadow and to a small stand of trees about halfway down to the lake.

It wasn't long before Guido appeared in the pasture, where he patted down the horses—the two thoroughbreds, the stallion and mare, were being frisky—saw me, pretended for a few minutes that he didn't see me, on the blanket, with the wine, cheese, and bread, and then turned and strode deliberately to me. He plopped down beside me, on the ground, not on the blanket. Without preliminary and showing no interest in what I'd brought, he reached out for me with both arms, embraced me, and rolled me away from the blanket. He wound up on top of me, pinning me to the ground.

Guido grabbed my wrists—in a painful grip—and thrust them over my head. At the same time, he forced his knees between my legs and spread them. We were basket to basket. I could feel him hard against me, and I'm sure he could tell that I was hard too. His mouth came down to mine and he possessed me in a brutal kiss.

There was no question that he was going to take me. And there was no indication that there would be much preparation before he did. My mind went to trying to remember how big he was. From the brief look I'd had of him stroking off in the sunset, I thought he was horse hung—long and thick.

He'd taken off his belt and tied my wrists together over my head, with the leather around the base of a small tree. This left his hands free to roam over my body, roughly grabbing and prodding me here and there. He rose up over me briefly, presenting a cock that was both magnificent and frightening for me to take in my mouth for several minutes. I nearly had to unhinge my jaw to take it. But take it I did. He left me no choice. I was frightened by him, though, and started working at the belt trapping my wrists over my head and to the small tree trunk.

At length, he shuddered and might have come if he hadn't pulled out of me and hovered over me there, panting hard, making me hyperventilate at how overpowering he was, muscular, hung. He lowered himself on my body and his mouth moved down my body to my nipples. I gasped and whimpered as he stripped my Speedo off and grasped and squeezed my balls. His mouth was on my cock and then between my buttocks cheeks, with my legs hooked over his shoulder when I heard the whinnying from the pasture and looked over at the horses.

The stallion had a massive erection, a good foot and a half long, and the mare had her tail up. He was nuzzling her neck and she was skittishly moving from side to side, seemingly not sure what she wanted. She nuzzled the stallion back and then vigorous pumped her head up and down, snorted, and push at him with her nose like she wanted him to leave her alone. He did move away from her then and

269

danced a wild circle around her at a bit of distance. The larger gray horse folded his ears down and moved away from the two smaller, sleeker horses. The stallion came in behind the mare and put his nose under her tail. She set her legs.

The stallion reared up and came down on the mare's hind quarters with his chest and front legs. I watched his massive erection poke at her buttocks under her tail and, finally, slide inside her. The mare held steady, hooves planted into the ground, while the stallion pumped her—but only briefly, four or five times, before he came off her. His massive erection was gone.

The cavorting horses weren't the only thing I saw when I looked over in that direction. In my peripheral vision, I saw Gordon sitting within the tree line not far from us. He was sitting at an easel and obviously had been painting Guido fucking me. So, we were both happy.

With a burst of adrenaline, I broke my wrists free, surprised Guido by rolling away from him, rising on my feet, and running into the pasture. I had no idea what I was trying to do. But it didn't matter. Guido caught me in the field, pushed me to the ground on all fours, covered me close from above, mounted me, penetrated me—painfully and deep— with his cock, and holding me in a firm embrace, pumped me and pumped me and pumped me.

The stallion had taken ten or fifteen seconds to seed the mare. Guido fucked me with the same intensity and in the same position as the stallion took the mare—to the extent that it was the image of the stallion and of his massive erection that went through my mind as Guido was fucking me—but he took ten or fifteen minutes of pounding away on my ass to seed me. When he was near to jacking, he moved a hand under my belly and stroked off my cock so that I came before he did.

When he had finished me, he fell over to the side, taking me with him, and, still buried inside me, held me close into his chest in a powerful embrace. I moaned and whimpered and listened to his heavy breathing calm down but then, after several minutes, grow ragged again. His hands went into motion, prodding and testing my flesh again. I felt him engorging inside me once more. He raised me back to all fours, mounted me again, and fucked me a second time, this time slower, deeper, with longer, more controlled strokes than the first time.

Looking over to the side, I saw that Gordon was still painting away. I wondered how many paintings he was getting out of these couplings.

Having come again, Guido rolled off me and pushed me down on my side. He stood, strode over to the blanket, picked up the bottle, pulled the cork out with his teeth, and began to drain the bottle down his gullet. All of the time he was breathing heavily and his eyes were boring into me, daring me to move.

I took the challenge. Painfully, and groaning, I pulled myself up onto my feet and started to walk uphill toward the terrace. He was on me in a flash, grabbing me and throwing me over his shoulder. As he was carrying me off in the other direction, my gaze went back to the pasture, where the stallion was mounted on the mare and having another go at her. She was just standing there, steady, taking that impossibly long cock of his. Gordon was still there at his easel too. Taking long strides, Guido walked into the trees, to his stone cabin. Locking the door from inside behind us, he tossed me down on the bed on my back, covered and entered me, and fucked me roughly again. He repeatedly fucked me over the afternoon, finally pushing me out of the cabin and telling me, in Italian, to come back only if I wanted what he had to give.

I went back to him three or four time a week over the next month, and each time he pounded my ass in multiple rough fucks. And each time I loved it, taking it as a balance of what I got from Gordon and Claude up at the main house when they used me in the limited way they could to feed their creativity and artistry.

I didn't begrudge how they used me, and over the summer Gordon taught me much about the art of photography. Guido taught me to include a touch of the wild and primeval in my subject matter. Together that was to win me many awards in subsequent years. The paintings he'd rendered from those sketches he'd made of Guido fucking

271

me in the pasture were a sensation at various underground exhibits.

As the summer was coming to a close, I was burdened with a conundrum. Claude was returning to Paris and to his concert tour. But Gordon wasn't returning to anything. He was continuing in exile on the shores of the Muhr am See. He spoke to me of loneliness and of not having completed his study series in oils of my nudes. He wanted me to stay. I could learn more about photography and have a better career by staying with him than going back to Cambridge. This was possibly true, but if I wanted to have the option of teaching I needed the university credentials. To stay with him would be to put all of the risk into a commercial art career.

And then there was Guido. How could I leave Guido? No one fucked me like Guido did. He almost—almost—had replaced photography in my list of priorities.

It was Guido who decided for me, though. I went to his cottage one afternoon in late August. it was not an unusual time for me to come. He wasn't alone. I knew that before I got to the cottage door. He was fucking a young man—younger than I was. I recognized him. It was Dieter, a waiter at the Vanilla Café we liked to frequent in Gunzenhausen. On top of that, the theme from Elvira Madigan, Mozart's "Piano Concerto Number 21," was playing on his radio. Guido had said he wanted me to stop fucking Gordon and Claude—to only fuck him. But of course I couldn't do that. I took the playing of what I'd grown to consider to be Claude's and my song while he fucked another young man as a message from Guido.

I turned and left, but not before Guido saw me standing in the doorway. He saw me there, but he didn't miss a beat in his pounding of Dieter's ass.

I swallowed my pride and came back three days later. His cottage was locked up tight and the horses were gone. Later that day Gordon told me, with a tone of victory in his voice, that Guido had moved on to another pasture and wouldn't be back here until the fall.

What Gordon thought was his victory, however, was also his defeat. Although it saddened me, I decided that my life didn't stop here. If I was going to be an artistic force myself, I couldn't be under the thumb of Gordon or the control of Guido. There would be other Gordons and other Guidos, and they would be more likely to be found in Cambridge and London than here on the shores of the Muhr am See.

In the end, I didn't choose either Gordon or Guido. I chose me. It had been a summer to remember—but it had just been three months of my life near the beginning of life, not at its end. I didn't forget to take the photo posters of Guido back to England with me, however, or to tell Gordon that I definitely wouldn't return the next summer.

~

About the Author

Habu is one of the pen names of a former supersonic spy jet pilot, intelligence agent, male model, movie actor, and diplomat. A wild youth in Southeast Asia was spent enjoying whatever sexual opportunities came his way, and much of his gay male writing is about recalling incidents from those days and inventing ones he'd perhaps have liked to experience. He now leads a very quiet and ordinary happily married family life.

An American, he is a published mainstream novelist and short story writer under another name and in another dimension of his life. He has written or cowritten (with Sabb) approaching 1,000 published short stories and over 100 published erotica e-books, primarily of gay fiction but also memoir, straight fiction and ménage fiction. His hand and creative writing can be seen in stories and books by habu, sr71plt, Dirk Hessian, Shabbu, and Stephen Kessel—among unrevealed others that might surprise readers. The fictionalized GM memoir *Flying High, Diving Deep* is loosely based on his life experiences. He can be found at the adults only gay male site www.BarbarianSpy.com, which he shares with Sabb and Dirk Hessian.

Our authors always like to receive feedback, and appreciate it when readers post reviews at distributors and other sites.

BarbarianSpy
FOR LITERARY HEAT

Not all books listed below may currently be on release.
* indicates the book is available in paperback and e-book.

BOOKS BY CHRIS CROSS
Multisexual Adult Romance
Pulaski Square
Chocolate in Vanilla (MF)2
Christmas with Chris (MMF) (MM) (MF)

BOOKS BY ALEX LOCKHEED
Transgender Romance
Meeting Jenna
Transgender Other
Being Sarah

BOOKS BY DIRK HESSIAN
Xtreme Historical Erotica
Dirk's Ancient Times Collection (Print only Bundle)*
The King's Men
Shores of Tripoli*
Prophecy of Noto
Pretender's Fate

General Historical Erotic Romance
Dirk's America's Founding Collection (Print only Bundle)*
Soldier,Spy
Ridden West
Deliver a Virgin
Clouds and Rain
Confederate Gold
Puttin on the Ritz
To the Hessian Hills
Fire Down the Valley*
Constantinople*
The Beautiful Way*
Blue and Gray
Colonel's Treasure
Beginning of Time
Labyrinth

BOOKS BY HABU
Gay Erotica
Memoir Faction
Flying High, Diving Deep*

Xtreme Erotica
Fist of Gold
Liaisons
Chain Gang Banged (Short Story)
Tramp Steaming*
Escape to Girne
Silas' Choice*
Last Call
Choke Hold
Apyko: The Greek Pimp
Visits of the Schlange
Second Coming: Emile La Cour Unleashed*
Vortex: Sacrificed by Curiosity*
Dark Angel Sounding (in e-book & included in Sounding:Ultimate Control paperback)*
Sounding: Ultimate Control (Print Only)*
Sounding Five (in e-book & included in Sounding:Ultimate Control paperback)*

Romance
Poison Pen
Need to be Needed
Key Westing (short)
Finding a New Sam
Bangkok Summer Seduction
The Photograph
Inevitable Case
Turn to Love
Rain Check
Built for Pleasure (Sci Fi)
Danny's Choice*
Pull of the Groove
Sugar n Spice Christmas
Friday Nights with Lenny (Christmas Romance)
Snowy, Snowy Nights (Christmas Romance)
Tank n Bull
Sail to the Sun
War Letters
Ravens Roost
Caribbean Cruise Top to Bottom
Arena Stage
Trading Partners (Valentine's Day)
Four Coins
Lower Than the Heart (Valentine's Day)
Brambleton
Finding Amnad
Platres Conclave

Other Novels/Novellas
Ranger Guided
Key Westing
Syrian Ram
Temptation's Clutches*
Descent into Chaos
Escape to Girne
Journey Through Abilene
Harmony and Dissonance
Stallion Station
Racing With the Devil (espionage suspense)
Prepared in Cape Verdi
Gilded Cage
House on Park*
Anything for Ambition
Dance of the Ravishers
Hard Knocks U*
My Neighbor's Spa*
Man's Man: Tales of a High Priced Gay Hooker*
Trip Money
The Indian Doctor
Sailorboy
Home to Fire Island

Murder Mysteries
Retribution (Hardesty)
Snitches (Hardesty
Gotta Keep Trying (Hardesty)
All Fools Day Foolery (Mike Kavanagh)
Inevitable Case (Mike Kavanagh)
Vanishing Laura
Death on a Ping Pong Table
Clint Folsom Mysteries Compendium Volume 1*
Death to Blonds - Stolen Judgment (Clint Folsom Mystery)*
Clint Folsom Mysteries Compendium Volume 2*

Gay Erotica Anthologies
Earth Cry*
Shunga
Habu's Christmas Balls
Eight in D*
DevilMENt
Silas' Choices*
Stallion Station (A Novella in Parts)
Eleven to the Dogs*
Fifty Seventy*
Spy Tails 001*
Spy Tails 002*

Doubled*
Doubled Again*
Tails in the Tropics*
Tails in the Med*
Tails in the West*
Rough Riders*
Grab Bag 1*
Grab Bag 2*
Grab Bag 3*
Grab Bag 4*
Grab Bag 5*
Grab Bag 6*
Grab Bag 7*
Grab Bag 8*
Grab Bag 9*
Grab Bag 10*
Grab Bag 11*
Beyond the Beaded Curtain*
The Sporting Life*
Fetish Galore!*
Literary Gay Erotica
Cairo Surrender*
The Handyman*
Homeward Bound
Journey to Mirage*
Bisexual/Menage/Multisexual Erotica
And Eat it Too
Two Men, One Woman*
Every Which Way
Summer of Denial
Death on a Ping Pong Table
Cruising Gigolo
13 Ways for Halloween
Luther*
The Indian Prince*
BOOKS BY SABB
Driver Reliever
Hiring in Hollywood
The Legend of Holleystone Grange
Surprise Encounters*
She is He
Wrong Man
Loyal to his King
Barbarian Tales - Book One - Traveler's Tales*
Barbarian Tales - Book Two - Journeys Begin*
Barbarian Tales - Book Three - The Inheritance*

Barbarian Tales - Book Four - Road to Persepolis*
BOOKS BY SHABBU
A Season in Galicia*
Blind Dates*
Velvet Interrogation
Finding Jason
Dirty Pool
Operation Black Jade
Cigars!*
Angel in the Barn
Gayly Complicated*
Despoiling David
The Tree of Idleness*
I Met a Man
Rough Road to Happiness
BOOKS BY STEPHEN KESSEL
Gay Romance
The Forever Man
Two Chances
BOOKS BY KIM BLACK
Lesbian Romance
Transfixed on Tammie (F/T lesbian)

www.ingramcontent.com/pod-product-compliance
Lightning Source LLC
Chambersburg PA
CBHW020736250626
47155CB00003B/786